W9-BCT-104

CHAPLIN & COMPANY

Chaplin & Company

MAVE FELLOWES

LIVERIGHT PUBLISHING CORPORATION

A Division of W. W. Norton & Company

New York • London

First published by Jonathan Cape Lts.,
one of the publishers in The Random House Group Ltd.

For information about permission to reproduce selections from
this book, write to Permissions, W. W. Norton & Company, Inc.,
500 Fifth Avenue, New York, NY 10110

For information about special discounts for bulk purchases, please
contact W. W. Norton Special Sales at specialsales@wwnorton.com
or 800-233-4830

Manufacturing by Courier Westford
Production manager: Louise Parasmo

Library of Congress Cataloging-in-Publication Data

Fellowes, Mave.

Chaplin & Company / Mave Fellowes. — First American Edition.

pages cm.

ISBN 978-0-87140-744-3 (hardcover)

1. Orphans—Fiction. 2. Mime—Fiction. 3. Neighborhood watch
programs—England—London—Fiction. I. Title. II. Title: Chaplin and
Company.

PR6106.E415C53 2014

823'.92—dc23

2013041286

Liveright Publishing Corporation,
500 Fifth Avenue, New York, N.Y. 10110
www.wwnorton.com

W. W. Norton & Company Ltd.,
Castle House, 75/76 Wells Street, London W1T3QT

1 2 3 4 5 6 7 8 9 0

For NPP and JPP

PROLOGUE

For Odeline at least, this is how it all began.

On a warm Saturday morning, nineteen years ago in genteel Arundel, a circus came to town. Coloured caravans and articulated lorries drove through the centre, past the shop fronts and striped awnings of Arundel High Street, past the Tudor facades and the quiet conversations of residents meeting on the pavement. On they rolled, over the bridge towards the southern outskirts, along the Causeway that links Arundel to its scruffier neighbour, the seaside resort of Worthing. The caravans and lorries turned off this road and bumped across to the far end of a field. Doors opened, ramps swung down. By midday the tent poles were up, carrying their huge folds of coloured canvas. Men with mallets worked their way around the sides, bashing rusty pegs into the ground. It was September, the end of the circus season; this was the second-to-last destination on their tour of Southern England.

If the circus's arrival had fallen on a weekday then things might never have begun for Odeline at all, for her mother's absorption in her work excluded any recreational inclinations between Monday and Friday. Work filled up her head completely. On the rare occasion that someone came to the door of the big house on Maltravers Street, they would not be greeted. Eunice Milk did not care for company. But most likely she never heard the bell over the much more urgent and noisy calculations inside her head, or the scratching and scribbling of her pencil working through the pages of her clients' account books. These fractions, decimals and percentages were more real to her. From Monday to Friday her mind made patterns of profits, climbed up and down numbers.

The weekends, however, were different. Eunice would plod plainly, big-boned and big-haired and blank-faced, down to the newsagent's on Saturday morning to collect the television schedule and then plod plainly back to her big house and lift her big body on to a stool at the kitchen table, where her pen pot stood. She would take out her biro and ruler. A chunk of tangerine hair would flop forward as she tipped her head to the pages. She would scan the columns for films and comedy programmes, and particularly for anything marked a 'Classic'. She drew a blue box around everything she wanted to watch. Her favourites were the old pictures – the romances (not the horrors). Her absolute favourites: the comedies where the funny men were always falling over, tripping up, bashing into things. It surprised her every time, even though she knew what the men were going to do. She liked the way they walked, those men in suits too big and hats too small. It made her laugh inside.

For the comedies, she would switch the television on long before the scheduled start time, and kneel by it waiting for the title to appear. The opening credits came and she would rush back to her chair, to sit with her ruddy, ginger-freckled face cupped in her hands. She watched and waited, and when the funny man came on, her face, usually so empty of expression, would ignite with pent-up laughter, her shoulders squeezed up to her ears. As he waddled obliviously into trouble she held her breath. She was ready to burst.

And then clonk, over he went and she would explode, hee-hawing and pounding her thighs with her fists. When the funny man was happy she would clap and clasp her hands, and when he was sad her face, her sighs, mirrored his. Sometimes, when the film ended with him still sad, she would flick away the tears from her cheeks, cross with the television for taking him away. But she couldn't bring herself to turn it off, however cross, in case he came back with a smile to wave her goodbye.

It was a picture of a clown that caught her attention that warm Saturday morning in the newsagent's as she paid for her television schedule. There were cards on the counter – advertisements for the circus. The clown in the advertisement had too-big shoes and a black hat like the men in the comedies, but his clothes were bright colours, squares of yellow and red, and his face was painted white with red lips and black diamonds for eyes. These black diamonds looked like something from the horrors, but the rest of him looked funny and the colours made her eyes dance, and so she picked up the picture from the pile on the counter and took it away with her.

So it began.

That afternoon Eunice Milk walked out of Arundel, down the High Street and over the bridge towards the Causeway road. She had a pair of scissors and a ball of string in the pockets of her blue-checked housecoat. Others were on their way to the circus too but she paid them no attention. Six foot tall and with her eyes fixed forward, she could see over their heads. Big-legged, she strode through them, her head of apricot hair jigging. When she saw the circus sign in blue and gold – 'CIRQUE MAROC! CIRQUE EXTRAORDINAIRE!' – she stopped and took out her scissors. She knelt down to the verge and snipped.

An hour later she was sitting on a bench in the big top, clutching a bouquet of wild flowers and long grass stems, looking up in wonder at the kaleidoscope of twisting, flipping, tumbling, turning figures above her. Two bodies in sparkling suits against the red and yellow triangles of the tent, swinging back and forth on the trapeze. One bent back and dropped, was caught, swung up and flipped, was caught. The sparkles made little dazzling explosions as they swept across her vision. So bright. Down below there was commotion, and through the heavy red curtains came an elephant, loping into the ring. Sitting on top, a boy in a blue turban and pale blue robes, holding a quivering cane over the elephant's shoulders. As the trapezes slowed, the elephant and the boy swayed on around the outside of the ring, the elephant lumbering from side to side, the boy switching the cane from right to left and back again, his mouth mumbling something inaudible under the gasps and jostle of the crowd. Eunice Milk sat upright and silent in the middle of it. She did not like animals.

At last the elephant pushed out through the curtain, and in its place burst a man in a yellow and red harlequin

suit – the man from the picture. With a white-painted face,
bowler hat and those too-big shoes. He looked surprised
to be in the ring, his black diamond eyes wide and worried.
He tried to get out again but couldn't find the opening in
the curtain. People began to laugh. He took a few steps
back and ran at the curtain – but bounced off it on to his
back. Eunice slapped her hand to her mouth, but he was
all right; he got up and dusted the sawdust off. And then
fell over again. She realised he was joking and let out a
squawk of laughter. He flipped on to his hands and knees
and began to walk, swaying side to side like the elephant,
with a glum face and one arm waving out in front. She
guffawed. When he reached the ladder at the edge of the
ring, he took the bottom rung in his hand and began to
climb. Up, up he went until he reached a tightrope that
crossed the ring to another ladder on the right-hand side.
He looked at the rope, and then at the audience with a
worried expression. They cheered. He held his nose and
prodded the rope with a huge-booted toe. It wobbled
violently and he snatched his foot back. He looked
terrified.

The audience shouted encouragement and Eunice began
to shake her head: no, don't. He produced a long cane
from behind the ladder and turned round to face the
tightrope, holding the cane across him with its ends
wobbling down. He shut his eyes and slid an enormous
boot on to the rope. Eunice was holding her breath, bolt
upright; the people on either side were silent too. The rope
shook and then was still. He brought his other foot round
in front of the first and tipped the cane to balance. Now
he was standing freely on the rope. He looked at the

audience and grinned, his painted mouth stretching from one side of his face to the other. He took another step, and another, and then he was almost dancing along it, stepping back and forth. The audience broke out into cheers, Eunice released her breath. Somewhere in the ring an accordion began to play. He took the cane in one hand and flipped his hat on top of it, twirling it round as he turned his head to the audience and lifted one of his boots sideways into the air. His hair was jet black and framed his painted face in corkscrew curls. The grin had dropped into a playful smile and as he looked down it seemed to Eunice that he stared directly at her and that his eyes twinkled. She smiled back and tipped her head to the side. She had never seen anything like him before.

That night she went back to watch the circus and sat on the same bench, waiting there long before the performance started. She kept her eyes fixed on the curtain. She ignored the ringmaster, she ignored the trapeze artists, she ignored the elephant. When he eventually came out through the curtain her shoulders gave a shudder. And when he looked down from the rope his twinkling eyes in their painted black diamonds were stars. Eunice dived into them and for her it was like falling through space. Her world was a distant speck in the night sky, far behind.

When he left the ring, she stood up and pushed her way out, not hearing the complaints of people on the benches around her. At the back of the big top was a patch of grass next to a caravan where the costumes were kept. He was climbing out of his red and yellow suit when he looked up to see a big-limbed, middle-aged woman with a helmet of fiery hair, standing plainly with her arms at her sides. Her cheeks were scrubbed pink and she was gazing at him with a wide, shining face, a full moon. She held an oddly cut bunch of flowers in one hand. Her head tipped to the side as she lifted her arm to offer them to him.

And so that is how this clown, this acrobat, this opportunist who was to become Odeline's father, found himself a place to stay while the circus was in town. Eunice Milk went back to the big top every evening that September fortnight, and when the performance was over she would wait for him outside. She forgot about her work: invoices were left unopened, tax receipts went unlogged. She walked past the stack of account books on the kitchen floor oblivious. During the days she attended him, fed him, watched him. At night she sponged the white paint and black diamonds from his upturned face and discovered such beauty underneath. His body was brown and taut, arms like ropes, she could see the ribs sliding under the skin of his chest when he breathed. She hadn't had anyone to look after before, and he was so hungry. She sat him on the chair at the kitchen table and gazed as he ate. He would bend down to the bowl and rush the food into his mouth. She reached out and felt the springs of his hair, the shiny black springs.

The circus left town at the end of the month and when he went she did not complain. It was not in her nature to ask for more.

ONE

London in August. From above, the city shimmers and glints in the sun. There is so much activity on its surface that it looks crawling, swarming with movement, as if it is one whole living thing. But look closer and this is just an impression given by the million little channels of movement that cross, curve, diverge and wind between buildings. These channels glitter. Look closer still. Sunlight flashes back from the windscreens and the roofs of the coaches, trains, lorries moving across the surface of the city. The machines chug out a quivering exhaust which softens the edges of the buildings and blurs outlines. It is thirty degrees of dry, dusty heat and London is baking.

It is a relief to notice the band of water at its middle, the cool ribbon of metal grey Thames which cuts through the hot, busy oval of the city.

The water snakes up, round and back on itself in its traverse from left to right. Look carefully and it is possible to see other smaller lengths of water, making less natural lefts and rights. Some connect to the wide band of the Thames but others come in from the outskirts, and stop abruptly somewhere near the centre. These waterways are manmade and tend to be set in straight lines and meet at sharp-angled junctions, like roads. They were

valuable arteries into the city when they were first
built, when water supported the loads that horses could
not, and reached places that the locomotives could not.
But now they are long unused, long unappreciated, long
unnoticed.

London has risen, built itself up like a toy city, stacked
itself, crammed buildings against the edges of waterways
and railways, so that from the ground these canals are
rarely seen. To cross a bridge and glimpse one is a surprise.
Life on these waterways is lower than life on the streets
around it. It is below the eyeline. A good place to hide.

Come down over the west of the city, above the patch of
sun-blanched green with its round dot of pond and long
pointed lake. Above this, snaking towards and away from
the railway that cuts into the city's north-west, is a
waterway that could take you all the way out to Birmingham.
Come closer down, to where this canal briefly touches the
raised section of the Westway, and closer still, until you
can see it emerging from under the road and winding up
to the right. This is where we join Odeline, who is making
her way along the towpath towards the canal junction of
Little Venice. Odeline the fledgling, wheeling her enormous
black cases along the paving slabs.

She makes for an unusual figure. From a short distance
away she looks like an overgrown boy dressed in his
father's clothes. Not that many fathers these days wear
the baggy pinstripe suits of a 1920s banker – or leather
brogues, which in this case are several sizes too big, even
for Odeline's size 9s. She has the height for the suit but

not the breadth and so the shoulder pads slip down, making the sleeves longer than they should be. The trousers are bulky under the jacket but held up by a pair of bright-red leather-buttonholed braces, which are probably Odeline's favourite accessory. More preferred, even, than her bowler hat, which she is not wearing as she walks along the canal. It is wrapped in tissue paper inside her prop box. Her hair is absolutely black and forms a bowl around the back and sides of her head. A crudely short fringe sticks out slightly at the top of her forehead. It looks like she has cut it herself, and she has.

The suit is heavy; she is terrifically overdressed for this sweltering day. People in the tower blocks behind the towpath are sitting out on their metal balconies showing shoulders and legs to the sun. It is a Sunday. There is the smell of their barbecues, the buzz of bass from their sound systems. But if Odeline is hot she is hiding it. Her face is set in its usual determined mask, with her dark eyes – huge and round and long-lashed – slightly hooded in the sun. She is refusing to squint.

At nine forty-five this morning she boarded the coach for London that would take her away from Arundel for ever. She was over an hour early but the coach doors were open, so she got on anyway and sat down at the front, stacking her cases on to the seat next to her. She held on to the handles and to her ticket. She is eighteen and she is an orphan. The roar of bus engines seemed deafening. Everything seemed too real, too loud, too colourful, too three-dimensional. The beige and brown carpeted stripes on the seat in front began to tremble, the sun was dazzlingly bright through the glass.

She checked through the papers in her bulging moneybelt. In the first compartment she has filed: two documents detailing the sale of her mother's house in Arundel (furnishings included), a blue booklet for a Post Office account which contains all her funds, and the receipt for her coach ticket. She has put a cash card in a separate compartment, next to a small brown solar-powered calculator. In the large pocket at the back of the moneybelt is a London *A–Z* and a letter confirming her first booking with Top Hat Entertainers in a Covent Garden theatre tomorrow night. Also in this pocket is an envelope containing London theatre tickets, with a receipt for payment stapled to the corner. She checks they are all still in there. And in a fourth compartment is a set of keys, an advert from a British Waterways magazine, and a letter from them with information about a houseboat named *Chaplin and Company*, which she has bought with a portion of her inheritance.

On the bus, she took her pince-nez out of her pocket, pushed them on to her nose and read through the contract. Passengers began to board and if they looked at her strangely, she refused to notice. In the *A– Z* she checked the route she had already memorised, to make sure.

Odeline's mother passed away six weeks ago, in pain but uncomplaining. Kidney stones. Her death was avoidable but she didn't go to the doctor. She was fifty-seven and healthy in all other respects, she just didn't want anyone prodding her like they did when she gave birth to Odeline. She hadn't known what was wrong with her and it wasn't in her nature to wonder. She bore pain the way she bore the rest of life, wordlessly, incuriously, and with half her mind somewhere else. Odeline's mother's face usually had an absent expression, like she was trying to work out an answer to something at the back of her mind. At the moment she died, this expression had lifted and her face was flooded, illuminated, as if she had finally found the pattern.

Eunice Milk has taken very good care of her daughter. In that Post Office account sits a small fortune. There is also a valuable life insurance policy. It turns out that she made a substantial profit out of her own death. As an accountant this might have been her greatest achievement.

The inheritance has given Odeline the means to escape. She thinks London will be her refuge. London understands talent, creativity, individual expression. This metropolis has been a stage for all the great artists of illusion and mime – from Maskelyne and Cooke to Houdini to Marcel Marceau. She wants to be part of this heritage, to walk the streets that her heroes and heroines have walked and visit the theatres where they performed. Finally, released, she will fulfil her vocation.

And for once be anonymous. Arundel is one of those towns that would describe itself as charming, well-tended, community-minded. There is nowhere more suffocating, she thinks, to an artistic temperament.

Walking along the canal, she is noticing things with the same intensity she has noticed everything since her mother died: the violent sparkle of sunlight chasing her along the water; the noise of her prop box wheels on the stone-flecked concrete slabs of the towpath, trundle and clunk, trundle and clunk; the clumsy splayed yellow feet of a moorhen perched on the side of the canal. And then suddenly an urgent tinny ringing approaching from behind her – she turns in time to pull herself and her boxes off the path as a cyclist flies past, bent determined over handle-bars, all black plastic and metal glinting in the sun.

She walks a little faster now and as she comes round a bend in the canal she recognises the boat from the advert in her moneybelt. As stated in the letter, it is the first in a line of boats on the towpath side, just short of an arched bridge with light blue railings which gives on to a wide triangle of water where the canal forks right towards Paddington and left towards Regent's Park. Little Venice.

The advert described the boat as 'one of the most hand-some houseboats on the water, with an imperial colour scheme, navy blue body with red detail'. Odeline does not like the word 'imperial', but thought the colour scheme sounded handsome enough. Of course, what really drew her to the boat was the name. It seemed like fate.

As she approaches she sees that the boat is less hand-some than in the picture, which must have been taken when it was last painted. Judging by its condition, this was some time ago. The red lettering has faded to pink and the paint has blistered and peeled off in patches. Somebody has attempted to cover up these blemishes, but the paint they have used is matt rather than gloss, dark grey instead of navy blue.

In the picture the boat's only neighbours were a pair

of swans by the bow. Now it is tail to nose with another even scruffier boat which has black smoke puffing out of its chimney, a wheelbarrow and a bicycle tied to its roof, and a dog stretched out on the deck. Odeline does not like animals. The dog, huge, grey and rangy, pulls itself up as a ponytailed man comes out of the cabin, the doors swinging shut behind him. He has muscular arms tattooed with swirling blue lines, and the shape of a bare-toothed serpent's head screams up one side of his neck. He is holding an axe in one hand and a hessian sack in the other. He looks at her straight and gives a nod which looks to Odeline like the nod of a murderer marking his next victim.

She walks quickly up to *Chaplin and Company* and steps around the mooring rope, which is tied to a hook sunk into the concrete of the towpath. There is a gap between the curved bow of the boat and the bank. She looks down, black water is swilling. The tattooed man is still watching, looming. She tugs up the knee of her trousers and places a brogue on to the boat, holding on to the cabin roof as she steps across.

She turns to yank at the handles of her prop boxes until they land with a thud on the deck. There is a step down to a pair of panelled cabin doors with a padlocked bolt across the middle. Her neighbour's axe is dangling. She stabs around for the key in her moneybelt, finds it, cracks open the padlock. The doors swing open. She pulls her prop boxes crashing down the step and into the cabin, shuts the doors and pushes across two flimsy locks at the top and the bottom.

The prop boxes are lying on their sides across the cabin floor. With their handles extended they are almost the width of the boat. Standing with her back against the doors she can feel the ceiling pressing at her hair.

The cabin is laid out before her. The floor is squares of orange carpet – areas of it below the portholes are bleached yellow. There is a white shelf unit in the corner on her left, and a low armchair on her right, upholstered in orange and brown 1970s fabric, also faded. Varnished wood planks run along the length of the walls and the ceiling. 'Chalet-style', it said in the advert. There are portholes set into the walls with short curtains in the same fabric as the armchair, and a set of curved gold lights on each side of the cabin. At the far end, on the right-hand side is a white wardrobe and in the left-hand corner is the kitchenette/breakfast bar: white wall cupboards above a U-shaped counter.

Odeline compresses the handles of her prop boxes and pulls them along to the counter. There are bubbled crescents in the marble-effect surface where it has been melted by hot objects. She inspects the kitchenette. There are more white cupboards under the counter. There is a hob with an oven beneath, and a gas canister inside the next-door cupboard. This connects to the oven on one side and a fridge on the other. But Odeline has come prepared. She's already bought food that doesn't require heating or cooling, so she won't have to rely on the hob, oven or fridge. This will save money: her research has shown that gas cylinders are extremely expensive to replace. £64 plus delivery. Although she has made a note to ask the canal warden about this. He or she may know of a cheaper source.

She checks the other kitchen cupboards. Their contents are disappointing. The British Waterways advert said that the kitchenette was fully furnished, but the glassware is kitsch and vulgar – tall and plastic with slices of lime cascading down the side – and the crockery consists of a set of eight lime green formica plates, coated in dust. In the end cupboard is a black bin bag full of metal parts. Spearing the side of the bag are some rusted barbecue tongs.

Opposite the kitchenette is the bathroom and she looks in. It is very small, and very dark. She pulls the light cord, a faux microphone at the end of a gold chain. A bulb flickers on above the doorway, and she sees that the walls, floor and ceiling are covered in black rectangular tiles. Almost directly below the shower head a green lavatory with a cracked plastic lid. There is a matching green sink by the door with limescale trails beneath the taps. Above the sink is a round mirror. Rhinestones are set into the rim and along the edge of a mirrored shelf which is fixed to the wall with ornate gold brackets. There is a border of green around the glass of the porthole. Mould.

She pulls her head out of the bathroom. At the far end of the boat is a step up to another pair of panelled doors, which must lead out on to the back deck. In the centre of each door is an engraved heart with entwined letters. I and F.

Odeline looks through a doorway on her right into the engine room. It contains the boiler for hot water, fixed to the wall backing on to the bathroom. There is a single porthole in here, and running beneath it a wooden ledge. The ledge is hinged and Odeline pulls it up to see the engine underneath, an oily bulk of metal spewing out pipes like tentacles. The diesel gauge points at empty. She shuts the lid; she has read the chapter about engines in her *British Waterways Narrowboat Manual* – but has not quite mastered it yet. She straightens up and knocks her head: the roof is even lower in here. Set into the ceiling of the engine room is what looks like another porthole with the same studded brass frame as the others on the boat. But on closer inspection, Odeline sees it is a compass, with the needle balancing on a brass pin set through the centre of its glass. The back of the compass is stained, spotted paper, with the directions painted around the edge in tiny longhand. It reminds her of the aged face and spindly numerals of her pocket watch. She taps the glass and the needle quivers. It is pointing to east north-east.

Her legs feel shaky. Must be hungry. She hooks the pocket watch out of her waistcoat and checks the time. Ten past eleven. She will have a snack and then unpack, before doing her first rehearsal session on board her new home.

In the top of the first prop box is a packet of cereal bars. She takes one out and unwraps it, and then opens the lower kitchen cupboards until she finds a white pedal bin inside one of them. The pedal doesn't work and she has to lift the lid herself, which is brown and chewed around the edges. There are two empty cigarette cartons wilting at the bottom of the bin, and no bin bag. She shoves the wrapper in and puts the bin back into the cupboard – she hates the stink of cigarettes. She goes to sit on the low armchair but it doesn't feel right: she's too far away from her belongings, and so she gets up and pulls at the fold-down bed. Its legs flick out and it lands with a crash, filling the space. She sits on the edge of the mattress and eats the cereal bar, and then takes a carton of pineapple juice from the top of the prop box, jabs the straw through the foil hole and drinks it in one go.

Unpacking. She takes the rest of her food provisions from the top of the box and puts them in the upper kitchen cupboards. She puts tins and powdered food on the bottom shelves and all other packets on the top.

Next in the box is her bedlinen, which she takes out and puts in a pile on the middle of the mattress.

Then her clothes, underclothes, two towels and her mother's sewing basket and toolkit. She puts these on the mattress as well.

Then a square, tan-coloured box, big enough to hold four account books, which she slides under the bed.

The rest of the prop box is filled with books and videos. She wheels it to the front end of the cabin and begins to put the books on the white shelving unit. She starts by arranging them alphabetically by title, as she had done on the bookshelf in her bedroom. Then she rearranges them according to subject – she has bought several new categories of book recently and this will make them easier to find. She starts with her mother's accounting manuals, then all her illusion books, her books on mime, with a separate shelf for her collection of Marcel Marceau books. Then anything falling under the title of 'Inspiration'. This includes the videos, which are old recordings of her mother's favourite silent films. She starts the shelf below with Canals and Waterways books, then anything to do with London life. A book called *Behind the Curtain* she leaves in its own category of one. She bought it in a rush at the charity shop thinking it was about theatre backstages; it had a white glove pulling back a red curtain on the front cover. But it was a book about Russia, and didn't mention theatres at all. The woman in the shop wouldn't give her a refund, so she has kept it (and read it) so as not to waste the money. £4. It is a hardback. She won't be so foolish as to buy a book again without checking the contents thoroughly.

So that is the first prop box emptied. She stores it in the engine room. The other stands upright at the end of the kitchenette counter. She flips open the lid and begins to unpack her costume parts and props. She takes out: a black waistcoat and white dress shirt on a wire hanger, hooking it over the rail of the wardrobe; three folded white vests, which she puts on the bed. The bowler hat in tissue paper goes on top of the wardrobe. A roll of posters, packet of Blu-Tack and the turquoise plastic jewellery box in which she keeps her make-up are placed on the kitchen counter. She will put the posters up later. She arranges the smaller props on the white shelves, displayed in front of the books: a packet of coloured handkerchiefs, a bouquet of fake roses, a pair of spectacles attached to a plastic nose and moustache, two pairs of white gloves, a pair of round mirrored sunglasses, a rainbow feather duster, a clip-on bowtie, a white quill, a top hat with no top, four boxes of chalk, a blackboard duster, a ball of string, a false cigar, a fold of false banknotes, a hunting horn, a bottle of black nail varnish, a harmonica. (She is teaching herself to play the harmonica. Half an hour's practice per day after repertoire rehearsal. She was not accepted into the orchestra whilst at school. But this, surely, was due to her general exclusion by teachers and pupils, rather than a lack of musical flair. After all, a gift for performance must entail an affinity with music.)

She also plans to teach herself to use her recently purchased roller skates, which she takes out of the box next and lines up at the bottom of the bookshelf. They are metal with yellow leather straps which clip over her brogues. When she saw them in the charity shop she felt like Charlie Chaplin in the toy department in *Modern Times*. She will have to find a smoother surface to practise on than the towpath, she thinks. The bumpy concrete slabs could send her off course, and she doesn't want to end up in the canal.

She leaves the larger props – a gentleman's cane, a blackboard, a collapsible wooden easel, an umbrella deliberately broken for dramatic effect – inside this second box, which she wheels into the engine room and parks next to the first.

She feels hungry again and eats a cheese slice at the kitchen counter. The cheese has sweated. Bits of it stick to the plastic. These have to be consumed soon if she isn't going to use the fridge.

Preparation for rehearsal, then. She takes the turquoise make-up box into the bathroom and balances it on the mirrored shelf. She lifts the lid and pulls the tiers up and out. Face paints and make-up are in the side trays, toothbrush, toothpaste and dental floss, cleanser, cotton wool and nail scissors in the lower compartment. She won't bother with full make-up now, but will perform her teeth-cleaning ritual. She does this before every rehearsal. It helps to switch her into the performance mindset.

The sink taps are squat and modern; there is a stripe of

limescale beneath the hot tap running all the way into the plughole. She turns the cold tap and water shoots out in spurts. She bends. Toothpaste on brush, she lathers for sixty seconds, spits and lathers for another sixty. She can hear the water trickling down the pipe and out of the side of the boat. Toothbrush back into the box. She takes out the dental floss dispenser and pulls off a short length. Bares her teeth and flicks her head up to find the left incisor, where she always starts. Her elastic lips are stretched wide and she can see both rows of teeth. She tries not to show them when she has to talk to people – they are in good condition but not as straight as she would like, and she considers them too messy for her face. They point slightly inwards, towards the back of her mouth, and are huddled together, hiding behind one another. She thinks this looks weak, vulnerable, retreating.

She flosses each gap once and then shuts her mouth. Closed, it is much smaller than you might expect, having seen it at full stretch. It is diamond-shaped and neat. She approves of it. The bow of her top and bottom lips is repeated in an upturned nose and pointed chin. Her skin is the colour of a tea biscuit. There is a speckling of dark freckles across her cheekbones.

She blinks.

Her eyes are the heaviest objects in her face. They are the eyes of a tragic heroine, she thinks. A forlorn clown.

She blinks again.

Her eyebrows are arched and black and there are four tiny crossed hairs in the centre. She used to pluck these for neatness but no longer does so (she thinks they add to the symmetry of her face).

Up close, her hair is black and brushlike. It juts out from each side of her head like the cap of a mushroom.

'You have arrived,' she says to her face in the mirror framed by rhinestones. Her voice is old-fashioned – clipped, learned from the heroes and heroines of the Saturday afternoon films.

'You have arrived,' she says, keeping her mouth small, lips covering her teeth.

'The adventure begins.'

TWO

Now leave Odeline for a while and move further up the canal. Past her tattooed neighbour, unfazed by her coldness, who places another log on the bench at the edge of his deck and raises the axe over his shoulder to split it. The axe sticks near the bottom of the log and he cracks the halves apart with his hands, which like his arms are decorated, marbled, filled in with ink, and chucks them into the sack at his feet. Go past him and the next two boats leading up to the bridge, where white-haired couples are sitting out on their decks, reading or listening to their radios in the sun. Past the boat filling up from the water pump near the bridge and the three bristly, rough-skinned figures drinking from cans and leaning over the blue railings looking on to the towpath, singing a low song. *And I'll be in Scotland before you.* One conducts with his can as he sings. *For me and my true love.* They are bulging figures in layers and layers of filthy clothes. Go on under the bridge, which is low and nesty underneath, and then out into the triangle of water.

Now the towpath widens. Go past the dark green barge with a wide double doorway. There are people sitting at tables on the stretch of towpath outside. A small plump woman rushes to collect plates of leftover salad and sandwiches, carrying them into the shade of the cabin, where she empties them clattering into the sink and puts the dishcloth under the cold tap to cool the back of her neck with. Water trickles down the back of her aertex, right down to the elastic waistband of her skirt. She puts the till receipt on to a metal tray and makes her hot, heavy way outside again. She has short, flat, lifeless hair, the roots are dark with sweat. She nods thank you to the customers, who have left a ten-pound note under the salt cellar and are picking up their bags to go.

Opposite the cafe is an island with a beautiful willow tree whose branches brush the water. The island is a refuge for canal birds; moorhens and ducks weave in and out of the branches to build their nests underneath. But keep to this side of the water and follow the customers as they walk off down the towpath, along the Paddington arm of the Little Venice basin. The towpath bends to the right, and here are a pair of heritage boats. They're not narrow boats but old schooners, maroon and oval-shaped with sails rolled round the masts. The sails haven't been unfurled for over forty years, when the boats were off-duty toys at the naval base at Plymouth. They were towed up to London by a tugboat belonging to the grey-whiskered, blue-capped man leaning an elbow on the side of the second schooner, the *Phoebus*. He is the canal warden for this stretch of water. There are three or four children on the deck of the *Phoebus*, peering into the cabin, and he is giving his usual spiel. Come a bit closer to hear. His voice is thick and his vowels are rounded, seasoned, fermented:

'Oh yes, well, the interior and all the wood you can

see, it's all solid mahogany. Solid. It's heavy stuff, about three tons of it on board, but there's no sinking her.'

He gives the side of the boat a flat slap.

'Some of the hardiest boats on the water, these ladies. She was originally used as a training vessel for the sailors stationed in Portsmouth, everyone had to learn to sail back then. And then they painted her up and kept her as an ornamental addition to the fleet. They'd bring her out on special occasions, like when the King came to visit and suchlike. So no, she never fought in a war, and neither did her neighbour. But they're tough old birds, you won't find many other boats built in 1910 in such good nick. And with all the original fittings.'

The children have already disappeared inside the cabin and have begun to fiddle with the fittings. They are disappointed by the absence of weaponry but still curious enough to play with the brass porthole catches and the funny dials on the walls. The man with the grey whiskers and the blue cap gives a belly laugh and turns round to share it with the children's parents. But they too have walked away and are making their way to a bench further up the towpath, talking amongst themselves. So he looks at his watch. He'll close up the boats after this lot, it's been a good day. He pats the cash in his shirt pocket.

This is the warden for the Little Venice Marina and the western stretch of canal which goes from here up to Ladbroke Grove. His name is John Kettle and he will be an irritant to Odeline. He is the kind of person who has ended up acting a caricature of themselves, in his case a friendly, twinkling, Captain Birdseye figure. This works well enough on the parents who pay for their children to clamber around on his boats. But the children aren't convinced. For a start he doesn't feed himself properly, so hasn't the approachable roundness and ruddiness that he needs for his role. He looks unhealthy, actually. His eyes are a washed-out blue and his discoloured nails betray a bad diet. His beard is tobacco brown around the mouth, teeth yellow. And the blue sailor's cap is faded and grubby, threadbare around the edge of the peak. There is a white line of sweat-salt around the rim where it jams tightly on to his head. Holding his brain in, he likes to say.

He keeps up a performance of jollity and manages to convince himself most of the time. He can't remember when it started to be an effort.

The children are joining their parents now. Before they go home they'll stop at the barge cafe for ice creams that will leave sticky messes and bits of wrapper on the ground around the tables. The small plump woman doesn't find it easy to bend down. The thickness around her middle feels solid and inflexible. She will lean heavily on the tables to pick up these bits of wrapper and the exertion will leave her heaving for breath and even hotter than she was before.

When the children and their parents have gone John Kettle closes up his schooners, dropping the heritage boat signs into their cabins before yanking the hatches across. He shakes a tarpaulin over each deck and clicks the button-holes on to their fasteners. He can't be bothered to do every one. A sloppy job but he doesn't care. It won't rain tonight. He shuts the doors and doesn't think to lock them – there's nothing inside worth stealing. He double-checks the cash in his shirt pocket. He will spend this tonight on whisky, leaning on the bar in the brick pub by the bridge, The Lock Inn. This is where he goes every night. Warmth from the lamps on the windowsills, the chatter of other punters, his drink swilling amber on the old wooden bar: these things will fill his head. But it is not yet opening time, and he is no good at entertaining himself. His mind flicks through things to do. He is not someone who is all right on his own. He finds it hard to be jolly without someone there to witness him being jolly. He dreads, in fact, the silence of his own company.

This dread feels like more than melancholy or boredom, it is something his mind runs from. This is how it comes to him in his dreams: he is on his own next to an enormous crack in the earth, the ground is dry and the horizon is empty of people in all directions. He knows what is coming before he even begins to hear the slow, steady approach of the creature crawling up to get him and take him down into that dark nothingness. The worst part of it is, he knows he will go. It is a pull like vertigo, it makes him want to jump. When that black leathery-winged monster appears out of its horrible lair, he will give no resistance, he will be weak and willing when it comes. He will let it take him in its talons and plunge. This dread is unspoken even to himself and keeps him looking, looking outwards for other people to shore him up against the pull of it.

And so the jolly part of him keeps up its chatter.

He decides to go and check on the new resident, that should keep him busy till opening time. He heads for the bridge, stopping in at the barge cafe on the way to say hello. The small plump woman who works there is foreign. She

is called Vera and he is relieved about this, not being good
with fiddly foreign names. She has a soft, kindly face, he
thinks. Commie accent but she seems to understand what
he says and speaks good enough English. 'Afternoon, Vera,'
he calls, propped against the cafe's doorframe. 'Belter of a
day.' She looks up from the sink and blinks slowly in reply.

Even on a day as hot as this the cafe owner, Mr Zjelko,
forbids her to switch off the toasted sandwich machine – it
takes a long time to heat up and the cafe sign promises
'EXPRESS SERVICE'. Mr Zjelko has a chain of cafes in
West London and sends his thugs to visit them unannounced,
to check his standards are being kept to. Vera knows that
she will be fired if she breaks one of his rules. Then what?

John Kettle feels his duty here is done, a few bright
words dispensed from a friendly warden. Is it Poles who
have a reputation for surliness? Or is that just the Russians?
In any case he can't remember where this one comes from.
Perhaps she never said. He has a feeling that she sleeps on
board, which would be against regulations, this not being
a residential mooring. He spotted her coming out of the
barge early one morning, raised an eyebrow. She looked
back scared as a rabbit in headlights. But rule enforcement
has never been his thing. Anyway, since that morning
he has popped into the cafe every lunchtime and received
a sandwich on the house. Which suits him fine. He always
gives her a wink as he goes out. Needn't worry, love. He
knows how to keep a secret.

On John Kettle goes under the low bridge, making his
crooked way towards the boat with Odeline inside. Even
when he's sober his walk is a stagger. He passes the two
cruisers who have been moored here for the last week. Both

retired couples. He salutes them and jabs a thumb over his shoulder at the trio of singing tramps by the railing. 'Sorry about those,' he says, 'locational hazard.' He passes the tattooed man's boat. Arrogant bastard is stretched out on his roof smoking something which definitely doesn't smell like tobacco. 'Police are on their way,' calls out John Kettle. Bloody gypsy doesn't answer. John Kettle can't be bothered to follow it up, too curious about *Chaplin and Company*'s new resident. He thrusts his nose forward and carries on.

Here's the old boat, then, a patriotic dame in red, white, blue. Weathered and bashed up but still she floats. Three hard raps on the roof and he pushes his face up against a porthole. The figure inside looks horrified. It stands frozen in a suit and a bowler hat, hands either side of its head, like John Kettle's pointing a gun. A handkerchief is sticking out of the cuff of its suit jacket. Behind the figure is an easel with a blackboard on it, covered in chalky writing John Kettle can't quite make out. 'Aren't you coming out to say hello?' he shouts through the glass. 'I've come to introduce myself.'

The figure looks blank and then whips the bowler hat off, clutches it with both hands, puts it down on the floor, makes a lurch towards the cabin doors, opens them, and ducks through the doorway to come out on deck. As the suit straightens he sees that it's a girl, a foreign-looking one, but she's almost a head taller than him. She is standing bolt upright and still as a statue. He sees now that her suit is in fact an oversized tailcoat that hangs off her like a scarecrow's. Must be thin as a broom. She's wearing scuffed black shoes with the laces pulled so tight they're bunching the leather. He brings his eyes up the baggy tailcoat – at the top is a pointy coffee-skinned pin-head with a mop of black hair. Big eyes.

'Submariner John Kettle,' he says and sticks his hand out. It isn't taken. 'I keep an eye on things round here,' he winks. 'What's your name then?'

'Are you the canal warden?' Her voice is as English as cut-glass. And about as friendly.

'That's right,' he replies. 'I know everyone on this little stretch, and beyond.' He leans in towards her and props himself on the corner of the boat. 'I can fill you in on who to steer clear of – those three pissheads up there for example. And him.' He tips his head in the direction of the next-door boat. 'No-good gypsy that one, with his greasy ponytail. Just this morning I saw him taking water from the lockhouse, pinching more like. I'd like to get a better look at his licence, bet it's dodgy as hell.' She doesn't look at the next-door boat but down at his grubby, oil-stained hand on her cabin roof. He removes it and shoves it into his trouser pocket.

'Where do I buy diesel for my boat engine?' Posh as a queen, she sounds.

He barks out a laugh. 'Ha! You'll have a job getting that engine going. Have you seen the date on her side? She's almost as antique as my two old ladies. I heard she'd been abandoned up by Scrubs Lane and British Waterways knew they'd get more if they sold her with a Little Venice mooring. She was towed down. I've never seen her go under her own steam. Anyway. What do you do?'

'I'm an artist.' No hint of a smile. Snooty way of talking, her mouth hardly moves. But he'll push on.

'Oh well, you'll find plenty to paint round here. Lovely

spots up the Regent's Canal, and Little Venice of course.
We get plenty of artists here, 'specially on weekends if the
weather's all right, come up to paint a nice canal vista.
Lots of them interested in painting my girls, the *Phoebus*
and the *Peggy May*, fine-looking both of them and classical models in the Edwardian style. You ought to bring
your sketchbook and pencils up. There's a good bench up
there to sit on, gives a sterling view.'

She doesn't look impressed. He rocks forward on to
his toes, feeling her height looking down on him, and
continues. 'So is it just you here then, no hubbie? They
said it was a single lady who'd bought the *Chaplin* but I
presumed there'd be a feller, unusual to find a boat run
by a lady on her own. You look young to be setting up
on the water, if I can say so.'

The girl's eyebrows press down and her forehead folds,
she is glaring at him. He takes a step back and opens his
mouth to say something but is cut off by a hand appearing
from the cuff of her coat. 'Your presumptions are chauvinist. Sexist. Ageist.' She flicks her fingers up one by one.
Bony brown fingers. The voice is shrill, out of date. Her
lips are tight and white-rimmed. 'Do not disturb me again,'
she says, and continues to glare as she steps back down
into her cabin. She slams the doors behind her. He hears
the locks shunt across.

Odeline yanks the curtains over the portholes. Enraged!
Violated! She huffs and she puffs and she listens to the
crossness of her sounds. Her rehearsal has been disrupted.
Presumptuous, bigoted little man! Her focus is lost.

She sinks on to the low armchair, her knees jut out in front of her.

The truth is that even before the interruption she was finding it difficult to translate her routine into this new space. The dimensions are unforgivingly tight and she had to adapt her preparatory exercises, moving sideways down the length of the cabin. And she can't stop *looking*. In her bedroom in Arundel her surroundings became invisible. When she entered the performance mindset she would leave her tawdry room with its beige waffle carpet and bumpy wallpaper. She would stop seeing her bookshelves, her costume rail, the posters on her wall. All she could see was the blinding brightness of the spotlight that shone upon her, and the bluish faces of her imagined audience illuminated in the darkness. She was on an empty stage, in a circular beam of light that followed her around as she moved. When she mimed she was contained in that circle. It was all she needed, all she knew.

She can't find that spotlight here. Light leaks in from every porthole, her attention is leaky and diffracted. Whenever she lets go and tries to transport herself, to really *go*, she bumps into something. Her wrist is still twingeing from knocking it on the gold wall light.

'It will be good discipline,' she says aloud, jabbing her trouser leg with a finger to make the point. To motivate. 'I must learn to move with smaller, tighter gestures. Marcel Marceau created drama in the raising of an eyebrow and I must strive for the same precision. The same subtlety.' She pinches her thumb and forefinger together and looks at their shape, their slender tawniness. She has expressive hands. 'It is not about grand or flamboyant gestures,' she tells herself, 'it's about timing. Everything is in the timing.'

Back to work, Odeline.

Stand up.

Put on your bowler hat.

Now watch as she becomes the mime.

She pulls a string of coloured handkerchiefs from her cuff and hangs them over the blackboard. Then rummages through her suit pockets, turning each one inside out. She shrugs at the audience. The pockets all empty. She takes off her shoes, peering inside each one and shaking them. They are empty too. She puts her hands on her hips, tips to the side and shakes her head, nothing comes out, she swings to the other side, nothing comes out. She clutches her face in panic. Her mouth is turned down in a tragic mask. All is lost! She drops to her hands and knees and begins to hunt underneath the audience's chairs, pressing her head down to the floor to inspect every inch.

'Ugh!'

A patch on the orange carpet stops her. It is a stain, sunk into the nylon fuzz, the shape of a heart, browny-red in colour. A disgusting stain, just where she was about to put her hand. She sniffs it and recoils. Barbecue sauce.

Late afternoon and the heat is letting go of the day. This is a noisy time on the canal, with geese honking their way back to their nests, beginning to flap and paddle with their feet and then setting off, flying low down the middle of the water. Their wings make a beating sound: tarpaulin flapping in the wind. The people who have been sitting out on the hot metal balconies of the tower blocks begin to lift themselves off their deckchairs, off their towels, and disappear indoors. Balconies will begin filling again with the things moved inside to make space for sunbathing: bicycles, children's toys, pot plants, bits of kitchen equipment. The canalside is empty, tourists have finished their visits. Parents head home, slowly, with their children tugging at their hands. The barge cafe is closing up and Vera is turning the tables on to their sides to fold their legs beneath them. She stacks them against the barge door, pulls the collar of her aertex to wipe the sweat from her top lip and takes a moment to look up. The sky is a brilliant blue with a criss-cross of white trails left by aeroplanes.

THREE

Walter Chaplin was a boat builder in Stoke Bruerne. In 1936 he built his first engine-powered narrowboat, the others of his fleet being butties and tugs built for local canal companies. He made it a smaller size of forty foot – better for solo steerers – with a raised rear deck to help navigation. He built the length of the boat as one long cabin with basic plywood flooring nailed over strutted supports. He laid a waxed canvas over this. He put the engine at the back of the cabin, and boxed it into a separate room with walls and a doorway. Then he lowered the roof of this room, in order to set a compass into the ceiling. He knew it was a vanity. He spent money on having the compass made, the needle set into the bowl of glass and the hand-painted wheel of directions. The frame of the compass was brass, like his portholes and the windlass he had made to match the boat, with the date inscribed, sunk deep into the handle. '1936'. Another extravagance. He allowed himself to order brass handles too for the tiller and cabin doors, and felt foolishly proud. After finishing every section he would step back and look. His pride swelled as he watched it take form.

Walter Chaplin and his wife, Ann, lived in a small bargee's cottage across the yard from his boatshed, although it silently felt to them both as though he lived in the boatshed and she in the house. His comings home at the end of the day felt more like visits. Past the age for children now, she missed the ones she had never had, and her sadness for them kept him at his work. He couldn't stand her disappointment, the reproach of it. When he thought up calm sentences to console her, he knew she didn't feel their comfort.

He had worked long, simple days building this boat; it was the first he could paint his name on. A long time ago he had dreamed of a boat like this one. Back then he imagined he would name her *Chaplin and Son*. The specialist enamel took four weeks to arrive from the warehouse in Glasgow and he had a sign painter do the lettering in the traditional Dutch barge script. *Chaplin and Company. Est. 1936*. Red with an outline of white on navy blue. A lot of the working boats were nondescript, barely stained. This one would be recognised.

The boat was commissioned to carry packets – mail, parcels and other deliveries – between Birmingham and London, and Walter hired a company of steerers who did the run. These were usually apprentices from other boatyards around Stoke Bruerne. An occasional packet run gave them a bit extra.

Then war was declared and the waterways were taken under Government control. Pill boxes were built along the length of the Grand Union and Home Guard manned the industrial wharves. *Chaplin and Company* was commissioned with wartime cargo and carried it proudly. Tons of aluminium ingots up to the artillery factories in Birmingham, coal and canned rations down to London.

It took the letters of Birmingham's fighting sons back to
their families. Hopeful and hastily written replies would
fill the return boat in elasticated bundles. Much bad news
was carried. Much sad news safely delivered. For Walt
these letters were his most important cargo.

Soon the young men Walt employed were all gone away,
and there wasn't a demand for new boats to be built. So
he himself would steer the boat between its two destin-
ations. If the job was to London he'd try and get within
reach of it the night before, so he could be in and out
quick the next day. He didn't much like the place. Too
many people, he thought. Made everyone a stranger.

The journeys took longer now because you couldn't
move at night, no headlamps allowed after dark because
of the bombings. He didn't mind being away for longer,
liked the quiet nights spent on the water. In his boat. He'd
use the engine room at the back as a cabin for overnight
stops. It was cramped but he built a fold-down bunk over
the motor and changed the glass in the porthole so that it
could be open without the rain coming in when the engine
smell was strong. He'd moor with his little cabin facing
into the canal so that any moonlight hitting the water
could come through the porthole and dance on the glass
bowl of the compass as he lay on his bunk, looking up.
He loved the weight of the windlass hooked over his belt,
would lie with his hand resting on it like the hilt of a
sword, run his thumb over the grooves of the date. He
listened to the night sounds of the boat on the canal, the
gentle washing of water at her sides and the creak of floor
planks as she tilted in the breeze. Sometimes he heard a
sound he couldn't place – a sigh that seemed to come from

the boat as a whole rather than any particular part. Even though he had put every inch of her together himself he couldn't pick out exactly what it was. It sounded as if she was exhaling, letting herself sink lower into the water. He felt it as her release, her change of pitch, her shoulders dropping after their day's work. Lying and listening to her sounds in the darkness, he felt more at home than he ever had in his own bed.

Walt had heard of crews of steerers who navigated the canals in the blackout, taking urgent coal, food and weapons into London. Floating invisibly beneath the noses of the German planes which had begun to cross the British coastline after dark. Sometimes, moored overnight, he thought he heard these crews passing his boat, just the very faintest chug of an engine and wet turnover of water. Other steerers on the Grand Union route said they were mostly ladies who crewed the night boats.

More evacuations were announced on the radio that spring, and he and his wife applied. Her idea. They were assigned a boy, thirteen years old, from North London they were told. They went together to Warwick Station and waited on the platform. Walt could hardly look at his wife's face, the tightness of it. Her hands tugged at her skirt. They were rubbed red and the nails bitten down. The train pulled in. A gang of children poured out through the doors and crowded together, not knowing where to go. The woman from the evacuation office came forward with a list. Walt and Ann strained to listen. The boy didn't step forward when his name was called and so was the last one standing on the platform after the others went, with a gas mask, a drawstring bag for a suitcase and the label ripped off the top button of his blazer. He held on tightly to the bag and mask as they led him away from the station.

The spare room had been set up once for a baby. There was a rocking chair and a cot in the corner. But the boy didn't seem to notice. When they went to check, that first night, he was just sitting on the bed looking out the window at the boathouse. When Walt's wife asked if the room was all right, he wouldn't answer or catch her eye. But he followed Walt over to the boathouse when Walt asked if he'd like to take a look. And watched quietly as Walt prepared the boat for the next morning's run. He followed Walt back into the kitchen when his wife called over to say it was tea. All three of them sitting at the table felt new, proper. And the boy ate all right. Just quiet.

Walt did a short run the next day and then came home. The boy still hadn't spoken and over the next few days they began to worry. When Ann came near the boy he seemed to shrink away from the surfaces of himself, away from being touched. And there was a problem with his schooling. All the evacuees were to be taught in a special class at Stoke Bruerne grammar. But the boy wouldn't go and Ann couldn't get him to go. When she tried, he snatched his hand back and looked at her with eyes of something worse than panic. She hadn't meant to be rough with him.

They had the mother's address in St John's Wood but got no answer when they wrote, no answer from the boy about her either. When they asked him how to find her he looked fiercely down at his knees. He reached his arms around himself and scratched, agitated. He wouldn't take a bath or be washed and his nails grew grubby and long like claws. He slept in his clothes. Ann didn't know what to do about it.

His left fist was always curled tight in his pocket. One day, desperate, she forced it out and found a picture there. The boy screamed and flew at her, scratching at her arm with some terrible strength but she held it up high. It was a studio shot of the boy looking up at a wide-faced, wide-shouldered woman in a cloche hat. Dark, thick hair escaped from a bun at the nape of her neck. She had her hands on his shoulders and looked directly back at the camera with a hooded, brazen gaze. Almost feral. Ann found it too much to look at and flicked across to the boy's face, which was creased by a fold in the photograph. His expression was lifted, illuminated.

The boy was still screaming. He grabbed her dress and bit into a chunk of her arm and she let the picture flutter down to the floor. He ran out of the bedroom with it and she heard his boots rapping away across the yard. Ann stood stunned. It had given her a shock to see him smiling. He didn't come back inside till after dark and began to whimper when she opened the bedroom door. So she left him. She felt a monster. The Evacuees Office said they would make contact with the mother but that as long as the boy was safe, that was the main concern.

Walt decided to try something. He took the boy on a short trip, one that took just a day, and kept an eye on him that way. The boy seemed to be all right with him, and all right with the boats. When Walt steered he would sit quietly, or lean over the bow watching the water. He still wasn't talking but he looked like he was thinking of somewhere else, and a little more peaceful. And at the end of the day, when they got home, the boy sat with them at the table and afterwards he took himself to the bathroom and came out cleaner.

Walt kept taking him out on the boat. Soon when they got to a lock the boy knew what to do and would jump to the towpath with the windlass hooked over his belt and run up to open the far lock. He managed it all right, he was stronger than he looked. Walt found he didn't mind the boy's company; he couldn't tell what was in his head but it was a quiet sort of company. He seemed interested in the boat and Walt was glad to show him all of it. He taught him to start the engine, how to wind the trickier lock paddles, how to mop down the cabin sides. He gave him a try on the tiller and showed him how to navigate through Blisworth tunnel by the beams of light from ventilation shafts. You had to stand straight and line up the point of the roof with the circles of lit water that appeared every ten metres out of the blackness. Walt enjoyed having someone to teach these things to. The boy had a good concentration. When Walt was talking through something the boy would fix his eyes on Walt, and then mime the way Walt did things exactly, looking up for his approval.

And Walt saw that Ann was relieved at the change in the boy. It began that in the mornings she'd bring their lunch packs down and send them off from the mooring. Walt would look back at her as they steered away, she'd give a wave which looked almost jolly.

Then one morning the boat was gone. Walt was about to go on a four-day run, to London and back. Too long for the boy. Ann said what would she do with him for four days and they'd spoken to the school teacher, asked her to come by, encourage him to go to school. The boy had helped load up from Stoke Bruerne depot the afternoon before; the cargo was sacks of mail and a delivery of tins for the Heinz factory at Harlesden. They had checked the fuel and the London route maps. When Walt got up before the sun that morning the boat was gone and no sign of it half a mile along the canal each way. Straight away he took his dinghy to look. He rowed back in a terrible black mood. What a time to rob your fellow man, he thought. His boat. And all the packets on board, he felt bad about them. All the letters. He rowed back into the boatyard and heard his wife calling; she was standing at the edge of the water. Before he reached the mooring he understood that the boy was gone too, and all his things gone with him.

Walt felt the responsibility of it and ran to the boy's room. The cot and the rocking chair sat there as they had always done. The bed was made up as it had been before the boy arrived. Nothing else. Ann was twisting her hands; there was no answer from the evacuation office this early but the police were sending someone. He couldn't wait for them. He woke his neighbour and borrowed a launch, took it down the water in the direction of the city. He asked everyone, stopped at all the places he'd stop when carrying cargo. Mostly people were just coming on to the water and hadn't seen anything but near Cosgrove a pair of boaters had seen his boat coming down that stretch an hour or two before. They said the boat was going fast and had its lamp on. They hadn't seen the steerer. At the

Bletchley Crown, the landlady, Bel, had seen the boy on the boat when she'd gone out to the cellar that morning. She'd thought Walt must be down below, and wondered why he hadn't got the boy into a jacket, something warmer than shorts and a jersey at least. She'd waved, but the boy didn't look and the boat went straight on. Whistled by. Yes, fast, she said.

Walt climbed back into the launch and felt his teeth chatter. He motored on as fast as he could, pushing the throttle hard. There had been more sightings; by his estimation he was an hour and a half behind the boy. He had a horrible idea that the boy was going after his mother and that he wouldn't stop for the blackout, but carry on straight into London with the headlamp blazing.

His petrol cut out at nine that night, and he towed the boat by its rope half a mile to Northchurch. They said there wasn't a chance of getting more until the morning, even for extra money. So he stayed in a boaters' inn that night, but he didn't sleep. Switching off the light and unpinning the blackout curtain, he looked out of the window. The moon was bright enough to paint the water silver, and make everything around it crisply visible. The long grasses on the other side were slices of pale grey and shadow, he could see the planks of the fence beyond that and the rectangles of roofs in the next-door village. So much for a blackout.

He could hear his own breathing, which came out rough and interrupted by his thoughts.

From the right-hand side, the Birmingham direction, came the slow prow of a huge boat, and it slid into his vision. But he blinked before he believed it because he couldn't hear a thing. The shape in black was a wide windowless barge and the moonlight made a seam of white along the roof. The chimney puffed smoke but it dissolved into the night the moment it came out. Not a sound. It glided on. And he saw a standing figure at the back, upright and still with a hand on the tiller. The figure looked forward. The face was in shadow but the silhouette showed a cap and an oilskin with the collar up, gleaming. There was movement at the front of the boat and a shape rose up from the lumpy shadows on the foredeck. It stuck a head over the roof and spoke in a hushed voice, a woman's voice. 'Berkhamsted, half a mile.' The figure at the back gave a nod and the prow pushed out of his vision and the rest disappeared after it, leaving an empty pool. It had hardly troubled the water. Two black stripes in the silvery surface.

Before dawn he walked down to the next boatyard, towing the launch. He waited on the step until the first worker arrived. They had no faster boat to spare. So he bought fuel and set off, in his head calculating the hours lost, the distance the boy might have covered. And hoping with every lock he came to that the boy might have stopped, or have been stopped, that he would find him on the other side.

As the day came it got lighter but no warmer. The sky was clear with a watery brightness that gave out no heat. He went for a long time without seeing another boat or another human being. The trees at the waterside were thick and the sound of bird calls rose and became almost a din. There was something unwelcoming about the water, the surface was untouched and the going felt heavy, as if it was resisting. He leaned forward and willed the boat on.

Coming through Uxbridge at just after ten that morning, it looked changed. Even from the last time he'd come through, a month ago. Reduced. The houses set well back from the towpath. He could see dents in their outline, gaps through to rows of houses he'd not seen before. As London became louder and closer he heard sirens overlapping each other, differently pitched. Some sounded desperate, others in the distance just a hummed note. And activity on the water. By Cowley a baggy canvas hose was being run down the towpath from an industrial barge, there was smoke and shouting coming from behind the other side of a corrugated warehouse. When he looked ahead at the skyline, towers of smoke.

At Bull's Bridge he forked left up the Paddington arm and just beyond the Hayes lock he noticed that the water level was going down. Wet black moss was showing on the concrete banks of the canal. Quarter of a mile on and he could see the low ledge at the side. That was usually covered by a foot of water, at least. There was a boat coming the other way, an ancient battered barge, steered by a thick-set woman wrapped in a rug. As their prows drew closer he opened his mouth to ask, but something in her expression stopped him. An old, deeply lined face. She twisted her head slowly from left to right. His stomach dropped with dread and he went on, gripping the throttle, pulling it back to slow as he came around the corner.

The first thing he saw was a boat, blown on to its side against the grassy left bank of the canal. His boat. The headlamp was on and shining weakly forward. The portholes were glassless, a line of black Os staring up at the sky. The sun caught the wet shine of the boat's bared hull, which, he saw, needed re-tarring. There were bald patches along the bottom. The brass-handled tiller stuck up awkwardly from the back. As he looked the boat creaked and the hull dropped lower until the boat tilted to upright, the portholes leaning up to face him, eyeless.

Walt looked at the wall of the canal, the water now visibly climbing down its surface. He turned to the opposite bank and what he saw made him yank the throttle back, cutting the engine. There was a screaming hole, a giant bite taken out of the concrete. The water was rushing into this, pouring through to a crater beyond it which was edged with brick and rubble and black soil. It was as if a handful of ground had been pulled into the earth. Sucked in. The water was filling it as fast as an open lock. On the towpath beyond the crater were objects that Walt could not at first make sense of: a clothes press, flipped back on itself, standing upright like a billboard; a mop with its string head flung over a crack in the path; a tin bucket with its mouth stupidly gaping at the water. He forced his eyes beyond these things. He was looking into a kitchen, stove and shelves and yellow-papered walls with pans hanging down on hooks. It was like the doll's house Ann had once wanted for the baby's room, with hinged walls that could open to show the rooms inside. He saw the underside of a staircase. A landing with a charred banister. Two floors up the browned underside of a bath stuck down through the ceiling. The houses on either side stood still and untouched and there was no one.

He oared over to his boat and clambered desperately

on, pulling open the engine room door. His bunk was down and the boy's drawstring bag was underneath in a pool of water. The gas mask looked up at him. There was shattered glass on the floor from the porthole but, above, the thick glass bowl of the compass was still intact. The needle quivered inside it. He pushed through to the main cabin and ripped up the tarpaulins he had packed around the cargo. The crates of tins were mashed against one edge, sodden brown envelopes leaked out of the sacks of mail. He burrowed madly through these things, thinking the boy was underneath, had been trapped there. Waterlogged crates collapsed in his hands and tins tumbled out. He grabbed them and threw them over the side. He scoured along the side of the cabin and back. He pushed his hands through his hair and over his face. He pulled up the tarpaulin completely. Nothing, and nothing when he climbed up on to the deck. Just an empty grass bank and that terrible scene on the other side. He looked up, to shout something. The sky was still milky and unmoving, a shut door. It would give him nothing.

There was a groan as the boat shifted on to a tilt. Walt was pitched backwards against the cabin door. He looked down; the water was low enough now to expose the muddy level of flotsam in the bottom of the canal. Wheel spokes and glass bottles distinguished themselves, other objects had merged their slimy curves and jutting corners into one inseparable brown mass. He wanted to look away. It sat at the bottom of his stomach as a sort of shame. It was what he was. What others were.

The launch was grounded between his boat and the bank and so he climbed shakily over it on to the grass.

He walked along the fence not looking back. He had a sensation like his ears were ringing. A panic, although it wasn't making him move faster; he felt like he was moving through a thicker element than before.

He knocked on doors and asked. The boy? He described the scene at the canal and people knew about it. The young woman had been killed by the blast, he was told. A seamstress, her husband in the navy. Walt was told her name, and it would be impossible to forget. June Levison. He kept on asking about the boy. He kept on walking, in through the outskirts of the city, kept on knocking. Houses were empty, sometimes half a street would be rubble. Often people opened their doors quickly, with anxious faces. It made him think about the letters. June Levison. No boy.

He spent that night in Shepherd's Bush Underground, on a platform with many other bundles that were people. Groups bunched together, a drunk tried to sing a lullaby to a crying child, boys hung their legs over the platform edge and smoked. He made himself check each face and met blankness, met exhaustion. He was frightened underground and felt ashamed to be. He tried to sleep in the same crooked position as he would in his engine room bunk. It took him hours and then he woke up, hopeless, the last one there. For a few seconds, looking over the edge of the platform into the dark pit where the tracks were, he thought he was looking into an empty canal. June Levison.

He wouldn't go back to his boat. He walked the miles through Acton and Greenford to Bull's Bridge and the dockyard. Got a lift back up to Stoke Bruerne. He passed

Uxbridge, Marsworth, Bletchley and looked at these places without recognition.

At home he went upstairs to the boy's room; he lay down on the bed facing the wall. Ann followed him up and sat by him in the rocking chair. She pulled a blanket over and stroked his forehead until he slept.

She went to the evacuation office every day hoping for good news, but no news came.

FOUR

Join Odeline on her first night in the boat. She has not yet managed to sleep, the newness of her surroundings has unsettled her. She tells herself it is anticipation. Look at her. Eyes wide open and hands clasped on her chest, she is lying in an antique nightdress flat on her back along the side of the bed closest to the wall. From the chest down she is a long thin column under the quilt she has brought from home, her large feet making a tent at the end. She forgot pillows, so her head is awkwardly back, and she lies straight, as if she has been arranged this way and told not to move.

Odeline looks around her cabin. It is illuminated by streetlights from the road beyond the towpath. The port-hole curtains are thin and don't seem to keep out any light at all. Everything is cast in an electric hue and is either orange or shadowy. She follows the arch of the roof from above her head to the far end and clears her throat to see if the sound echoes as in a tunnel. 'Ahem.' It doesn't.

Her stomach gurgles and she puts a hand on to it over the quilt. She had the rest of the cheese slices on cracker-bread plus tinned pears for dinner and still felt hungry afterwards, but didn't want to use up any more of her provisions.

She blinks. Her eyes do not want to close. Inside her
there is an unarticulated feeling that she should be on the
lookout. Not so much a sense of danger as an utter clue-
lessness regarding her new surroundings. She has no idea
whether she is completely safe or completely exposed.
Her mother's toolkit is on the kitchenette counter and
as she was getting ready for bed, she found herself putting
the screwdriver under the quilt next to her. Self-defence,
she told herself, a sensible precaution.

She can hear noises from outside and tries to work out
where they're coming from: a soar of aeroplane overhead;
the occasional lap of water – birds perhaps; voices moving
along and away – people passing over the bridge; brief
fade-ins and fade-outs of pop music – the door of the pub
up by the bridge opening and closing.

And suddenly a horrible tuneless hollering which makes
her freeze, and she holds her breath to listen as it gets
louder.

'I'm an artist,' it says, although the vowels are garbled
and dragged.

'Aaaartist,' the voice says again.

Odeline freezes; it is that grubby bearded warden.

'Oooh my, I'm an aaaaartist!' Closer now. He is wheezing
with laughter.

She makes an irritated face to herself and sniffs, but her
heart is knocking against her chest. She reaches for the
screwdriver handle and finds herself holding it downwards
and tight in her fist, like a knife in a horror film.

'I only thought it would be nice to welcome you to the
community.' He sounds angrier. 'I only thought it would
be NEIGHBOURLY,' he ends with a shout.

Then there are three knocks on the cabin roof. 'Halloooo? Is her majesty in residence?'

His voice has gone old-womanish now and she can hear him breathily stumbling towards the other end of the boat. The cabin walls are so thin! Maybe he can even see her through the flimsy curtains. She closes her eyes tightly, shrinks under the quilt. She has heard of these things happening in London: Rape and Murder. She finds herself thinking she is going to die the most alone person in the world. At this moment in time, there is no one alive to whom she is not a stranger.

The warden is carrying on his chaotic rant, and it sounds like he has stepped on to the boat, shouting through the door.

'No need to be so BLOODY UNFRIENDLY.'

As she jerks upright in her bed with the screwdriver held high, ready to defend herself, she hears the door of the neighbouring boat burst open and a new voice, deep and well-spoken.

'Enough. And get off her boat. Much more of this and they'll take your licence.'

'Licence! I'd like a close look at yours, bloody New Age Cossack.'

'They will, they'll have it off you. You'll have woken half the street up there. People will complain again.' The tone is relaxed, almost a drawl.

'Crystal ball tell you that? Bloody gypo.' She hears him trip over the side of the boat back on to the towpath. 'You're the one they should be getting on to, I might bring 'em along for a look at your dodgy boat. And that manky dog.'

'Go home and let the girl be.'

'Oh but she's an artist, don't you know? An aaartist.' There is silence and then a few quick steps on to the towpath from the next-door boat and a low purr which Odeline thinks is machinery and then realises is a dog's growl.

'All right, all right,' the drunk voice says, and she hears footsteps staggering off. They fade, and then she hears them again, echoing under the bridge.

'Take no notice of him,' her neighbour calls across. 'He's just a sad old boozer. Comes up here pestering people.' He pauses. Gently: 'Are you okay?'

Odeline doesn't answer; she is still upright with her screwdriver poised, too scared to move. Her head is shrunk into her shoulders, her eyes stare straight ahead at the cabin doors. Her mind is a flashing white screen. What would it be appropriate to say? The ease with which these voices travel through the boat makes her feel horribly vulnerable. She is sure this man can hear her breathing, so she stops.

'Just let me know if you've any more trouble,' he says, and she hears his cabin door click shut. She blinks and breathes out. Slowly she allows herself to fall back on to the bed but her heartbeat, it seems, is pulsating the whole cabin. She replays the scene in her head.

'A Life-Threatening Encounter,' she says to herself, in a breathy whisper. Whilst 99 per cent of her is still terri-fied, 1 per cent is secretly impressed by the drama of it. She feels like the heroine of an Alfred Hitchcock film. She thinks back to those few seconds and they are accompanied by orchestral bursts; high, jarring notes. She can see her silhouette in angular black against an electric orange background. A title in jagged white lettering.

'A Close Call,' she whispers.

Gosh.

But quickly the adrenalin drains away. She drops the screwdriver to the floor. She looks around at the narrow cabin, the tiny kitchenette, the fuzzy orange carpet. What kind of vessel is this on which to launch a life? She is yet to locate the feeling of nomadic freedom that was meant to come with living here, the urge to spread her wings. Just a dizzying sense of nothing being solid. This boat and I are the same, she thinks: unprotected, foundationless, sinkable.

This is not winning thinking, Odeline.

Staring at the ceiling, she flicks her mind on to the plan for tomorrow. She has her first London performance at 7 p.m. in the famous theatre district of Covent Garden. The thought of it brings a pinch of panic. She is excited at the idea of a new audience but also uneasy at not knowing what to expect. Will it be the London audience she has imagined all these years in her rehearsals? The open-minded cosmopolitan avant-garde, the still and attentive rows of faces in the darkness, watching silently and then erupting into applause at the end of her repertoire, rising to their feet one by one to pound their hands together. Encore! Encore! And will she be able to expand her repertoire here, from illusions – the tricks that are second nature to her now – to the purer art of mime? Mime has been her private passion up till now. In Arundel she was billed as an illusionist only. More commercial. But surely a London audience is ready for higher art forms? She has been rehearsing her mime routine fiercely in the last few weeks for just this moment, this evolution.

The theatre is called 'The Globe'. She can't picture it. Whenever she tries to, she just sees her old classroom at school with the gridded blackboard globe on the desk, and her fifteen-year-old self being asked to go up and chalk Great Britain according to the latitudes and longitudes. She had drawn it upside down and south of the equator and everyone had laughed, including her geography teacher, Mr Binwell. Ignorants. Why should the world be depicted one way up rather than another? Why should the shape of Britain be sitting comfortably on its haunches whilst Africa and India and Latin America wobbled uncertainly on their points? It was an imperialist depiction. She hopes her classmates felt threatened seeing their smug country destabilised and sent to the bottom of the map. Perhaps that was the source of their jeers.

She checks her pocket watch next to the bed. It looks like half past eleven, but the antique glass makes it hard to read in this orange light. She is wide awake still. So she rolls on to her front and slides out the beige cardboard box from beneath the bed. From it she takes a pencil and the account book, opens the book, and begins to update her expense forecasts.

Odeline's mother taught her the importance of good accounting. She showed her how to balance a book, set profit against loss, detail a week's expenses, how to mark off a page with ruler and pencil and set out the numbers in neat little columns and rows, down and across. These columns and rows provided for the Milks.

Provincial England, genteel England. Nobody needed an unmarried mother in their town, or a dark-skinned girl in their child's classroom, but everybody needed their tax bill minimised. Eunice Milk walked from office to office at the end of every month, waiting on doorsteps for secretaries to hand over boxes of receipts and invoices without looking her in the eye. Then she would sit all day at the kitchen table, with the battered brown boxes stacked at her elbow, tapping at her calculator. Her expression would be quiet but her fingers struck the buttons like little hammers. She was so fast it sounded to Odeline like a hailstorm hitting the window. Odeline used to imagine the numbers appearing as they were punched in, forming a cloud around her mother's head that became denser and darker with figures, pound signs and decimal points. When she got up to stop work Odeline would picture them all dropping to the table and her sweeping them up and emptying the lot into the wastepaper basket.

Odeline's mother was the only female accountant in Arundel and though she had many clients she had few acquaintances. The Milks received no invitations. They were not acknowledged on the High Street, in the post office, or in the queue at the bank. They kept the shutters of their big red-brick house closed, to prevent townsfolk prying. They had no friends, but they did not want any. In the playground Odeline had her brush-black hair tugged, was chanted at and asked questions. 'Mop-head,' they called her, and 'Odd-bod.'

She would not respond.

She always took a book out with her in the lunch break. She would sit on the school steps reading, and never look up. And so they left her to her own devices. Over the years she looked on thankfully as the other children tangled themselves in friendships. They were like the tiny ants she watched rushing relentlessly back and forth over the miniature muddy ups and downs of her mother's garden. It all seemed such an effort, and so pointless. Odeline knew that she was different, that she breathed a rarer air.

Her mother's pale brown receipt box sits on the carpet next to Odeline's bed now. In it are some of her mother's personal items. Odeline's mother was not attached to the material world, she paid little attention to it, but these are things she used or looked at every day.

From her mantelpiece, all of Odeline's school photographs from five to eighteen: Odeline, easy to spot, bigger and darker than the other children, in all of them unsmiling and standing a head taller than the rest of her year group. Also from her mantelpiece, an envelope of Odeline's school certificates and a word-processing qualification from Arundel library. From the kitchen table, her mother's Arnott's biscuit tin containing the pencils (always HB blue) for working through those towers of account books. In the tin too are rubbers used down to the size of a pea, her folding ruler and two blue sharpeners. Everything in the tin is dusted with pencil lead. The lead that would coat Eunice Milk's hand as it moved across the page, quickly, column to column, a rapid scribble followed by the abrupt swish of skin on paper. She used to press so hard that the lead splintered and her fingertips would be speckled with black. At the end of every page she blew the dust off the paper with a puff before turning over to the next.

Underneath the biscuit tin are some of the logic puzzle books which Odeline's mother received monthly, with page after page of number grids and mathematical scenarios. Most puzzles are completed tidily and with no written workings. She did one puzzle at 11 a.m. every day with her glass of fruit juice and plate of frosted sponge biscuits. It would take her five minutes to complete.

On the blue account book which Odeline has just picked up, a business card taped to the front reads 'Arundel Magic'. The company logo: a top hat and wand. This is the business that Odeline's mother set up when Odeline was sixteen and had enough of a repertoire to work on weekends as a professional illusionist. Her mother ordered eight hundred of these cards and pinned them to noticeboards all over Arundel, in the post office, church and the supermarket, in the bank and the butcher's, the doctor's surgery and the town hall. Eunice Milk, who'd always seemed not to notice that anyone else existed, gave them out to people she passed on the pavement. She didn't explain, gave no sales pitch, just pushed them into people's hands and walked on. She'd include one in every box of accounts she returned, and even put them in the envelope with her cheque for the gas and electric bills. Arundel Magic was perhaps one of the most widely advertised small businesses in Sussex.

Odeline was hired for several children's parties around Arundel but her repertoire was too advanced for such a limited audience and these jobs were not successful. (She is an artist not a children's entertainer. She is not a balloon

sculptor or a whoopee-cushion prankster.) Her mother
would have her costume ready the night before each job,
freshly ironed and laid out on the armchair in the television room. She would polish Odeline's brogues and
inspect the suit with a needle and thread pressed between
her lips, darning any parts of the old tailcoat and trousers
that appeared to be thinning. She would admire Odeline
as she left the house, fists squeezing with excitement. But
as Odeline pulled her box of props down the slope of
Maltravers Street on her way to each new job, she felt no
such excitement. And when she rang the doorbell of
another pointlessly pretty Arundel house and heard the
children shrieking inside, there would rise in her a shaking
anger at her mother for all the stupid excitement, for
getting it wrong, for limiting her to this stupid town,
for offering her only Arundel with its lack of imagination,
its lack of opportunity.

Sometimes she turned away before the client had even
opened the door, pulling her prop box quickly down the
street before she could be seen. But more often she stayed
and performed, just to get paid her fee. Standing in front
of a wriggling herd of children in someone's sitting room,
beneath bunting and paper chains, she would move half-
heartedly through her repertoire, checking her pocket watch
after every one until the forty-five-minute act was finally
over. Sometimes she didn't even bother getting all the props
out. What was the point? Her audience were more interested
in stuffing their faces with cake and jelly. So degrading.

When she got home she would ignore her mother as
punishment, going straight upstairs to her room and shutting the door. But her mother never seemed to notice.

Even after hours had passed, she never came upstairs to make amends. When Odeline eventually came down for dinner her mother would smile at her brightly in the same way as she always did, pat Odeline's place at the table as she always did, tip her head to the side and gaze at her as she ate her dinner, just as she always did.

At Odeline's last engagement, a child's eighth birthday, she had been dismissed mid-repertoire by the child's parents. It was another twee sitting room in another twee Arundel street. The parents must have spent a fortune on the party, helium balloons filled the ceiling and there were trestle tables with plastic tablecloths piled with food. The children kept on getting up to wander to these tables, bringing back packets of crisps and rustling sweets. Even some of the adults were talking while she performed. So she told them to shut up. And then lost her temper, when the children began to heckle. They were a pack of bourgeois imbeciles! And so she told them that too.

The clients had refused to pay, despite several subsequent claim letters, and Arundel magistrates' court had refused to take the case.

After this she received no more jobs.

This is reflected in the Arundel Magic profits, which, no matter how hard her mother scribbled, rubbed and tapped, could not be balanced against the necessary expense of props, costumes and educational literature from which Odeline learnt.

Yes, Odeline has come to London to find her true audience – but also to see this account book balanced. She

bought the narrowboat and its mooring with the proceeds
from the sale of her mother's house. The remainder has
gone into her Post Office savings account. But she will
not be living off this. No. She will be successful and self-
sufficient in her own right.

She has itemised her deficit on the page as follows:

Arundel Magic Deficit as of 1st August	−£442.11
Other Expenses [London, Narrowboat-related, Career-related, Provisions]	
Literature/Research [London]	£16.20
Literature/Research [Narrowboat]	£8.47
The Professional Magician [annual subscription]	£12
Stamps for Correspondence	£16.60
Theatre Tickets plus booking fee	£63
Transport	£35
Tourism Allowance	£50
Laundry costs	unknown
Top Hat Agency Subscription	£90
Food Provisions [Long life]	£29
Food Provisions [Perishable]	£11.93
Gas Cylinder	unknown
Diesel	unknown
Deficit TOTAL	−£774.31

She has allowed herself two months to earn this sum
back, and after that would like to move into her budget

plan 'A', which is based on her taking four work engagements per week. This, she has calculated, will lead to entries of between £360 and £440 in the profit column at the end of each month, after all necessary expenses. Any less than three work engagements per week and she will have to fall back on budget plan 'B', which would make profits negligible, even if she reduces expenses. She looks forward to the day when she can open this Arundel Magic account book, run her finger down the right-hand column and feel proud.

This is one of her aims. Here's another:

In that pale brown receipt box there is also a card: it is the advertisement for the Moroccan Circus that came through Arundel nineteen years ago. It is faded now but otherwise in good condition – it has been well kept. 'CIRQUE MAROC' is written across the top, red letters on a yellow banner, and underneath is a picture of a white cat leaping through a red hoop. A Harlequin stands in the centre, holding a placard on which is written the main attractions:

CIRQUE EXTRAORDINAIRE!
Les frères BOUM-BOUM
Le Jongleur PI-KA-TA
ODELIN le clown (Exercices au Trapèze)
AKBAR et ses CHATS
Le SINGE et le PERROQUET
et Madame FATIMA clairvoyante

Odelin the Clown.

There was no mention of Odeline's paternity as she grew up and something had always stopped her asking. But Odeline knew the seeds of her existence must have come from somewhere more spectacular than mere Eunice Milk, the accountant, with her cardboard receipt boxes and HB pencils. Sometimes she felt she was trapped inside one of those beige boxes, forced to live a small life of endlessly repeated routines. Boiled egg and toast for breakfast. Every morning. Her mother checking the weather forecast on teletext for Odeline's walk to school. Every morning. Her mother standing in the doorway until Odeline reached the end of Maltravers Street. Every morning. An hour of homework on the kitchen table before dinner. Every night. Tinned soup and rye biscuits with cheese slices for dinner. Every night. Hot chocolate in the mugs with the Pierrot clown before bedtime. Every night. Weekend routines were just as repetitive. Down to the newsagent's on Saturday morning to collect the television schedule. Sponge fingers and fruit juice at eleven. Wafer ham and cheese-slice sandwich in front of the afternoon film. A walk down the Causeway road on Sunday morning. Tinned fruit and Neapolitan ice cream for pudding on Sunday night. Odeline did not fit this life. She was different. She knew there was something *spectacular* in her own blood, and soon found a theory to support this.

Unclear as to the precise conditions of parenthood, she'd imagined that her mother had achieved an immaculate conception like the mother in the Bible readings she heard in school assemblies. This interpretation appealed to a girl who sensed she was in some way set apart from the other children. The more Bible readings she heard, the more she became convinced of it. Jesus, she learned, was revealed as God's son aged twelve when he addressed the Pharisees in the Temple. During the lead-up to Odeline's twelfth birthday she practised a slow, low public voice which might be appropriate for a child of God.

Her birthday fell on a Wednesday, and there was no Temple in Arundel, but that morning she walked on past the school gates and into the wilderness of Arundel Park, where she sat beneath a plane tree and *listened*. She closed her eyes. She tuned out from the earthly distractions of dog-callers and traffic. She awaited the seed of her father inside herself, pressed an imaginary ear to the opening in a tiny shell deep within her chest. Orange blobs fuzzed in her eyelids where the sunlight came through the trees. After a minute or so, the blobs went a dark red colour, and she realised she'd been listening so hard she'd forgotten to breathe. She drew in a deep breath.

'Hosanna in the Highest,' she said to herself, dizzy.

Then, as she sat there, something in her opened up and she felt as if she was growing taller, as if her shoulders were physically rising up, as if her body was being stretched from the tree root she was sitting on. Up and up she seemed to go, and there was a clean cold vacuum at the top of her head that was pulling her skywards. Up and up, and she thought that if she opened her eyes she would be looking down from a great height, down along an elongated torso that was swaying in the wind next to the other trees. The calls of the dog-walkers were distant now, and she heard a rushing of something in her ears.

'The breath of God,' she said to herself. 'Alleluia.' She lost
her balance then and tipped backwards, knocking her head
against the trunk of the plane tree. Her eyes sprang open
and were flooded with the luminous green layers of the
giant leaves above her. She stayed tilted back, and looked
up without blinking for about a minute, her arms flopped
at her sides. She felt held in the palm of her father's hand.
Her eyes were circles of wonder.

When she finally forced herself up, aching, from under
the tree, she thought perhaps years had passed since she
had sat down, she felt so utterly different. She walked
back into Arundel town reborn, still with that same light
feeling, as if angels were gently wheeling her along. She
ate her packed lunch on a bench opposite the church and
then went inside.

It was a cool, dark, empty place in which it was difficult
to translate the ecstasy she had felt in the bright greenness
of the tree. The statuettes of the crucifixions along the walls
were quite alarming. But this is my father's house, she told
herself. I must try to feel at home. She parted the curtains
and looked into the vestry – it was bare but for a cupboard
and a toilet sign with an arrow. She climbed up into the
pulpit and said, 'Hello.' Her voice came back to her impressively deep. She sat in the front pew, looking up at the
enormous window of men in their colourful robes, and
meditated on her new prophet status. She felt as if she had
plenty of wisdom to share. She wished she had brought a
pen to write some of it down. When the stained glass lost
its glow and the church became even darker she got up
and walked solemnly down the aisle and out through the
church doors.

At home her mother was bent rigidly over account books as usual, heavy clumps of tired ginger hair jiggling with the effort of pressing figures into columns. She had not heard Odeline come in. There was a tower of beige boxes at each elbow, and the hair, now fading, shot with grey, had started to match their colour, so that it seemed they were three parts of the same machine, two thick trunks with a vibrating ball between. Odeline looked at her mother's head with a forgiving smile and closed her eyelids slowly in a gesture of omniscience and understanding. She wondered how her father had made his divine visitation. Perhaps via an angel. She imagined a stained-glass window of herself, her father and her mother, in long coloured robes, making the two-fingered blessing of Christ.

Odeline's passion burned brightly but did not last for long. She received no divine instruction, despite daily requests for it. She bought a copy of the Bible and began to study it from the beginning, hoping to find some kind of personal message, a reference, perhaps, to a girl from Arundel. She read five verses every morning before breakfast. She enjoyed the discipline of it and all the biblical names and the rhythm of the language, but after three months with the Old Testament, she noticed she was feeling more and more despondent at breakfast, often not hungry for her boiled egg and toast. The stories left her crushed. It was a saga of endless punishment! She felt no kinship with this undemocratic, thunderous, irrational deity. In fact she disapproved of him. All the stories seemed to be about men. Women, if they featured, did particularly badly.

When Lot's wife was frozen into a pillar of salt, Odeline closed her Bible for good. A little older and more worldly wise, she replaced her immaculate-conception theory with an adoption theory. It still explained her difference from the other children, and the feeling that she came from somewhere else. And it was easier, she had to admit, to imagine her mother interacting with adoption forms than angels.

So she thought up a new set of grand and exotic origins for herself. Her parents were the exiled monarchs of Ethiopia, banished into the desert and unable to care for their only and highly precious daughter. Her parents were deep-sea explorers, brutally murdered by giant squid in the Marianas Trench. Her parents were genius code-breakers, imprisoned underground by the Communists and forced to decipher one thousand codes a day – they gave up their lives to smuggle her to safety. The Messiah complex never quite wore off.

But then, before her mother's cremation – a discounted early-morning slot at the mortuary, as outlined in her will – Odeline was handed a bag of clothes and her mother's purse by the mortuary assistant. As she waited for the ceremony in the brick foyer, she opened the purse and found an account slip folded at the sides to make an envelope. Her name was written across the front in her mother's hard-pressed capitals. Inside were folded two things. The first, her birth certificate. Odeline Eunice Milk. Born: 6.50 a.m., Arundel Maternity Ward. Years of elaborately imagined origins dispelled in an instant. Behind it, the immaculately preserved circus flyer with the name Odelin the Clown outlined by a neatly ruled blue box. She looked at the dates the circus came to Arundel, and counted nine months forward to her birth date. One world closed, another opened.

Odeline had shaken her head when asked if she was waiting for other attendees, and was shown into the chapel. She took a seat at the back, and stared down at her father's name on the flyer in her hand. She ignored the entrance of the mortuary assistant, the words of committal, the noise of the conveyor as it drew the coffin through the curtain. She kept her eyes fixed on the flyer, her mind focused on the film running in her head, the great moment of reunion with Odelin the Clown.

Later, at home, she looked up the Cirque Maroc in her *World of Magic Compendium* and found it listed under 'Travelling'. So she spent the next few days composing a letter and found she hardly had time to think of her mother at all. She wrote it out several times and posted a copy to every circus agency in the *Compendium*. After that she busied herself with administration. She followed the instructions her mother had left in the stapled pack of papers under the toolkit in the kitchen, entitled 'IN CASE OF EMERGENCY'. She went to the bank and the lawyer's office and read out the instructions exactly as they were written. She walked around Arundel like an automaton, carrying the pages in one hand and a shopping bag in the other (Eunice Milk had included a list for Odeline's weekly food shop). She took the death certificate to the post office and made herself the major signatory on the savings account. She went to the estate agent's and put the house on the market with all the contents included. At each of these places she left a small stack of Arundel

Magic business cards; the instructions recommended not
wasting these valuable advertising opportunities.

The instructions suggested that she rent a smaller house
for herself. But the discovery that her father was a nomad
inspired her to deviate, and she began to look into more
itinerant ways of living. Caravans were her first thought
but the ones she saw were either extremely ugly or required
horses. The idea of living on water occurred to her in a
Eureka moment. She bought a *Waterways* magazine and
very much liked the appearance of the traditionally decorated houseboats. When she found the *Chaplin and
Company* listing she felt destiny's hand as strongly as she
had in those moments walking back from Arundel
Common.

She has yet to hear from her father, but before leaving
Arundel sent a fresh batch of letters to the circus agencies
with the return address of the British Waterways building
at Lisson Grove. Again and again, she plays out the
moment of their meeting. It can only be days away.

It is thoughts of her father that finally allow her to fall
into the half-dreams that lead to sleep. And as with every
recent night, these half-dreams are of him. She has a clear
idea of how he will be: she worked it out like one of
her mother's accounting calculations. Her qualities minus
her mother's must equal her father. She sees the three of
them in adjacent columns on the page, he making the
balance on the right-hand side marked 'Profit'. Her mother
was gingery fair with mottled pink skin, and she is black-
haired with butterscotch skin. Therefore he will have hair

that is pitch black and skin that is smooth, deep brown. Her mother was tall and big-boned, and she is tall and slight, so he will be slight, although tall too – Odeline wants him to be tall. And perhaps slight is not the word, more *athletic* in physique. He is after all an acrobat. And therefore deft and highly coordinated, which would explain Odeline's gift for movement – her mother was an extremely clumsy woman. And her mother, though gifted with numbers, of course had no imagination. Odeline is all imagination. Her father will be pure imagination too. Her kindred spirit. He will be her artistic mentor and her springboard into the world of performing arts. He will look at her solemnly (according to her calculations, her father will have dark soulful eyes, bottomless pools of wisdom) and know that she is his daughter, that she belongs to him. That her star is aligned with his.

A breeze travels along the canal and gently rocks the boat on the water, making it sigh. Odeline looks into those imaginary eyes; they become bigger and bigger until she tips into their dark, serene, bottomless pools, and into sleep.

FIVE

The boat is breathing. It is never still. Through the day and through the night, it is always moving, nudging at the bank, in, away. Things that live on water are like this. There are rhythms. Because water is never still. Even this water, contained by concrete, shadowed by buildings, locked out from the sea. Like all water, it is in love with the moon. Night after night it yearns towards the moon's glow like a body arching, making invisible tides. Through the month it rises and falls and repeats and repeats, like deep and shallow breaths. The wet green line creeps up the concrete bank and creeps back again. People don't notice. They don't see the boat breathing. But people are the same. As long as there is breath they are never still. So the boat rises and falls, and it sighs as it falls. It is always moving.

Walt Chaplin knew this as he fell asleep on his bunk at night, that what he was listening to was the boat breathing. He heard the creaks of planks ageing, cracking in the heat, closing in the cold. He knew that her nails would rust, her paint would crack. He and his boat, neither of them would last. Time would wash them both away. Time would wash it all away. He knew the boat was never still.

SIX

Lunchtime and the canal junction is busy. The two cruising narrowboats by the bridge have moved off from their moorings and come into the Little Venice pool. They are waiting, with engines chugging, to pass through a narrow neck of waterway that leads north-east up towards Lisson Grove. Steering through this now is an open-sided narrowboat that has travelled down the canal from Regent's Park. 'ERIC'S TOURS' is written in red along the edge of the awning. A man in a golf visor is leaning against the front of the boat with a videocamera, other tourists are taking pictures out of the side. At the back, the tour guide is holding the tiller and a small black radio which is connected to tannoys at four corners of the awning. He is a tanned young man with sideburns, wearing wraparound sunglasses and a T-shirt which also says 'ERIC'S TOURS', in red. He brings the boat around the little island in the middle of the pool and into the bank next to the barge cafe. 'Time for lunch folks!' he calls into the radio. He hops out and winds the bow and stern ropes quickly around the mooring stones, and then holds out a hand to help the ladies – portly, middle-aged, rich – on to the towpath, pushing his sunglasses on to the top of his head so he can give them a proper smile. Eric from the tour boat company always brings his customers to the barge cafe for lunch. He has a deal with Zjelko.

Vera has seen the tour boat approaching and is at the kitchen counter, peeling clingfilm from a tray of sandwiches. All of the cafe's nine metal tables are outside today, and she has kept five reserved. She takes a selection of soft drinks out of the fridge and puts them in a bucket with ice at the bottom, and then balances a stack of foam cups on top of the sandwiches. She loops the bucket handle over her arm and picks up the tray. When she goes outside, Eric is seating his tourists around the tables. He motions to her to hurry up, mock-complaining, 'My poor passengers are thirsty! Typical British weather eh!' Some of his boatload laugh, others are fiddling with their cameras and telephones. Vera puts the tray down and people lean in to take sandwiches. Eric takes the bucket from her arm and goes round offering the soft drinks. She follows him, dealing out the cups. It is just as hot as yesterday. She is wearing a V-necked mauve T-shirt and you can see her chest and arms reddening. Nobody says thank you. Eric hands her back the bucket and says, 'Mr Z said we'd have ice creams too.'

Vera nods. 'I have plenty. In the freezer.'

'Okay. Bring them out in five. I want to get going quickly.'

Another table have left and Vera goes over to clear up, stacking the plates on to a chair and putting their discarded newspaper under her arm while she wipes the surface with a napkin. Inside she throws the napkin and ketchup packets into the bin, but keeps the newspaper. She glances through the doorway – all her customers are still eating. She puts the newspaper on the counter and flicks the pages over, scanning the articles. There is nothing. No international news at all. It is the wrong kind of newspaper. She puts it into the bin as well, pressing it down into the bag with her knuckle. There is a small flap of window at the back of the boat. She goes over to face it, leaning her hips against the sink and tilting her head back so that the air can cool the creases of her neck. The radio is playing its *Summer Lunchtime Ballad Hour*. Always the same station. This is the rule.

There is a whistle from outside and she is moving again, opening the freezer and putting handfuls of ice creams into the soft drinks bucket. She carries the bucket outside and Eric takes it from her, doles out the ice creams. She stands and waits in the beating sun, the soles of her feet aching flatly in her trainers. Pigeons are pecking at sandwich crumbs around the tourists' chairs. A man in a sun visor and sandals shoos them with his plastic bag.

Chugging out from under the bridge now is the wide black bow of the refuse barge, its pan filled with objects picked out of the canal: a car bumper, the silver cage of a shopping trolley, a wooden chair, a door, foam squares from a mattress, rubbish bags ripped and spilling, card-board boxes sodden and collapsed. The whole length of the barge comes into the sunlight and dark smoke coughs out from a pipe at the rear cabin.

'I think we're done with these,' says Eric, pointing to the sandwich tray. She leans forward to take it and stacks the cups and empty drink cans on top. Eric claps his hands, 'Shall we enjoy our ice creams on board, folks?'

The tourists begin to zip up their rucksacks and camera cases. Vera hooks the bucket back over her arm and carries the tray away into the kitchen.

There are new customers inside wanting ice creams and drinks. She serves them, punching numbers into the till, counting out change – even the coins feel hot in her hand – and then goes outside to wipe the tour group tables. Eric's boat is pulling away from the bank, turning its nose towards the top of the pool on its way back to Regent's Park. Another pair of customers ask for the bill. She clears their table and comes back with the till receipt on a metal saucer. They give her a note and wait for change. More customers arrive and sit down outside, pulling their table a few metres over so they have a better view of the Little Venice pool. She carries the chalked menu board over. Sparkling water and two paninis. Inside, she heaps salad on to the sides of two plates and, sweating, shuts her eyes as she waits by the machine for the paninis to toast. She lifts them out with tongs and slides them on to the plate. Sprig of parsley on top (Mr Zjelko is particular about presentation). She delivers them to the table with the bottle of water and two cups. Takes the metal box of sauce sachets from an empty table and gives them that too. Strains to bend for a used napkin stuck to the leg of a chair. And then back inside.

The microwave clock says it is 12.58 and so Vera looks outside to check she is not needed before going over to the radio, which is in the corner of the counter, next to the till. She turns the volume down before twisting the dial to the World Service. After a minute she hears the beeps for the news programme. She looks outside again and then, keeping her finger on the dial, bends her head to listen.

News from England.

News from America.

News from the Middle East.

She turns the volume up, listens for the next feature. They must have a report from home soon.

She hears a step behind her and turns around into a big, polo-shirted chest. She looks up, tripping back into the cafe counter. It is one of Mr Zjelko's men, one of the crew-cut giants he sends to check on his establishments. The other one is standing in the doorway, blocking the brightness from outside. He is also wearing a polo shirt, and three-quarter-length trousers with flip-flops. How did she not hear them? She spins round and jabs at the radio, gets fuzz. She twists the dial to try to find the station. Gets dialogue, twists it further. Mr Zjelko's man reaches a heavy, muscled arm around her and turns off the switch at the wall. Silence.

'The aerial is broken,' says Vera, 'I am trying to find the station.'

These men have no names. The one by the door steps into the cabin and comes towards her. He looks into the bucket on the counter and takes out an ice cream, unwrapping it as he goes back to the step. He leans against the side of the doorway. Takes a bite.

The man in front of her flexes his jaw. He is burly-faced, the middle section of his nose is flat and he has military-style dog tags sitting in the neck of his polo shirt. His biceps stretch the sleeves.

'So. What do we tell Mr Zjelko?' he says thickly, in

English. Since she was hired, no reference has been made
to where she comes from. And they refuse to speak to her
in her own language, though she knows this is their
language too. But this is how they all do business.

The man carries on, manoeuvring his huge, blunt
features into a look of concern. 'He will be so upset when
he hears that his favourite radio station is not being
played. Mr Zjelko takes very seriously the atmosphere
in his cafes. He gives instruction to always maintain this
atmosphere.'

Vera opens her mouth but doesn't say anything. She
has backed herself against the counter, gripping on to it
with her elbows up behind her. She keeps her gaze fixed
on the polo-shirted chest in front of her, stops it from
flicking back to the low double doors at the back of the
cabin. Her hiding place.

Zjelko's man opens his hands to his sides and looks
round at his friend in the doorway. He's hamming it up.
'How can he continue to employ a person who cares
nothing about this? Who cares nothing for the atmosphere
for his customers?'

The man in the doorway shrugs. He is holding the ice
cream stick out between his thumb and forefinger. It is
dripping on to the cafe floor.

'I know the rules,' Vera rushes. 'I am just looking for
something. There are no customers inside today.' She
gestures to the empty cabin.

He sighs and she can smell beer in the exhalation. 'I
really don't want to upset Mr Zjelko,' he says. The man
in the doorway shakes his head slowly, regretfully.

Vera closes her eyes. 'Please.'

Silence. Brightness and chatter uninterrupted outside.

The man steps back and puts a fist inside his other hand. 'Mr Zjelko takes pride in his establishments. He needs employees who will respect these environments he has worked to create.'

Vera nods her head.

'There are so many who would like to work in Mr Zjelko's establishments.'

She nods her head again.

He gestures at the radio and she turns around to switch it on at the wall, and twists the dial until she finds the station. *More sunshine songs on their way for you now . . .*

'We will see you soon.' He ducks his head and steps out of the cabin. The man in the doorway drops his ice cream stick on the floor and turns to follow. They walk away through the tables, huge square heads stacked on top of dense chests, the pink palms of their hands facing backwards like apes.

Vera goes to the sink and turns the hot tap on full so that it thunders into the metal tub. She loads in plates, bowls, cutlery, panini tongs, and shakes washing-up liquid all over them. She lifts things out, sluicing them with water. She grabs bunches of cutlery and grips them tight so that they dig into the fat flesh of her hand, drops them clanking on to the drying rack. She doesn't bother to turn the tap off, keeps it running and steam rises to wet her face and cloud the rectangular window above the sink. Hot thundering water to block out the noise of the radio, to block out everything.

So she doesn't notice until she turns around for the dishcloth that there is another visitor standing behind the counter.

The figure makes her half laugh in surprise. It is a tall girl dressed in men's clothes, a caramel-skinned girl in a baggy shirt, braces and billowing trousers, with a long neck like a stalk, a crooked mop of black hair and blazing eyes.

'I'm sorry,' says Vera. 'You give me a shock.'

'Do you serve hot chocolate?' the girl says, glaring. She is upright as a stick, her lips puckered forward, hardly moving. Vera wonders if her face is frozen from an illness.

'Yes.' Vera points at the drinks board above the till. 'Two pounds forty.'

'Oh.' The girl drops her head and turns to go out. She looks so thin, Vera can see the sinews of her neck, the bony corner of her shoulder under the white shirt.

'Take a seat,' says Vera, pointing to the stool. 'I can make you one for free.'

'Okay,' the girl says, and returns to the counter. Vera rips the top off a sachet and shakes the chocolate powder into a foam cup. She switches on the hot water and looks up at the girl, who has swivelled her small head to the right and is looking out of the porthole window. Her black thatch of hair touches the cabin roof. She turns back to Vera, rolls her eyes up in thought, and then brings a small blue spiral-bound notebook, an A–Z and a biro out of her trouser pocket on to the counter.

Suddenly, words are fired out like little barks. 'Are British Waterways who I should make a complaint to about an assault on my boat?' The voice is much older than the girl.

Vera shrugs. 'I don't know about that.' She presses her palm to the side of the water dispenser. 'Your water is taking a minute to heat up, okay?'

The girl opens her notebook, folding the cover behind it, and picks up the biro, taking the cap off and slotting it on the top end. Vera notices numbers down the side of the page, each next to a line of narrow writing.

'Do British Waterways offer lessons in steering?' she continues in the same barking tone.

Why does this girl think I am the person to ask, thinks Vera.

'I don't know about that either, I'm sorry.'

The girl looks at Vera blankly. A pause, then another question.

'How far is it to Covent Garden?'

'Oh, you can take the bus, number 23 to Trafalgar Square, then you can walk from there. It's not far.'

The girl dips down over the counter and scribbles into her notebook. She holds the biro oddly in her left hand, curling her forefinger around the body of it. She straightens up.

'Do you know where to buy gas cylinders for on-board use?'

This is an interrogation.

'For the cooker?'

'Yes.'

'You can get them on Harrow Road. From the hardware store by the crossroads, that way.' She points towards the back of the boat. 'Sometimes my boss sends me.'

'How much is a fifteen-kilogram cylinder?' The girl's voice breaks on the word cylinder, it wavers and ends in a squeak.

'The one I get is sixty pounds, I don't know how many kilograms. It's this size.' Vera opens the cupboard next to the oven and steps back to show the red tank inside.

The girl looks at it and then bends down to write. Her handwriting is as tall and stick-like as she is. At the end of every word she makes a curl from the last letter. She flips upright again, the biro still hooked rigidly by her finger and pressed against the page. Vera can see the words 'CONVENIENCE STORE' written in capitals next to the ball of the pen.

The next question:

'Where is the nearest convenience store?'

But before she can answer, a shadow falls across the threshold. They both look round. It is John Kettle, wet-lipped and grinning desperately. He is on the towpath, but sways as if at sea, and holds on to the barge's doorframe for support.

'Good afternoon, ladies!' He smells stale. He is in the same crumpled clothes as yesterday but his hat is gone and a strand of yellowed hair is pasted across his bald head. The beard has been shaped into a greasy point. A baggy cigarette hangs from his fingers. Vera nods to him but the girl has jerked her head back round towards a porthole and is staring furiously at it. Vera notices the girl's hands gripping her notebook and pen. They are shaking.

'I was going to introduce you two but I see you've beaten me to it. Vera, this is our new resident artist.' He makes a presenting gesture and then slaps his hand to his lips and sucks at the cigarette. It has gone out. He pats his shirt pocket and finds a lighter, slumping against the doorframe as he uses both hands to try and get the thing lit, pushing the spark with his grubby thumb. The paper catches and he straightens, grinning again, pleased with himself. Sucks at it and coughs out smoke. Vera thinks of the refuse barge.

'You know you can't smoke in here. It's the rule.'

'I'm bloody outside, aren't I?' He looks down at his boots on the step and jabs a finger at them. Then lifts his chin and squints to focus on the girl.

'Aren't you going to say good afternoon?'

He leans his head in her direction, the girl swivels hers around even further towards the porthole and sniffs.

'Eh? Just a hello?'

Nothing.

'Not interested in making friends?' He winks at Vera, who doesn't wink back. The girl doesn't move. Vera shrugs at John Kettle, hoping he will be on his way. He looks at the cabin floor and then turns, manoeuvring himself around in the doorway and staggering off. Vera hears a scrape as he bashes into one of the metal tables outside.

'Well done,' she says to the girl. 'I can never get rid of him so quickly.'

The girl brings her head round and checks the empty doorway. She looks at Vera and it is like someone has animated her frozen face – her eyebrows are now halfway up her forehead, the eyes are stretched open.

'Is that man dangerous?' she spurts in a shrill, broken voice, her mouth wider and more elastic than before, showing small, inward-pointing teeth.

'I don't think so. Just unhappy.' Vera feels the hot-water tank and then fills the girl's cup to the top and puts it on the counter. 'Here you go. You ask about a convenience

store. There are some by Paddington Station – carry on
along the towpath and you come to the back of it.'

The girl stacks the notebook on top of the *A–Z*,
replaces the cap of the biro and then clips it on to the
cover of the notebook. She takes the cup and moves
towards the entrance, no nod of farewell, making an exaggerated stoop as she ducks under the doorframe. Vera sees
that her huge trousers are held together at the back with
a crooked line of safety pins. As she listens to the clip of
the girl's shoes on the towpath, she thinks she hears a
small thank you, but can't be sure.

SEVEN

In the ladies' toilets of the Globe, Odeline is packing her props into their box. She lays out three silk handkerchiefs on the baby-changing shelf – red, white, black – and folds them carefully. As she reaches for the red one the hand-dryer turns on and blows them all to the floor, into puddles of water under the sink. She has to get on to her knees to pick them up and feels a darned patch of her trousers give way. She looks down: beneath the bumpy stitched square across the knee she can see a slice of skin. She squeezes the cloth together, pinching the skin beneath it so tight that her fingers shudder. Her mother was in charge of costume repair. Couldn't she have darned it properly? Can't Odeline kneel down if she needs to without her suit falling apart? Professional mime artists should never have this problem. She stands up and chucks the wet handker-chiefs into the bottom of the box without wringing them out.

The job has not been a success.

After this morning's hot chocolate she'd followed her *A–Z* successfully to Lisson Grove. She said each street name out loud as if it was destiny, and saw her figure stride along the pavements of Maida Vale, over the zebra crossing of Edgware Road, as if watching herself on film. The other characters on the streets were minor parts, extras. The backdrops of mansion blocks, shops, restaurants and market stalls, brilliantly painted sets. She felt this to be a seminal moment in her life: she was on her way to collect the first correspondence from her estranged father, celebrated international artiste Odelin the Clown.

The British Waterways building was in an industrial yard on a road opposite the Lisson Grove bridge. Odeline opened the door into a small foyer with framed photographs of canal scenes on the walls. She could see someone's silhouette through the frosted glass of an office door ahead. There was a rack of wooden pigeonholes on the right-hand wall. Names had been written on card and slotted into brass plates by each one. She found 'MILK' but there was nothing in the pigeonhole, nothing in the one below either. She checked the names on the post in the other pigeonholes, just to be sure her letter hadn't been given to another person by mistake. Nothing. She considered knocking on the office door and asking the person behind the frosted glass about lost post. She stood and watched the blurry shape move around behind a big dark rectangle, which was presumably a desk. Heard a telephone ring and a muffled voice speaking. But when the telephone call ended Odeline decided not to knock. She had something else to deliver, which required anonymity: a formal complaint about the warden, written on her notebook paper, folded inside an envelope she had made out of another page of the book, sealed with Sellotape. She pushed the complaint under the office door and walked quickly out of the building and away from the industrial yard. She had signed it 'A Person Who Wants To Be Left Alone'.

She reasoned with herself on the walk back. Obviously her letters were taking some time to reach her father. It must be a complicated business, delivering post to someone of a nomadic persuasion. Presumably they had been sent ahead to somewhere he was about to arrive, some exotic circus location. Perhaps they were going abroad! This would definitely take longer – luckily she had enclosed sufficient postage for this possibility. She had bought stamps for as far as Australia and China from the Arundel post office and included them in the packets. Once her father reached his next destination and found her letters there, his response would be lightning quick. Charged with paternal feeling. And that would be that, the reunion of two artistic soulmates, father and daughter would inspire themselves and others for years to come. As she walked back to the boat she became overwhelmed with anticipation for this moment. She felt sure that her next visit to Lisson Grove would be the changing point of her life.

When she got back to the canal, she had to stay on the lookout for the warden in case he tried to accost her again. She looked over the bridge railings and saw him a safe distance away down the towpath, leaning on the side of an old sailing boat, talking to a pack of children. She crossed the bridge and looked along the other stretch of canal towards her own boat. There were two pigeons on the roof, pecking at the patchy paint. Next door the tattooed man was sitting on his front deck, leaning against the side of the cabin with what looked like a handmirror squeezed between his knees. He was wearing the same khaki shorts and vest as yesterday and had his hair pulled back again in a ponytail. She could see the ornate drawings running down his arms and legs even from here. Next to him on the deck was a bucket of water and he was swishing a razor about in it. Half of his face was smooth, half covered in soap. She dipped around the end of the bridge and came down to the towpath, walking quickly past his boat, gaze fixed on the ground. It didn't work.

'Hello,' he said, keeping his eye on the mirror as he drew the razor down his cheek. She stopped, felt pinned to the spot. He turned his head. His deep-set eyes were looking directly into hers. The half-face of white soap made his lips seem very red, clownlike. 'Hope you haven't had any more trouble.' His voice was quiet but definite. She remembered it from last night: relaxed, almost sleepy, but authoritative as it dispatched John Kettle. Maybe this man was a hypnotist, who controlled people by talking to them!

'Hello,' she said, confused, and broke away, walking quickly to the far end of her boat. She stepped on, shooing the pigeons who flapped down on to the towpath. She cracked open the padlock, unhooked it, opened the doors and ducked inside, then kept the latches shut for the rest of the morning. It was hot. Sunshine streamed through the portholes, but she didn't open them. She wanted to be watertight, all hatches plugged to the outside world.

It was rehearsal time, but she'd decided not to do any harmonica practice. She was worried someone would hear. She had heard her neighbour playing violin music early this morning – it was as clear as if he had been playing it just outside her cabin doors. Instead she flossed and brushed and then ran through her repertoire for the evening whilst envisaging her audience. They were cultured, quiet, appreciative, and applauded sincerely at the end of each set piece. She practised a series of bows. The rehearsal went well and afterwards she did a prop check to make sure she had everything for the job. She did.

For lunch: six cheese slices on crackerbread. And then she made her way into the city. It was only half past three. But she wanted to get to Covent Garden in good time, to look around. One of the oldest books in her collection is a pictorial history called *Great London Theatres*. She has had this book since she was ten and knows all the descriptions by heart. (It was one of the books she took to the playground to fill lunchbreaks.) The illustrations and photographs are in black-and-white and she has coloured them in her imagination, gilding the outsides and filling their auditoriums with rich red velvet. The Globe is not featured in the book, so she had deduced that it must be one of the great *modern* theatres of London. All of the theatres in *Great London Theatres* were built before 1900.

And so her prop box trundled once again along the bumpy slabs of the towpath. She was dressed in full performance outfit: brogues, black trousers held up by red braces, white collarless shirt, black bowtie and waistcoat, minus her tailcoat, which she hooked with a finger over her shoulder. There was no room for her bowler to go in with the other props so it sat on her head, at a bit of an angle. There was no sign of her neighbour now, and John Kettle was safely occupied with another pack of children. As she left the canal and went up to street level to find the bus stop she felt jaunty, full of promise. Off to seek her fortune.

In the ladies' toilets of the Globe, Odeline unscrews the easel legs and folds them back on themselves, using a pair of braces to keep them together. She slots the easel down the left-hand side of the box, next to a theatrically broken umbrella, on top of the small blackboard which goes flat across the base. She pushes in the tiers of the plastic make-up box and shuts the lid. There are dirty tissues all around the sink – she has tried to scrub her make-up off as quickly as possible. She can still hear the brawling outside. She felt like just flinging in the easel legs, any which way. She feels like ripping open the box of chalk and writing 'WHO CARES?' on the blackboard.

When she'd followed her *A–Z* from the bus stop to Covent Garden she couldn't believe how many people there were. She thought it must be a political protest, of the type she'd heard could happen in London. Taxes. Redundancies. Anti-war. But then she realised the crowds weren't heading anywhere; people were wandering aimlessly. They all looked so scruffy. Londoners ought to be several degrees smarter than Arundel folk. But old-looking shirts, jeans ripped and baggy, big black boots – all these people looked like tramps! She kept an eye out for punk rockers. There were pictures of them in her *Visitor's Guide to London* and she hadn't seen one yet. Which was a relief.

Her plan was to tour the theatres, but first she decided

to have a more general look around and joined a wave of
people heading towards the centre of the Piazza. This, said
the *Visitor's Guide,* was the site of the old fruit and vege-
table market. She kept one hand on her moneybelt as she
walked, remembering that other line in the *Guide* – this
was an area *awash with pickpockets.* The prop box was
hard to manoeuvre in a throng and she kept it close behind
her. But still people tripped on it and pushed into her.
They didn't seem to notice, though. Nobody said anything.
She felt dizzy with how close the people were.

The patterns and checks of their clothes made her vision
quiver.

She looked up as she walked between the giant pillars
of the Market building, and was calmed by doing that.
She fixed her eyes on the huge plain slabs of stone, silent
above the bustle of the people. Their blankness helped.
But then she couldn't look away. She found a way to push
herself into the corner of the building and kept on looking
up. There was something about the building's wall, the
colour and flatness of the stone, that gave her a feeling
she knew. She leant against it. In a world that vibrated and
wobbled and barged, it was still. Unspeaking. She found
herself thinking of her mother, and she didn't know why,
and soon found she wanted to move on.

At one of the market stalls she saw some Buster Keaton
prints and pushed her way to the front. They had a whole
series from *Steamboat Bill Jr.* She picked out five. But
when she checked the price she was horrified. £15 each!
They could *never* be justified in her accounts, even if filed
under 'Inspiration'. She put them back and got away from
the stall. Other stalls were equally expensive. On one sat

a leather notebook that cost more than her coach ticket to London. The only things reasonably priced were postcards. She bought one of a pair of punk rockers, both with green spiked hair and nose rings. The message said 'WELCOME TO LONDON'.

She heard operatic singing now and followed it to some railings looking over a courtyard where two ladies were standing next to a speaker. They were dressed in baggy sweatshirts and tights with big boots, but the sound they made was beautiful. They sang to each other and to the people sitting at tables down there, and their voices intertwined then stretched away from each other and then came back together quite perfectly. Odeline closed her eyes and her heart split into two swallows that flew with the music, dipping and soaring then changing direction. When the singing stopped she was still soaring. Only at the buzz of the speaker did she open her eyes. The singers had picked up baskets and were going round the crowd, asking for money. She walked away quickly.

Outside the market, in the large paved square, were a pair of stiltwalkers, one dressed as St George, in chainmail and a sword, the other in a suit of green scales and a flame stick. They were fighting in slow motion, St George wielding his sword and then ducking as the dragon raised the flame stick to its mouth and bellowed fire. It was very impressive and there was a crowd gathered around them. Odeline would have liked to get closer but then saw a man in a damsel-in-distress outfit rattling a donation pot around the crowd. Everyone was after her money in this place.

There were other attractions in the Piazza: a juggler; a still and very fat man painted gold like a statue; a gorilla standing on a box in King Kong pose, frozen with a blonde doll upside down in its fist. The sun pushed down on all these things, and the air was close with heat. Most people were sitting or lying on the cobbles to watch, half absorbed in ice creams, drinks, cigarettes. Odeline thought that she would never allow an audience to eat, drink or smoke during a performance. It was disrespectful. Also, it made it impossible for them to applaud.

The huge clock in the Piazza chimed five o'clock. Time to start her tour. She would go first to the Theatre Royal. She has read much about the career of Mrs Jordan, the great actress who made her name here. She has been enraged by the tale of Mrs Jordan's mistreatment at the hands of men. She can remember by heart the paragraph on page 14 of *Great London Theatres*, below the picture of a young Mrs Jordan in her London stage debut:

Abandoned by her father in Ireland, Dora Bland was forced on to the stage as a child to support herself and her mother. She was abducted and impregnated by the tyrannical stage manager of the Cork theatre, and fled to London to escape him. In 1786 she appeared in A Country Girl *at the Theatre Royal and was immediately adored for her great talent and charisma. She adopted the stage name Mrs Jordan, in reference to her escape across the Irish Sea, her River Jordan.*

Odeline has always found this final line particularly romantic. She likes the thought of having a dramatic stage name. 'Odeline' is good but she has always felt the surname 'Milk' lets her down – she has never liked drinking milk and the word makes her think of the grotty newsagent's in Arundel with its humming freezer of dairy goods and racks of trashy magazines. Perhaps, like Mrs Jordan, she could change it to something referring to her escape from provincial entrapment? Redwing, after the coach company that carried her to London?

Here she was, then, below the towering columns and white stucco facade of the Theatre Royal. She tipped her head to the side to look at it. The illustration in *Great London Theatres* shows a gleaming temple sitting stately and solitary at the top of a street. But it sat there today grey and dull, squeezed between two buildings covered in scaffolding. Up close the columns were scuffed and cracked. She marched under the portico and pushed a door. It stuck and wouldn't open. She tried another. Through the glass she saw an old man hoovering the foyer. He wagged a finger. 'Closed,' he mouthed, and tapped his watch. She didn't like his manner and gave the door a kick. His face blinked in surprise and she turned away. Regulations are mediocrity's means of suffocating the gifted, she thought.

She walked round to the Royal Opera House and gazed up at the glass arc of the Floral Hall next door. This was not a disappointing sight. It was a great fan of white and refracted light. Inside she could see the painted top of an enormous set background, huge treetops with light coming through the canopy. She thought of that afternoon under the tree on her twelfth birthday, and then of her hours in the darkness of Arundel church. This was more of a church to her now, this flower market building – this filled her with real exultation. A church of the arts. Impassioned, she went to see inside the Opera House, but the entrance was cordoned off for a private function. One day, she swore, she would return as a guest of honour. With seats in the Royal Box.

She walked back into the Piazza and round to what her *Visitor's Guide* told her was St Paul's Church, the 'Actors' Church'. It had tall black windows and to Odeline looked like a big tomb. There was a sandwich board outside saying 'CLOSED'. She stopped and put her tailcoat on, tired of carrying it. Suddenly tired of everything, she pulled the prop box handle to the ground and sat down on top of it, leaning an elbow on one knee and sinking her chin into her hand. She felt glum for some reason.

She heard a metallic clink and looked down to see a coin had been flipped down at her brogues. It was a 50p, which wobbled then dropped flat on the cobbles. She looked around but couldn't tell who had thrown it. 'Nice outfit,' a spotty boy in a tracksuit said. 'Can you do the Chaplin walk for us?' She got up quickly and pulled her prop box after her. 'That's not it,' she heard him shout, and then heard laughter. She couldn't tell if it was at her or at some-thing completely different.

The Globe took some time to find. Odeline had been looking for a theatre. Not a pub. There was just one customer at the bar, a white-haired, crumpled figure, who for a second she thought was the canal warden come to accost her, then realised was just another drunkard. This one was older, red-nosed, spine curved in a collapse against the back of the bar stool. He mumbled into a pint of something. Seated in the window was a family with knapsacks out on the table, speaking what might have been German. She waited for the barman to come to her and asked where the venue was for tonight's performance. Obviously there was a theatre of the same name, or a bijou space attached to the pub – she'd read that was fashionable these days. The barman was also German-sounding and seemed to have some trouble understanding her question, but then directed her upstairs. She followed him up, hauling her box one step at a time. On the staircase wall were theatre posters, pasted on top of one another. Odeline saw old posters for ballets at the Opera House, Shakespeare at the Old Vic, and countless comedy shows which looked, frankly, quite tacky. She imagined her own poster; perhaps she would be in Art Nouveau silhouette, juggling signature props: a rose, cane, handkerchief, umbrella.

Upstairs was no theatre. To the right of a small bar was a raised and carpeted platform which, according to the barman, was the stage. He presented it with a bored flourish which irritated Odeline. She sniffed to show her disdain. Either side were heavy red curtains which, he pointed out, didn't close. He seemed to think this was funny. At the top was a tasselled safety curtain, which, he pointed out, didn't lower. This amused him too. It looked like a Punch and Judy box. She imagined the barman up there as Judy, herself as Punch, hitting him repeatedly over the head. Facing the stage was a single table with a few empty chairs scattered around it. She asked when the audience's seating would be set up. He told her this was it. She told him the stage was too small. He agreed. She asked where her dressing room was. He said she could change in the toilets. She told him this was not good enough. He shrugged, said she could have one free drink on the house. She didn't thank him and he went back downstairs, still shrugging to himself.

It was an hour before she was due to perform. She went over and stood on the stage – it was an even narrower space than the cabin of her boat. She tried reducing some of her movements, whilst keeping the mime as expressive as possible. It was hard. She put her props in position and then went to the ladies' toilets to begin her preparation.

Her disappointment at the venue was nothing compared to what she felt on seeing her audience. Her first thought on emerging from the toilet was that they were insane, they were shouting so loudly. And then she looked around for a television showing some kind of sport – why else would they cheer like that? But quickly she understood that they were just drunk. So this was her audience: twelve men sitting around a pub table, brightly dressed in Hawaiian shirts and garlands. They yelled and stamped their feet as one man in the middle of them, who, to Odeline's horror, appeared to have been stripped and put into a coconut bikini and grass skirt, was forced to drink from a line of drinks on the table in front of him. He grinned desperately, raised his glass and looked around his companions before taking a sip. They all pounded the table and in corresponding gulps he finished the rest of the drink. 'Next!' someone shouted and the man in the middle laughed loudly. To Odeline the laugh sounded hollow. It sounded like the laugh she would make if forced to laugh just at that moment.

An instant later, she was taken to the stage and introduced by the barman.

'Gentlemen, your evening's entertainment!'

No one heard; they carried on forcing the man to drink. A pack of wild animals, thought Odeline, mad with the scent of blood. She pictured them around a carcass, tearing it apart.

She began her repertoire and was grateful, so grateful, for the low and tiny platform she stood on, though she wished she could lower the faux safety curtain and disappear. Her movements were minuscule, so eager was she not to be noticed. She raced through the rose illusion at double speed, producing it from the cuff of her coat almost as soon as she'd hidden it there, and didn't bother with any of her accompanying facial expressions.

But during the next trick her audience began to pay attention. A bald-headed man in the seat closest to the stage stood up and made some lewd Hawaiian dance moves towards her. They all laughed and she pretended not to see, looking down as if to check her watch.

She wasn't wearing a watch.

'Time to get your kit off?' shouted the bald man, with an exaggerated opening of his top button. The men gave a pantomime jeer.

'I can't hear you!' said the bald man.

They shouted louder, and Odeline could feel their eyes on her, up and down her full height, burning through her tailcoat, waistcoat, trousers. Her insides shrivelled.

'Come on, Charlie!' she heard a voice shout. She looked around: the barman was nowhere to be seen. A Hawaiian garland landed at her feet.

'Kit off!' another one shouted.

They started a slow clap. She stood still as a statue looking round the table of faces, and it was as if the sound had been turned off, so loud was the throbbing in her ears. Puce, manic, they leered forth at her and at each other.

For a second her eyes caught the gaze of the man in the middle, the one in the coconut bikini who'd downed the drink. He was not clapping or shouting but looking back with a deadened expression. He nodded at her slowly. Then stood up swaying, raised his hand and picked up the next glass from the long line in front of him. He drank this, then the next, and the next, three in a row, then sank back into his seat. The men turned back to him and began to cheer again. More glasses were slid up the table in front of him. He made as if to push them away and was chanted at to drink. As if underwater, his eyes half closed, he focused on the glass closest to him, taking it slowly and tipping it down his throat. As the glass dropped back to the table he blinked, and shunted further down in his seat. The men roared.

Odeline picked up all the props she could in both arms and ran off into the toilets.

Her props are now packed. She flips shut the fasteners on the box and picks up her bowler hat and umbrella. Outside the heat has cracked and there is a release of rain – huge hot drops hit the windowsill of the ladies' toilets. She pushes through the swing door and makes it through the top bar quickly without anyone seeing her, then thumps down the stairs with her case. People from the downstairs bar are blocking the way and she says excuse me a few times without being heard and so squeezes herself against the wall to pass. She doesn't want to be seen – she feels she has been excessively looked at this evening, obscenely looked at and assessed. The people in the bar all seem to be shouting over the sound of each other. When she looks up she sees only hairstyles, sweaty foreheads, open mouths. She accidentally clips a glass off the top of the cigarette machine with her umbrella handle and feels the contents splash over the bottom of her trousers. She feels a pinch of fear that the glass's owner might come after her and squeezes on along the wall, keeping her head down. She feels any moment they might all turn round to point at her, and there she will be, scurrying like a rat towards the door.

At last she reaches it and is out on to the street, where the noise of the bar closes behind her. The cobbles are shiny with rain, reflecting the streetlamp across the road. Odeline puts her hat on, and then takes it off, feeling stupid. And then puts it on again, because of the rain. She opens her umbrella and two prongs stick upwards, leaving the material flapping down on one side. Her upset at the evening, her disappointment at the job, her disappointment at everything, she carries it all in her shoulders, which are braced and raised up, almost to her ears. She walks off down the rain-slicked cobbles. A sad silhouette in an over-size suit and bowler hat, walking crooked as she pulls the heavy box behind, the broken umbrella doing little to keep her dry.

EIGHT

The sound is a throttle sound, the sound of an aeroplane flying very low overhead, so hoarse and close that he thinks to duck in case it takes his hat off. The sound doesn't fade, it just stops. A bloody doodlebug, he thinks. He had better be alert. He holds his breath to listen harder but hears nothing and then gives up and the sound starts again. It is his own exhalation, thick and wheezing from the drink and all the fags. He gets the giggles and his chest slumps off the bar. He shunts forward again on the stool, sets both his arms down to stay upright. The giggles come out like haws, like a donkey laughing at its own joke. I'm a bloody doodlebug, he thinks. I'm a cockadoodlebug.

'Got an air raid shelter, Frank?' he says.

'What?'

'Give us a refill,' he says, flicking the top of his glass.

'Go home, John,' says the man leaning against the till. The Lock is almost empty now, there are a pair of girls finishing drinks in the corner and a man and woman at the other end of the bar, dolled up like they've been some-where special.

'Okay, I'll have a rum. Like a pirate. I've got enough for a round.' He pats his shirt pocket. 'Where you going?'

The barman has walked off to clear the last of the glasses from the tables.

'Self-service now is it?' He leans up off his stool and tries to reach the spirit bottles on the wall opposite. The stool tilts and crashes beneath him and he gets his foot tangled in the rungs. Keeps himself up by holding on to the edge of the bar. The stool has got him by the ankle. Get off me, you bloody thing. The foot won't disentangle itself and he kicks the stool against the base of the bar. The woman at the other end smirks into her boyfriend's shoulder. Bloody stuck-up bitch, he thinks. And then shouts. That takes the smirk off her face. The boyfriend comes over in his shiny suit.

'What did you say?'

'Fed up of being looked down on by bloody stuck-up women. Think you're so superior. You're not so bloody superior. She thinks she's bloody superior to you, pal. I know that type'.

'Fuck off,' says the girl. A flicker of indecision crosses the boyfriend's face and then he steps closer. He is broad and towers above John Kettle.

'I should probably knock you down right now, you little shit. But I'm going to give you one chance to apologise.'

'Babe, he's not worth it,' the girl says.

'See, pal,' says John Kettle, 'she thinks she's bloody better than everyone.' The boyfriend grabs the scruff of his shirt and all but lifts him off the floor.

'Ten seconds, you little shit.'

'I wouldn't,' slurs John Kettle. 'I'm a doodlebug. I'll come and blow up your little house and everything in it.'

The two girls from the corner scuttle out. 'Babe, leave it, please,' shouts the girl.

'All right,' says the barman, coming over and putting his arm between Kettle and the boyfriend. 'He's not worth it,' he says to the boyfriend. 'He's a sad old pisshead, making trouble. Not worth it'.

The boyfriend puts John Kettle down with a push that sends him tripping back over the chair and on to the floor. 'Crash,' says John Kettle. 'The bomb has landed.'

'See?' The barman taps his head. 'Just a mad old boozer.'

'You shouldn't let him in here,' says the boyfriend, still angry.

The barman shrugs. 'He's been a customer a long time.'

'If he's pissing off your other customers, you shouldn't let him in.' The boyfriend looks down at John Kettle nodding off into his chest. 'Pathetic.'

The girl comes up to them. 'Come on, let's go.' She takes his hand. He hovers for a second and then turns away. The door slams shut behind them. The barman takes John Kettle by the crook of his arm and helps him up.

'Time to go, John,' he says. He props him against the bar and gives his face a couple of soft slaps. John Kettle's head rolls forward and then jerks upright.

'What you kicking me about for? I said I'd pay for it.' He taps his shirt pocket. 'Forty-five quid,' he says, 'in one afternoon. I reckon that's pretty good. How much do you earn?'

'Not enough,' says the barman. 'Come on, out you go. It's past twelve. Back to your boat.'

'Hold on, hold on, I had a drink coming', says John

Kettle, indignant. 'A whisky. A risky whisky. Easy on the water.'

'Bar's closed, John. Go on, back to your boat.' He steers John Kettle towards the door, supporting him as he stumbles to the right and then the left.

'That fellow pushed me pretty hard, Frank. Should I have taken him down?'

'I don't know who Frank is, mate, but he's not here.'

'Frankie?' John Kettle asks, staring at the barman. He's found himself looking for Frank a lot recently, after a few.

'Not here, mate,' says the barman, and gets him out the door. He points him in the direction of the canal and pats him on the back. 'Goodnight, John. We don't want to see you in here again tomorrow, all right? Take a day off.'

'Righto,' says John Kettle, confused. The door swings shut and after a few seconds the lights go out. Goodnight, Frankie. It is a warm night and the street is empty and still after the rain. Puddles in the road shine back at the moon. There is no one about. It is too quiet. His thoughts echo back. He stuffs his hands in his pockets and walks up the street towards the canal, scuffing his boots on the pavement. Too bloody quiet. A couple of men come round the corner and he stops, lights up, all smiles, ready to greet them. Are they submariners come ashore for the night, like him? But they cross the top of the road and go on, away, and so he raises his fingers to his brow to give them a formal salute. A sign of respect for fellow sailors.

He shuffles on. He is making his way deliberately slowly, almost sulkily. Going back to his boat: a cold prospect. He'd rather stay up here on the street, where people might pass by. The canal is too silent at night. The emptiness is a magnet that pulls him towards it. Reels him in. Reeling around reeling him in. Dizzy just thinking about it.

He hears a clipping beat of shoes on the pavement and enjoys it alternating with his own irregular shuffle. Tap tup shhhh tap tup, louder and louder, and then it overtakes him and he gets a flash of bowler hat and downturned face as she passes and who should it be but Madam from the *Chaplin and Company*.

'Well, what a surprise, so late in the night –' he stops and tries to say. Her tapping stride does not break for one moment and she walks away from him like clockwork, pulling her rumbling box behind her.

'It's me, John Kettle,' he calls after her, taking hold of a lamp post to help himself shout. She turns right and taps down to the canal. He hears the tap-tup echo as she goes under the bridge and then die away as she walks out the other side. It is as if she put up a cold thin wall down the middle of the pavement as she passed, so that he couldn't be seen or heard. He thrashes out to punch it down. Still the silence, getting louder in his head. Luring him like a bloody harpy. He can hear the wings. Something in him wants to reach out and welcome it.

He makes a noise in his ear with his finger, and then does it with the other one too. Scratches his head so he can hear his fingers on his scalp. He gets a sudden picture of himself slumped against the railings, itching like he's got the fleas. Feels rottenly horribly sorry for himself. He's feeling: low as a snake. Low as a snake. That's the phrase chasing round the edge of his head. Low as a snake. Since the visit this afternoon.

There have been complaints. One complaint in particular. *Threatening behaviour.*

The case is being referred – he could lose his licence.

They'll be finding a new warden for Little Venice.

He walks to the bridge and up the arch of it till he's standing in the very middle. He is looking down the western arm of the canal, away from the Little Venice pool. Under the moon the water is a path of light, leading down to the next bridge and then winding left, with the full-leafed trees protecting and overhanging at either side. The noises from the roads – sirens and traffic on the overpass – don't touch the canal. It is still and silent. Horribly silent. There are two narrowboats to the left and one to the right; all look closed up, closed to him, a door shut in his face. He takes hold of the railings on this side of the bridge and hauls himself up.

He doesn't want to be facing his *Peggy May* for this.

NINE

Odeline has reached the deck of her boat when she hears the flat splash of weight hitting the water behind her. It startles her. It sounds heavy and she immediately has a vision of a swan dropping like a stone from the sky. Do birds die in mid-air? She looks back and sees the water below the bridge disturbed, sloshing against the sides of the canal. In the middle is a humped mass, dark and wet, a glint in the moonlight. It is not a swan. Its shape is oval and it shifts about now in the water. She thinks then that it is perhaps some giant turtle or sea creature, that the splash has been caused by the lashing out of a huge tail. She steps off the deck of her boat on to the towpath, feeling safer on land, but then steps back on as she hears loud barking from inside the boat next door.

The door opens and out steps the tattooed man. 'Jesus,' he says, jumps on to the towpath and starts to run towards the bridge. He is wearing a vest and shorts – and, Odeline notices, no shoes. It is like someone has coloured him in: even in the darkness she can make out the inky shapes coiling his calves. She hears him say it again: 'Jesus.' Is he going to wrestle the creature, or save it? She puts her hand to her mouth as he jumps feet first into the water and takes a few strokes to the shape in the middle. He puts an arm over the top of it, seems to be trying to turn it. When he does, she sees a head flop up out of the water and realises: it is a person. A body. Her chest jerks. She lets go of the prop-box handle with her left hand and hears it crash to the ground. Her neighbour is holding the body by its arms, hoisting the head and shoulders up, kicking back towards the side of the canal. 'Hey. Please. Could you come and help?' he calls out as he reaches the bank. He looks over to her. 'Come on!'

Mind blank, she obediently begins to run. Her heavy, wet trousers flap around her legs and she feels her feet sliding about in the brogues. She gets to the bank and kneels down by the water's edge, tucking her legs underneath her. She looks to her neighbour for an instruction. One arm, swirling with gothic script, is out of the water, gripping the bank. His hair runs sleek and wet down the side of his neck. He has a thin, aquiline nose which points down like an arrow, pressing his lips together in a line above a dented chin. His features shine like marble in the moonlight.

He is trying to lift the body up on to the bank. Odeline looks at the heavy wet bulk leant over his shoulder, a humped embrace.

'Just hold him up while I get out.'

She doesn't move. He looks up at her.

'If you put your hands under the shoulders,' he says, 'we can keep his head out the water.'

Odeline obeys and puts her arms out. He hooks the body up on to her hands and rests the soaked head on Odeline's knees. And she is looking down on the face of John Kettle, his mouth open and teeth showing in a grimace, the whites of his eyes visible under not quite closed lids. Wetness has silvered, flattened, elongated his stained beard. His shirt clings to the shoulders and torso and then billows out where it touches the water. A wilted five-pound note edges out of the breast pocket.

Her neighbour has lifted himself out and is putting a hand under John Kettle's limp arm.

'Take his other shoulder,' he says, 'like this.'

Odeline does as she is told. They pull up hard and the heavy frame comes dripping out of the water. Paunched stomach, trousers sticking to thin legs and boots that flop outwards as they come on to ground.

'We can put him here, gently down.' He places his hand under John Kettle's head as they lay him on the path. 'Okay, he needs an ambulance.' He pulls a fabric case from his pocket and unbuttons a toggle at the top, pulling out a mobile telephone. When he flips it open, water trickles out. He presses the buttons but nothing happens. 'Fuck.' He looks up. 'Have you got a phone?'

Odeline shakes her head.

'We'll have to use the phone box,' he says. She nods her head and straightens. He has dark, deep-set eyes and a steady gaze. He pushes the wet hair off his face and she sees that he has two thin gold rings through his left eyebrow.

'You know the one by the bridge?' he says, pointing.

She nods and sets off, tripping over her feet as she runs up the ramp. The phone box is fetid, the floor thick with cans and food wrappers. Obscenities have been scratched on to the wall and the telephone itself. She picks up the handset and presses 999, but finds it hard to speak to the voice at the other end. She can't think of the address but eventually manages to explain where she is. 'The Lock Inn,' she says, seeing the name of the brick building lit up on the other side of the road. When she puts the phone down she looks through the glass of the telephone box down to the canal. Her neighbour is bent over the wet mass of John Kettle's body, breathing into him and then turning his head to listen.

When the ambulance arrives for John Kettle he is breathing but not conscious. Odeline stands by dumbly as her neighbour explains how they found him. The ambulance drives away, blue light flashing, and her neighbour rubs his face with his hand. He looks over at her.

'You okay?'

She nods.

'We deserve a drink, I think,' and the line of his mouth widens into a thin smile.

She nods.

He heads for his boat. She thinks she probably shouldn't get on to a stranger's boat but finds herself following him and stepping on to the front deck between a dogbowl and a pile of stacked wood. There is no space for the prop box, so she leaves it prostrate on the towpath. He asks her to excuse him while he changes into dry clothes. When he opens the cabin door the grey wolf-like dog comes up the step to greet him.

'This is Marlon,' he says, turning to Odeline, who has stepped back to the edge of the deck, ready to jump down on to the bank. 'Okay, come in then, boy,' he says, pushing the dog's shoulder gently back down the steps.

As he clicks the doors shut behind him Odeline's legs

go numb and she sinks slowly down to sit on the side of his boat.

John Kettle's face, calling 999, and the ambulance people asking questions: it's taken her back to six weeks before, to the night her mother died. The world is scrolling madly in front of her eyes as it did then. She hears again the groans coming from her mother's bedroom, and again tries to ignore them. She had been in the middle of rehearsing. She remembers wishing her mother would be quiet, but then feeling uneasy when the groans became louder.

These were new noises. Usually her mother went to bed silently: the most Odeline heard were the sounds of the chain rattling across the front door and the mug of hot chocolate being placed on the bookshelf outside Odeline's bedroom. But for the past few nights Odeline had opened her bedroom door and found no mug of hot chocolate on the shelf. All the lights were still on downstairs and she'd hear the groaning. And that final night it was worse. Much worse. Louder than ever.

She remembers going into her mother's room. She sees again the image of her mother's pale moony face, waxed with perspiration, the roots of her hair dark with it. Her mother's eyes, usually impassive, darting around desperately. Her eyebrows twitching with surprise, as if trying to decipher a conversation only she could hear. When Odeline suggested a doctor, her mother's head switched left and right on the pillow, and so Odeline just sat with her, a straight dark figure on the side of the bed, still in her tailcoat and trousers.

Her mother was calmed by this. The groans quietened and her eyes, though glazed, fixed on Odeline. Odeline had felt a tug at her sleeve and looked down to see her mother's fingers pulling a red silk handkerchief from the cuff and laying it over her daughter's knee. When she looked up her mother nodded at her, very faintly. Odeline picked up the handkerchief with her right hand and stuffed it into her left fist, only for it to disappear when she opened her palm. Her mother nodded again. Odeline produced the handkerchief from behind her ear. Her mother screwed her eyes up in delight. She tugged the handkerchief on to Odeline's knee again. Odeline repeated the trick. Her mother smiled, her lips pale. She pressed her finger into Odeline's leg. Odeline stood up and pretended to straighten her other sleeve, pulling a red rose from the cuff. She mimed surprise. She looked at her mother, who blinked back, mirroring the surprise.

And now Odeline performed a simple mime – one she had performed for her mother since childhood: trying to smell the rose, sticking her nose out for it, only for her hand to move it further away. She craned her neck forward, becoming almost horizontal, the rose still just out of reach. Eventually she swiped at it with her other hand, which stuck to the outstretched hand, and at the same time knocked the rose free to catch it with her teeth. She looked back at her mother with a showbusiness smile, the rose clenched in her mouth and her arms still stuck out in front. Her mother's face cracked into a smile reflecting Odeline's. She wheezed with silent laughter.

The other trick Odeline knew her mother loved was the glove mime and so she did this, slipping a white glove on to her right hand, collecting the bowler hat from her prop shelf and bringing a chair over from the corner of the room to sit on. At the point that Odeline mimed despair at having lost her left-hand glove, her mother would always gesture at her head – *The glove is under the hat!* But this time Odeline looked up and her mother's face was a mask of sadness, her mouth pressed down at the edges and her eyes glassy wet. Odeline hurried on and found the glove. She mimed joy and celebration, pushed her left hand quickly into the glove, made both hands dance. Her mother's face melted back into a smile – she clasped her hands together and gave a long blink of relief.

Her mother seemed tired now but when Odeline turned off the light she became agitated. So Odeline switched on the old television unit at the end of the bed and pushed a video in. And then sat in the chair next to the bed to watch. It was an old Marx Brothers film, turned to mute because her mother didn't like the music. It was the one with Harpo as the Professor and Groucho as Captain Spaulding. They had seen it a hundred times before.

Her mother watched the beginning as absorbed as usual. When Groucho danced she moved her head in time. When Harpo came on she squeezed her fists with excitement. But the next time Odeline looked over, she was asleep with her hands across her stomach, her chest slowly moving up and down. So Odeline switched off the light and went out quietly, leaving the film running.

She had abandoned her rehearsal, having been forced out of her performing mindset, and decided to read instead. Half an hour later she was sitting up in bed with *The World of Mime* when she heard, quite clearly, a sound she knew well. It was the shutting of a plastic-bound accounting book, followed by the slap of the book being added to the pile of finished ones. It was a sound Odeline heard every day. She got up and crossed the corridor to her mother's bedroom. The video was still running: the scene where Harpo is trying to box Mrs Rittenhouse and Chico is the referee. The room flickered with the screen's white light and illuminated her mother's face, which was caught in an expression of revelation, mouth and eyes gratefully open – she had just been told a wonderful answer to a long, puzzling question. Odeline had never seen this expression on her mother's face, and was shocked by it. And by the stillness of her body. She went forward and tugged at the sleeve of her nightdress. The arm dropped back lifeless. She said, 'Mother', quite loudly, and there was no response. She stepped forward and listened, there was no breath.

She had gone out and shut the bedroom door behind her. After calling 999 from the telephone in the kitchen she sat on a stool at the kitchen table and didn't go back up. When the ambulance arrived Odeline let them in and then went back to the kitchen while they did their business upstairs. Before driving her mother away they came into the kitchen and asked her questions she couldn't answer. When they had gone she sat there for a little while longer and then went back up to her mother's bedroom, where the light was on and the bed empty. The film was still running.

She flinches when the cabin door opens and her neighbour comes out on to the deck. He is wearing a fresh grey vest – tight over his torso and trim at the waist – baggy trousers and sandals. His head is wrapped in a turban of towel. He is carrying two metal tankards. 'Try this,' he says, and hands her one. Odeline does as she is told. It is a warm, creamy, liquor-and-coffee taste that runs down her throat. In response, a hot ache floods the back of her mouth and nose and suddenly she is crying, hotly and breathlessly, her shoulders out of control and twitching, working up the tears. She doesn't know what is happening to her, but can't stop it. She is disgusted by the sounds she is making: as if some grunting creature is trying to crawl up her gullet and escape. The drink has sloshed over her hands and on to the deck. It occurs to her that she has been drugged: the drink contains a weeping draught, designed to throw her out of control. She looks through bleary eyes and jerking breaths. Is this man a danger? He is still standing in the doorway of his cabin but looks so surprised in his turban that her worry subsides. The crying slows to a whimper. She hiccups once, and then her body is silent.

He sits down on the side of the boat opposite her, holding his tankard in the palm of his hand. As well as tattoos along both arms, he also has copper bangles and bits of rope around the wrists and biceps. He says quietly, 'It's okay, you know. The ambulance people said he's going to be fine.'

All Odeline can do is nod, and sniff. Her mouth has gone to blubber. She keeps her eyes on the decking, which is painted with wiggling lines, one main artery running down from the left-hand corner, with small channels branching off it and then splitting into smaller forks in turn. Along the lines are lots of little crosses.

'That's where we are now,' says her neighbour, leaning forward and pointing to a fork in the line near Odeline's right brogue. 'Here's Little Venice –' he circles a black triangle where three lines meet – 'with the Regent's Canal coming out the top.' She is struck again by how deeply and easily he speaks, pronouncing every part of the word without trying too hard. It is how she imagines an aristocrat might speak. 'The map helps me for navigating,' he says. 'I'm always losing the paper ones.'

'Oh,' says Odeline. Her voice sounds squeaky by contrast. Her lips feel loose and so she tightens them to cover her teeth.

'I mainly stay on the Grand Union,' he goes on, 'just for the landscapes. It has so many changes from top to bottom.' He points to a cross far beyond her left foot and asks, 'Have you been up to Braunston and the Buckby locks?'

Odeline shakes her head.

'The most incredible old architecture around there. And some lovely quiet parts of the canal. But then London has so much. I can never stay away for long.' He smiles slightly. 'I've got a bit of a thing about maps.' He pulls his vest across to show his right breast, which is hairless, a mound of smooth flesh. She feels heat fill her face. There is a map inked on to his chest, with riverways and hill ranges. 'Wiltshire,' he says. 'I used to live down there on the Kennet and Avon.' He pulls his vest back over. 'Why did you choose to come here?' he asks, then checks himself. 'Sorry, we haven't even met properly. I'm Ridley.' He touches his chest. 'You've met Marlon, and this is our boat, *Saltheart*.' He pats the boat's side. 'We three have been travelling together for a long time.'

'Um, my name is Odeline,' she starts, her eyes back on the decking. 'I came here because my hometown was . . . very limiting.'

He nods and she carries on.

'I couldn't, I wasn't, appreciated there. I wanted to bring my art to a new audience.' She looks up, but then remembers tonight's audience and lowers her head again. 'Actually, it seems the audiences here are even more philistine than in Arundel.'

'What art is it you do?' he asks, taking the towel off his head. His dark hair falls down behind his shoulders.

'I am a mime,' she says, 'although my training is as an illusionist.'

'Oh like, you know,' he says, thinking, then gets it: 'Marcel Marceau!'

'You know about Marcel Marceau?'

'Yeah, I used to like him in those films. Beautiful, quite sad. And amazing *movement*.'

'You don't like him any more?'

'Well, I can't watch the films any more. I used to have a projector.' He takes an elastic band from his wrist and pulls his hair back into a knot at his neck. 'But I sold it to buy a new fiddle. My old one got so beaten up. I went to an auction and bid for the best one there. Ex-orchestral.'

Odeline looks blank.

'But,' he goes on, 'I've probably still got the Marceau films. You should have them. I'll take a look.'

He gets up and goes into the cabin, leaving the door open. Odeline puts her head to the side to peer in. The boat is wider than hers and has bowed sides, so the walls of the cabin are rounded. This might be what her *British*

Waterways Narrowboat Manual identifies as a Dutch barge: *A curvaceous version of the traditional English narrowboats and more of a challenge to steer.* She can hear him inside, opening drawers. The floor is wood-planked, and the walls are a rich dark red colour. In her view Odeline can see a leather armchair and, along the wall, what look like old maps in brass frames. It is how Odeline would imagine the interior of an old admiral's cabin: smart, warm, nautical. She cranes her head further forward and sees the corner of a brown suede rug on the floor, and a small wooden dresser with kitchen utensils hanging from it. There is a sack of chopped wood next to an iron stove in the centre, with a pipe leading up to the chimney in the roof.

'Found them,' says Ridley, appearing at the door, and hands a large brown paper bag to her with both hands. She takes it on to her lap. Inside are five film reels, actual reels of acetate wound around a grey plastic spool. Odeline takes one out and holds a tail of film reel up to the light from the cabin doorway. In the first square of black acetate is the pale figure of Marcel Marceau in his white suit, spotlit on the otherwise dark stage, head bent to his right palm, left toe *en pointe* in his ballet pumps. It is the beginning of *Bip, the Bird Keeper.* Odeline looks up at Ridley.

'Its him!' she says.

Odeline has nineteen books on Marcel Marceau, and four by him. These twenty-three are the most treasured books in her collection, even the ones written in French, a language she has yet to learn. Three of them her mother bought full price from a bookshop – she hadn't been able to resist, despite the impact on the Arundel Magic accounts. But most were bought from the Arundel Hospice shop, or when the town library sold off books that people no longer wanted to borrow. Some of these were in poor condition but Odeline has done her best to preserve them, fixing torn jackets with Sellotape and sticking in loose pages. She has crossed out all the names of previous owners and borrowers and written her own in clear, unjoined-up letters, making her signature curl from the last letter of each word. *Odeline Milk. Please Return to 61 Maltravers Street.* It is an impressive collection, by any book collector's standards. They filled a whole shelf of the tall metal bookcase in her room in Arundel.

Marcel Marceau's story has been more of an inspiration to her than anything else. And it is the start of his story which resonates most powerfully. As a young boy growing up in the town of Strasbourg, Marceau saw *City Lights* in the cinema and became obsessed by Charlie Chaplin. He used to do an impression, wandering around his neighbourhood in an ill-fitting tailcoat and bowler hat like Chaplin's Little Tramp. Odeline has always wondered if he was as bored and limited in his hometown as she in hers. Growing up in Arundel, she had felt the other lives she was not living as if they were ghosts haunting her own. They were more potent and colourful than her own beige existence. Alternate worlds in London, Paris, travelling circuses, bohemian salons . . .

In Odeline's view Marcel Marceau is a point where all the influences of mime and illusion come together. He is her link with all the artists who came before. She imagines strands of light travelling over centuries to meet in him. He contains everything, from Japanese theatre to the slapstick of Stan Laurel and Oliver Hardy. Bip the Clown has the tragic mask of Greek theatre, the stylised gestures of Noh, the diamond eyes of Harlequin, the white face of Pierrot, the deftness of Houdini, the wild hair of Harpo Marx, the misfortunes of the Little Tramp: he is every mime that has ever been!

Odeline has always dreamed of seeing Marcel Marceau on stage. In Arundel this seemed as distant and impossible as a trip to the moon. But she lives in London now. Those three theatre tickets in her moneybelt are front-row seats for a matinee performance at the Royal Albert Hall in sixteen days' time. Why three tickets? Because she plans to sit in the middle seat and not be constrained or bothered by people either side.

The tickets cost an enormous amount of money, more than all her Marceau books put together, including the full-price ones that were not from the hospice shop or the library sales. But the experience will be beyond value. Marcel Marceau! She would like to talk to him about her ideas – she has, after all, studied his work intimately, improvised variations of her own. Perhaps their paths will cross that day. Perhaps she will be the next strand of light beaming forward for the art of mime.

TEN

After the bomb, *Chaplin and Company* sat crookedly in the bottom of the canal for two days.

On the first evening, as the daylight went, its headlamp shone weakly at the opposite wall of the canal, reaching towards the cracked towpath and the open kitchen beyond. As the rest of the bank faded into darkness the kitchen stayed illuminated. It flickered and glowed in the lamp's light. The old walls looked golden and were patched where things had already been removed by neighbours and relatives. The bath no longer hung down through the ceiling. The pipe from the stove had been taken and there was a brown vein leading up to the ceiling where it had touched the wall. Things looked tidier, cleaned up. The table and chairs were still there. They had been set back upright in the middle of the floor, expecting dinner.

The lamp weakened over the next few hours until it cast just a faint glow towards the kitchen. As if the room was very slowly receding. At some time past nine the light spluttered and died. Then the boat and the house spent the night in darkness, while other parts of London occasionally flared into life. Explosions, fires, swinging torchlight.

The next morning the children of the canalside houses

leant over the bank and tried to hook things out of the
mud. They looked across at the boat and longed to get on
to it, see what was behind the cabin doors, climb on to
the roof. But it would mean dropping down into the canal
bed and they were afraid. They'd heard the mud was a
mile deep and would swallow you up. They'd heard that
the woman's body had looked pale as a statue when they
found her under the rubble, covered in brick dust. They
peered into the crack in the concrete and the crater in the
garden. The canal company men arrived for the repairs
and sent them away.

For the rest of the day these men filled the cracked
concrete and fenced off the woman's garden without
looking into the house more than they had to. They knew
what had happened to her. They went down by ladders
into the basin of the canal and managed to haul the launch
upright. The canal had been dammed in both directions
and they began to let water in from the Paddington end.
The *Chaplin and Company* was not too damaged to float;
it creaked upright as the water level rose. The water didn't
wash the mud and black grit from its side, and the brass-
handled tiller, broken, wasn't fixed. Eventually the boat
was towed to an empty warehouse at the back of
Wormwood Scrubs, where it was hoisted out of the canal
on to a trolley and wheeled inside. When the way was
passable again, it would be sent back to Bull's Bridge for
full repair. But a week later an explosive dropped on the
Glaxo wharf at Greenford, killing – along with several
others – the canal company manager overseeing the repair
operation, and with that *Chaplin and Company* was
forgotten.

So she sat. The empty warehouse had belonged to a small carrying company that went under before the war. Its entrance faced the water and the houses behind looked away from it, uninterested. Its corrugated roof was rusty and holed, pigeons scratched around on it by day and built their nests in its eaves. A few other discarded vehicles lived inside: a bust bicycle frame, a rusted pulley that lay on the ground near the front entrance and a cart with metal wheels whose planks sagged and were split in the middle. The boat sat in the centre of these, tilted to one side on her trolley, her upfacing side covered in canal mud.

So she sat. The roof leaked in bad weather and water hit the boat, running through the glassless portholes into the cabin and engine room. It ran between planks and collected in pools – the wood on the tipped side of the boat went dark and soft with water. The heat of that summer made the water fetid. The freeze of the following winter turned it to ice, and the boards of the boat blew up and bumped. The ice cracked the varnish and the colours of that upturned side began to fade. The white lettering of *Chaplin and Company* discoloured to brown, its red border became pink.

The boat was a shelter for some that winter. Water voles whose burrows were frozen found their way up and into the boat, and bit into the drawstring bag which lay beneath the fold-down bunk in the engine room. Inside were two vests, a pair of shorts, a cotton shirt and a boy's evacuation papers. These things gave warmth and so the water voles survived winter. Birds built their nests in the dry corners of the decks and under the edges of the cabin roof. The warehouse floor and the top of the boat became thick with pigeon droppings. Old feathers curled on the ground. The tin sound of hail or heavy raindrops on the warehouse roof sent the birds up in fluttering panic around the building, like rocks thrown up by a bomb.

For the rest of London, the tin sounds of gunfire ended suddenly one Tuesday and the city came out in flag colours to celebrate. And, for those who had not yet, to mourn.

ELEVEN

Since childhood, Odeline has never moved in her sleep.
Her sleeping position has been as much an expression of
her willpower and design as the rehearsal schedules or
each day's outfit. She has woken to the world every
morning just as she left it the night before, on her back
and poker straight, diagram straight. Her eyes blink open
on the chime of seven, her hands clasped in the same
position on her chest. On waking she shifts them to
her sides and pushes down in a full body stretch before
flipping back the quilt and swivelling up to a sitting
position on the side of her bed, ready to start her movement exercises.

But this morning, her third day aboard *Chaplin and
Company*, she wakes in a very awkward position. Her
lower body is on its side, but her chest is twisted round,
facing down, and her arms reach up and forward, over her
head. Her mouth is open and she is wearing all her clothes,
including shoes. Her quilt is on the floor – not next to
the bed, but right across the cabin, next to the kitchen
counter. Also, it is nearly eleven o'clock. She is shocked
at herself. She closes her mouth, shifts quickly to her
customary position, clasps her hands across her chest.

And begins to process the night's events.

Curiously, the horrors of the Covent Garden job and the unconscious face of John Kettle do not present themselves as the major events. What happened after preoccupies her more. She is briefly mortified by her crying episode, but then recalls her neighbour's quiet reaction and thinks perhaps it was not so bad. She reaches for the paper bag on the bed next to her and feels the hard wheels inside. She can't believe she now possesses original Marceau film. She can't believe she has met someone who knows about him, even if this person cares more for fiddle music. This is what London is for! This man Ridley is no threat: he is an ally. A fellow nomad. In fact, she feels safer lying in her boat knowing that he is only a few metres away. And, most thrillingly, this Ridley has friends on the Grand Union Canal at Kensal Rise who have gatherings every Saturday night, with music and performance. He said it: she'd be welcome there. This is it, then, her entrée into the city's artistic community. But at the same time the thought is half terrifying. Who are these other performers?

Ridley seems to know a lot about the canal. She asked him about steering lessons and he said there was a programme in Camden which gave free training on the community boats. She will go and apply there tomorrow. Free training will be good for the accounts – she can remove money allotted for steering lessons from her expenses column. It will make up for failing to collect her payment from the job last night.

Last night's job. She is going to have to register with a different entertainment agency. A proper one. How to go about this? Top Hat Entertainers was the only agency advertised in the back of *The Professional Magician* that was specific about not catering for children's entertainment. And the magazine subscription is quarterly, so she doesn't get the next one until October. But she has to pay back the first instalment of her £774.41 deficit long before then. She has to find proper work. Otherwise she will have to busk on the streets of Covent Garden, like George and the Dragon or the Opera Singers, performing to smoking, eating, distracted shoppers, forced to go round with a begging bowl asking for money. Still, that would be better than being shut in a pub with a pack of drunken, drooling animals. She shivers. Last night was worse than any of the children's parties in Arundel. She looks down at the knee of her trousers – the darned patch has ripped wider. It is now flapping completely open, showing a whole square of skin. She must have done this kneeling down by the canal. In the rescue.

She remembers Ridley's boat, the canal map painted on the deck, and the careful decoration of ivy vine painted round the cabin doors. She remembers the name of his boat, *Saltheart*. Poetic. The outside was scruffy but what she saw of the inside was handsome and well kept. She looks at her orange carpet squares and the cracked varnish on the walls – unimpressive by comparison. She wonders if she could copy the Grand Union map from her canal book on to the rear deck. And she would like to frame some of her mime posters properly and paint the walls a strong colour. Dark red would be smart.

She is full of resolve now and swings herself up off the bed, goes into the bathroom and pulls the microphone lightcord. But when she looks in the mirror her jaw drops

open in horror. White make-up is still thick at the edges
of her face, in her eyebrows and the crevices of her nose.
The two Marceau-style red dots are smeared across her
cheeks. The only areas of completely clear skin are below
her eyes, where tears have run into the greasepaint in
dribbly shapes. She looks like a debauched clown. What
must he have thought?

She takes her sponge from the mirrored shelf and
squeezes it under the tap, then pulls it across her face until
the make-up is gone and her face is gleaming. She blinks,
checking the creases around her eyes are clean, and wipes
the sponge along the lines of her eyebrows.

Next she changes into clean clothes: fresh pinstriped
trousers, a white vest, her red braces and a waistcoat. She
leaves her torn trousers out on the kitchen counter to
mend later.

She will go and thank Ridley for the film reels. She will
be a composed and rational version of the night before;
she might even make some lighthearted allusion to the
make-up. Then she will make her way to the British
Waterways building to check for her father's letter. She
gets dressed quickly and checks her appearance three separate times in the bathroom mirror. When she gets to the
cabin door she stands for some time holding the handle
without turning it. Her heart is beating in her head – it
sounds as though someone is rhythmically boxing her ears.
When she drops her hand the heartbeat recedes but then
throbs louder when she lifts her arm to the door again.
She has never experienced this phenomenon before.

Eventually she twists the handle down and steps on to
the deck.

But there is an empty space by her stern. Ridley and his boat are gone.

She looks left and right but they are nowhere to be seen.

The canal is quiet compared to yesterday. The only thing she can see on the water is a procession of swans swimming parallel to the bank. The only things on the towpath are the three tramps, sitting on the bench up by the road, drinking cans with plastic bags at their feet. There is a shopping trolley behind the bench piled high with objects. Odeline can see a tennis racket cover sticking out of the top. The weather is still brightly sunny but all three tramps are wearing several skins of clothing. The one on the left of the bench is in a wool hat – his face and hands are puce, as if the clothes are too tight. He looks angrily sunburnt. The middle tramp is narrower, the top half of his face obscured by the hood of a black cagoule. The third has black skin and grizzled, matted hair that sits like a beret on its head. It. Odeline can't tell if it is male or female. It has slim ankles sticking out from a belted beige mackintosh. Female?

The one in the wool hat is looking back at Odeline and raises his can. He begins to sing in a crooning baritone.

'Strangers in the night, exchanging glances . . .'

Odeline turns away. Is she to be accosted daily by drunkards in this place? She can't remember seeing one drunkard in Arundel. They were probably cleared off the streets by the prim ladies of the council, put in vans and delivered to Worthing. She is about to step back on to her boat when she sees another figure coming towards her along the towpath. Lumbering, a crabby gait, it is the fat little woman from the barge cafe. She is looking straight at Odeline and her face is pained with effort – in fact she is walking quite fast. She holds her hand up as she gets closer, a greeting or a plea for Odeline to stay where she is, to wait until she has made her hot, heavy way along the strip of towpath to reach her.

'I close the cafe for one minute. I hear there is an accident last night, with the warden. In the canal? I hear the siren,' she says, and then bites her lips together as if she's said something wrong. Her accent is thick and clunky, but she speaks English fluidly, not searching for the right word.

Odeline looks at the woman. Her eyelids droop at the corner of her eyes, so she appears permanently concerned, sympathetic. She has soft cheeks hanging either side of her mouth. They sag over her jawline – and wobble when she talks. 'Yes, me and Ridley.' Odeline gestures to the space beyond her boat where his had been. 'We found him.'

'Is he alive?' asks the barge cafe woman. She looks emotional. Odeline wonders why she cares.

'I believe so,' she says, 'though –' she is trying to remember exactly what the paramedics said – 'he was not *exhibiting signs of consciousness* when we put him in the ambulance.'

'Do you know –' the barge woman talks as if she is trying to slow the words down as she speaks them – 'do you know, if he doesn't come back, do they send a new warden? And last night, are the police here?' She wipes her forehead. 'I'm sorry for the questions.' She seems exhausted though it is not yet midday. And very hot: she is wearing a heavy floral skirt with tights and trainers, and a zipped turquoise shellsuit top underneath which she is visibly sweating. Even to Odeline the outfit looks strange.

'No, we just called an ambulance. There were no police,' says Odeline – but then looks up to see, as if she has just introduced him, a policeman, buttoned, and striding in black uniform out from under the bridge.

The cafe woman follows her gaze and jumps at the sight. She turns to Odeline and grabs her hand. 'Please can I go in your boat? Please?' Odeline doesn't know what to say and looks down at the desperate upturned face and then at the fat little hands holding on to her fingers. She takes her hand back and puts it into her pocket. The woman turns round to the policeman – young, well built, filling his uniform – who says:

'Good morning, ladies. I'm looking for a lady by the name of Vera, a foreign lady, the waitress from the Venice cafe, just beyond the bridge.'

'This is her,' says Odeline, stepping aside. She doesn't want to be held as an accomplice in whatever this woman has done. This is turning into the most eventful twenty-four hours of her life. Is she about to witness an arrest?

The woman has her head down. 'Miss Vera,' starts the policeman, 'we have a patient in intensive care at St Mary's Hospital. Do you know a John Kettle?'

Vera nods her head, still keeping her eyes down.

'And you are aware that he was taken to hospital last night?'

She nods again.

The policeman takes a notepad from his jacket pocket, flips open the cover and reads as if from a script.

'Mr Kettle was brought into hospital unconscious and

in a critical state. He claims not to remember the circumstances leading up to the incident, and it is not certain
whether it was a genuine accident, whether someone else
tried to harm him, or indeed whether he tried to harm
himself.' He looks up. 'Do you follow me?'

'Yes, sir,' says Vera in a quiet voice.

'However, Mr Kettle denies trying to harm himself, and
there is no evidence to suggest that this is anything but
an isolated incident as a result of overdrinking. He has
completed a psychiatric assessment and is due to be
discharged, on the condition that he is escorted home by
a relative or friend and enters an approved alcohol
programme. This will be followed up by a visit from social
services. There being no close family, he has named you
as an acquaintance or neighbour who would be able to
collect him from hospital today, and to sign the discharge
form.' Here he makes a writing gesture with his hand.
'Would this be possible?'

Vera looks up. 'I can't do the forms,' she says, making
the writing gesture back.

'Well, perhaps your friend here could come with you?'
The policeman nods to Odeline.

'Me?' says Odeline, horrified.

'I can't leave the cafe,' pleads Vera to the policeman.

'Could your friend here keep an eye on the cafe then,
while you're away, and you could get the hospital reception to help with the forms? It is you he's asked for. He
is said to be in a fragile state.'

'Okay,' Vera shrugs, eventually. 'I can go.'

'I am not working in that cafe,' says Odeline.

'Well, the whole thing won't take long anyway. Only

took me ten minutes to walk up from the hospital to here. Why not go after the cafe closes, Miss Vera. And perhaps your friend here could then assist you with the forms. What time's the cafe close, please?'

'Five o'clock,' says Vera.

He unclips a pen from his uniform pocket and twiddles it over his fingers down to the notepad. 'Okay, ladies, so can I report back that you will both be there to discharge John Kettle from the Victoria and Albert Wards at St Mary's, Paddington, shortly after five o'clock. And he'll need some clean clothes. I believe his boat is open, so if I could leave you to arrange that?'

Vera nods imperceptibly.

'I am under no obligation to collect that man from hospital. I refuse to go,' says Odeline.

The policeman takes off his helmet. He has short blond hair and a precisely squared jaw. His eyes are sky blue and look directly into hers.

'Madam, this gentleman has suffered a nasty shock. It would be very much appreciated if you could assist this lady in bringing him home. I suspect that is the best place for him. He has, I understand, been a little distressed at being kept in hospital. If you could find it in yourself to help, it will take under an hour of your day.'

He keeps his crystalline gaze fixed on her. Odeline finds herself shamed and nodding.

At five o'clock Odeline is leaning on the railing opposite the barge cafe while Vera locks the doors. The day has been a failure. There was no letter from her father in the

pigeonhole at the British Waterways building. She knocked
on the office door, but the officious woman inside said
she was unable to answer any enquiries about lost letters
as post wasn't her department. She gave Odeline a number
to call for General Enquiries. Odeline, irritated, had
requested to make an official complaint about the state of
her boat. In her opinion, British Waterways misrep-
resented the vessel. The woman had given her a form to
fill in. *Tawdry*, wrote Odeline, in her stick letters. *Shabby.
Bathroom unsatisfactory. Portholes grubby*. She remembered the promising description in the advert. *Poor
paintwork*, she wrote. *Highly personalised interior. No
traditional fittings. Disappointing decor. MISLEADINGLY
ADVERTISED. COMPENSATION DUE*. Odeline
promised to visit the office daily to check the progress of
their response, and slammed the door.

On the way back to her boat, across Edgware Road
and along the streets of Maida Vale, Odeline had felt as
if people were deliberately ignoring her, just as they had
in Covent Garden. In Arundel people's eyes would linger
on her, they would look her costume up and down. But
when she scanned the pavements on her walk home from
the British Waterways building, she realised: she wasn't
the most startlingly dressed. She watched the shopkeepers
and market sellers as she walked by. Their gaze passed
over her quickly, lingering instead on the barely clad, the
girls in cropped tops and cropped shorts, the ones in big
sunglasses making a noise. Perhaps people would notice
her if she was wearing her new yellow-strapped roller
skates, wheeling and spinning down the pavement. But
these pavements were crooked and bumpy, filled with

hazards, and there were cars zooming along the roads. It would be as dangerous to practise here as on the towpath.

Back at Little Venice she'd gone to the telephone box by the bridge to try the General Enquiries number. There was a new foam carton in the bottom of the telephone box, with half a baked potato in it. The whole box stank of tinned tunafish and Odeline had to hold the door open for the best part of a minute before going in. Once inside she picked up the receiver and reminded herself of her courage last night in making the 999 call. She dialled and reached an answering machine. And then tried two more times, still getting the answering machine. The payphone did not return her money. The three calls cost her £1.80 in total.

Ridley's boat was still gone. She went back on board *Chaplin and Company* and ate some jelly squares for lunch with a carton of tropical fruit juice. She decided then to mend her trousers, and took out her mother's sewing basket, opening it on the bed. In the padded underside of the lid were rows of needles and pins arranged according to size, and a clear pack of 'O.MILK' nametapes. The reels of cotton were in rows around the sides of the basket, in the middle were scissors, thimbles and an unstitching device on top of squares of cloth. Odeline picked up the squares. They were all black and white: the thick black cotton of her suit material, the fine white cotton of her shirts. Clinging to one of the black squares was a wiry reddish hair.

The sewing was not as straightforward as she had envisaged. It took almost ten minutes to thread the needle. She sewed a patch on to the trousers and then had to unpick it when she realised it should have been sewn to the inside. Her stitching was loose and ugly and she did the knot too tight at the end, so the patch was slightly bunched.

She spent the remainder of the afternoon rehearsing, although her concentration was continuously disrupted by the flashbacks of the bald sweating man in the Hawaiian shirt, jeering up at her, the sound of fists pounding the table, the eyes looking down the length of her, boring through her suit. She also found herself listening out for the engine of the *Saltheart*, but to no avail. Eventually she gave up for the day, and went over to the barge cafe at four forty-five.

When she arrived the last customers were leaving. As they walked away a pair of pigeons fluttered down on to the table to peck at their leftovers. 'Shoo,' said Odeline, rattling a chair to scare them off. Pigeons were so pushy and ill-mannered. The towpath was busier now, with cyclists jangling by and some children in school uniform sitting on the bench making a noise. Vera came out and started pulling the tables over to the barge doors, stacking the chairs on top. It looked like hard work and, after standing watching for a minute, Odeline had walked over and helped with a few. She didn't know why. It wasn't like she needed to. When they had finished, Vera had turned and said, 'Thank you', in a very warm way, and patted her arm. Odeline had found this embarrassing and went to lean on the railing.

Now Vera is bolting the doors shut. She has to fasten one door from inside and then comes out and pulls the other one shut. 'Okay,' she says as she turns the key. 'Shall we go and find the clothes?' They walk over to the first of John Kettle's boats, the *Peggy May*. The tarpaulin is fixed at the front but folded over so that most of the back deck is open. 'I think this is the one he lives on,' says Vera. Odeline looks at the boat and its stained tarpaulin in disgust; she has no desire to set foot on this odious man's property.

'Thank you for helping me,' says Vera, looking up at her, with that same embarrassing warmth as a moment before.

It wasn't my choice, Odeline wants to say, but doesn't. Instead she says, 'You're welcome.' Something about this woman makes her feel she has to be falsely nice – maybe it's because of the free hot chocolate yesterday morning. This is exactly why I never become obligated to people, exactly why I never owe, she thinks.

Odeline finds herself stepping on after Vera. She loses her balance and clutches Vera's shoulder – the boat is much less stable than a narrowboat.

'Okay?' says Vera.

'Yes. Thank you,' says Odeline. Again, too nicely.

They go down into the cabin, which has grubby windows in heavily varnished frames. There are dull brass dials on the dashboard and a small wooden steering wheel with an anchor engraved in the centre. Old coins and empty packets of tobacco are jammed in the crevice between the dashboard and the front window. The wood floor is black with dirt and there are some pieces of broken glass in the corner. Vera steps down carefully and opens a low door to the left of the steering wheel. 'Ugh,' says Odeline, peering in. Inside is mostly dark but they can see a small shelf with a ball of yellow string and some rusted cans of oil. On the bottom shelf are some stained blue overalls rolled up into a ball. The floor by the door is covered by a mass of twisted clothes, half of which look wet. They can see the corner of an old mattress at the back, with what look like cartons next to it. The smell coming out of this place is babyish, the soured smell of old milk.

'Ugh,' says Odeline, again.

'It is disgusting,' agrees Vera.

'Just take the overalls,' says Odeline, and Vera does, shutting the door quickly. They back up on to the deck, Odeline stooping and holding herself away from the walls of John Kettle's filthy cabin. Vera takes a plastic bag that is snagged on the corner of the deck and shoves the overalls into it. As she steps off the boat it lurches violently and Odeline has to grab hold of the cabin roof until it subsides and she too can climb down.

'I think we go straight down here for the hospital,' says Vera, pointing down the towpath. She has hooked the plastic bag over her arm. The soggy overalls are heavy, stretching the handles. Odeline remembers John Kettle's wet face in the moonlight and shudders.

'Are you okay?' asks Vera.

'I saw him, just before,' she says. 'On the street. He was trying to talk to me. I pretended I didn't see him.'

'What is he saying?' asks Vera.

'I don't know because I couldn't understand. His words were slurred. I think he must have been drunk.'

'He is a very troubled man,' nods Vera. 'Very troubled. Sometimes it seems he is bothering you and all you want is for him and his troubles to leave you alone. To just stay away.'

'Yes,' says Odeline.

'Shall we walk?' says Vera, and they turn on to the towpath. There are a pair of ducks paddling by, one leading the other. They bob alongside Vera and Odeline for a few metres, then turn away into the middle of the pool.

'I checked in my *A–Z*,' Odeline says. 'We have to follow the canal and turn off when it bends to the left.'

'Oh, okay,' says Vera, nodding.

Odeline takes the *A–Z* out of her trouser pocket and flicks the pages around the spiral. 'I'll get to the page, just to make sure.'

'Good idea,' says Vera. She is panting slightly. 'Can we walk a little slower?'

'Here it is.' Odeline shows her the page.

Vera nods again, wiping her temples with the cuff of her shellsuit top. Then she stops and grips Odeline by the arm. 'I can't do a form,' she says. 'When we get there. If we have to fill in a form for him.'

Odeline pulls her arm away and carries on walking. She is not sure what Vera means. Perhaps she can't write English. 'Fine,' she says, and now they are going under a big bridge, with cars zooming overhead. In the amplified darkness, Odeline can hear the click of her brogues against the background roar of traffic. Vera's trainers don't make a sound. As they come into the light, Odeline checks the *A–Z* page. Two more bridges to go until they turn off. She remembers now the queries she jotted into her notebook this morning, and takes the opportunity to interrogate her companion.

'Underneath carpet squares, are there always floorboards?'

Vera shrugs, the plastic bag swings. 'How do I know?'
Odeline walks faster.

'In boats or in houses?'

'Boats. For example, a narrowboat.'

'I would say probably yes.'

'How much is paint?'

'How do I – for boats?'

'Yes.'

'I don't know exactly. I think you can get it cheap from
the hardware store.'

They reach a section of canal where two or three narrowboats are moored on either side. Odeline scans the names;
none of them is the *Saltheart* – where has it gone? They
are walking next to a length of corrugated fence with
cranes sticking up from behind it. On the far bank the
towpath is walled by a white office building with small
square windows looking on to the canal, and beyond that
some wooden warehouses.

'How long does it take for a letter to reach a destination
abroad?'

Vera blows out, tries to catch her breath. 'Uh, probably
a week to Europe. Outside Europe, I would say up to
two weeks.'

'Could it be longer? For somewhere really remote?'

'Excuse me. I must stop for one moment.' She takes off
her shellsuit top. Underneath she is wearing a baggy mauve
T-shirt. The collar is darkened with damp.

'Could it be longer?'

'I expect so, yes.' Vera flaps the sleeve of the shellsuit
to fan herself, and they walk on.

'Where are details of entertainment agencies listed?'

Vera squints up, eyes crinkled, shaking her head – she appears amused by this question.

'You are working me hard.'

'Do you know the answer?'

'Are you needing a telephone number?'

'Yes.'

'There is no computer, but we have a telephone directory in the cafe. You are very welcome to look.'

Odeline sees the bend in the canal. 'Turn here,' she says, sticking her hand rigidly forward to show their route. They walk down a narrow cobbled passage between two buildings and come out facing a line of brown brick buildings, a quiet street with cars parked down the sides. Through a gateway between these buildings Odeline can see the back of an ambulance. She looks down at her *A–Z*. 'Left,' she says, signalling with a straight arm flung out to the side. They walk past a yard with large square plastic bins, and metal trolleys piled with laundry. The tarmac surface looks smooth and newly laid: possibly a good site for roller-skating practice. She could push one of the bins along as a stabiliser. But then she notices the 'TOXIC CONTENT' stickers on their sides. Perhaps not.

Protruding from the centre of the next building is a blue porticoed entrance. It is busy here, with people walking businesslike in and out. They all look perfectly fit and well, and mostly young. This is not how she imagined a London hospital. 'In here,' she says to Vera, indicating the entrance, and puts the *A–Z* back into her trouser pocket.

Inside there is a smell of antiseptic and everything is lit, almost blindingly, by strip lights in tight rows across the ceiling. They go to the information desk, Vera's shoes squeaking noisily on the rubber floor, and are told to join a queue. Odeline stands in front of Vera in the queue and picks her pocket watch out of her waistcoat. The ceiling lights make bright bars across its glass face and she has to shield the watch face with her hand. It is five twenty-five. She has better things to do with her life than stand in queues. Time has value too, she thinks, just like money.

When they at last reach the desk, they are directed to a building further down the street, and as they approach it, Odeline tenses. On a square of pavement outside a set of double doors are an assortment of ill people. Some are in wheelchairs, some lean on crutches and some are attached by tubes to wheeled metal posts like the end of a clothes rail. They are nearly all old and nearly all wearing the same disgusting apricot-coloured tunics, their sickly, scrawny limbs poking out of them as they cluster outside in the sunshine. They look like they have been in the sun too long, wrinkled like prunes. Disgusting. Odeline drops back behind Vera, who doesn't seem fazed by this sight and is walking towards them quite happily.

Ugh! Some of them are smoking!

Odeline feels like retching. She is going to have to cross the paving to get to the entrance. She wills the little army of diseased aliens to wheel off and disappear. Shoo! Vera is still marching on. Stupid *fat* woman. But Odeline is forced to follow, and as she gets closer she takes a breath and holds it, looking straight ahead at the electric doors, which open to let Vera through. But just as Odeline gets to them, they close, and she releases some of her held breath as she pushes and kicks at the glass, trying to make the door open. A wrinkly hand appears by her hip and she freezes – she can see one of the wheeled poles and a corner of apricot tunic. The hand extends forward and pushes a button, the doors click and open.

'There you are, dear.' The croaking voice breathes cigarette smoke towards Odeline's nostrils, and she snorts, pushing it away as she trips through the doors.

TWELVE

John Kettle has not been a good patient. This is what he has been told by the ward supervisor, a small Oriental woman who he pretended not to understand. He looked around when he did this but nobody laughed. She pursed her little mouth and clipped off back to her desk. He is fed up with lying here in a paper nightie, his mottled arms sticking out – it's like he's wearing a bloody woman's dress. He feels ropey, his stomach feels uneasy. His tongue is puffy and sour in his mouth. And he doesn't like being patronised by these bloody doctors. They asked him about 'feelings of depression' and he said that being stuck here all day was enough to make anyone depressed. That old boy in the bed next door looks dead already, he said. They didn't smile.

Now the doctors have left, all he can hear is the laboured breathing of that bloke next door and the scratching pen of the ward supervisor behind her desk. This is his audience. He thought hospitals were supposed to be busy places. He can hear the low buzz of the strip lights along the ceiling. He feels itchy with the silence, so leans forward to grab his medical notes from the clipboard at the end of the bed.

Upon admittance the patient's blood-alcohol level showed at 0.47.

The patient was monitored for late Cardiac Arrhythmia and administered a dextrose/saline drip.

The patient has exhibited some gastrointestinal symptoms as a result of swallowing contaminated water. The report recommends tests for E. coli, Faecal Coliform and Faecal Streptococci and a prescription of antibiotics according to the levels of toxicity.

The patient did not regain consciousness for 6 hours and appeared disorientated and incoherent on waking.

The patient will be required to complete a psychiatric assessment before being discharged.

The patient refused to complete the self-report questionnaire and is therefore subject to a psychiatric evaluation interview (PEI).

He flicks over to the next sheet.

Psychiatric Evaluation Report:
The patient exhibits signs of stress and depression manifesting in hostility and attempts to inhibit or frustrate the interview. The patient initially refused to confirm his name, responding to the interviewer's requests with incorrect identities, for instance 'Adolf Hitler', 'Greta Garbo'. The patient repeatedly evaded the initial straightforward enquiries of the interview, questions such as 'How are you today?' were repeated with exaggerated references to the interviewer's accent and gender. The patient seemed to be playing to an

audience in the ward, and when questioned about the incidents leading up to his admittance to hospital became hostile and silent. The patient refused to look at the interviewer and would only answer with head gestures to signify 'yes' or 'no'. The patient does not remember the incident. The patient does not remember where he was drinking on the night he was admitted to hospital or if he was drinking with other individuals. The patient does not usually drink large quantities of alcohol. The patient does not know how much he usually drinks. The patient would not say he was a heavy drinker. There have been no previous incidents of this kind. The patient has not previously discussed any problems of this kind with his GP. The patient would not say he was feeling depressed or frustrated on the evening he was admitted to hospital. The patient is happy and fulfilled in his work. The patient has no financial anxieties. Nothing had occurred to make the patient particularly distressed on that evening. The patient has no history of alcohol in his family. The patient has no family. The patient has no spouse or companion. The patient has a normal network of friends, colleagues and acquaintances.

Patient 66719343 agreed to attend a community alcohol awareness programme and has named a close friend who will be able to accompany him home from hospital.

'What a lot of balls,' he says, loudly, and chucks the clipboard down the bed. And then kicks it on to the floor. Some visitors at the other end of the ward look up and murmur at each other. He drums his nails on the bed tray and looks around. Everything is pastel – the walls are lilac and the bedclothes a pale orange, which seems a particularly gruesome colour to cover the grey breathers underneath. They look degraded by it, such an infantile colour.

He hears the ward supervisor rustle out of her seat and turns to see the squat shape of Vera from the barge cafe and the tall girl, the artist, in the reception area.

'Oh look, it's Laurel and Hardy!' he calls out across the ward.

He sees the weird girl's lips tighten and feels his joke wither. He is ashamed to be seen like this, especially in front of the girl. Vera is holding a blue bundle in her arms which he recognises as his old overalls.

The ward supervisor brings Vera and the girl over. He is made to get out of bed in front of them, and walk across to a curtained cubicle to change into the overalls. He feels better in the overalls than the paper frock, even though they are damp and stained. He is given a plastic bag bulky with the clothes he came in with, and picks out his boots from there, even though they are soaking wet. In the cubicle is a small mirror and he tries to sort his hair out a bit. His skin is yellow under the strip lights and his lips darkly purple. He doesn't look at his eyes, can't.

He comes out and the ward supervisor leads the three of them to the lift in silence, her hair in a perky little black bun. 'Didn't catch her name,' he jokes to Vera, jabbing a thumb.

'Are you okay?' Vera asks him as the supervisor presses the button. There are other people getting into the lift, also going to the ground floor. He mimics her worried expression. 'Arrr you hokay?' he says, in a Commie accent. 'Oh yes. Don't you worry about me.' He gives a little laugh. The weird girl sniffs. Nobody speaks while the lift goes down. The supervisor leads them across the foyer to the front desk. 'You taking us all the way home?' he asks. She ignores him, clips off behind the desk and comes back out with paperwork.

In the foyer he waits with the bag of clothes while the two women fill in the forms – for some reason it takes a long time and the girl ends up doing it. Vera walks away from the reception desk saying she is too hot, but then goes outside and stands in the sun. He follows her out and looks around. More of the living dead on the pavement out here, sucking on cigarettes in their apricot tunics. Thank God he's out of there. A couple walk past with ice creams. 'Belter of a day,' he says. Vera doesn't answer. She is holding her tracksuit top over her arm and her hands are clutched at her waist. She has her eyes closed.

Odeline marches out and past them. John Kettle and Vera follow her along the street and round the corner on to the cobbled path leading to the canal. They turn on to the towpath: one, two, three.

They pass the Paddington warehouses, which are more like farmyard barns in the soft six o'clock light, old brown planks and corrugated roofs. The water is busy with moorhens and ducks. John Kettle is almost keeping up with Odeline; Vera is wheezing some way behind. Clusters of pigeons are perched on the canal ledge, pecking at something. Tails upturned and with grey wings closed, they look like mussels on a rock.

Odeline says spikily, without turning round, 'I think you should find Ridley and thank him.'

John Kettle scoffs: 'That gypsy off the *Saltheart*? I would have thought he'd let me drown. No morals that lot.' He turns and grins at Vera for confirmation, but she just shrugs.

Odeline spins round. 'Well, perhaps he should have. But instead he got in the water to save you.' Her mouth pokes out with anger. 'He got in the water, you know. And broke his mobile telephone. And did the resuscitation. You know, in my opinion, he shouldn't have bothered. You are pathetic. *Pathetic.* A crude, ungrateful bigot. Typical philistine, chauvinist, middle-aged, offensive, racist bigot. That –' her eyes blaze – 'is what you are.' She spins back round and walks on. John Kettle reels, punchdrunk, his stomach lurches. Closest he's felt to seasick in forty years living on water.

Looks at the horizon to steady himself. Follows the line of tower block, bridge, advertisement hoarding. Rotten. How rotten he feels.

He murmurs something into his beard.

'What?' Odeline says and stops.

He can't speak. She marches off again and now he calls after her, 'I'm terribly sorry! I'm terribly sorry, Odeline! I know I'm a fool! I say stupid things, very stupid things. I don't even think. I'm sorry!' His voice is strangled. But at least Odeline has stopped.

'I am grateful,' he begs, 'I am.' He looks down at his feet. 'Thank you a million times. And for coming to get me. You don't know what it means.' He turns to Vera, who has caught up, and grabs her hand, pumping it up and down. 'Thank you, you don't know what it means, that you two came to get me. I've no one in the world.'

Vera extracts her hand from his. 'It's nothing,' she says.

'It doesn't matter where you sleep, I would never report it,' he pleads.

Vera flinches.

'If I've ever offended you I'm sorry,' he says, feeling desperate.

'You should think before you speak,' says Odeline, walking back towards them.

'Yes,' he says.

'You don't respect other people's lifestyle decisions. Or their privacy.'

'You're right, I know, you're right.'

'And you need to clean your boat. It's disgusting,' says Odeline.

'I don't take care of it,' he says, miserable.

'All right, let's go,' Odeline says and they walk on, slower this time. John Kettle is on her right and Vera has stepped away from him on to Odeline's left, and so they travel the last part of the towpath together, their shadows stretching back behind them as they go under the bridge by the Little Venice pool.

That night John Kettle fills two black bags full of rubbish from his cabin, and takes them up to the bins on the road. For the first time in months, he goes back to his boat without a drink. He feels too wrong in his stomach for anything anyway. He lies down on his mattress but doesn't sleep. Instead he listens to the night sounds of the canal, the wash of water against the side of the boat. In his windowless cabin it is pitch black, just the open hatch letting a small slice of moonlight hit the end of the mattress. He allows himself to think of earlier times on other boats.

There was a time when he was better at life, when he had belonged in it. He thinks back to those days. Life had a structure, you knew where you were. You turned on a wheel. None of this thinking, being chased by your own thoughts. Just the simple rotation of each day: cleaning the cabins, manning the boat, banter in the canteen between watches, onshore leave to look ahead to. When he tries to picture these days, there is always someone beside him. Always at his side, within pinching distance. Constant chatter. High-pitched chatter. I'm your shadow, Kettle. Who smells like a petal? Submariner Kettle. And John is in his bunk again in Portsmouth, low down in the belly of the boat, feeling the gentle rise and fall. Hearing the boys call out to each other. Frank singing a dirty tune. There once was a girl from Chester. John knows the song – it makes him chuckle as his head rolls to the side and he follows the rise and fall of the boat with his breaths, hears his own throaty snore rumbling.

He sleeps better with them around him. They're talking, they'll talk on into the night. Frank doesn't like to stop talking. Hates going to sleep. But John can snore through it. Out cold, out like a light. Laid out. Miles below the surface. Miles below.

THIRTEEN

In a field outside the airport town of Luton a circus is being set up. Men wearing shorts and vests are unloading from huge lorries parked along the fence at the back of the field. Metal poles and huge plastic crates full of wiring are passed down from the back of the lorries. Fake hay bales are being stacked outside on the grass.

In the middle of the field, another group of men are pushing a great wooden pole into the air. The end rising into the sky has a tangle of ropes, wires and pulleys attached to it. The men push the pole vertical and then two hold it fast while the others walk out with the rope ends to peg them down. There is another huge pole ten metres away which they will put up next.

At the entrance to the field an arc-shaped sign lies flat on the ground. It is painted yellow with red writing, and has battered edges. It reads, in old western script: 'CIRQUE MAROC! CIRQUE EXTRAORDINAIRE!' Painted cats jump through the hoops made by the letter Q. The sign is shiny with dew. It is early morning and the sun is not strong yet. A few metres back from the sign are flatpacked stalls folded out on the grass, with wooden awnings that have been painted to look like striped fabric. Beside them are plastic boxes of circus souvenirs: diabolo sets, juggling

balls, postcards, red noses. One box is full of small harlequin dolls, with black diamond eyes on a white face, long
clown shoes, and a red and yellow suit with O on the
front. On their heads are bowler hats. These dolls are
stitched and filled, stiffly, with wadding. They sell for
£19.99 and cannot stand upright without being leant
against something.

In a semicircle in front of the lorries, hiding them from
view, is a row of traveller caravans. Some look more like
carts with roofs, being plain wood with no windows and
only a flap for an entrance. Others are more ornately
decorated, with carved and painted detail around the
windows and proper fold-down steps. The biggest is in
the centre and slightly set back. It is dark green, with gold
rosettes around the windows. Its wheel hubs are brass
rosettes and its roof and sides are prettily bowed, much
like the shape of a Dutch barge. On platforms either side
of the steps are brass pots planted with real-looking red
tulips. The door is green with a gold border and has a
small oval window, a red curtain drawn behind it.

A tiny, brown, muscular man in tracksuit bottoms and
a vest comes to the door, lifts his fist and hesitates. In his
other hand he is holding an envelope. He knocks.

'I'm preparing . . .' comes a low, sing-song voice from
inside.

'Sorry, Monsieur, it's Mignon.'

'Hello, little one.'

'There is a letter for you, Monsieur.'

'Oh? Does it look, ah, official?'

The small man looks at the envelope, addressed and
underlined in blue biro:

<u>ODELIN THE CLOWN</u>
<u>C/O THE CIRQUE MAROC</u>

'No, Monsieur, it's just handwritten.'

'All right. Could you slip it under the door for me, Mignon. Thank you.'

The small man pushes a corner of the envelope under the green door. 'Thank you, Maestro,' he says, and makes a little bow before turning away.

There's the sound of footsteps approaching the door, a pause, and then the envelope disappears.

FOURTEEN

The morning after they collect John Kettle from hospital, Odeline arrives at the barge cafe to look through Vera's telephone directory. She is wearing her wing-collar shirt with waistcoat and trousers, and brogues on her bare feet. Looking out of the porthole this morning, she judged it too warm for socks. She asks for a hot chocolate and says she is prepared to discuss the price, but Vera insists on making her one for free.

'As long as there are no customers inside,' Vera says, 'it is okay.' Vera is wearing her mauve T-shirt again, with the flowery skirt and trainers. The T-shirt looks cleaner than yesterday and Odeline can smell washing powder. Vera tells her she is the only person who orders hot chocolate in August and smiles, but Odeline doesn't see what is so amusing. Hot chocolate is her favourite drink. It is therefore a good way to start the day.

Vera pulls the telephone directory from behind the blaring radio and puts it on the counter in front of Odeline. 'Have a seat,' she says, indicating the stool. Odeline would have, but now she has been told to, she doesn't want to sit down. So she stays standing, the ceiling tickling the top of her head, and gets out her pen and notebook, opening it on the latest page. Vera is putting a croissant on to a plate for a customer outside.

'What happens if you swallow canal water?'

Here we go. Vera takes a deep breath. 'I think it makes you sick.'

Odeline wrinkles her nose. 'Do birds defecate into the water?'

'Certainly. And the rats.'

'Rats?'

'Oh yes. Rats love the canals. Excuse me.' She lifts the tray and takes the customer's breakfast out. Odeline leans over the counter to check the kitchen area and then looks around the floor behind her. She shudders. There is a wall at the back of the cabin with low doors in it. That's the kind of cupboard where a rat would lurk.

'What happens in there?' she asks, pointing at the cupboard as Vera steps back into the boat.

'That is where the tables are stored,' says Vera, her smile gone. 'Do you find anything in the directory?'

Odeline looks around the cabin floor once again and then opens the directory. She flicks the pages over until she reaches Entertainment. She bends down to look through the listings but the radio is singing in her ear and she keeps losing her place. She looks up again.

'Do the rats come out at night or during daylight as well?'

'Sometimes you see them in the day.' Vera is stacking cold drinks into the fridge from a cardboard box; she holds the fridge handle and strains to bend down for each can.

'Do they come aboard boats?'

'I don't think so.'

'Why do you play this annoying radio music?'

Vera laughs. 'Yes, it is annoying. It's the rule. I have to play exactly this station at exactly this volume.'

'Perhaps that's why the customers don't want to come inside.'

Vera laughs again. 'You might be right.'

Odeline writes the telephone numbers for six entertainment agencies into her notebook. She finishes the hot chocolate, leaves the foam cup on the counter and walks up to the telephone box by the bridge. She holds the door open for a few seconds to air it before going in. She takes the coins from her moneybelt and arranges them in columns according to denomination on top of the telephone. It is a feat of mental coordination trying to conduct a telephone call whilst at the same time judging which coin to put in next. She can't just use up all the 10p coins, because then she might waste 20p and 50p coins on a call which ends prematurely. It is disingenuous of the telephone company not to give change. It is quite clearly a conspiracy to make more money. But she is no fool. She will not fall into their trap. She decides to start with a 20p coin and ask her opening questions quickly, hanging up if the answers do not sound promising. If she thinks the agency sounds suitable, she will use a 50p to ask further questions. She will keep the 10p coins for situations where she is reaching the end of the call but anticipates one or two more exchanges before it is over. Whatever happens, she will not replace the receiver until she hears the line cut out – the telephone company will make no unearned profit out of her.

Afterwards, she writes the results of each call into her notebook.

Call 1: Magic Wands
Answering machine. 20p not refunded
Call 2: Rabbit in a Hat
For artists who work exclusively with animals. 20p
Call 3: Send in the Clowns
90% of bookings are children's parties. 20p
Call 4: Abracadabra
Answering machine. 20p not refunded
Call 5: Silent Stars
Exclusively adult event bookings. Registered. £1.40
Call 5: Feathers
Exclusively adult event bookings. Require show-reel. 70p

Not particularly successful, on balance, but she will try Magic Wands and Abracadabra again tomorrow, pursue work through Silent Stars and do some research into making a showreel. Perhaps another telephone directory will have more Entertainment listings. But these telephone costs are going to be considerable, and she did not anticipate this in her budget forecast. She will have to make adjustments.

She has two more calls to make. The British Waterways General Enquiries number keeps her on hold for over a minute, at full rate. The machine clicks down 10p every five seconds. When she finally connects to the Customer Services department she would like to complain but doesn't, because of the extra cost this would incur. The Customer Services woman assures her that their mail service is reliable and that there are only three delivery points in London, so it is unlikely that a mistake has been made, and in any case, a misdirected package would be reported and re-delivered. Odeline hears the line clicking and lets it go dead. £2.70. She forgot to ask whether they have processed her letter of complaint about the tawdry state, personalisation and misleading advertisement of *Chaplin and Company*.

Her second call is to the Canal Community Centre in Camden. She has brought her National Insurance card and NHS Immunisation booklet with her in her waistcoat pocket, in case they require identification details, but it turns out to be surprisingly easy to book a free steering lesson. They have a slot available tomorrow morning. All they need is her name. She double-checks the lesson will be free and hears the man confirm this just as the line cuts out. £1.30.

Back by the canal she looks both ways, up and down the towpath. Last night she had an alarming dream about Ridley – that she rescued him from a bald man in a pub, a man who was trying to kill him. She beat the bald man away with an umbrella and carried Ridley in her arms over the cobbles of Covent Garden, to safety. She remembers looking down and seeing his shirt ripped and his bare tattooed torso, inky and dark and throbbing.

There is no sign of Ridley or his boat. Or, thankfully, John Kettle. But the drunks are back in their spot by the bench. Just two of them this time, the man in the wool hat and the one wth the grey matted hair, who is rolling a shopping trolley as if it is a baby's pram. On closer inspection, she is definitely female – today she is wearing a short-sleeved floral dress and has a pair of sunglasses perched on the grey thatch of hair. There is a pillow balanced on top of the junk in the trolley, and a fan of empty tennis racket covers flops over the end. The man in the wool hat is slumped low on the bench with his hand around a bottle. They are singing low notes, their voices winding around each other. *A hundred and one pounds of fun, that's my little honey bun.*

The woman rocks the trolley, back and forth, back and forth.

Inside her boat Odeline can still hear the singing, but it stays at a low, constant pitch, and after listening for a minute at the door, she decides it is less annoying than the bursts of shrieking and squawking from the canal birds, who today seem to be constantly landing on or launching off the water, as if it is an airport runway, and all the time making noisy announcements about it. She goes to the bathroom to perform her dental hygiene ritual before rehearsal. When she pulls the microphone light cord the wall light flashes and then puffs out. She tugs at the microphone again and again, but the light has fused. Infuriating. She has to brush her teeth in the light from the porthole. How is she supposed to enter her performance mindset with this racket? But then she has a eureka moment. She grabs the make-up box and takes it to the kitchenette counter, then lifts up the tiered compartments and rummages through the eye pencils and facepaint sticks at the bottom. Aha! Earplugs! She squashes one into each ear, and holds her breath to listen. The birds' squawks are distant, muted squeaks. Now she can concentrate.

She has folded her bed up against the wall in preparation for rehearsal. This morning she Sellotaped some of the strips of the Marcel Marceau film reels to the portholes so she can see them clearly against the light. She goes to a porthole and stoops to look at the line of stills inside it, bands of black acetate with punched holes down the side, frame after frame showing the artful poses of her hero. More than that, the minute and artful transitions between poses. As her eyes flick down the reels, his ballet-shoed toe turns out, extends, a pose becomes a step, becomes a leap, becomes a pirouette. All the while the rest of the body, the arms, the face, the hands, are changing too. Every inch of his body engaged. None of her books have shown her this. Each image in the books is finished, a frozen statue like the painted buskers in Covent Garden. But in these reels no two frames are identical. He was never, in fact, still. Now she tries to copy these movements, frame by frame, adjusting hands, arms, turning her torso, twisting her chin, extending her leg, her toe. She tries to invoke the great master, the white figure moving in his circle of spotlight on the stage. In just fifteen days she will be there, in the front row of his audience, watching him.

The next morning she is woken abruptly – birds again. This time they are scratching and cawing on the roof of her boat. She was in the middle of rescuing Ridley from a huge wolf-like dog. The birds woke her just as she and Ridley were pressed together in a telephone box, the dog barking outside. She fetches a brogue from under the bed and stands up to knock the heel against the ceiling. Usually Odeline's day sets off the minute she wakes – she is up and dressed within minutes. But this morning she sits back down bewildered on the side of the bed, still half in the dream. There is a warm sloshing in her stomach and her

skin is still prickling with alarm at the memory of the
giant dream-dog.

Her pocket watch says ten o'clock. She has woken
ninety minutes later than planned. There is no time to
rehearse, to telephone the other entertainment agencies,
or to go to the British Waterways Office to check her
pigeonhole. She had intended to do all these things before
going to Camden for her steering lesson. She does have
time to stop in at the barge cafe en route, though; she
would like answers to a few more queries. She gets dressed
and straps her moneybelt around her waist – she packed
it last night with her A–Z, notebook and biro, change for
the telephone and the solar-powered calculator, so she can
forecast her telephone costs for the accounts book on the
bus to Camden. The moneybelt is quite heavy and jangles
when she climbs out of the cabin doors. She stands on the
deck and swivels her head in periscope fashion. Still no
sign of Ridley or the *Saltheart* in either direction. An old
couple have moored their boat next to hers and she feels
like telling them to move, that they have taken someone
else's spot. She wonders if Ridley remembers telling her
about the music and performance gatherings on his friend's
boat – she had been full of anticipation for that. Perhaps
he has travelled on to that other canal, the one drawn on
his chest, and won't ever come back.

When she comes out from under the bridge there is a
squawking frenzy in the water at the end of the barge cafe.
Seagulls and moorhens are pecking at each other, their
wings batting the boat. Just as it subsides, Odeline sees a
fat wrist appear from the small flap of window and drop
something into the water. The squawking and flapping

sets off again. It is a very jarring sound. When she gets to the cafe doorway, Vera is standing by a chopping board at the sink, cutting crusts off squares of bread.

'Won't that encourage the rats?' says Odeline, over the racket.

Vera jumps away from the window and then starts to laugh, bringing her hand to her chest to calm herself. She is wearing a pink aertex over a huge denim skirt with buttons down the front. It is shapeless and hangs in loose folds above her trainers and pink ankle socks. 'Oh, Odi, you do give me a shock.' She leans back against the sink. 'I am glad it is only you.'

Only, thinks Odeline, staying on the doorstep. What does she mean, *only*? And no one has ever shortened her name before. She didn't give Vera permission to start making up nicknames. Is it because of the hot chocolates – does Vera think that gives her the right?

She opens her notebook and unclips the biro from the cover. She will make her enquiries and then move on.

'Which shop sells lightbulbs for bathrooms?'

Vera's thick mouth widens – she is smiling to herself. Odeline wants to ask what is so amusing, but would rather have the answer to her question.

'It depends which bulb you need. You can take the old one out of the light to check the size.'

'Do you know how to make a showreel?'

'A showreel?'

'Yes.'

'What is this?'

'For actors. To show examples of what they can do.'

'Oh, okay.' Vera opens a bag of bread and counts out

six slices. Odeline wants to stamp her foot. *Answer the question.*

'Well –' Vera brings the chopping board and bread over to the counter, unsure – 'I think you need a camera. For the filming. And then you need to edit the films into small parts.'

'How long does it have to be?'

'The whole thing? I would say a few minutes. I don't know. I never see a showreel.' She opens the packet of butter next to the barking radio and starts buttering the squares of bread. 'Are you making one?'

Odeline looks down at her notebook and turns a page. 'Do rats attack human beings?'

Vera is smiling again. 'No.'

'But they have teeth.'

'Yes, but only for eating.'

'Do rats carry diseases?'

'Yes, I think sometimes.'

'Deadly diseases?'

'I never hear of that.'

Odeline steps forward to lean on the counter and write. She hooks her finger around the biro and presses her small, deliberate letters into the page, beneath the query entitled *Rats: Deadly? Not through direct attack*, she writes. *Possibly through disease.*

When she looks up there is a foam cup of hot chocolate next to the chopping board. 'For you,' says Vera. 'And this,' she says, taking a flat croissant out of the microwave with some tongs and putting it on a plate. 'You are too thin. You need some more weight.'

Odeline looks at the pink aertex stretching across Vera's

bosom, at the roll bulging over the elasticated top of the denim skirt.

'Maybe not as much as me,' says Vera, patting her middle.

Odeline wants to refuse the croissant, but her stomach feels hollow and the smell of it is buttery and delicious. She hasn't eaten hot food since she arrived on the canal. That first evening, there had been a moment when mouth-watering smells from the barbecues in the tower blocks had wafted into her cabin and she had thought about setting up the barbecue in her kitchenette cupboard – but when she'd looked inside the bag it was such a tangle of rusty metal parts that she'd shut the cupboard door again. She picks up the croissant and bites the end of it, sinking on to the stool at the counter. She looks down to check her final query for Vera.

'Have you seen the warden?' she asks, her mouth full.

'Not since we bring him from the hospital.' Vera is layering slices of cheese on to the bread. 'I see him working on his boat but he doesn't come by the cafe. At last –' she puts ham slices on to the cheese – 'some peace.' She places a slice of crustless bread on top, and then uses the tongs to lift the sandwiches on to a plate. 'Excuse me,' she says, going outside.

Odeline looks out of the porthole at the island on the far side of the pool. She picks up her hot chocolate and blows on it before taking a sip. There are a pair of upright grey and black birds standing on the bank between the drooping branches of the willow tree. They are like senti-nels at the edge of the water. When Vera comes back into the boat Odeline asks her what they are and Vera tells her they are herons. Odeline finds them aesthetically pleasing, especially the flick of black feather at the back of their heads and the way their necks extend. They look more like the ink paintings from her book on Japanese theatre than actual flesh and blood. The looped tips of the wings are scribbled, like calligraphy. They are certainly superior to the screeching seagulls and moorhens Vera gives left-overs to. She is sure that the herons would never lower themselves to fighting for scraps with those sorts of birds.

Odeline is finishing her hot chocolate when Vera suddenly spins around from the sink window and goes to grab the croissant plate and the chopping board from the counter. 'Please, you have to go outside now like a normal customer.' She makes a lunge at the radio and turns the music up even louder. 'Please, can you go now? I am in trouble if I give you things without charging.' She leans over and shuts Odeline's notebook and gives it to her. 'I'm sorry. I'm sorry.' Odeline takes the notebook and clips her biro on to the front. She stands back off her stool, looking at Vera, who is flushed and frantic now, wiping the counter with a teatowel. 'I see you later,' she says, looking up.

'I've finished anyway,' says Odeline, putting the foam cup down. Vera snatches it, wipes beneath it and puts it in the bin. 'See you later then,' says Odeline, stepping up and out of the boat. As she walks to the bridge, two shaved blocks of head come out from underneath, two sets of puffed-up chests and burly arms swinging in time with each other.

She travels up to Camden by bus and uses her *A–Z* to find her way back down to the canal. When she telephoned, she was told to look out for a boat called *Nelson's Victory*, which would be moored opposite the floating Chinese restaurant at Primrose Hill. She locates the boat easily and with some disappointment. It is a modern design in mint green, with a shiny white roof and large white plastic handles on the windows. Fire exit signs are stuck to the glass. Next to the name is a silhouette of Nelson himself, done like an old-fashioned portrait in a white oval. He is gallantly posed holding up a telescope, an admiral's hat and ponytail leading down to epauletted shoulders and slender frame, with one knickerbockered leg thrust forward, like on Nelson's Column.

She walks to the bank and looks down into the boat. There is a fat man in a sweatshirt on the rear deck, leaning against the tiller with his fists jammed into his pockets. He appears to be in his own world, tapping the toes of his trainers together. He is wearing a baseball cap from which flows a shock of white hair. He has a heavy moustache, also bright white, and, from what she can see, very red cheeks. The moustache droops down at the sides of his mouth. Walrus, thinks Odeline.

'I'm here for my steering lesson,' she calls down.

The man looks up quickly and then appears to hover from one leg on to the other before answering. She half expects a honking noise to come from below the moustache, and is surprised to hear a quiet Scottish accent.

'Yes. Please come aboard.' He gestures on to the deck without catching her eye. All she can see is the moustache moving up and down. 'My name is Crosbie. I'm one of the Community Boat Workers.'

Odeline steps down on to the deck and introduces

herself. 'I am Odeline. I've just moved on to a narrowboat but I haven't steered one before.'

The teacher bends to check the rope tying the boat to the bank. He breathes in deeply, then, still facing the mooring hook, says, 'The Community Boat Scheme is aimed at teaching all levels.' He stands up straight and looks around, tapping his fingers against his leg.

Odeline says, 'I have read my narrowboat manual but I don't know anything about the engines or the mechanics. I'd like to understand all that, so as to be fully prepared in the case of an emergency. I've brought my notebook.' She picks it out of her trouser pocket and shows him.

The teacher breathes in again and nods, looking down at his feet. 'The Community Boat Scheme recognises the importance of teaching emergency procedures,' he says. He sounds as if he has learned these statements by rote – there is no variation in the tone of his voice. He takes yet another deep breath and announces the start of the theoretical part of the lesson. He points along the roof of the boat to its nose.

'The steerer's gaze must be directed at all times towards the bow of the boat. Maintaining this eyeline is the most important thing to remember when steering. The rest of the boat will duly follow.'

These lines sound familiar; Odeline is sure they are direct quotes from the Introduction in her *British Waterways Narrowboat Manual*, having read it cover to cover several times before coming to the canal. She looks along the line and squints as though she is looking through the sights of a rifle. She imagines a line going forward from her eye, down the roof and off the end of the boat.

At the moment it would be hitting the bottom of the floating Chinese restaurant.

Before she has a chance to note down this first point, the teacher trips back into his robotic mumble. 'This boat is six foot ten inches wide, which is the normal width for a narrowboat. The steerer should keep that in mind when passing other boats. But it is recommended to always allow a boat's width of extra room as some narrowboats are built wider.' He pauses. He sounds short of breath, but Odeline realises it is the way he speaks, with a little gasp before saying anything. That and the blushing cheeks make him seem shy. 'Boats always pass to the right of an oncoming boat. The port sides pass each other.' He taps the left side of the boat. Odeline quickly unclips the biro from her notebook and writes '*Port to Port*' under the title *PASSING*. She likes the sound of nautical terminology but is not yet sure what all the words refer to.

The teacher bends down and hooks his finger into a brass pull on the deck. 'This is where your engine is,' he says, pulling the hatch open and looking down into a pit of grimy painted machinery. He begins to indicate the different parts of the engine: the batteries, the isolator, the valves, the grease pipe. Odeline scribbles in her notebook. She will look up these parts in the *Manual* later on. He goes on to point out the weed hatch inspection compartment, the water tank and the calorifier, and then various constituent parts of those. All this time he keeps his eyes fixed downwards on the engine compartment, and keeps one hand in his pocket. Odeline wonders if he has something wrong with his arm like Nelson.

He announces the beginning of the practical part of the

lesson and unties the boat from its mooring, wheezing
under his baseball cap and moustache. Odeline positions
herself at the stern, plants her feet wide for stability and
takes hold of the tiller. It shakes in her hand as the engine
comes on, and she can feel the vibrations through the soles
of her brogues.

So, so, so exciting.

She doesn't know what to do with her other arm and
so puts it on her hip, making little squeezes to her waist
with the thrill of it. The boat begins to move forward and
the teacher recites a line she recognises from a caption
below one of the diagrams in her *Manual*.

'For left-handed steerers, an orientation to the left is
made by pulling the tiller towards the body.'

She does this and the boat swings slowly away from
the bank. She opens her eyes wide and keeps them firmly
on the line along the roof of the boat. She is heading for
the opposite bank and pushes the tiller away from herself
to bring the boat straight.

He mumbles another pair of sentences from the
Manual:

'The accomplished steerer will make minor and repeated
adjustments to the tiller position whilst maintaining the
forward eyeline. Some new to steering find this coordination awkward at first.'

Odeline, in fact, finds it comes quite easily. She feels
perfectly coordinated and hardly breaks her eyeline as she
makes the minor adjustments. They float slowly around
the top of Regent's Park. The houses on the park side are
high up and very grand, like enormous white cakes with
decorative icing. Odeline imagines women in ballgowns

and long gloves fanning down their steps. On the opposite bank of the canal are low rows of narrowboats and barges, stacked up against the side. A jumble of boats, all shapes and colours, all within inches of each other. Set back from the towpath are little boxed gardens for each mooring. Some are beautifully done with tiles, wooden chairs and hanging lights. They pass one with a pair of women sitting on deckchairs in their underwear next to a smoking barbecue, bodies cooking in the sun. Odeline sniffs and looks back along the line of the roof.

'I would hate to live so packed in with other people,' says Odeline, imagining sunbathers' faces lining up to look through her porthole.

Her teacher doesn't reply, but directs her into a mooring at the end of a row of boats. She manages to come into the bank smoothly and at a perfect angle. She is impressed with herself. The teacher shows her how to rope the boat to the mooring hooks, the final stage of this first lesson. She also finds this easy, although the rope ends are covered with manky weed and she doesn't have anything on which to wipe her hands. She ends up shaking them over the side of the boat.

'So what is there still to learn?' she asks.

'The next stage in the Community Boat Scheme is to practise turning manoeuvres, including steering in reverse. The following stage is to learn locks.'

'When could I come for another lesson? Do I have to book it on the telephone again?'

He bites his moustache and nods, which Odeline takes as a yes. 'All right then,' she says. She doesn't really know how to say goodbye to this man and ends up giving a sort of salute. He salutes back and immediately looks down. 'See you then.'

As she walks away she feels more than satisfied at how smoothly and precisely she has steered the boat. She had thought she would find it difficult but it is the second thing in life which she realises she might have been born with a natural gift for. She is looking forward to the next lesson.

From her *A–Z* she sees she can get back home along the Regent's Canal towpath. As she walks away from the grand houses and the busy moorings, the towpath becomes potholed. The foliage along the edge is overgrown – chicken wire and plastic bags sit on top whilst cans and broken glass spill out from the bottom. She comes to a tunnel with graffiti covering the walls and walks quickly through, listening out for what might be in there. She hears a steady dripping, water leaking through the mossy joins in the concrete. Out into the sunlight and walls rise up high on either side – she can hear traffic above and sees the backs of billboards facing the road. This city's hidden places are dark and stink of neglect, thinks Odeline. Arundel was a one-dimensional place but London has two faces, one as dirty as the other is shiny. The bits hidden from view are not taken care of. She wonders if this is true of the people in London too.

FIFTEEN

The floor of the warehouse was thick with feathers, pale and rippled like sand. In the centre, tipped away to one side on a trolley, was a long boat. It was covered in a crust of white and grey droppings like barnacles on a shipwreck. If he twisted his head to the rust-bitten hole in the wall, he could see cabin doors at the near end of the boat, and also the brass underside of a tiller. The roof of the warehouse was corroded and shafts of sunlight streamed through the holes and came down on to the boat. Flecks and feathers swilled in these slanted columns of light. The air seemed thick and swaying, as if water. Donald could hear his own breathing. Around the boat he could make out the relics of other contraptions, long gone, collapsed and rusted, half subsumed in feathers. But the boat itself was held up whole on the trolley. Donald felt as if he had come across something perfectly, magically preserved.

He didn't know how long he had been standing there looking. He straightened up and brought his pen up to the paper on his clipboard. The warehouse was derelict – it should certainly be destroyed. He pressed the nib of the pen to the paper, but couldn't move it. Perhaps he needed to go in, he thought, to assess who the boat belonged to. This might have implications for the site report.

He went round to the high doors at the back of the warehouse and pulled at the padlock. It was locked, rusted shut. He looked up at the corrugated doors spotted with rust. The wood around the hinges was splintered and mouldy. He prodded it – his fingers sank in and came away muddy. Then he gave the bottom of the door a push with his shoe and it came away from the hinge. When he pushed further the door came away from the top hinge too and creaked back, leaving a space big enough for him to enter. The top hinge fell from the door frame and clanged against the door, setting off a beating of wings inside. He heard the birds scrabbling at the roof and then, in a moment, it was quiet again.

He budged the door open an inch further and went in, not really expecting the boat to be there, thinking it might have been his imagining. But he found himself facing the back of it: solid and real above the floor of feathers. He walked up to it. He saw four brass portholes along the side and flaked blue and red paint – he couldn't make out the words that had been once written along the side. The decking at the back of the boat was rotten, the planks buckled and split. He climbed up on to a wheel of the trolley, reached over the side and pushed the cabin door open.

He was looking into what must have been the engine room, with some sort of dial on the ceiling, and a tipped fuel can in the doorway. Beyond that the main body of the boat was a long empty cabin. There was a tarpaulin, stained and green with age, rucked up against the side, and some collapsed crates in the corner. Donald stepped back down to the warehouse floor and moved round to the stern of the boat. He brought his hand up to the tiller and scratched off some of the dirt encrusted around the top. Underneath was a warm gold colour. He carried on scratching until he had made a line of gold in the dirt.

He did not know how long he stayed with her, but at last he managed to drag himself away, pulling the broken warehouse door back into position. He decided not to mention the boat in his site report; he didn't know what to write about it. He was aware of feeling strongly about it. And he wasn't the kind of man who felt strongly about anything. He was not a man of conviction, as his father said.

Donald Fallagh was the son of a politician, now retired, formerly MP for Harrow West. Once a formidable orator, Patrick Fallagh was dying now and only moved between the armchair and the bed. He ate his meals from a tray on his lap. But he still brandished rhetoric from his armchair, jabbing a discoloured finger at whoever was there to listen. Once a week this was Donald. He had a flat in Pimlico but came home on Sundays. He sat in the other chair by the fire while his father talked. His father's vision for Britain had not materialised and neither had his vision for his son, who held a junior position in the Ministry of Transport. Under a Labour Government. Donald was made to understand that these things were the results of his own weakness. He felt his father's disappointment as disgust, and was forced to know it weekly, sitting by the fireplace. He was a flimsy betrayal of the old man in the chair opposite. A real man would have achieved something by now. A real son would have leapt up and sworn to uphold his father's legacy. But Donald just sat there, looking into the fireplace. He looked down and scratched at the piping on the armchair cover, or sipped at his teacup long after it was empty. His mother was a quick shadow in and out of the room, clearing the food tray, stoking the fire, fetching an extra blanket.

That Sunday, Patrick Fallagh looked even weaker, his body seemed shrunken in its clothes and his face had become a sort of grimace, toothy and wet-lipped. He still roused himself to speak, but his ranting was less constant – it came in shorter volleys and then tailed off. Donald did not squirm at the silence as he usually did. He found he had allowed his mind to go back to the warehouse by the canal. He was imagining what would happen if he didn't submit a report for the warehouse, if he didn't put it forward for demolition. If he went back to see the boat.

The following Saturday, he arrived at the warehouse with tools and kit for cleaning. Once inside the doors, he approached the boat slowly, treading gently on the carpet of feathers as if she was asleep. He had brought a bucket of water and started by brushing down her sides. The top layer of paint had come off with the crust of dirt and bird droppings, but in the underpaint the boat's decoration was legible in red script against a blue background: *Chaplin and Company, Est. 1936*. Donald felt as if he'd unearthed treasure that was three hundred years old, not thirty.

He'd checked the hull. It seemed intact. The structure of the main cabin was also in good condition – it was only the outer planks which had gone bad. In the engine room he had found a fold-down shelf with a cloth bag underneath, which was half disintegrated and full of droppings. There was a gas mask beneath this with the glass missing from both eyes. The face of the mask was cracked rubber, the strings green with mould. And he was able to decipher the dial set in the lowered ceiling of the engine room: a hand-painted compass, its needle still balanced on its point, trembling towards south-east.

The debris in the main cabin consisted of old tins, crates and sacking. Donald didn't feel these things were his to dispose of. He put them into one intact sack and left it in the corner of the warehouse behind a bicycle whose frame was iced with rust and droppings.

His mind went over these things as he sat opposite his father the next day. Patrick Fallagh wheezed and ranted. But, again, Donald was immune. Instead of rehearsing responses to himself, he rehearsed pulling up the rotten wood from the decks of the boat, polishing the brass around the portholes, finding paints to trace the outline of the letters along her side.

Every Saturday he went back and worked on the boat. He worked late, driving a hook into the ceiling of the cabin and hanging a hurricane lamp to see by. The lamp's flame lit the cabin waxy yellow, a warm capsule in the black of the warehouse. Donald's world shrank to this as he worked through the night. Sometimes, as he sat back against the boat's walls, pausing between tasks, he imagined he could feel tiny movements in the boat, as if she were on water. Or yearning to be.

He worked hard. He replaced the timbers on the decks and varnished them. He scrubbed and painted. Repaired the roof, re-tarred the hull. As he worked he heard the pigeons scratching on the roof and during the day some would clamber through the rusted warehouse holes and sit watching him from the eaves. He felt proud of his work, a balloon inflating bit by bit inside him. But in the weekdays he would grow terrified: that on Saturday he might go back to find her gone. He left a loose plank above the doorway to the engine room and kept his tools inside. He also put the gas mask into this gap, and the remains of the drawstring bag – he wasn't sure why: perhaps he felt they simply *belonged* to the boat.

During the weeks he read about narrowboat building and steering and looked at diagrams of engines, careful to hide the books from colleagues at work. He ordered new parts for the boat's engine and learned how to install them. All this felt audacious and irresponsible and pointless, given that the boat might be claimed and destroyed at any time. But he didn't want to think about what he was doing. To think would be to puncture the feeling it was giving him.

Donald restored the boat in eleven weeks. In the twelfth week his father died. He received a message on his desk at work and telephoned his mother. He was given leave. He went home and saw his father laid out on the bed in a suit with his hair greased back as it never had been. The eyes were sunk and the jowls had a sort of weight to them, seeming to pull the lips slightly apart. Teeth just showing. His fingers were paper white but still looked full of life. Donald felt that if he touched them they would grip hard and never let him go.

After the funeral Donald took his mother home and

stayed the night, sitting awake in the armchair by the fireplace. The next morning he went directly to the warehouse. He went to the doors at the far end and kicked at them. It worked. They split easily from their hinges and with a great groan fell backwards together into the canal. Sunlight rushed in. He pulled the base of the doors up to make a ramp and water sloshed at their edges. Donald went to the back of the trolley and pushed. The wheels creaked and began to turn. They sang. They hit the edge of the ramp and began to tug forwards. He let them go. The trolley ran down the ramp and off the end it dropped. The boat breasted the water and levelled itself, rocking backwards and forwards, making waves that washed over Donald's shoes and the ends of the fallen doors. As it settled in the water he heard a sound like a sigh come from the bows of the boat and felt his lungs release too, his shoulders drop.

He was able to reach the trunk of the tiller, grabbed it and lifted himself aboard. He saw the trolley wheels sinking below the surface of the water. When he opened the cabin doors, the hurricane lamp was swinging side to side from the hook in the roof. He let her level, stood at the ignition and stopped his breath to pray as he pulled the engine on. He opened his eyes again to hear the first tugs of the motor as she came to life.

SIXTEEN

John Kettle unfolds the piece of paper again and looks at the map. It has been badly photocopied and sits at a slant near the top of the page. There is a large arrow pointing to a cross at the centre of a jumble of rectangles. The line of a railway track winds along the top of the map. Underneath in faded type are details of the first meeting. *Your Community Alcohol Awareness Programme will be directed by Rev. A. Pillet.* So they are sending him off to be preached at by the God Squad. He is going to need a drink after this.

He has followed the towpath, then walked a minute or so inland, through the housing estates and clusters of tower blocks. He is in the middle of one of these clusters now, standing on some threadbare grass next to a bin that has had its front panel ripped off. It is impossible to tell where he is on the map. Little roads lead off in all directions between the patches of grass – every time he's followed one it's taken him down another dead end and he's found himself in a grubby courtyard, two or three tower blocks looming over him with God knows who living inside. And dog shit everywhere. Packs of kids on bikes wheeling past, so close some of them hit his shoulder. They pedalled off before he could yell. Feral rats. Delinquent youth. *Why aren't you in school?*

John Kettle stuffs the map back into his pocket and checks his watch. Quarter past four. He is late. Can't be helped. The God Squadders can wait a bit. He rummages through his other pocket. Forgot the tobacco, damn it, he could do with a smoke. He lifts the cap from the front of his head and wipes his brow with the sleeve of his shirt, then jams the cap back down. He walks across the grass to join another road. This one has speedbumps, so it could be the way out. He turns the corner and sure enough there's the bloody church, sitting in a square of grass with a pathway leading up to the porch. It looks more like the house of Dracula than the house of God. The huge square stones are blackened with dirt and wire grilles have been fixed over the windows. There is a crescent-shaped flower-bed opposite the front of the church which has one skeleton plant in it, and is spotted with little plastic bags. More dog shit.

A painted sign sticks up next to the flowerbed. Welcome to St Philip's. The service times have been sprayed out by graffiti.

Bloody hell, John Kettle says to himself. What a dump. He walks into the porch and twists the iron door handle, hearing the latch echo inside. The door creaks open: a horror film. This is a bloody bad joke. Do they really send people to this place for help? He peers around the door. The inside of the church is lit yellow by blazing floodlights strapped to the top of the stone columns. There is almost no light coming through the windows – he can see the tight grilles through the panes of stained glass. The altar is empty apart from a pair of gold candlesticks with chains shackling their bases like handcuffs. The main body of the church is filled with two banks of orange plastic chairs, arranged in rows with a blue carpet running up the middle. At the back of the church there is an area enclosed by bookshelves and beanbags, with an ethnic rug in the middle. Five plastic chairs are arranged in a circle, and four of them are being sat on. In the chair facing the door is a young bloke in a dog collar. He gets up when he sees John Kettle and paces over, his hand outstretched. The sleeves of his black vicar's shirt are rolled up above the elbow, he is wearing blue trousers with brown lace-ups and has little round wire-rimmed specs. Looks like some grub just off to university.

'Hi, welcome.' He blinks through the specs. 'You must be John?'

'If you say so,' says John Kettle, shaking the bloke's hand, a surprisingly firm grip. Still looks about twelve though. Bald arms, thin hair in a side parting and pink cheeks that surely haven't seen a razor. 'Bit spooky this place.'

The vicar laughs. 'It's not the most idyllic setting. I'm sorry if you had trouble finding it. These estates are quite a rabbit warren. Anyway, here you are. Come and meet the group.'

'Aye-aye, Captain.' John Kettle tips his hat, and then takes it off and smooths the hair over the top of his head before fixing it back on and walking over.

Oh God. It's that rank old tramp, the black one, from by the canal. She's sitting in a chair one away from the vicar's, wearing a belted mackintosh, probably nicked, and her hair matted and hanging in a sort of bob, like she's got a net on. He can smell her: body stench mixed with sweet-reeking alcohol. He walks round to the empty chair to the right of the vicar's, and sits down, looks at the shelves around the edge of the ethnic rug, stuffed with children's books and toys.

'Hello, Warden.' The tramp. Her thick, curling voice has an edge of laughter to it. He looks over and she is smiling. The chapped lips are stretched back to show big, yellow teeth. She is sitting stately, pleased with herself, her hands clasped beneath her bosom like a headmistress. She is square-shouldered and square-jawed. And square-bodied, although that could be the bulk of all her stinking clothes. She appears to be wearing checked chef's trousers under the mackintosh. They are too short and reveal bony ankles in black tights going into loafers with gold snaffles – the loafers planted outwards like duck's feet on the carpet. The shoes look new, probably nicked too. She raises a grey eyebrow and the skin of her forehead creases blacker.

'So, you have got yourself in trouble too?' Her voice is regal and she speaks slowly, enjoying the words, rolling them out.

He looks around to the other two in the group and rolls his eyes, but gets nothing back. The woman sitting next to the tramp is blank-faced and upright in the plastic seat. She is tall with ash-blonde hair falling in two panels from a centre parting and a big necklace of amber beads. Like a young hippy. But she's probably fifty-odd, and dressed in crumpled, beige clothes and God Squad sandals. She has high cheekbones and big pale blue eyes, and is looking back at him without seeming to focus. Probably high on drugs.

The final member of the group is the boy on John Kettle's right, who is leaning forward, rubbing his shaved head with his hands. He has a rucksack on the floor beside him and is tapping the side of it with his suede trainer. Druggie too? He looks too neat to be a down-and-out: the hoodie is baggy, but it looks clean. But you never know. The boy brings his arms down to lean on his knees; the sleeves are cupped over his fists. John Kettle feels the wad of notes in his breast pocket and looks down to check it's buttoned.

'Right.' The vicar is sitting cross-legged with an open folder on his knee. His trousers have ridden up to show pink and green striped socks, schoolboy socks. 'John, we started doing introductions but we'll go through them again to make sure you're up to speed. This –' he gestures to the pale woman – 'is Inga. We're doing just first names here.' The pale woman doesn't move and he extends his arm to the grizzled, stinking, mackintoshed figure next to her. 'This is Mary.'

'We know each other,' the tramp says in a low voice, bowing her head graciously to the vicar.

'We don't know each other,' says John Kettle. 'She annoys my residents. Singing and caterwauling on the towpath all day.'

'Better than keeping them awake all night,' says Mary, delighted, letting out a hoot of laughter.

The vicar puts his hand up. 'Okay, this is very unusual, for two group members to know each other. Even vaguely.' He blinks at John Kettle through his little round specs. His eyes are slightly enlarged behind the lenses, like in joke-shop glasses. 'Is this going to be a problem? We can swap one of you to another session if you think it could prevent you from engaging with the work here.'

'Won't make any difference,' John Kettle says. 'She doesn't bother me.'

'Mary?'

'I'm happy,' she says, stretching her fingers and clasping them again, shuffling back into her seat. Like a rancid old hen.

'Okay. If you're sure.' The vicar looks from one to the other, his cheeks flushed like a choirboy's. 'Okay, let's carry on. John, this is Chris.' The lad nods at John Kettle, raises his hand and looks back down at his trainers. 'Everyone, this is John. And, last in the circle –' the vicar puts a hand on his chest – 'I'm Alwyn.' John Kettle sniggers. Vicarish name.

'I was saying to the others, John, just before you came in, that, as we do first names only here, that includes me. No Reverend, no Father. We could be princes, doctors, hardened criminals, but when we come here we leave our status at the door.' He looks round at the group. The pale woman nods – it's the first time John Kettle has seen her move. 'Whatever goes on in our week, whatever we do or don't do, we just have to make one commitment, to turn up here twice a week. Sunday midday and Thursday at four. Or thereabouts,' he adds, smiling at John Kettle. 'Does that make sense to everyone?'

'Hardly rocket science,' says John Kettle.

'Great. The other thing to mention is this –' the vicar puts a finger inside his dog collar. 'We can ignore this. This is my day job. It needn't be relevant here unless you want it to be. Feel free to ask any questions but I'm not going to bring God into the work we do here. It's for each person to find their own way, not for me to give you mine.' He looks up at the church. 'This venue is free, that's why we're using it.'

'So it's not a Christian course?' asks the lad on John's right, huddled into his hoodie as if it's cold. 'We're not here to be reformed?'

'You'd have a job reforming this one!' Mary wiggles her head.

'No, it's not a Christian course. And this is definitely not a prayer group.'

The lad nods to himself, gives half a laugh.

'Thank God for that,' says John Kettle.

'Yes,' the vicar smiles, and runs a hand through his hair, combing it back into its side parting. 'People are usually relieved when I get to that bit.'

He stands up and rubs his hands. 'Right then. I'd like to start with a little exercise. It might seem a bit odd but hopefully you'll see the point of it.' He nods around the group but only Mary is looking back, beaming at him like a halfwit. The lad is watching his toes wriggle in the end of his trainers and the pale woman is looking down her nose at her string of beads, her fist closed around the end of it. She's got a cold look about her. Snooty, a bit like Madam from the *Chaplin and Company*, but she's frailer, more willowy in her floaty clothes. She doesn't, for instance, look like she's got a broom up her arse.

He checks his pockets again. God, he could do with a smoke.

The vicar picks up a green crate from a seat by the back

wall and brings it over to the group. From the crate, he lifts out a potted plant on a terracotta tray and hands it to the pale woman, then gives one to each of the other three and takes one for himself before sitting down. John looks down at the frilly blue flowers in his lap, the thick stubby leaves. There is a plastic tag sticking out of the soil which says *Busy Lizzie Perennial*.

'So there is one more thing I'm going to ask you to do. As well as turn up to our meetings. I'd like you to take this away with you today and keep it alive. It needs water once a day, just enough to fill the tray, and it needs to be kept in a sheltered spot. Inside near to a window is ideal.'

'Is this a joke?' says John Kettle, looking round at the others holding their plants on their laps like a bunch of bridesmaids. 'Fucking pot plants? Excuse my French.' He sees a flicker of a smile on the pale woman's lips. Maybe she's not so snooty.

'Mine smells lovely,' says Mary, leaning forward to sniff.

'Bear with me, John,' says the vicar. 'The point is, it's something for you to remember. Every day, you're making time to do this. It may seem stupidly simple, it may seem pointless –'

'Too right.'

'– but in remembering to look after something as small as a plant, we can begin to remember how to look after ourselves.'

'I look after myself just fine, thank you.'

'Hmmmm,' pipes Mary, raising both eyebrows and pouting her flaky lips.

'You shut up,' he growls through his beard. 'Dirty old witch. Stinking pisshead. Excuse my French again.' The pale woman doesn't smile. 'What's the problem, blondie, are we not amused?'

'John, if you're frustrated with the situation, then direct your abuse at me, not other members of the group.'

'All right then. Alwyn.' John Kettle stands up. 'You can keep your bloody plant. Keep it for another one of your mad drunks or druggies. Or why not stick it in your lovely flowerbed out the front?' He slams the pot down on his seat and soil spills everywhere. He pushes the sleeves of his shirt up his arms. 'I don't need a bleeding awareness programme. I don't need first-names-only with some speccy pipsqueak. I don't need to sit in the kids' corner with the beanbags and the train sets. I'm not one of your nut-jobs.' He taps the side of his head. He is gathering momentum, getting louder. He can hear his voice booming in the empty church. 'I don't need to be stuck in here with a bunch of tramps and zombies, sniffing bloody flowers. I've got work to do. I've got things to keep an eye on.'

Eye on, eye on, the church vibrates with his last note.

'Okay, John,' says the vicar, putting his pot plant down on the carpet next to his chair. 'I know what happened last week. They passed on the report.' John Kettle winces and looks away towards the fluorescent-lit altar and the glaring lights. He can hear the whine of the electrics. The vicar is speaking in a stupid, muted voice.

'Everyone here is in a different situation.'

John Kettle's fingers are twitching. He can't remember the last time he felt more like laying someone out. The vicar stands up and puts an arm out but doesn't touch him. Wisely.

'You may consider others to have bigger problems, or that there are better ways to spend your time, but all we ask is that you come along. As far as I understand, that was one of the conditions of your release from hospital, is that right?'

John Kettle spins around. 'Fucking Nazis, haven't got a bloody clue about a person's life. All the other stuff he might have to do. Four p.m. on a Thursday afternoon? Some of us have proper jobs. Reverend. This is a fucking waste of time.'

Time, says the church, backing him up.

The vicar lowers his arm to his side, and says very quietly, 'The report mentioned that you had had your position suspended, is that right?'

. . .

'Is that right, John?'

. . .

'John?'

. . .

Eyes so tired.

Suddenly. So tired.

He rubs them.

Mouth aches. He lets it go loose. Rubs jaw, hears the bristles scratch.

He drops his head, jams his hands into the pockets of his trousers. Starts to rock back and forth, a nodding donkey, a cresting ship.

Shoulders curl in.

'Sit back down, John.' The vicar leans over and lifts the pot plant from his seat, brushing the soil off with his hand.

John sits down and takes it back on to his lap. Shall he

do what he's told? Doesn't know any more. What are the others doing? The woman opposite is looking down at the ethnic rug. He doesn't want to look at Mary. He catches eyes with the lad on his right, who flicks his glance away, starts chewing on his lip.

The vicar is leaning forward, his elbows on his knees. He pushes his glasses up his nose and blinks, big-eyed. 'No one has to engage with any of the work we do here, if it makes them uncomfortable. Everyone is welcome to tell me where to go if I cross a line, or get something wrong. That's almost bound to happen. This is a process – I'll be trying my best but I'm sure to make mistakes. Some of the exercises might not work for some of you –' he looks around the group – 'but I'd just ask that you give each one a try. Does that sound fair enough?'

'I say so,' shrugs Mary.

'Shall we start again?'

'A clean slate,' she announces, emphasising the 't'.

'Exactly. Great. Okay. I'd like us each to look at our plants.' He lifts his to eye level and turns it around in front of his face. John copies him and lifts the plant up with both hands. 'Really closely, under and all around it.' John turns it around the same way as Alwyn. 'Really notice the stalks, how many and their texture.'

Six rough stalks.

'The shapes of the leaves and their colour.'

Round-edged, dark-green leaves covered in fine, grey fur.

'Their underside.'

John tilts the pot up to see underneath. Light green, shiny as plastic.

'How many flowers, and the different colours.'

Six flowers with heart-shaped blue petals. Purple smudges like ink stains spreading from their middle. Nucleus of small bright-yellow beads. So many and so small he can't count.

Alwyn brings his plant down to his lap and the others follow. 'So the idea of this is that in seeing our plant, in looking at it and really seeing it, knowing our plant better, we will be more inclined to remember it. To remember to look after it. Now we know our plant, it is harder to forget about it.'

'Objection,' says Mary. 'I don't know about that, Alwyn. I forget about everything. No long-term memory. It's my special talent.'

'Absolutely everything?'

'Except the words to songs.'

'That sounds like another special talent.'

She shrugs and pouts her lips out. 'I suppose so.'

'So could you all put your plants down now, just on the floor or somewhere.' Alwyn lowers his to the floor and John copies. The pale woman twists and puts hers on top of the bookshelf behind her. 'I want us to look at our hands, to really look at them, and see them.' He lays a hand, palm up, on each knee. John does the same. His hands are thick and stubby and deeply lined. The palms are a rough, rubbery red and separated from his leathered forearms by deep creases across his wrists which make them look as if they have been screwed on. There is dirt in these creases, and in the deep tracks across his palms, which are cross-hatched, woven like ropes. Each puffy section of finger is scored with vertical lines.

'Have a look at how they move.' Alwyn opens and closes his fingers like the tendrils of an anemone.

John does the same, and sees his yellow, overgrown nails: thick with dirt, rimmed with muck, bowed like claws. The nails on his thumb and forefinger are striped brown from the fags. As long as a whore's! He shuts his fists and looks to the right. The lad next to him has his hands face down on his knees, the cuffs are halfway up the hands and he's not doing any of the movements Alwyn demonstrated. He's just staring at them, shaved head hanging forward like it's too heavy for his long, white neck. The fingers poking out of the cuffs are long and white too. John can see chipped blue varnish on the nails, just at the ends, as if they have been dipped.

'So the idea is the same here. That in knowing something better, we are more likely to care for it. To look after it. These are our hands.' He lifts his up either side of his head, fingers splayed. John starts to copy, and then sees that none of the others are doing the same and drops his hands back down to his lap.

'They are different to everyone else's. No one else has the unique shape, pigmentation, the same fingerprints as we do. Our lives are in these palms, this pattern of lines is our experience.' Alwyn links his fingers and leans forward. 'We overlook ourselves so easily. So many things in life tell us they are more important than caring for ourselves, coming back to ourselves. We can lose touch with ourselves just as easily as we can with friends and family members. And it's when we become strangers to ourselves that we neglect ourselves most harshly.'

Mary raises a finger. 'But it's also true, is it not, Alwyn, that sometimes when we look too closely, we don't like what we see.'

The pale woman gasps, very faintly, and lifts a hand to her mouth. She is staring at Mary's hand, which hangs in the air, poking up from the cuff of the mackintosh, making its point. There are raised welts crossing the back of the hand, sticking out pink and shiny from the black skin in crossed lines like a tally chart. John looks down to Mary's other hand, which is sitting like a claw in her lap, similarly striped and swollen.

Alwyn cranes forward towards Mary. 'What happened to your hands?'

'Oh, these old things.' Mary flutters her hand in the air and then puts it inside the other one. 'So long ago I can't remember. I told you that was my special talent.'

'Those wounds look recent.'

'Well, these things take time to clear up. Sometimes they *flare up*.' She chuckles and shifts back in her seat.

'Mary, did someone else do that to you?'

'Oh, I expect so.'

'You remember who did it?'

She rolls her eyes up to think and makes a little whistle with her mouth. 'I couldn't possibly say. It could have been any one of them.'

'Them?'

'The angry people. They don't like you sleeping on their street.'

'Can you remember where it happened?'

She shakes her head and whistles again, the matted hair makes a brushing sound against her mackintosh collar. 'No, sir. I rotate. And I don't keep a diary.'

'Did you report it?'

'My memory is full of holes but there are some things I am sure about. I can safely say that I did not.'

'Have you been attacked like this before?'

'Oh, many times.' She cocks her head and bats her eyelashes at him.

'And never gone to the police?'

'Perhaps the first time, but that really is too long ago to remember. Stop testing the old girl.'

'Okay. I'm sorry. I would like to help you find somewhere safe to sleep.'

'Save your energy, young man. I like my rotations. Many have taken this challenge and failed. I am an impossible situation.'

'I would like to try.'

She shrugs. 'Alas, another ship heads for the rocks.'

At the end of the session John Kettle carries the pot plant back through the estates and along the towpath back to his boat. He holds it out in front of him, in both hands. He puts it on the section of deck by the cabin wall, where it will be sheltered, and fills the tray with water. He sits on the deck next to it and rolls a cigarette to smoke. And then goes up to the Lock for a drink. He deserves it.

SEVENTEEN

11 a.m. on the last Sunday in August: Odeline's seventh waking on board the boat *Chaplin and Company*. Sunlight streams fully through the portholes (she forgot to pull the curtains across). Her head is throbbing and she is hot in her nightdress. She kicks the quilt down to the bottom of the bed, but doesn't sit up and start the day. Instead, she sinks back into the events of the day before. They are even more vivid than her dreams.

Ridley is back. The *Saltheart* hadn't been there yesterday morning as Odeline made her way to the barge cafe. But suddenly, while she was watching Vera pour hot water into her cup, he had appeared in the doorway.

'Hello,' he said. That easy, rumbling voice. He was standing squarely on the step with his hands in his pockets. His hair was tied back and he was wearing a short-sleeved shirt with a green vest underneath and khaki-coloured trousers. No shoes. His feet brown and sinewy, surprisingly clean. The right one was tattooed with busy bars of music, notes crammed into the lines. He dropped his head to see what she was looking at and said, 'Fiddle music.'

Odeline hadn't known how to be. 'Hello,' she said, and leant against the counter. The radio was playing some noisy song with explicit lyrics. *From your head down to your toes* . . . She picked up her hot chocolate from the counter and gulped at it. The liquid scorched the roof of her mouth.

'So, John Kettle is okay,' he said, raising the eyebrow with the two gold rings in it. 'He just said thank you to me. Amazing!'

'Amazing,' Odeline had repeated, and taken another sip of her drink. It was still scaldingly hot, but she needed something to do.

'So,' he said, 'do you remember I was telling you about my friend, the one who has the parties on her boat in Kensal Rise? There's one tonight and I was planning to go along, if you wanted to join. They welcome new performers. I don't know who will be there but it could be interesting for you. And there's usually good music.' He turned to Vera. 'Perhaps you would like to come as well?'

'Me?' said Vera, tucking her hair behind her ear.

'Sure. It's not all performers. Some people just come along to watch and listen.'

Odeline looked at Vera in her mauve T-shirt and huge denim skirt. Surely she would be out of place at such a creative gathering.

'I don't know,' said Vera. 'I don't know. I have jobs.'

'Well,' he shrugged, 'I'm relaxed. I'll be leaving at seven, if anybody wants a lift over. You are both very welcome to come.' He stepped back and took his hand out of his pocket to wave goodbye, his wrist thickly bound in its ropes and copper bangles. He then spun himself around on the ball of one foot and walked off smoothly through the cafe tables, swaying his hips to dodge a chair. He was very elegant in motion, Odeline thought. A dancer, a will o' the wisp. She couldn't believe she had only spoken two words. For some reason her brain had switched off. She wished she'd asked where he'd been.

'Are you really going to go?' she said to Vera, who was leaning into the cupboard under the sink. She imagined herself and Ridley trying to whisper to each other under the willow tree like Romeo and Juliet, with Vera as the fat chaperone in the background.

'I don't know. I have to make sandwiches for tomorrow. And Mr Zjelko gives me a shopping list. We have run out of everything here.' She took out a thin baton of black bin bag, unrolled it and shook it out. 'Including these.'

Odeline took a sip of her hot chocolate, which was at last the right temperature. She had been so surprised to see Ridley that she had forgotten to ask for all the crucial information about tonight. The dimensions of the space, for example, or the time allotted for each artist.

'How big will the performance space be?'

'Tonight?' Vera flips the bin lid back and hooks the bag around the rim, leaning on the fridge to press it down inside.

'Yes.'

'How do I know this, Odi? He says it is on a boat, so . . . I don't know. Same as this?' She uses the fridge handle to pull herself up again.

'So no stage?'

'I don't know. It sounds, you know, like a party.'

Odeline couldn't imagine how this would work. Would people be drunk, like the Covent Garden job? Would Ridley be drinking – and would it be safe to travel on his boat if he was? Should she take her *A–Z* in case she needed to get home independently? What time would the gathering end? Was it safe to travel alone from Kensal Rise late at night? But then maybe she wouldn't have to travel alone . . .

She put her hot chocolate down on the counter. 'If you want I can help with your jobs, so you can be ready in time for seven o'clock.'

At quarter past seven they were on board the *Saltheart*, travelling up the canal towards Kensal Rise. With Odeline's prop box inside the cabin, there was room for them all on the wide steering deck at the back of the boat. Ridley steered, leaning back against the wooden rail around the deck, with one leg lifted underneath himself – like a heron – bare foot pressed against the rail. He had changed into a different shirt from earlier – this one was striped and collarless with bells for buttons – but he was still wearing khaki trousers and no shoes. He hadn't read his *Manual*: he didn't maintain the eyeline over the roof of the boat, instead looked around at the buildings as they passed them, and at the mug of beer which he held in his left hand. Odeline sat on the right-hand side of his boat, holding on to the rail as they chugged along. Vera sat on the left with her hands in her lap. She had her eyes closed and her face lifted to the low evening sun. Ridley didn't talk much either at the start, just offered them a drink, which they both declined. 'I want to keep a clear head,' Odeline had said, 'for my performance. What size is the performance space?'

He'd shrugged. 'I don't know. It's just a boat.'

She was wearing her tailcoat with a wing-collared shirt and red braces holding up her pinstriped trousers. She had decided not to wear the waistcoat as well because of the warmth. She wasn't wearing full make-up, just some eye-liner and rouge for the cheeks. She had rubbed some rouge on her lips as well, thinking of Ridley. She didn't want to look too manly. It had been hard to see the effect of the make-up in the bathroom mirror with the light broken – she hadn't yet managed to get the cover off to see what bulb was underneath. Brushing her hair had made it stick out more, so she had splashed handfuls of water on it from the tap. She had brought her bowler but hadn't put it on yet, and picked at the rim now as she looked around. The light glowed orange on the buildings. She remembered passing these high tenement blocks the day she arrived.

'This is my favourite time of day,' she said, pursing her rouged lips.

Ridley nodded, his arrow nose pointing down and his mouth pressed shut, and they steered on, past a black-spired church with barred windows, past a shopping trolley marooned on the towpath by the tenement blocks, under a high bridge where children leant over the railings, past a wall with 'NOT OUR WAR' scrawled in spray paint, a big peace sign underneath. At the bottom of the wall sat a wide barge with an engine cabin at the back and a long curved bowl making up the body of the boat.

'What's that?' asked Odeline. Ridley told her it was an old coal vessel, now used to pick up rubbish from the canal. 'But you can see they hardly bother.' He went quiet again. Odeline agreed. The canals seemed a dumping site for every kind of rubbish and unwanted thing. Earlier in the week a rusted trolley had appeared poking out of the water next to the bridge and it still hadn't been picked up.

'So you saw John Kettle,' she tried.

This seemed to work. 'Yes!' he said, turning to her. 'He was really busy. The heritage boat signs weren't out but he seemed to be doing loads of work on his boat. He'd redone the lettering, looked much better. And was planting stuff, I think. There were pots and bags of compost on the deck.'

'Is he still the warden?' asked Vera, opening her eyes and turning round.

'I don't know,' said Ridley. 'I expect it's under review. There've been a lot of complaints over the years, but they might give him one last chance.'

Vera turned her face back to the evening sun and closed her eyes once more. It occurred to Odeline that she had never seen Vera still, only ever in action: puffing, pouring, lifting, serving, scrubbing. Even her walk looked like a kind of heaving. Tonight her hands rested in her lap and her expression was lighter than usual. If it wasn't for her outfit, the zipped-up shellsuit top, skirt and trainers, she would have looked almost majestic.

'Do you think he's still getting drunk?' Odeline asked.

Ridley shrugged. 'I don't know. He didn't look well, but no worse than before. Thinner perhaps.'

'Stupid man,' she said. 'Why can't he look after himself?'

They went on, past a small park with teenagers sitting around on skateboards, past some prettily kept allotments, past some nice-looking houses with prim gardens coming right down to the water and people sitting out on their roofs. Luminous green mould grew out from the banks here in bulging shapes – it looked solid and walkable as grass. Objects were stuck in it: a half-sunk wine bottle, crisp packets, a football. 'Duckweed,' said Ridley. 'We get this problem in summer.'

They passed an enormously high tower block that looked like something from an awful future. It had a second, thinner tower attached to it, like the twin engine of a spaceship, ready to discard once it fired through the atmosphere into outer space. Odeline imagined the tower block and all its inhabitants on their way up to the moon, faces looking out into space from every window. It was an awesome and terrifying building: the sun moved behind it and she shivered.

She looked down at the bars of music across Ridley's foot. His big toe was tapping in time to the turnover of the engine.

'How much does a tattoo cost?'

'Oh, it depends, on the size, the design. I've got a friend who does mine for free. For the art.' He looked down, lifting his ringed eyebrow. 'Are you thinking of getting one?'

'Does it hurt?'

'Depends where you have it. Bum's a good place to start. You hardly feel a thing.' He laughed. Odeline thought quickly of something else to say. She could feel her face burning.

'Why, why do you have them?'

'Because I'm always leaving places and I travel light. They're all the things I want to take with me. Stuff I don't want to forget. A Chinese Dragon –' he pointed to the reptile head screaming up his neck – 'for my martial-arts stuff. The years in Wiltshire'; he touched his chest between the bell buttons: Odeline could see a corner of the map. 'Favourite tunes, here and here'; he pointed to his foot and lifted his left sleeve to show more notes on his forearm. 'Unicorn and serpent from my family crest'; he pulled at the leg of his trousers and Odeline saw a set of hooves and a forked tail curling up his calf. 'Sunset in the Orkneys, here'; he turned and lifted his shirt to show the bottom of his back, keeping a hand on the tiller. There was a wedge of land jutting towards a horizon with a craggy stone in the foreground. 'Favourite quotes, up here'; he pushed up the right shirt sleeve to show her the rings of gothic script around his bicep. 'And so on and so forth.'

'How many do you have?'

'Far, far too many to count. Even got them on my head, from when it was shaved.' He lifted up a flap of hair behind his ear to show Odeline more inky symbols.

'Wow.'

Past the tower block and on, they reached a part of the canal which was built up on either side and backed on to by buildings. Most were padlocked warehouses or high houses of brown brick, their windowless backs to the canal. The blindness of these buildings gave the canal a sinister feel. The towpath was narrow and the warehouses pressed right up to it. Not somewhere you'd want to walk alone.

She was relieved to have seen no sign of the big grey dog, Marlon. She asked where it was, which was a mistake. Ridley whistled and the grizzly shape lifted itself from the roof and picked its way around the wheelbarrow, hosepipes and bits of wood strapped to the top. It hopped down on to the deck. Odeline froze. 'Sit then,' said Ridley, and the dog sank down, lying over both of their feet. Vera leant forward to pat Marlon and then went back to her still pose. Odeline spent the rest of the journey keeping herself absolutely still as well. She didn't want to annoy the dog. She could feel its dirty grey fur touching her ankle, and she wasn't wearing socks.

At the end of this sinister section of canal they reached a huge supermarket building with a long yellow roof. As they passed it, the canal opened up with trees on one side and a jumble of gravestones on the other which went back as far as she could see. It looked scruffy for a graveyard. They pulled in next to a large orange barge with white lotus flowers painted on the side. It had portholes with split glass, like bifocal lenses, and the bottom sections were flipped open. It was much higher in the water than *Chaplin and Company* or the *Saltheart*, as if it had two storeys. As Ridley shut down the engine they heard chatter and noise coming from inside the boat. He asked Odeline to steer in whilst he jumped on to the towpath with the rope. She did it nervously but perfectly and hoped he was impressed.

He led them to the orange boat. As they made their way along the towpath Odeline tried to walk separately from Vera, her shellsuit top and trainers. She didn't want Vera to ruin her first impression. They came to the front deck and two small girls in identical green tunics ran out of the cabin. Not a children's party, thought Odeline. *Please.* The girls looked at the new arrivals and arranged themselves at the edge of the deck facing each other, lifting their arms as a barrier and shouting in unison, 'Friend or foe!' Odeline stiffened.

'We are friends,' said Ridley, and ruffled the hair of one.

They looked at each other and screeched, 'Then you may enter!' and slowly lifted their arms, making noisy creaking sounds, a barricade opening. The three of them stepped on to the boat, down the steps and into a crowded cabin full of adults. The doors at the far end were open and people were sitting on stools and kitchen sideboards and benches running along both sides of the main space. There were bodies everywhere: far less space than on the tiny stage in Covent Garden.

'Ridley!' shouted a woman, and it seemed like everyone stood up – and Odeline doesn't know if it was the rocking of the boat or the confusion of people, but from this point her memories of the night become various and bombarding.

Lying on her sunlit bed, she wants to remember it right. She puts them in order.

She remembers:

A man dressed like herself: in tailcoat, wing-collar and brogues, but with a white bowtie, who kissed Ridley on both cheeks, introduced as Philip. This man Philip clasping her and then Vera's hands and going through the names of a group of people sitting and talking at the far end of the cabin. She can't remember any of the names now. There was the tall blonde actress with plaits around her ears and another brown-haired girl with a fringe and a rectangular mouth who he said wrote poems.

She remembers:

A wall-hanging of the sun shining on a fat buddha surrounded by bright-blue clouds. This was in the corner of the cabin. Pale pink-and-purple crystals hanging from thread like sugary stalactites in front of it, twirling from right to left.

Lace over the portholes and the orange glow of the low sun burning through it.

Being able to stand up straighter than in her own boat – there was air between her head and the ceiling. She put her bowler on and it still wasn't touching.

Angela, the owner of the boat, hair piled up on her head with the two small girls attached to her skirts, also kissing Ridley on both cheeks. 'You brought friends, how wonderful! Help yourself to nibbles –' she waved her hand at the tray of pastries being carried around by one of the identical girls.

Odeline watched this Angela taking Ridley's arm and smiling at him. She had wiry eyebrows in thick commas across her forehead.

'Is there a schedule for the performers?' asked Odeline, but Angela had already turned away. She had a lotus flower tattoo on the back of her neck, coloured with violet petals and voluptuous green leaves.

She remembers:

Someone thrusting a plastic cup into her hands filled with ice and an amber liquid which burnt cold on her lips.

Vera taking a sip from her drink and closing her eyes for a second. 'Rum and ginger.'

Ridley touching plastic cups with her and then Vera. He had found a place for them to sit on a bench by the door, and then went over to the other end of the cabin to sit on another bench next to Philip-in-the-tailcoat. She couldn't hear what he was saying over there because of all the noise from other people, but he was much more talkative than he had been on the journey. Vera started talking to the rectangular-mouthed girl about her poems. The girl was showing her a book with her picture on the back. Odeline was being softly pressed by Vera into the corner of the cabin and wriggled to get more room. 'Sorry,' said Vera, and moved up.

Odeline took another sip of her drink. Sweet and pungent. It made her nose feel as though it was going to start running. She looked down to check that the white handkerchief was in her breast pocket. She might need it. She took another sip.

She had not been this close to this many people in a confined space since being in a classroom at school. It felt strange. Her mind flipped inside out like an umbrella in the wind and new thoughts started to blow about. How must she appear to all these people? Did she look superior to them, or stupid? How should she sit in order not to look stupid? No one was talking to her – were they intimidated or had they not noticed her? What would they make of her performance? Did any of them know a thing about the art of mime? Or perhaps they were all experts? She looked down at her frayed cuffs and the hands with their pink nails and caramel fingers. Her skin was a shade darker than anyone else's here. Did being different mean she was better than them or worse?

The small girls knocked past her as they ran back upstairs. 'Friend or foe!' she heard from the deck.

A grizzled voice replied, 'Foe.'

'Overboard!' came the shout, followed by shrieking. A rugged old man came down the steps with an accordion.

He had badger hair: black and silvery white. Ridley stood up to embrace him.

As the badger-haired man played his accordion the woman Angela stood and people shifted themselves to the far end of the boat to give her room, squeezing on to the end of benches, sitting on each other's laps. She began to dance with hands on her hips and her skirts opening out. Wisps of hair flew out as she spun her head. Her lace-up boots clipped round and round to the beat of the music. She was Toulouse-Lautrec's dancing barmaid. The children linked arms now and spun round fast. A two-headed monster in a green tunic. Ridley slapped his khaki trousers in time to the music. Philip and the actress clapped. Vera nodded her head. And on Angela went – round and round and round. Odeline felt fuzzy and hot-nosed. She wished they would all keep still.

After the music the actress with the plaits stood up and announced: 'Juliet's last speech!' The room cheered. The actress then spoke loudly, with a pained look and for a long time, and ended with a stab to the heart and a death rattle as she sank back into her seat. Ridley was smiling. Angela leant forward to clap, and the room ignited again, applause and cheers and chatter. Odeline had another sip of her drink and squeezed her nose to make sure it definitely wasn't running.

Next the rectangular-mouthed girl got to her feet and the room stilled. She read a poem very quickly without looking up. Odeline can't remember any of it.

Then the man Philip had stood up in his outfit: a fitted version of her own. Vera's eyes closed and her fat little hands fell open on her lap as he sang something from the opera.

Odeline closed her eyes as well and she felt the voice soar inside her, like when she heard the singers in Covent Garden. She felt his voice collecting all the feelings from the bottom of her stomach and carrying them upwards. She could feel the boat rocking and Vera's heavy breathing next to her. Philip's voice continued to swirl around her until it reached its climax. There were more cheers and congratulation, and then slowly the room fell quiet.

She opened her eyes to find Ridley asking if she wanted to perform something. Panic. Her prop box was still in his boat! She swivelled her head around, looking for a way out. But everyone was looking at her, expectant. A cabin full of faces waiting. No, she thought. I am not prepared. I have to set up. Every single illusion in the repertoire requires props. It will take at least thirty minutes to prepare. And even then, I cannot possibly perform in such a small space. But without planning to, she had stood, as if someone had yanked her up with a string. Like a rag doll she dropped her head and her baggy sleeves hung at her sides. She could feel the cuffs in her curled fingers. She was a scarecrow, a straw man, a puppet. Wait. Wait. She thought of Marcel Marceau's face and the wide-eyed blankness of it. Wait. She thought of his colours, his black and white and red. Wait. She thought of his spotlight on stage and the circle of light. Yes. The circle of light. And she began to move. She became the mime.

She remembers:

Saying 'Bip, the Birdkeeper', without remembering to keep her mouth small.

Uncovering the cage and seeing the bird, its yellow and green feathers. A wonder. Her eyes rejoice.

Bending her head and listening to the bird sing. Her ears rejoice and rejoice.

Opening the door of the cage and letting the bird hop out on to her finger. Making an O of delight with her lips. Her heart rejoices.

Letting the bird fly and come back to land on her finger. They bow to each other. Hello, little bird, hello, little bird.

Flinging her hand up and letting it fly again, the little bird, this time flying higher and further away, making circles in the sky. Watch it soar, watch it turn, before it comes back to land on her finger.

Stroking the tiny head and cradling the light-boned body in her hand. Feeling the soft feathers almost invisible to the touch. Feeling the heart beating, tiny drumsticks knocking inside the tiny frame.

Lifting her finger to whisper to the bird. Looking at it, looking at the little bird and leaning her head towards it. For one last time. Her heart is sad.

Throwing her hand high into the air. Watching the bird fly away. Watching it out of sight.

Sending her arm across in a wave – but it is gone.

It is gone.

The bird is gone.

One tear of sadness. She follows it down her cheek with a finger.

She remembers:

Sinking back into her seat. A moment of quiet and then the whole cabin is applauding. Looking up, all the faces are smiling at her. The two girls in green have come to sit at her feet and are clapping with their hands in the air. 'More! More!' they cry. They are looking up at Odeline the way her mother used to, eager and open-faced. A hotness floods the back of her eyes. Her mouth turns down. Her mother was the only person who ever clapped for her like these people are clapping. Still they are clapping. Her mother leaning forward to clap after every trick and holding her breath for more. Her moon-faced mother, shining up at her. Her mother's pale-blue eyes that could speak so clearly and ask for one more, one more, and seemed to say each one was even better than the last and how proud, how proud.

This memory is an ambush, it catches in her throat and bends its way upwards. Odeline cannot do any more – she hangs her head. Her chest is heaving and hot tears are filling her eyes and spilling out. Her nose is now very definitely running, streaming, and she grabs for the handkerchief, presses it to her face. Vera beside her squeezes her arm. 'Very good, Odi!' she is saying. 'That is very good!'

She remembers:

Hearing Ridley beginning to play his fiddle, moving the bow forward and back over the strings. Steadily forward and back. As he played she felt herself calm. Forward and back. It soothed her. The upward motion of tears inside her weakened. She hiccuped once and then they stopped. Looking up at all the faces, they had turned to watch Ridley. The woman Angela smiled at her, calling the two girls back over. Vera asked if she was okay. Odeline nodded and turned to watch Ridley play. Decorated forearms, wrist poised, fingers long and dexterous.

At the end of his tune, he let his arms drop. And then lifted the fiddle again, nudging it under his chin. He tucked his bow between his knees, smiling over at her and Vera, and then looking around the group. 'People might know the words to this.'

He began to pluck, fingers moving in a wave over the bridge of the fiddle – a sad melody. Vera's hand tapped at Odeline's leg, 'Oh I love this one.' Ridley played two rounds of it and then took the bow from between his knees. To Odeline's horror, Vera's voice joined the bow then, as it began to move across the strings.

I am sailing, I am sailing, home again, 'cross the sea.

The sound of the voice was embarrassing: it was warbling and thick. It sounded as though it was struggling in her throat. But as she went on the voice straightened and came out in a line, thick still but steady, and holding the notes. *I am sailing, stormy waters, to be near you, to be free.* Vera began to sway, nudging Odeline further into the corner with her soft shoulder and cushioned hips. The shellsuit rustled as she swayed. *I am flying, I am flying, like a bird, 'cross the sky.* Ridley looked at Vera as he sawed the bow back and forth. Everyone looked at Vera – none of them seemed embarrassed at the voice, at her appearance.

I am flying, passing high clouds, to be with you, to be free.

Odeline twisted to look down at Vera next to her and saw how her face lifted up as she sang, how her forehead furrowed as she pushed each note out and took deep breaths in between. The light from the porthole lit up the wisps of hair around her face like fine, fiery wickerwork. She looked beatified, a saint in one of the stained-glass windows of Arundel church. Odeline could not help being glad for Vera then – she seemed to have forgotten all of

her heaviness in this moment. She looked as though she
had forgotten where she was. She was singing to someone
somewhere else.

*Can you hear me, can you hear me, through the dark
night, far away.* Philip started to sing the song too, and
Angela. They knew the words. *I am dying, forever trying,
to be with you, who can say.* More people joined, swaying
in time with Vera. *Can you hear me, can you hear me.*
Then the badger-haired man stood and slowly pulled his
accordion open, meeting Ridley's note with his own. He
played as if the machine were an extension of his breathing
chest, stretching the thing out and then pushing it back
in, rising and falling. His head thrown back, hitting the
keys with his fingers. Ridley with his fiddle stood up to
face him. They played and the others sang and swayed.
The two girls were slumped against Angela, who had her
arms lifted above their heads, waving from side to side as
she sang.

On the way home Odeline asked to steer and Ridley let
her. It had been difficult to maintain the eyeline along the
roof of the boat because of the wheelbarrow, logs and
other things strapped to the top, so her navigation had
not been as accurate as during the lesson. Also it was dark
and there were distracting noises on the water. But Ridley
said they were only birds. He leant back against the rail
beside her and she copied him, letting it support the small
of her back. His patterned neck was silver in the moonlight
and its shapes were slightly pronounced under the skin,
like braille. He occasionally guided the tiller back on

course. At one point his hand bumped hers and shot a shivering line up her arm.

Odeline had felt like talking, just talking and talking. She wanted to know what Ridley thought of her performance. 'I thought it was very impassioned,' he said.

Impassioned. 'What else?'

'Very pure, very concentrated. You looked as if you had completely transported yourself. It was really good.'

'Do you think everyone thought so?'

'Oh, without a doubt. Didn't you hear them clapping?'

'It was my first mime performance in public.'

'Really? Well, you looked like a pro.'

'I was Bip, the Birdkeeper. Marcel Marceau.'

'I remember that one from the film reels.'

Vera had been silent the whole way back, sitting in the dark. She left them to their conversation. Odeline was aware she was talking more freely than she ever had before. She noticed that the sentences came out easier, and it didn't feel necessary to practise what she was going to say in her head before saying it. She wanted to tell Ridley about her father. 'Shall I tell you a secret?'

'Please do.' She saw his mouth open into a smile, teeth and eyebrow rings glinting in the moonlight. He nudged the tiller back to the straight position.

'My father is a famous performer. Odelin the Clown. I'm going to perform with him one day.' She saw Vera turn to listen. 'One day soon in fact. I just need to find him.'

'You don't know where he is?'

'He tours with the Cirque Maroc. I've contacted him through various circus channels. I'm just waiting for my letters to reach him. Its takes a while, you know, when someone's on the road.'

'Oh, don't I know about that. Letters take about a year to get to me.'

'A year?'

'Well, months perhaps. I make sure some letters never catch me up. The typed ones, for example.'

'Typed ones?'

'Official stuff. I can't be doing with that. I travel light.'

'Are you on the run from the law?'

'Ha!' He threw his head back and grimaced at the moon. 'You make it sound so romantic.'

During the journey she felt her body split away from her mind and it had brought strange feelings. Her shoulders wanted to be close to Ridley as they stood together by the tiller and her free arm gesticulated as she talked in the hope of brushing against his. These feelings weren't unpleasant but they were alarming – her body had never acted of its own accord like this. It had always been subject to her mind and obedient to its plans. Now it seemed to have leanings of its own which could override everything else. She didn't know what it would decide to do next.

When they reached Little Venice, Vera stepped off the boat and said thank you to Ridley and goodnight to them both before walking away under the bridge. Odeline was annoyed that the journey had come to an end. She wanted it to go on and on. Ridley collected her prop box from inside and lifted it on to the towpath. Standing on the path she said thank you and then, without practising the move in her head, leant forward and pushed her lips on to his. In the half-second that their lips were touching she became aware, for the first time, that she was taller than him. Then her whole consciousness flooded to her lips and to the sensation of their mouths pressing like two cushions against each other, the uncomfortable prickle of his stubble framing it. And then she was aware of his hands on her shoulders, tilting her back to upright, and the view of him smiling as her face came away.

He said goodnight very quietly and stepped back on to his deck. She towed the prop box back to her boat feeling that the dress rehearsals were over and her life had finally begun. Back in her cabin she became aware of a sudden terrible hunger and had eaten an entire packet of cracker-bread with cheese slices, a cereal bar and a tin of tropical fruit pieces. She had felt wide awake, but lay herself on the bed anyway, and within a few moments had fallen into a thick sleep.

This morning seems as blessed as the night before, with the light filling the cabin like a new beginning. Odeline doesn't bother to check the clock. She doesn't bother to make a plan for the day. It is Sunday – the British Waterways Office is closed, the entertainment agency answering machines will be on. There are no jobs to do. She is a magnet for good things – she will just walk around and let them happen.

She pulls her nightdress over her head and wriggles out of it. Pulls on the underpants which are on the floor next to last night's outfit, and the trousers beneath them. She puts on a white vest with her red braces and a waistcoat, leaving the wing-collar shirt – it is too cumbersome. Today she wants to feel light on her feet. She slides her feet into the brogues and ties the laces in a double bow. She goes to the bathroom and looks at herself in the mirror above the sink. The bathroom lamp is still broken but sunlight from the porthole hits one side of her face, dramatically. She puts her hands casually in her pockets, tips her head to the side like Chaplin's Little Tramp and allows herself to smile. It looks new on her lips. She remembers Ridley's wide smile.

When she opens the cabin doors brightness floods in and she feels the heat hit her. But when she gets up on deck and looks around for the *Saltheart*, it is not there. She looks both ways. He has gone. *Again.* There is just the wide-bowed rubbish barge chugging along the canal towards her, its curved bowl giving an insolent black grin.

She kicks the side of her boat. Why does he have to disappear every time she makes a connection? Slippery, non-committal, he's a featherweight.

Then she remembers the orange drink in the plastic cup, all those sips, and wonders if, last night, she had in fact made herself ridiculous.

This thought nags at her all the way to the barge cafe. Vera stops wiping the counter and motions her to a stool on the other side. 'A special hot chocolate for the star of the show,' she says, taking a can of whipped cream from behind the microwave.

Odeline sits on the stool. 'The star?' she says.

'You are a very talented girl, Odi,' says Vera, nodding. 'Big talent.'

Odeline practises the smile again.

'You will go far. I know it.'

'Your singing was very good as well,' says Odeline. The compliment feels strange in her mouth, but she is grateful for Vera. She decides that Vera is probably a very good judge of things.

John Kettle appears in the doorway. This is the first time she has set eyes on him since they returned from the hospital. His shoulders are slumped and he is wringing his hat in his hands. His grey hair is overgrown and swept back, part of it sticks up from the top of his head like a crest. He looks old. 'Hullo,' he says, mashing his face into a grin. 'Good morning, ladies.' He smiles frantically at them both.

'Hello,' nods Vera, 'nice to see you.'

Odeline takes out her notebook and opens it.

'Hullo, Odeline.'

'Hello, John Kettle,' replies Odeline, looking down at her book.

'Odi,' says Vera, softly.

Odeline turns her head to the doorway and says, flatly, 'Hello, John Kettle, how are you?'

'Doing well,' he beams. 'Ever so well. I've really cleaned up the boat, you know.' He says it like they should be impressed.

'I noticed,' smiles Vera, indulging him.

'Well, I'll see you ladies later.' Odeline hears his voice break. 'I've got a meeting to go to.' Odeline watches him walk off, chaotically, sees him knock into a table as he goes, not noticing the pepper and salt grinders that topple and slowly roll off the table. His whistling echoes from under the bridge.

When she turns back round Vera is looking at her in

that way she does, her eyes crinkled with amusement, and this annoys her. So she asks, 'Why didn't you want to sign your name on the forms when we were at the hospital?'

And Vera's smile goes, as she knew it would, and the air between them chills. Vera gets down from her stool and starts, in silence, to clear away the tea things into the sink and then goes outside to rearrange the table John Kettle has knocked. She doesn't make eye contact on her way out. Odeline sits at her stool feeling like a tall tree in a blizzard – the silence is very confusing to her. She doesn't know what to do in this situation. She doesn't know whether she has discovered a terrible thing, or done a terrible thing herself. She steps down from the stool and, looking straight ahead, walks out past Vera, who is bending over the table with one hand holding her side like it hurts.

When Odeline gets back to her boat she sits on her bed and tries to push down the panic that is flapping around inside her. She knows Vera is hiding something. She behaved suspiciously at the hospital, and she has never said where she goes at night when she shuts the cafe. What if she is a convicted criminal? What if she has connections with the shady East European organisations she read about in *Behind the Curtain*: the Stasi, the KGB? What if Odeline is arrested as her accomplice and sent to prison? Is she being followed? She has heard that you have to share cells in prison – she could never rehearse in front of some criminal. How many years do you serve for being an accomplice?

She gets up and begins to straighten the Marceau reels on the portholes. If Ridley was here he could defend her.

She hears a quiet knock at the cabin door and freezes, perhaps she should pretend she is not here.

'Odi, I am sorry. You deserve an explanation. I can explain it all.'

Odeline goes to the door and unlatches it. Vera is on the deck and looks extremely apologetic: she doesn't look like a criminal. But Odeline steps out into the open to talk to her just in case. They perch opposite each other on the low ledge around the side of the deck – Vera's fat hands gripping the edge, Odeline's long legs bent upwards either side of her like a grasshopper – and Vera begins to explain her situation.

EIGHTEEN

Eighteen months ago I am working as an English teacher at the secondary school where my father is headmaster. He has been headmaster for twenty-one years. He and my mother are well-known figures in the town, and respected. They are old-fashioned people. Like many in their generation, they may be holding some prejudice from twenty, thirty years before, but they never speak this in public. They would never cause an offence. They are peaceful people.

It is unusual for a woman to hold an academic post, but my parents encourage me to study and then to take the job. My younger sister does what most girls do, and marries after school. She has always been in competition with me I think – she is pleased to beat me to a wedding. But marriage and children do not feature in my plan. I want to concentrate on my English studies and earn enough to travel. I want to see Paris, Berlin, Rome, Amsterdam, and, most of all, London. My parents have never travelled beyond the borders of our country and they think it is a wonderful ambition for me. They say they want a postcard from every capital city in Europe.

Three years ago, the President dies, and after that frictions start to grow – along the old lines. Resentment from a generation ago. Angry words in Parliament become insults spat in the street, graffiti on the doors of shops and houses, brawls in the bars after dark. The spark is hate. It carries and burns. It rages. There is a new vocabulary, talk of pride, rights, blood, a homeland, and this language is growing more and more normal. Tomo, my brother-in-law, brings it into our house. He tastes the words on his tongue as he speaks them. My seven-year-old niece is using these words. People march on the streets with flags, singing old nationalist songs that half of them have never known and have to learn from scratch. They relish the hatred. They pass it on. They allow their fifteen-year-old sons to sign for military service. These boys just do not turn up to class one day. In total a quarter of my senior class leaves school early to join the army.

Others of my students are enlisted as local vigilantes. Children help set fire to shops belonging to their class-mates' parents, and force neighbours, who they have lived beside all their lives, to leave their homes.

My parents do not approve of what is happening. They do not hang a flag from their window and they never go to a demonstration. Tomo brings his angry talk to the dinner table: he comes home full of joy at the story of someone losing their business, or the vandalism of a reli-gious house, but my parents do not respond. My mother might offer more potatoes around the table and my father might change the subject to work.

'You know, Vera, I am reading about a new syllabus they have introduced in France.'

What my parents say to each other in private, I never know. With my parents these things are always unreadable to me.

Eighteen months ago there is a riot at a football match
on the outskirts of town. Hundreds of people are injured.
Many shot or stabbed, or teargassed by the police, who
are thought by Tomo and his friends to be with the other
side. He comes home that night boasting that he has ripped
out a stadium seat to hit a policeman. He is covered in
blood and has his nose punched in. Never has he looked
so happy.

After this things are getting worse. Some people from
the town have a relative killed in the riot and they hear
that my brother-in-law is boasting about how many he
has punched. It is also known that my father has been
involved in the old protests, in the 1970s. People think
my family need to be taught a lesson.

On winter mornings, my father goes to warm the car
engine before driving us to the school. So, on this morning,
when I leave the house, he is already sitting in the car on
the other side of the road, with the engine turning over.
He is looking straight ahead with his hand on the wheel,
as if he is driving. There are insults scratched into the
bodywork of the car, obscene words and shapes. A back
window has been smashed in but hangs there, lines
spreading from the smash in a cobweb. The wipers are
stolen and broken stumps poke out from the base of the
windscreen. I get into the car. My father releases the hand-
brake to drive. He does not say what has been done and
so neither do I. He drives as if nothing is different to
yesterday: slowly, steadily and talking through my timetable for the day. When we arrive outside the school he
pretends he does not see all his students looking at the
words and shapes on his car. It must be a humiliation for

him, but he does not show it. He takes a few moments to comb his hair and moustache in the mirror, polish his glasses, wish me good luck for the day, as usual, and then we both go into school. I miss assembly that morning and so this is the last time I see my father.

My mother comes to the school at lunchtime and together they drive to the next village, where her brother, my uncle, has a garage. They have arranged to have the car fixed and take the bus back into town.

On the way to the next village, the car skids and rolls down a bank. My parents, they are both killed. When my uncle looks at the car afterwards, one wheel is very loose and he thinks the vandals might be removing it. But also it is raining, and perhaps my father cannot see without the windscreen wipers.

From the moment I hear of the accident, my parents are no longer belonging to me. People straight away begin to tell me what to do. I have to make sure the people who murdered them are punished. My parents are martyrs to the cause of independence. I should write to the President to have this recognised. I should organise a memorial to them in the municipal square.

I can do none of these things. I cannot cry but I feel like I am fat with tears. I feel like I have sunk, I am sitting at the bottom of the ocean, my head is full of water.

The funeral is organised by Tomo. At the service, my parents' coffins are draped in flags and people sing a nationalist song outside the church. After the wake there is a fight in the municipal square which Tomo is involved in.

That night we receive a brick through our window.

I do not go back to work for a time. I spend days sitting

in my parents' room, trying to take the information of
their death. Something inside is being very stupid, very
obstinate. I am thinking normal thoughts about them, as
if they are alive, and then interrupt myself to try and force
the fact that they are gone, but something in my head will
refuse it. My sister is downstairs most of the time with
her daughter and leaves me alone. She doesn't know what
to say. She thinks I have turned into a simpleton. When
the new headmaster comes to visit, I can hardly string a
sentence. Not good for an English teacher. He passes on
sincere condolences of the other staff. The school will
grant me more leave. Everyone is still outraged at what
has happened, he says, and so sad to be losing their beloved
headmaster.

All this time Tomo is holding meetings around the
kitchen table, making plans to kick more people out of
the town. My sister and I are the figurehead of this movement, he says, we must lead the demonstrations. My sister
goes. She takes her daughter, just seven, to witness doors
being axed, people kicked and thrown out of their homes,
swear words being painted over shop windows. The other
side is just as bad. One night someone leaves a bleeding
pig's head on our doorstep.

After a time, my sister and her husband move into my
parents' room. I go back to work. Outside the school
gates is a line of dead flowers, flags and crosses in the
mud. Nobody has cleaned it up. In the classroom I find
a mixture of praise and obscenities scratched on to my
desk. Martyr's daughter. Fat traitor bitch. Pictures of my
father are pasted on to flags and stuck on the walls. Many
students tell me that vengeance will be visited on his

murderers. I do not know what to say; they must wonder why I am silent.

I am not fit to teach but people are patient. I go through my lessons like a robot and mostly my students are quiet and obedient. Over half of my class are now gone, either to the army or thrown out of town.

I am floating through my timetable for a few weeks and then one morning something snaps. One of my students has written an assignment with a title, 'How to Kill an Immigrant Pig'. It is violent and childish like a cartoon. But it brings out such an anger in me that I tear it in front of the class and fling it in that boy's face. I tell him he is more stupid than a pig himself if he thinks this is a clever thing to write. I am getting hot with anger. I tell him that the new President and his cronies are a bunch of pigs who are turning the country into a hell. I tell them that my father would be ashamed. They are so surprised that none of them say one word and I leave the classroom. My face is wet with tears and with sweat.

In the bus on the way home I am alive for the first time in many weeks. I feel that I have broken back into myself. I sit solid at the front of the bus, holding my backpack on my lap. The fact of what happened to my parents hits like a wave smashing again and again. I sit and hold tight to my backpack, I can weather it. I am back inside my body, and my thoughts are moving again from one thing to the next and to the next, no more flipping backwards and forwards and chasing in circles. My mind is returned.

On the next morning I am greeted at the gates by the new headteacher, who tells me never again to step within the walls of this school. I have betrayed my father's

memory and spat in the face of my parents' sacrifice. He
is trembling and dark red with rage, holding his arms tight
to his sides as if to stop himself from an attack. For a
second I am confused, this morning I am looking forward
to my classes for the first time. I am still stupid to the
workings of this new system, I have forgotten the rules.
Anyone who shows a thought now that is different to the
mob will be reported, thrown out, punished. This is the
new law.

I take the bus back to my side of town and walk home.
My sister is out, but I only have a few hours before my
brother-in-law comes back for lunch. I put my clothes in
a bag. I am packing up my books when Tomo, thirty
minutes later, comes through the door with his two bully
pals and grabs me by the face, pulling it close to his and
whispering his insults: fat whore, traitor, communist,
immigrant-lover. His pals stand behind nodding their big
heads like dogs. I don't know why I am not afraid. He
continues and I am thinking, really this man's vocabulary
is limited. He is picking up my books and tearing pages,
asking, 'Is this where you get your traitor's ideas, bitch?
Is this why you can't find a man and have children? Did
these books take away your appetite?' He takes me by
the hair and pushes me out of the house. I fall on my hip,
hard – I can still feel it today. I am picking myself off the
street when he throws my bags through the door. He spits
and slams it shut. I can hear him shouting at his friends
as I walk down the road. I am in pain but I don't care. I
don't feel afraid but free, completely free and light.

I go to the house of a colleague and persuade his wife
to let me in. I stay for a few days but I know they are

wanting me to go, they can't look in my eyes the whole time I am there. So I take the bus to the capital, where I stay in a hostel. I think about finding a job but: I am sick of my country. The only thing that holds me is the feeling that I am leaving my niece and my sister at the mercy of two monsters: Tomo and this new stupidity. But I go.

When I first come to the UK I stay in a special hostel for visitors from my country, and I work there as a translator. Every day I check the database for my sister's name, to see if she has left. My plan is to find other teaching work. There is a programme which helps organise visas for foreigners who teach or translate for international business. I am there for only one month before a boy arrives from my town. I don't recognise the boy but he tells them something. I am thrown from the programme and they say they no longer have a room for me at the hostel.

This is a year ago. For five months after, I live in hostels and do basic jobs for very little money. Some of the hostels are not safe, and sometimes at these basic jobs they ask questions and are catching foreigners who do not have the right documents. And I do not have the right documents. I hear of Zjelko from the other workers. He pays almost nothing but will give work without asking questions. He has bars and cafes.

In December I go to ask Zjelko for a job. Just a temporary solution, I think, until I can think of another plan. I go to a bar on Elkstone Road as I have been told. The Portobello Queen. It is a fashionable place, they have cocktails, art on the walls. They take me to a table in the corner and tell me to wait. I am there for past one hour when this cowboy comes and sits opposite. Oil in his hair, open shirt, pointed boots. He says his name is Mr Zjelko. He looks me up and down and perhaps he is disappointed. He turns his eyes to the window and looks at the girls on a table outside. He curls out his tongue, puts a mint on it. How is my English? Can I cook? Can I serve? I answer. I must be saying the right things. He needs someone to run the most important establishment in his portfolio, he says: a cafe on a barge in a tourist destination. I am lucky, he says, that the position has recently been vacated. He makes quoting marks with his fingers as he says the word 'vacated'. All he usually has for women is cleaning work.

NINETEEN

As Vera tells her story, perched on the side of Odeline's boat, John Kettle is sitting in his seat at the Alcohol Awareness Group, between Alwyn on his left and Chris, the young lad with the rucksack, on his right. Opposite is Inga, wearing another crumpled beige outfit and her hippy beads, and Mary, who is wearing a buttoned blue floral dress, the collar faded and stiff with sweat, and a burgundy-coloured towel around her shoulders.

When John walked up to the church porch, Alwyn had been holding the door open for Mary to wheel her trolley inside. She bumped it across the stone floor and parked it behind the door. 'Oooh, 'tis chilly in here,' she said, and began to rummage in the trolley, piling the pillow and tennis racket covers at one end until she found the burgundy towel. 'Aha!' She lifted it high and then wrapped it around her shoulders like a shawl, before clicking over the flagstones towards the circle of chairs, her stick legs moving like a wind-up toy, the snaffled loafers planting outwards on each step.

Alwyn had seemed pleased to see John and pumped his hand up and down, 'John. Hello. Welcome!', and gestured for him to join the others. When John sat down his eyes dropped to Mary's lap. The wounds had closed but her hands were still ridged with pink lines. She saw him looking and moved them beneath the towel. 'Good morning, Warden,' she said, stretching her big, chapped lips in a smile. There was a shadow next to her mouth which could have been a bruise, or just a patch of discoloured skin like the bluish strip on her forehead.

'The bonus of today's session,' Alwyn is saying, 'is that we have some refreshments left over from this morning's family service, so if anyone would like some squash or a biscuit –' he points to a tray with a jug and stack of coloured cups on top of the bookshelf behind Inga and Mary – 'please do help yourselves.'

'Well, I certainly will,' says Mary, pulling the towel higher around her shoulders and rising out of her seat. 'Can I help anyone else?' She looks round the group. Inga shakes her head. 'I'll have a squash, why not?' says Alwyn.

'Anything for you, Warden?' Mary proffers a red cup in John's direction.

'I'll have a squash too,' he says, tipping his head at Alwyn, who catches his eye and smiles back.

'Two squashes, on their way. And what about the paperwhite gentleman? He looks like he would benefit from a biscuit.' She waddles across the ethnic rug with an open packet of digestives and the lad lifts his shaved head and shoots a hand out from the cuff of his sweater to take a stack of biscuits from the top. He makes a murmur of thanks and pushes one of them into his mouth, cupping his other hand underneath to catch the crumbs. He has a collared shirt under the sweater, jeans with an ironed crease down the front, and the same pair of brown suede trainers. Not the uniform of a druggie. Gobbles the biscuit down and puts a finger in his mouth, to pick at a metal brace around his teeth.

'Thank you, Mary,' says Alwyn as she hands him a yellow cup full of squash, and John the red one. She takes a purple cup for herself and sits down with the packet of digestives in her lap.

Alwyn takes a sip and leans forward to continue. 'So, in our last session we thought about the idea that by getting to know something better, we are more likely to care for it. I'd like to look this time at the ways in which we neglect, or do damage to, ourselves. This is an Alcohol Awareness group and so I'd really like to talk about what alcohol does to us. What is its effect? Maybe in the short term it appears that it is helping in some way, or acting as a distraction, suppressing or managing or even solving what seems like a larger problem. Perhaps we feel it keeps us company. But we're all here today because it isn't helping. It doesn't, in fact, solve any problems. Does it?' He pushes his glasses up his nose and looks around the group. His magnified eyes are blinking through their round lenses. John Kettle shakes his head. Mary takes another biscuit.

'I'd like us to take a journey together. A journey of awareness. In becoming more aware of the damage we do to ourselves, I hope that we might become more reluctant to do it. I hope we can undo some of the habits we've constructed which do us the most harm.' He sits back in his seat and uses his cup to gesture to his right. 'John, could you start us off? What does drinking do to you? Do you feel it helps in some way? Could you describe what it feels like to want a drink?'

'Haven't had a drink since Friday night,' says John. 'Skipped the pub last night.'

'Well, that sounds great. Would you usually go most nights?'

'Yep. And I didn't go last Tuesday. So that's two nights off.'

'So you've managed to disrupt your routine a bit. That's really good news.'

'The plant's coming along well too. I've remembered to water every day. Thinking of getting a few others, she looks so nice out on deck.'

'So that exercise seems to have worked. That's great.' Alwyn nods. 'Would you mind if we went back. Could you talk us through your decision not to go to the pub?'

'I have a puzzle for you, Alwyn,' interrupts the pale woman, Inga. Her voice is low and coldly accented. She pronounces his name with an 'h'. Halwyn. 'What if a person has no interest in looking after themselves?' She is motion-less as she speaks, her hands sit forgotten on her lap. They are old woman's hands, frail and veined, sunken. There is a gold band on her ring finger, underneath a silver band with a large amber stone set on to it, marmalade-coloured and cut in the shape of a heart. The rings look too heavy for her bird-boned fingers. 'What if a person no longer cares?'

Alwyn nods at her to carry on but she is looking at the beanbag in the corner beyond him. Her words are tone-less, as if she can't be bothered to give them emphasis or colour. 'I don't have a problem with alcohol.' Halcohol – it is horrible to listen to. John shifts in his seat and has a sip of squash. Scratches his beard to hear the crackle.

She is still going. 'I don't even like the taste. I could

stop drinking without a problem. But I don't even care enough to stop.' John moves his finger to his ear and rustles it around. Why doesn't Alwyn say something?

'If I drink, I become stupid, and I can pretend he is with me. I lost my husband.' Her right hand moves up to take hold of her bead necklace. 'I turn the music loud and we are dancing.'

She flicks her eyes up to Alwyn. They are pale blue, puffy and lashless. Naked. John looks away towards the crate of toy cars in the corner.

'So life has no more value than these moments. I am jealous of the animals.' Hanimals. 'They can take themselves away to die when they are ready. When they have nothing left. I want to do that.'

'Shall I tell you my theory?' Mary has decided to contribute, her mouth full of biscuit. 'Men want fantasy, whilst women cannot help but be stuck in reality.'

'Okay, Mary,' says Alwyn, saying something at last. 'Do you mind if I just follow up a point with Inga?'

'Please,' says Mary, gesturing to her right and swallowing the biscuit.

Alwyn shifts forward in his chair. 'Thank you for speaking so openly, Inga. Thank you.' He pauses and chews his lip and then looks up again, his cheeks as rosy as a doll's. 'Could I ask you a question?'

'Sure.'

'You say you feel that life has no value for you now.' He keeps his spectacled gaze fixed on her. 'Do you feel that you, yourself, have no value? Are you not worth *something*? Something that would merit trying to make life better?'

'Mmm,' agrees John, nodding his head. Inga looks at him, her eyes empty, and then switches back to Alwyn.

'I know that life cannot be good now,' she says flatly. 'And no, I do not deserve any better than this.'

Mary raises her grey eyebrows, impressed. 'This lady is under no illusions.'

'Your second statement there,' says Alwyn, pointing his finger. 'Why don't you deserve any better?'

Inga looks back at the beanbag. 'I left him. I was coming back, but I disappeared. For a while. And I would not tell him where. I was very angry.' Hangry. 'Very upset. And he died waiting for me. I broke his heart.' Her hand grips hold of the necklace beads and John can hear them being ground together. It is a sound like one glass being twisted inside another, a bottle unscrewing, the strained squeak of polishing a valve with wire wool. He can hardly bear it.

TWENTY

In a gypsy caravan with a velvet interior, on a mahogany desk with brass-capped corners and a leather blotter, a brown hand, small, muscular, and creased with lines, holds a fountain pen over a blank piece of paper. The fingers are slender, and almost every one is stacked with rings: tarnished silvers, dull golds, and brightly twinkling false jewels. The hard-padded fingers of the right hand drum out a beat on the paper, rumpapum pum, rumpapum pum. Rumpapum pum. And then the forefinger of the left hand hooks around the pen and begins to write.

MY DEAREST ODELINE,

The script is large swirling capitals in green ink. He ends the last letter of each word with a flourish.

HOW ABSOLUTELY WONDERFUL TO HEAR FROM YOU. INDEED, TO HEAR OF YOU.

Rumpapum pum, rumpapum pum.

YOUR EXCURSIONS INTO THE WORLD OF ART AND PERFORMANCE SOUND INTRIGUING.

Rumpapum pum.

I AM SORRY TO HEAR ABOUT THE PASSING
OF YOUR DEAR MOTHER. I HAD NOT SEEN
HER FOR SOME TIME. I WONDER, WHAT HAS
HAPPENED TO THE LOVELY HOUSE IN
ARUNDEL TOWN?

Here the hand draws a child's picture of a house with five
windows and smoke circling out from the chimney. And
then hovers above the page for a second.

I WOULD BE MOST HONOURED IF YOU
WOULD BE MY GUEST AT A PERFORMANCE
OF THE CIRQUE MAROC.

I ENCLOSE A TICKET FOR THE AFTERNOON
PERFORMANCE THIS SATURDAY.

Three taps on the paper. Pum, pum, pum.

IN ANTICIPATION OF OUR REUNION,

YOURS IN ARTISTRY,

ODELIN OF CIRQUE MAROC

The 'O' of Odelin is huge and has a dancing loop
at the top. The forefinger of the left hand uncurls itself
from the pen and puts it down on the leather blotter. Both
brown bejewelled hands wait for the ink to dry and then

fold the paper twice. It is shoved into a large brown envelope along with a circus ticket, and then the British
Waterways address in Lisson Grove is written in green
capitals on the front. The letter is not stamped – Odeline
will have to pay the 76p postage when she collects it. This
is a sum she will forget to add to her accounts.

TWENTY-ONE

Tuesday morning, day nine aboard the *Chaplin and Company*. Odeline wakes up extremely late and has to rush to her second steering lesson, tucking her shirt tails into her trousers as she runs across the bridge to the bus stop. As last week, there is no time to get a hot chocolate, to ring the entertainment agencies, or to check her pigeonhole on the way as she had planned. She will have to do these after her lesson, again infringing on valuable rehearsal time. She does, though, look along the Little Venice pool as she crosses the bridge for any sign of the *Saltheart*. She has been checking for it several times a day. Every day there are new boats moored along the bank, cruising past: full-length narrowboats, old Dutch barges, modern houseboats with sun decks, and none of them is the *Saltheart*. No sign of it this morning either. She is annoyed with herself for checking so often. Ridley has no permanent mooring – he said himself that he never stayed in one spot for long. What did she want from him anyway?

Camden. Her teacher, Crosbie, is just as awkward as before, but the lesson starts well and her talent for steering is just as evident. She comes away from the bank expertly and holds a steady line down the centre of the canal, keeping a boat's width between the *Nelson* and the line of moored narrowboats on her left. But she finds herself frustrated by her fat and taciturn teacher. He is again wearing a sweatshirt and baseball cap – his white hair streams out in a triangle beneath it – is breathing heavily, and has one hand permanently jammed into the pocket of his baggy jeans, which are belted beneath his low stomach by a piece of yellow rope. His face is stodgy like dough. He is an entirely graceless figure. And again his only conversation is mumbled quotations from the *British Waterways Narrowboat Manual*. She looked up his instructions in the *Manual* after the last lesson and found them all in there, word for word.

And Odeline wishes she could talk to him. To anybody. She wants to tell someone Vera's terrible story. Odeline thinks there must be something that can be done; it is outrageous that Vera is living as an outlaw when she has done nothing wrong. Wiping tables and washing up plates: it must be a punishing existence for someone with an able mind, a person who is such a good judge of things.

Odeline suggested, immediately after hearing the story, that Vera go to Downing Street to appeal directly to the Prime Minister. He would surely be swayed by the story. But Vera laughed, and then became serious; they would put her straight into a police cell followed by an aeroplane back to her country. So Odeline has instead advised that Vera lie low while she comes up with a plan. She feels there is an opportunity for heroism here. She hopes Ridley will be back to witness it. Vera thanked Odeline for her concern and said she has become very good at lying low.

Odeline knows she cannot talk to her steering teacher

about Vera. She decides to see if she can coax him into talking about boats. 'What's that for?' she asks, pointing at a raised metal grille about a metre along the roof. There is no answer and she looks quickly at her teacher before turning back to the correct eyeline. His jaw is juddering silently up and down, making the walrus cheeks wobble. She looks again: his eyes are lifted to the peak of the baseball cap, as if he is scrolling through his internal narrowboat manual for the answer.

'Is it a chimney?'

He begins to shake his head, his bottom lip drops from under the moustache and tries to form a word. No sound comes.

'Is it a vent?'

'No,' he says. 'The steerer's gaze must be directed at all times towards the bow of the boat.'

God, thinks Odeline, swivelling her head back to the right position. She could hardly steer off course in four seconds of not looking. Ridley had completely ignored the eyeline rule when he'd steered them to the gathering. He'd been looking everywhere but ahead. The eyeline didn't even exist on his boat, there was so much strapped to the top of it.

'I'd like to point out that your instructions about the engine were wrong,' she says. 'On my boat, the engine is in a compartment at the back of the cabin, not under the steering platform, or the poop deck, or whatever you called it.'

Surprise surprise: no answer. She keeps on holding the tiller straight, changes her stance to settle her hips against the rail, as Ridley had done. And then Crosbie speaks,

speaks his own words, in a low Scottish voice scratching through the moustache.

'Your boat must be a traditional model. What year was she built?'

'It says 1936 on the side.'

Another silence. Perhaps that's it. But no, he pipes up again. 'I have built my own boat in the traditional style from 1936. Boats built at that time have a separate boatman's cabin for the engine.'

'Someone told me I wouldn't be able to drive such an old boat,' Odeline says. 'Will the engine still work?'

He clears his throat. 'In the world of waterways, *driving* a narrowboat or barge is referred to as *steering*.' Unbelievable! This is the first line of chapter one in the *Narrowboat Manual*. Odeline has read it at least fifteen times.

'I *know that*,' she says. They are cruising past the huge white houses – the decorated cakes – behind Regent's Park. She wonders if anyone ever makes it past a second lesson with this infuriating man. 'So, will the engine still work?'

'I have installed an engine from that year on my boat. I modelled the engine room as an exact replica of a traditional narrowboat.'

She remembers now exactly how Ridley stood on their sunset journey to Kensal Rise, and picks a leg up underneath her, heron-like, pressing her brogue against the metal rail.

Then she has a eureka moment.

'How many free lessons am I allowed under the Community Boat Scheme?'

'Three.'

'Could I have my last lesson on board my own boat so that I can practise steering on it?'

No answer.

'Would that be possible?'

'I will have to check the regulations.'

She thought bureaucrats lived behind desks, not on canal boats.

'I don't see why it would be a problem. Don't you think it makes sense seeing as my boat is very different from this one? Seeing as it's a traditional model.'

Silence. Then, 'No, I don't see that it would be a problem.'

She gives him the location and name of her boat and asks if she will see him there, in little Venice, at the same time next week. He is silent again. It's a very long and profound silence this time. It occurs to Odeline that he might be slow to understand things. She turns to him and asks more clearly, shaping each word carefully in case it helps him to lipread. He moves to prop himself against the edge of the boat. His eyes are doing the scrolling thing again, squinting upwards. His mouth has dropped open to show the red bottom lip and nothing is coming out. He looks as if he has been hit in the face.

Odeline finds herself feeling a little contrite.

'I'm sorry,' she says.

He doesn't answer.

She thinks perhaps it is time to end the lesson and pulls into the bank.

'I'm just pulling into the bank,' she says loudly.

He still doesn't move.

'Are you all right, Mr Crosbie?' she says. And then, 'I

don't mind if you want to check the regulations first.' She wonders if he has gone into some kind of spasm, but she can see he is breathing, quite fast in fact. She throws the rope on to the bank and gets out to knot it around the mooring post as he has taught her. She says goodbye and gives a small salute. He doesn't salute back and so she walks off down the towpath.

When she turns around to check, he is still in the same position, shoulders hunched and propped against the side of the boat. Both fists are jammed into his pockets. Perhaps he is just a bit of a slow case, who runs out of words if made to talk too much. She rather hopes he won't turn up at her boat for the third lesson. She might try to find a new teacher – perhaps there is another Community Boat Scheme elsewhere. Hopefully only a single bus journey away, so she won't have to pay two fares.

August has slipped into September, but this day is as hot as any in high summer, and as she walks back home along the towpath, Odeline feels her feet sweaty and sliding in her brogues. She has a thought and then dismisses it, and then it pricks her mind again. With a feeling like she is breaking all the rules, all her own rules and all the rules of London and Arundel and everywhere else, with a feeling of defiance and a surge of something like spontaneity, she unties the laces, loosens the cracked leather and takes off her shoes. She hooks two fingers into the heels, stands up and looks down at her feet, which are brown and long and quite perfect. She takes a few steps forward and the towpath concrete is hot on the soles of her feet, slightly rough.

But the roughness is pleasant. She walks on. She is a

hippy, she thinks, she is a tightrope walker, she is a shoe-less joe. She is free.

An hour later she runs, shoes on, past the customers at the tables outside the barge cafe, knocking over a potted plant outside the door. Inside Vera is at the counter, arranging salad on to a plate next to a panini. Odeline waves the letter in Vera's face – she is too excited to know what to say. Her forehead is corrugated with delight and the concentration of running in the sweaty, slidey brogues. Vera realises what the letter is and her face opens into a smile which Odeline beams back. Odeline feels as though someone has hooked a coat hanger inside her mouth. It is straining so wide it is almost painful. She looks at the salad dressing on Vera's fingers and decides she mustn't let her touch the letter. Instead she holds the letter open in front of her friend's face. Vera seems to understand: she keeps her hands next to the plate as she reads the letter carefully, nodding as she looks down the page. When she gets to the end she looks up, her droopy eyelids creasing even more than usual.

'Odi,' she says, 'I knew he will write.'

'He sent a ticket,' Odeline says, her top lip catching on her teeth, which have gone dry she has been smiling so long. 'I'm going, this Saturday!'

'It is wonderful news, Odi.'

'I don't know whether to take everything with me. What happens if I join the circus straight away?'

'Have your meeting first. You can always come back to collect your things. Where is the circus?'

'Luton.'

'Not so far away then.'

'How shall I get there?'

'Oh, there will be trains, or buses.'

'Bus is usually cheaper.'

'Well then.'

'But I'll take my props. Because I've got to show him my repertoire.'

'Good idea.'

'Where is the nearest launderette?'

'I think there is one on the corner of Harrow Road.' Vera points a finger over her shoulder. But then her face reddens as she hears a voice outside. She bats her hand at Odeline. 'Zjelko! Please, you must go!'

Vera dives into the fridge and pulls out another bag of salad, rips it open and begins pulling the leaves out and frilling them around the sides of plates. Odeline folds her letter carefully back into its brown envelope, snug next to the ticket. She steps towards the door. A man with oiled black hair, a blue shade of stubble and a leather jacket is winding his way through the tables outside, speaking a foreign language into his mobile telephone. His bottom lip pouts out as he talks. He is holding the phone delicately, a little finger protruding like a classy lady drinking a cocktail. Ferrari, says the label on the breast of his jacket. He reaches Odeline, looks her up and down, winks a pink-rimmed eye and makes a gesture to allow her past, clicking his phone shut as he does. She wrinkles her nose in a sniff of disdain as she walks past. He smells of coconut.

'Ciao, Vera,' she hears him say in a velvety accent. 'How many customers today?'

But today Odeline has more important things to think about than low-life gangsters. She dashes under the bridge with her beautiful brown envelope – she must prepare a routine to show her father this Saturday. Perhaps she will be a member of the Cirque Maroc by the end of the week!

When she gets back to her boat she finds two plastic pots balanced on top, planted with brightly coloured flowers, one orange and the other mauve with a purple stripe. Plastic tags jammed into the soil read 'Busy Lizzie Herbacious Perennial'. Whoever put the pots there has spilt soil all over the roof. She takes them off and ditches them on the other side of the towpath – they are extremely silly looking plants. She will have to borrow a cloth from Vera to clean the roof. But this can be dealt with later.

She goes inside and sits down on the bed. She unsticks the gluey flap at the end of the brown envelope and takes out her father's letter. Unfolding it, she reads again the wonderful words, runs her eyes over the green-ink capitals, the magical drawings. She looks at the stick-like letters, the decorative curlicue at the end of every word. She runs her hand over her own name, written by him. Odeline. Odelin. She feels her face break into a smile again and feels the muscles of her chest open and lift as the rest of her body rejoices as well.

TWENTY-TWO

Alwyn looks at his watch. 'Still no Mary. Did she mention to any of you that she wouldn't be coming to this session?'

Inga shakes her head and the young lad on John's right does too, sinking back into his sweater. The sleeves are looped over his fists as usual, and he has tucked his rucksack under the seat as if trying to save room. He is wearing jeans with the crisp line of an iron down the front as last time. They sit neatly over his suede trainers.

'I've not seen her all week,' says John.

Mary hasn't been on her usual bench by the canal. He's seen the other two there but no sign of her, not even her trolley, which she sometimes leaves under the bridge.

Alwyn blinks at Mary's empty seat. 'Odd. She's been very punctual at the last two. Oh well, shall we make a start anyway? Perhaps she'll join us at some point.'

John puts his hand up to speak. 'I could go and have a look for her. I know her usual spots.'

'That's kind of you, John.' Alwyn lifts his glasses and rubs his eyes before slotting the glasses back on to his nose. 'Perhaps you could keep an eye out for her after the meeting, if she doesn't appear. I'd like to know she's all right. I'm sure we all would.' He looks around the group. 'But let's get on with the session now. There are some questions that came up last time that I've had a few thoughts about.'

'I can't make it to the next session,' says Inga. Her voice is flat and her eyes swollen. Her beige crêpe shirt hangs off her shoulders as if they are the wooden frame of a chair. 'I have a shift on Sunday.'

It's that voice again. The way she talks without trying. John has been to the pub for a drink every night but one since Sunday, but hasn't been himself there. They even said so. He's just sat staring at the bar. Every time he's had a drink all he can think about is Inga and the way she told that story, the way the words just came out of her, so *dead*.

'What do you do, Inga? Do you mind me asking?'

'No, I don't mind. I work in the supermarket, up by Ladbroke Grove.' She replies like a reflex; there is no space between Alwyn's question and her answer. 'I work on the checkouts.'

'How long have you worked there?'

'Since he died. There was no money.'

'So you work there every day?'

'Usually I do the night shifts.' Voice as flat as if she was reading the shipping forecast.

'That must be tiring. And then you sleep during the daytime?'

'If I can. Or I go walking.'

'Where do you go?'

'Always the same place.' Halways.

'Is it somewhere to do with your husband?'

'It is the place I left him.'

'What do you hope for, when you go back?'

'I don't hope. I go because when I am walking there, I imagine I can feel him waiting.' She offers up these terrible answers as if they're nothing at all.

'And when you get there?'

'Obviously there is nothing.'

'And so you turn back.'

'Yes. I go to the wine shop. And I try another way of pretending he is still alive.' It's the way she says it. *It's the way she says it.*

'It sounds like a very cruel way to treat yourself. Almost like torture. What would happen if you didn't go out for this walk every day? If you didn't go into the wine shop on your way home?'

She lifts her bony shoulders in a shrug. John Kettle wants to surround her feet with flowers, to distract her and make her smile. Make it better.

'Am I right in thinking it was your employers who signed you up to this course?'

'Yes, that is right. It was the management.'

'Because drinking during the day meant you couldn't cope with the night shifts?'

'They said people could smell the alcohol. But I never made a mistake on the checkout. So.' She shrugs again. She looks so tired. John Kettle is tired – he rubs the bridge of his nose, smears his eye with his fingers.

'How about swapping some more of your shifts to the daytime? I know it's not a solution to much but it must be disorientating, working all night and trying to sleep when it's light.'

A pause. 'Maybe. I could try.' She sounds exhausted now, the voice is lower, slower. Waterlogged.

'It's just an idea. I know it's not getting to the heart of the problem. But it could be a way to get into a better sleep pattern.'

'Maybe.' She waves her hand. She is done.

Alwyn pushes his glasses up his nose. 'You have been really open with us, Inga. I want to thank you for that. Have you found it helpful coming here? Beginning to speak about things?'

'It gives me something to do.'

'Yes.' Alwyn swivels around in his seat. 'What about you, Chris? We haven't heard much from you yet. Is there anything you've witnessed here which has seemed relevant to you? Have you found it helpful coming so far?'

So tired. Like Inga. So tired. So lonely. Pull it together, John. Pay attention.

The boy uses his sleeved fists to push himself up in his seat. His shoulders are still curled in. His trainers begin to tap-tap-tap-tap.

'It keeps my parents off my back.'

So bloody lonely. Steady, John. Hold steady.

'Was it your parents who signed you up for the course?'

'Yeah. My dad's waiting in the car round the corner.' He lifts a hand to fiddle with that metal brace across his teeth.

'So you've had some trouble with your parents?'

John sees Alwyn nodding his head and does the same. He links his fingers over his knees like Alwyn. *Keep busy. Keep busy.*

'Yeah.'

'For drinking?'

'And failing exams. And this . . .' He brushes a sleeve over his shaved head. 'And this . . .' He points to the chipped blue enamel John Kettle saw on his nails last time. John Kettle looks hard now at the line where the blue meets the pink, the jagged line.

'How old are you, Chris?'

'Seventeen.'

Tap-tap-tap-tap-tap.

'So old enough to do whatever you like with nail varnish.'

'Yeah but that's not the point is it?' His voice has gone surly and quiet.

'What is the point?'

'It's a sign, isn't it? Of something else.'

Just bloody desperately lonely.

'I didn't know that,' said Alwyn. 'A sign of what?'

Chris looks down. His trainers stop moving and rest on the rug. 'My parents think this is a reform group. A Christian group. They think I'm being fixed.'

God Squad, God Squad, that's what Frankie used to call them. Had a rhyme – a rhyme for everything, Frankie: There was a young girl from Stadricka, whose knickers could flicker a vicar's ticker.

'Why do you need to be fixed? The drinking?'

'It's what I did when I was drunk.'

Oh, we used to drink, we used to get so drunk. Staggering along the docks, gripping shoulders, yelling out our songs.

'Chris?'

'I fucked up, didn't I? I got drunk and had a go at someone.'

'Had a go?'

Just hold on Submariner Kettle. Hold on till you get out.
There is such a hotness, such a grip in his throat.

'Made a pass. Made a move.'

'Isn't that what seventeen-year-olds do?'

There was a young girl from Stadricka, there was a young girl from Stadricka.

The lad looks down and pulls his hands back into his sleeves. 'Yeah, but it was a guy. So.'

A door swings open to a night many years ago. John has shored his whole life up against it since, just to keep it shut. Now he sees the way this boy can't look up, the way he's hiding himself in the folds of his clothes, the shoulders curved in with shame, and he jerks his arm out to take the poor lad's shoulder, he grabs it, grips it with his fingers, rocks it, and the boy looks up, stunned like an animal braced to run, but John grips harder and pulls the shoulder back proud and tells him, the words bumping over the memory stuck in his throat, over the regrets, all the regrets, over the sobs:

'You didn't do anything wrong, son. You didn't do anything wrong.'

TWENTY-THREE

It is the afternoon of the first Saturday in September. Odeline is sitting on a bench inside a huge red and yellow panelled tent in a field outside Luton. Around her the audience are noisy and jostling, children are squirming on parents' laps, people are edging along the rows of benches to go to the portable toilets outside or to fetch ice creams. None of this is apparent to Odeline, who has her face turned upwards in wonder towards the roof of the tent. A man in a diamond suit and a bowler hat is standing on a platform at the end of a wire which connects the two poles of the big top, his arms held out. He slides an enormous shoe along the wire. Wobbling, he brings his other shoe around in an exaggerated arch through the air, and places it ahead of the first. This causes the wire to wobble violently from left to right. Odeline whips her hands to her mouth. The man freezes and the wobbling subsides. He steps back and Odeline's shoulders drop – he is not going to go. But he leans backwards and takes a cane from the ladder at the back of the great pole. He holds it out horizontally. And then walks forward again, this time more sure of himself, swinging his shoes around each other with a kind of rhythm.

From somewhere an accordion begins to play and his

walk becomes a dance – he is stepping forward and back in time to the tune. He flips the cane upright and throws his bowler hat on the top, twirling it around as he turns to face the audience, and his face breaks into a grin. The audience cheer and clap but these are all distant sounds to Odeline, who is looking into the black diamond eyes of the man on the wire. His hair is speckled with grey and frames his face, which is painted white and heavily creased as he smiles. And it seems he is looking straight back at her. And those eyes, the black painted diamonds, are twinkling at her, and as they twinkle they seem to expand and they are all she can see. It is as if she has dived into the night sky and is falling through it. The rest of the audience are tiny applauding figures, left far behind.

As he turns to walk back to the ladder, Odeline stands up and pushes past the other people on the benches to get to the aisle and then runs to the exit. She runs round to the back of the big top, ducking under the guy ropes. She sees a metal fence and squeezes through a gap in it. There are a cluster of caravans and cages around the tent's stage entrance. She weaves through them and pulls back the tent canvas just as Odelin the Clown is taking his exit bow, backing through the red curtain. The audience's applause follows him out. He stands up and flips his bowler back on. He steps carefully out of the enormous shoes and flicks them to one side with his foot. And then turns around to see her.

'Hello,' she says. 'I am Odeline.'

She is dressed in her complete outfit, including waistcoat, wing-collar shirt, braces and tailcoat, despite the warmth of the day. Her shirt has been freshly laundered and her suit dry-cleaned. Her shoes are blacked and buffed and she is wearing her bowler hat, like him. A mauve flower droops from her breast pocket. She took the window seat on the coach to Luton this morning and it has wilted in the sun.

He comes towards her, holding out both his hands, which are heavily jewelled and glint like the glitter on his harlequin suit. He is not a tall man: the top of his bowler is about level with her nose. But he is lithe, as she has expected. He walks weightlessly and with the grace of a classical puppet, lifted gently by strings. He is coming towards her, and his face is lined and his eyes are dancing. He is holding out both his hands and she lifts hers to meet them. He takes her hands and squeezes. She feels the stones and the sharp settings of his rings pressing into her fingers. When she looks down she sees that their hands are the same colour, pale brown, and the same shape; they have the same slender fingers. But where her hands are smooth, his are lined, a well-used version of her own. She thinks of her mother's hands, which were large and freckled and pink as raw sausages. So ungainly compared to the elegant butterscotch fingers that are holding hers now.

'Hello, my dear,' he says, 'I am so happy you have come.'

'Hello,' she says again, feeling overwhelmed. Her breath is coming in shallow gulps. She remembers to keep her mouth small so as not to ruin the neatness of her face by showing her teeth.

'Did you enjoy the show?' He lifts an eyebrow and his eyes laugh as he speaks.

'Yes, thank you,' she says, and is knocked off balance

by a pair of midgets in sultan costumes who run past and tumble through the red curtain. She hears a cheer go up from the audience.

'Come,' says Odelin the Clown, and motions towards the caravans outside. As they walk out of the tent he clasps his hands behind his back. He treads carefully as he walks. There is something that surrounds him, a charged aura that is more than the glitter of his suit. Odeline is in the presence of greatness.

'Yes,' he says, 'it was remarkable to hear of you, to receive your letter. And amazing that you have followed in my footsteps despite never knowing of my existence. The artist's gene must be a strong one, *oui*?' He looks up to wink at her.

'Yes,' she says, feeling short of breath. 'I would love to show you what I have been working on . . .'

'*Bien sur*, you must, you must.'

'My prop box! I left it at my seat.'

He stops and gestures back towards the big top, 'Off you run, my dear. Come and find me when you are ready. My home is the green caravan at the edge of the field. Come and find me.'

Odeline walks quickly around the big top. The circus is finished and the audience are spilling across the field towards the stalls. She goes to the tent's main entrance but is repeatedly forced backwards by the flood of people. Children eating ice creams barge past her and she backs out to make sure they don't smear her suit. She holds on to her moneybelt, which is strapped tightly around her waist. Crowds equal pickpockets.

When the bulk of the audience are out she nips through

the entrance and goes back to her seat. Her prop box is standing there next to the bench – faithful prop box – with a ziplock plastic bag untouched on top. Inside the bag is a cream cheese and tomato panini, a fizzy drink and three chocolate cookies wrapped in cling film. Odeline had been on deck this morning polishing her shoes when Vera appeared on the towpath with the bag in her hand.

'For you, Odi. You might not get a chance to find something to eat today.'

'Oh,' Odeline had said, straightening, with one hand inside a shoe, the other holding the brush. 'I was going to take some cereal bars.'

'Well, take this too. It can fill you up better.'

'Okay.' Odeline put the brush down and accepted the bag. She couldn't think of any questions to ask. Vera was wearing the shellsuit top with the floral skirt, socks and trainers. A variation on the same outfit. 'If I don't join the circus straight away, I'll be back soon to collect my things.'

'I am keeping a look out for your boat.'

'Thank you,' said Odeline, and didn't know what should come next. 'Lie low!' she tried, but it sounded empty, like something John Kettle might say.

Vera smiled. 'I can do that.'

'Goodbye then.'

'Goodbye, Odi. I hope it goes well with your father.'

Vera walked away, rocking from side to side in her heavy, lumbering way, and Odeline wondered when she would see her again. As Vera's squat figure went into the shadow of the bridge, Odeline felt like calling out. She opened her

mouth, but then shut it again, she didn't know what she
might say. She twisted back down, picked up the brush
and carried on polishing the toe of her shoe, pressing harder
now as she pushed the brush from left to right.

As she walks back through the caravans with her box, the
ziplock plastic bag looped around the handle, she tells
herself to observe and remember all the things she is seeing.
All the colours and the sounds of people in their costumes
milling around the back of the tent. Acrobats are sitting
half out of their leotards in the sun, clowns are washing
the paint off their faces in buckets by the steps of caravans.
A man is throwing handfuls of feed into a cage of flapping
white geese. No one takes any notice of her. Some time
in the future she will be asked about this day, this great
reunion. Or perhaps she will write it all down herself in
an autobiography.

    She finds the green caravan, large and ornate and slightly
set back from all the others. There are green-painted steps
leading up to the door, which has a bowler hat hanging
from the handle and a window in the shape of an O. This
is where she belongs. She pulls her prop box up to the
bottom of the steps, takes off her own bowler hat, reaches
up and knocks on the door.

    'I am disrobing,' comes a sing-song voice from inside.

    'Sorry. It's me, Odeline.'

    'Take a seat, my dear, I will be out in just two minutes.'

    Odeline looks around her. There is nowhere to sit – the
steps are too narrow – just grass which is grubby with
cigarette stubs. She tips the prop box on to its back and

drops down on it, resting the bowler hat on the corner. She can't decide the best way to appear when he comes out. She tries a nonchalant pose with her legs stretched out and crossed at the ankles, hands in her trouser pockets. But actually her legs then just look too long; they stretch right across the patch of grass in front of the steps like a barrier. She brings her feet back and leans forward on her knees in a pensive pose, cupping the sides of her face. But the lowness of the prop box makes her knees stick up like a squatting frog. She crosses her legs at the thigh and clasps her hands around her knees, but this pose feels too feminine, too debutante. She pushes herself up and tries to bring a foot up to sit on, but clips the edge of her brogue on the catch of the prop box, and tips backwards, hitting the ground hard and with some bewilderment. As she scrabbles, her father comes out of the caravan door and closes it behind him.

'I see you have some of the clown in you,' he says. He is wearing a collarless green shirt with red embroidery, loose striped trousers and green velvet slippers. A Moroccan ensemble, thinks Odeline. His face is wiped clean of its clown make-up and is beautiful. Brown skin sun-weathered, with high cheekbones and a prominent mouth drawing back to reveal very white teeth. His eyes are as round and glittering as planets. They are deep-set under a solid brow, which curves back into a long forehead, framed by that thick arch of hair which spirals out in black and grey corkscrews, each tuft twisted into a point at the end. They are like the curling flames around the face of the sun, she decides: Odeline has never seen such hair.

She tucks her tailcoat under her and finds an unlittered

patch of grass to sit on, leaning back against the prop box with her knees together and her hands clasped around them. Her father sits his small frame on the top step of the caravan and looks down at her.

'We have much to talk about,' he says. 'Odeline.' His accent pronounces her name differently: Oh-dey-line. 'Odeline, I am truly sorry to hear of your mother's passing. She was a very kind woman. Tell me, when did she pass?'

'Um, on June the twenty-third,' says Odeline. She doesn't really want to talk about her mother, at least not about this aspect. She wants to hear about the great love affair that led to her conception.

'At home?' he asks.

'Yes,' says Odeline.

'So she stayed in Arundel all those years, in that lovely house?'

'Yes,' says Odeline. And then, to move the conversation on: 'After she died I found my birth certificate, and the picture of you from the Cirque Maroc.'

Her father's eyes soften. 'She came every day. Every day she would be there to collect me and take me home. You must understand what that meant, to me at that time. I was a penniless artist. I had learned my tricks in the main square in Marrakech. That is where I learned to entertain. I wore bells on my ankles and performed acrobatics in the dust. I drew large circles of people, Odeline. I shook a tin around the audience afterwards, most people walked away. It was my dream to be picked up by the Cirque, but they paid nothing. They fed us nothing. We had to work and do all the menial jobs, just for one meal a day. Cleaning the tent, slopping out the animals. It was a hard beginning. But,' he shrugs, 'it taught me to work hard.'

Odeline nods, she is hooked on his words. These are the sort of exotic origins she always knew she had.

'Now we take care of everybody in the Cirque,' he continues. 'And the artists are expected to work hard at their acts – we have others to take care of the menial workings. Like Luis.' He gestures past Odeline to a large-bellied man in a dirty vest, shorts and flip-flops, who is carrying a mop and bucket towards the big top. 'The Cirque has always been a family, but now we take care of our children. It is I who have been largely responsible for this change. Of course, it is more expensive like this, but also more in the spirit of artistry, more . . . *démocratique*.'

Odeline nods, it seems like a good idea. Although circus work for one meal a day does hold a certain romance.

Her father sighs and makes a comedy frown. 'Yes, it is expensive.' Odeline smiles with delight at this clowning, such an expressive face.

'So when your mother met me, I was this thin –' he holds his thumb and forefinger together – 'with no energy to develop my art, I was in a state of exhaustion. Surviving on only love, for the art of the circus. This was my only sustenance. Your mother saved me. She took me in, she fed me. She was kind to me.' He pauses. 'I think, in her silent way, she understood me.'

This is a wonderful story. But Odeline still cannot imagine these two people, her mother and father, together. She cannot see that big, pink-skinned, large-limbed woman next to this small, stylish, dynamic man. Her mother would not even fit on the caravan step. Her mother had a heaviness, a width, a vacuity – she cannot be cast in the role of romantic heroine. But perhaps she looked different then, thinks Odeline. Perhaps she was lighter and had more subtlety in her movements. She must have been. Because the only formation Odeline can imagine her parents in otherwise is her neat little father sitting on her mother's big lap, plain ventriloquist and colourful dummy. She blank-faced, he animated.

Odeline's father tips his head to the side and brings his fingers together carefully. 'Did your mother leave me anything, when she passed? A bequeathment, a message, anything?'

'Um, no.'

He tips his head further, and says quietly, enticingly, 'I thought that was why you might have been contacting me?'

Odeline doesn't know what to say. His eyes are twinkling and it feels as though he might not believe her.

'So, what has happened to that lovely house? Are you living there all alone?' He makes another sad clown face, his bottom lip stuck out.

'No,' says Odeline. 'I live on a narrowboat on the Grand Union Canal at Little Venice. I chose it for its name, it's called *Chaplin and Company*.'

'So the house is . . . empty?'

'Sold,' says Odeline. 'Mother left instructions for me to sell it.'

He pauses as if to think this over. And then his mouth stretches into a smile, wide lips and white teeth.

'And what are you going to do with all that money, my dear girl?'

Odeline takes a breath and then tells him what she has never told anyone, not even Vera.

'Well, before I knew about you, my plan was to get some experience performing here, in England, to widen my repertoire and also to experience a freer life, a nomadic lifestyle. I was going to start in London. And then I was going to move to Paris and live in a loft apartment with wooden floors and a high ceiling that echoes. I thought I'd keep it completely empty as a rehearsal space, with just a huge mirrored wall and shelves for my props. And I was going to study at the Ecole de Mime. I wanted to see the Moulin Rouge and Toulouse-Lautrec's paintings of La Goulue. And walk across the bridges as the sun goes down. I thought I could find other artists and form a troupe. We would devise sequences and perform them in theatres, proper theatres. We would only grant interviews to publications we respect. But that was before I knew about you.'

She pauses. Her father lifts up his hands in mock astonishment. '*Mon Dieu!* What grand plans, for one so young.' And then leans forward to whisper, 'I've always found Paris a little overrated! Well,' he continues, 'enough of this chatter. Would you like to have a guided tour of the Cirque Maroc?' He stands up and pads down the steps, offering Odeline his arm.

'Shall I leave my prop box here?'

'Yes, yes, it will be fine.'

'Can I show you some sequences from my repertoire after the tour? Some of the things I've been working on.'

'Absolutely.' He squeezes her hand. 'I can't wait to see it.'

They walk arm in arm towards the big top across the
threadbare and sunbleached grass, past caravans, Portaloos
and open-air washing facilities. Her father walks slowly
beside her and it feels as though they are making a stately
procession – there is much activity with people carrying
things back and forth, but everyone stops to nod to him
before they cross his path. 'Monsieur,' they say, before
moving on with their crates or cardboard boxes or armfuls
of costumes. 'Maestro.' He nods his head slowly back. As
Odeline and her father walk, she imagines a circle of shim-
mering gold around them.

'Tonight is our last performance here,' he explains.
'Tomorrow morning we are on the road again. You must
stay, if you like, for the party tonight. Would you like to?'

Odeline pumps her head up and down. She would like
to very much. They come to a square white tent at the
back of the big top and her father pulls a flap of plastic
back to let her in. 'This is our prop box,' he says, '*la
Costumerie*.' Odeline ducks her head under and then tries
to straighten but the canvas roof is too low, and, she
notices, rather grubby. She tilts her head to one side so as
not to let it touch her hat.

'So, my dear, you are one of the fortunate few to be
granted a look behind the red curtain.' In front of them
are rows of clothes on metal rails, colourful, jumbled,
jostling. Odeline spots the red and yellow diamonds of a
harlequin suit, the gold ensembles of the acrobats, and a
ringmaster's scarlet tailcoat. 'We don't have a ringmaster
any more,' says her father. 'The concept is outdated,
un-*démocratique*. But we keep the outfit as part of the
collection.' She follows her father down a gap between

two rails. They both have to walk sideways so as not to knock the hangers. 'These are costumes from throughout the history of the Cirque Maroc. There will be some here from your mother's time.'

Odeline is awestruck at the number of outfits in here. On each rail there are a hundred different colours and textures crammed together. Sequin, lycra, leather, felt, frill: she lets her hand run along them as she walks along. She imagines the creative possibilities opened up by having access to even one of these costumes. All the improvisations she could work on, so many new ideas.

She can't help but notice, though, that it is musty in here, as if these clothes haven't been washed. And that some of the costumes are stained and threadbare around the neck. It smells more and more stale as they move deeper into the tent. At the end of one rail they come to a huge plastic crate – this area gives off a particularly sharp odour. Odeline brings her shirt cuff to her nose and breathes through it. In front of her is an enormous pyramid of shoes: clown's brogues, glittering heels, a ringmaster's patent pumps, flat leather slippers in every colour, some turned up with embroidery and bells at the toes. She looks down at her brogues. Even though polished, they look tired and uninspiring. The leather is cracking across the creases, and peeling to grey. She would like to swap her old shoes with any of the pairs from the crate and see where they took her.

She follows her father towards the far end of the tent, which is less musty. There is a faint smell of cigarettes, though, and a breeze coming in from an opening in the canvas. 'We have several *costumières* who work with us,' he explains, 'they mend the outfits, and look after them when we are on the road.' He points to a white plastic chair and a table in the corner of the tent, with a sewing machine next to a pile of clothes. A can of Lilt sits on a magazine next to the sewing machine, with a packet of cigarettes.

'Marie is our chief *costumière* . . . She should be here?' He taps the table with two fingers. 'Marie?' he calls, in a sing-song voice. 'Where are you?' He turns and flashes a smile at Odeline. 'Perhaps outside,' he whispers. He lifts back the canvas flap and Odeline sees a woman squatted on a crate outside, sucking on a cigarette. She has tight black jeans with studs down the side of the leg, and spiky yellow hair which is dark at the roots. Odeline wonders if this is a punk rocker. When she sees Odeline's father she jumps up and flicks the cigarette on to the ground, stamping it into the grass with the toe of her trainer.

'Sorry, sir,' she says, in rounded Irish vowels, 'just a quick burn.'

Odeline's father bows his head slowly and smiles, opening the flap of the tent wider to let her back in. 'Sorry, sir,' she says again as she nips past them to her seat. She pulls the top garment from the pile of clothes and pushes it under the needle of the machine.

'Marie makes sure we are all properly dressed when we come through the red curtain. It is important work. Each artist used to have responsibility for their own costume, but now, with Marie and her team, we all have more time to give to rehearsal. So, it is more expensive for the Cirque to have hired the *costumières* but, I think, it has improved the quality of our performance.' He brings his thumb and forefinger together: 'We are sharper now.'

'Yes,' says Odeline. This makes sense to her, although, personally, she would not want anybody else handling her performance outfit. Or for it to be kept in a communal tent with everyone else's. Getting smelly.

'You must come and see our souvenir stalls,' says Odeline's father, leading her out of the tent. They walk around the side of the big top, past a pair of musclemen in black nylon shorts who are juggling skittles between each other. 'You see, more time for rehearsal.'

He leads her towards the circus entrance, a large gate at the far end of the field. The arced signs – 'CIRQUE MAROC! CIRQUE EXTRAORDINAIRE!' – are weathered, the blue has faded, the gold flattened to yellow. Immediately before this is a cluster of caravans with striped awnings and open sides. The first one they pass has a plastic pond inside, numbered rubber ducks floating on the surface and small fishing nets propped against it. On the back wall are computer games in blue, pink and gold packaging. 'We find we have to have some of these fairground-style attractions,' says Odeline's father, 'just to help with funds. It is not authentic circus entertainment,' he shrugs, 'but we have to adapt to the modern audience.'

The next caravan has a newer Cirque Maroc sign painted in old circus script. There are juggling balls and mini big tops for sale, and small harlequin dolls which Odeline realises are models of her father, with bowler hats and a red and yellow diamond suit with an O on the front. Her father picks one up. 'Perhaps you would like one of these, as a souvenir?'

He hands it to the stall keeper, a boy with a shaven head. 'Nineteen pounds ninety-nine,' says the boy. 'Do you want a bag?'

'No, thank you,' says Odeline, and untucks her shirt to access the moneybelt underneath. In the second compartment there is £100 in various denominations. She takes out a twenty-pound note and hands it over. It is more than she has spent in one go since buying her coach ticket to London. The boy gives her the doll and the one penny change, which she zips back into her moneybelt.

'*Mon Dieu!*' says her father, looking at the clock at the back of the stall with mock alarm. 'It is so late! I must prepare for tonight's performance. Only one hour!'

'When would be a good time to show you some of my repertoire?' says Odeline. 'Some of the things I've been working on.'

'Of course, *chérie*, there will be plenty of time later for that. I cannot wait to see it. But now I must go to prepare. Please, feel free, continue looking around the stalls. I'm sure there will be so many things you will like. And then maybe you can take your seat in the audience. Just give my name and they will give you the best seat in the house!' He takes her fingers and kisses them. Once more, she feels the cold edges of his rings pressing the palm of her hand. He looks up and winks at her before spinning on his toes and walking back to the tent. Odeline puts the doll in her pocket and then walks along the stalls. A few circus-goers – parents with children, couples – are still here wandering in and out of them, picking up items. She keeps a safe distance. She doesn't want to be persuaded into buying anything else.

Further along there is a stall called Hemptastic! selling

clothes made from organic materials. The folk shirt that Odeline's father was wearing is here in various colours, and the striped trousers. The stallholder, a woman with long grey hair who is getting customers to sniff soaps from the display, is wearing a similar outfit. So they are not from Morocco. There is a rack with leather sandals in different styles. Some have straps over the toe, others around the ankle. Odeline goes closer to look at them. She thinks of Vera and how much cooler these would be for her feet than those hot trainers. What size would Vera be? She picks one sandal up but puts it back down when she sees the price. She doesn't know if she'll be going back to Vera again anyway.

She checks her fob watch. Half past five. She should probably go and take her position for the next performance, just to make sure she does get the best seat. There's a sudden rumble in her stomach. She realises she has left her picnic with the prop box. She buys a chocolate bar from the ice cream stall. It is double the price of a chocolate bar in London.

Ten minutes later she is sitting in the second row of benches in the big top, directly opposite the red curtain. Perfect. Around her the benches are empty of people but dotted with cans and sweet wrappings from the last audience. Perhaps it is because the sun has gone in, but the roof of the big top looks dull. The yellow sections are more of a mustard colour, and have grimy lines along the folds. She is close enough to the ring to see that its sandy floor is in fact mud with sand sprinkled over the top.

She feels a discomfort in her belly, as if the chocolate bar she's just eaten had something wrong with it. She tries to quieten her mind and follow the sensation. For some reason it leads her back to the computer games in the stall by the gate, and what her father said about having to adapt to the modern audience. Her stomach twinges again and she shifts around on the bench. There is an uncomfortable image in her head: a page of the Cirque Maroc's accounts, with a full column of outgoings, requiring more incomings. Odeline has always pictured her ideal balance book as an almost empty page, with minimal outgoings meaning she could be less dependent on incomings, and whatever cash came in could be moved straight to the profit column. Her mother's only outgoings were food, VHS tapes for recording her weekend films and educational items for Odeline. But perhaps this idea of self-sufficiency is naive. Why should her mother have it right? Her father, with his wisdom and years of experience in the artistic world, is surely more enlightened. And he hadn't seemed impressed by her Paris plan. Perhaps it is just not possible to live the way she has envisaged, needing little, spending little, maintaining her boundaries. Perhaps she will have to change and adapt like the Cirque Maroc. Perhaps, if she joins them, she will have to compromise some of her ideals as well?

TWENTY-FOUR

She is sitting on the ground, facing away from him. He can make out her figure in the dark from about fifty yards away. There is a gap in the houses on the opposite bank where a streetlamp shines through, weakly yellow – otherwise this section of canal is pitch black, invisible to the grid of windows in the looming tower block behind. He wouldn't usually walk this far up the path – John must be two miles from home now – but he's kept his word: he's been looking for her, and now he's found her. He can see her legs in the chef's trousers splayed out in front of her, the snaffled shoes pointing outwards – the hands of a clock at ten to two. She is wearing a red football shirt. As he gets closer he reads the white lettering across the back: 'GIGGS'. The grey beret of hair is nodding back and forth. A figure is crouched beside her. John Kettle sees a white hand on her shoulder, a patterned arm, a blue-black shoulder. It is Ridley, in vest and shorts, bowing his head down to Mary's.

As John Kettle gets to them, Ridley looks up. 'I think she's been attacked. She won't say.'

'Bloody hell.' John plucks the baggy cigarette out of his mouth and chucks it into the water, rushing to bend down in front of Mary. Her head is hanging forward now.

'What happened, Mary? Did someone hurt you?' He looks up to Ridley.

'I found her like this about half an hour ago. Can't get anything out of her.' Ridley picks up an empty bottle from the ground next to his foot and shows it to John. Brandy. A red-shirted arm comes out and takes the bottle, and Mary throws her head back with the mouth of it pressed to her lips. The arm sinks back into her lap when she realises it's empty.

'Hello, Warden,' she says, lips flattening against her tombstone teeth as they stretch open. There is a shining swell below her right eye, which is puffy and almost closed. The eyebrow is crusted black and purple.

'Bloody hell. Bloody hell. What is this?' John spins around to Ridley. 'Who did this?'

'She says she can't remember.'

'She says she never can,' says Mary, breathing brandy. 'She has the memory of a *fish*.'

John gets on to his knees, looks again at the eye. There is whiteish gunk between the lids. It isn't a fresh wound. 'When did this happen, Mary?'

'If I had to hazard a guess, I should say it happened on a Thursday.'

'I've been looking for you since Thursday. You didn't come to the group.'

'I was making a journey of awareness,' she says, rattling the bottle at him. Her head flops forward again.

Ridley says, 'I think we need to see to her eye, but I didn't want to leave her alone. And she wouldn't move.'

'She would not be moved,' says Mary into her chest.

'She has found her resting place.' The arm extends again and flaps around for something out of reach.

'I'm moored up at Kensal but I could run and get something to clean it up with,' says Ridley. 'If you stayed with her. Won't take long.'

John nods, looking at the bony ankles jutting out of the chef's trousers, skin scaly dry.

Ridley stands up. 'She wouldn't say what else they did. But the trolley's been kicked about, definitely.' He points behind him and John can see the trolley sitting crookedly in the undergrowth. It looks like a wheel is missing and the metal caging along the sides is bent. The front has given way entirely, crumpled.

'Write-off!' says Mary.

'I'll keep an eye.'

Ridley jogs off and John bends down.

'I'll stay here and keep an eye on you, Mary,' he says loudly.

'Thank God for that.' Mary raises her bottle. 'The blind leading the blind. I'll keep my eye on you as well. I've only got one left!'

'Your eye will be all right,' says John, loudly again. 'Ridley's off to get something for it. It'll clear up in no time.'

'He is a nice young man,' says Mary. 'Maybe I could get a patch.' She puts the bottle down and tries to twist round on to her side. 'Bedtime for the old girl.' But her hand fails to support her weight and she hits the towpath with her shoulder. 'I'm very tired,' she says.

'Stay where you are, Mary,' John Kettle says. 'I'll make your bed up.' He goes over to the trolley under the trees.

The back wheel is missing so he lifts up that corner to wheel it over. Stuffed into the end of the trolley are the tennis racket covers. He sees there's a bench in the darkness to his left. John pulls out the racket covers and lays them along the bench, as he has seen Mary do many a time. Then he lifts out the pillow and the burgundy towel, laying the towel over the racket covers and putting the pillow at the head of the bench. The duvet is underneath some magazines, the cream mackintosh and a knot of black wires, so he stacks these things at one end of the trolley and tugs the duvet till he's got it out. Then he drapes it over the trolley handle and bends down next to Mary. He pushes his arm through her elbow. 'Right, lass, you ready?'

'What's happening?' she says, her eyes closed.

'Heave!' He pulls her up until she's sitting on her haunches. She balances there, teetering slightly. He takes a breath and smells the sharp, sweet alcohol, the low stench of her body. Then hooks his hands under the arms of the football shirt – 'One, two, three, heave!' – and lifts her up to sit on the bench.

She plants her feet apart on the towpath for stability. 'Don't break your back,' she says, chin in her chest again. 'The old girl weighs a ton.'

'That's all my lifting done. You just lie down now. Sleep it off.'

She folds on to her side and he picks her legs off the ground, laying them along the towel. He lifts the duvet off the trolley and places it over her. Tweaks the pillow down under her head. And waits for Ridley to come back with the stuff for her eye.

TWENTY-FIVE

Later on this same night, from inside the telephone box
on the Little Venice bridge, a man is watching a boat. He
has been watching since it got dark, with both hands
holding binoculars steady against the glass. The image
through the binoculars is blurry around the edges but
sharp at the centre. The boat is well lit by a streetlamp.
The lamplight makes the ripples of the water yellow and
its shadows black. It discolours the paint of the boat's
exterior but keeps its form sharp. The man makes adjustments to the angle of the binoculars to look, again, from
one end of the boat to the other.

The front of the boat is furthest from him. He moves his
binoculars back from the snub nose, the short front deck
and blunt prow, along the side. The bowl of the boat is
sitting below the towpath level and is barely visible, but the
tops of the orange buoys wedged between the boat and the
bank are luminous in the lamplight. There are four along
the side, in the same positions as the rope bumpers used to
be. Above each one is a brass porthole – through the binoculars the man can see the three screws in the brass frames,
but the glass glares from the streetlamp and he cannot see
through. He can't tell if she's inside or not.

Between the central two portholes is the painted name

in an arc. He knows the shapes of these letters. They come through the binoculars with a clarity that is almost too much. They pinch the breath out of him. He blinks, and they are still there. As he watches, they begin to shimmer.

It has started to rain. He sees the surface of the water speck. Hears the flat sound of drops on the roof of the telephone box.

He brings the binoculars back to the cabin doors. They are the same as they were – double doors in the blue of the boat – but now they have a lock bolted at the top and two white handles, most likely plastic, where they used to be brass. The paint looks patchy around the locks and he can see that one of the handles is split. The thought that the boat has not been well kept stirs something. For a few seconds his view of the boat loses its sharpness, shakes slightly. He can hear his breathing get faster.

He brings his binoculars along to the back deck, which is a lighter wood than it used to be: it must have been restored since then. The planks are well lit in the lamplight. He looks over them one by one. They have been fitted decently enough but the edges are water-darkened, which tells him that they have not been treated for a long time. They have not been nurtured as they should have been.

Again a cloud passes over his sight and his breath tugs at his chest. And again something within him strains, although he doesn't know what this is. He wouldn't have the word for it. He is someone who has learned to speak, but not to speak to himself. He feels a pull, a strong leaning from inside him towards the boat. And also a pull back, to the time he saw it last. When he saw it last in the fire's light. Saw it last half afloat in the bowl of the canal. He feels no different to the boy who stood on the bank and stretched his mouth to howl noiselessly, water pulling at his jumper, streaming down his legs, one cold, stiffening hand clutching the windlass in his pocket. He ran away from it that night in the smoke and the chaos, leaving his clothes in the drawstring bag, his gas mask. If he goes back to that moment he can hear his own blood pumping and the muffled sirens as he heard them then through newly deafened ears. He can see his shoes pounding sound-lessly along the slabs of towpath, the laces soaked, undone and hitting the stone. He can smell the smoke from the fire chasing him, about to catch him up.

He brings the binoculars down and leans back against the wall of the telephone box. Puts his hand on the warm, bent, dented metal of the windlass in his pocket, rubs a thumb along the numbers in the handle. The boat has returned to him. She has restored herself and come back to him. For all the changes, there is no doubt she is the same boat. He knows every inch from memory; he could shut his eyes and move around the shape knowing the place of each screw and each join. This is what he used to do at night in his room at Walt Chaplin's to quieten himself. It became a habit.

For the last two years, he has given his days to building this boat again. He came back to London because he'd grown used to the way cities left him alone. He took a job doing repairs on the community boat at Camden. This allowed him access to tools and a boatshed. He bought a forty-foot narrowboat from a scrapyard and stripped it down to the shell, replacing any rotten wood in the frame. He built the cabin and laid plywood flooring over the joists. He used old pine for the decking. He fitted the engine into the cabin at the back of the boat, and built a fold-down bunk over it as Walt Chaplin had done. He found old brass portholes and screwed them to the cabin walls – and one to the ceiling, after he'd painted the compass points around a circle of paper. He found a brass handle and fitted it to the tiller. He varnished the interior and the decking and took his time painting the outside. He matched the colours to his memory: blue, with white letters and a red outline.

But the boat he has been building these last two years doesn't feel *right*. It looks right – he has remembered everything precisely and his drawings have been accurate. But when he is on board and closes his eyes, he knows it is not her. This boat he has built is silent. It doesn't have the sounds of Walt Chaplin's boat, the little creaks and sighs that were the small murmurs of someone gently listening. He had known that Walt Chaplin felt it too. He had heard him talking to her sometimes, seen his head and lips moving silently as he steered. The boy had talked to her too as he lay over the bow watching her blunt nose push through the water. Watching the water fold away to let her through. He had practised talking to her and she'd listened. She had been his companion.

A knock on the glass of the telephone box and the man jerks up, hitting the edge of a glass pane with his binoculars. He does not find it easy to interpret the signals given out by faces or voices. He doesn't know what means anger, what means friendliness, what means wariness. This has made life difficult for him and it has felt safer to keep himself away from other people.

Two boys in tracksuits outside – one wet-haired, the other with a rain-darkened hood over his head, holding a rolled cigarette in its shelter. 'You done in there?' the second one mouths through the glass. The man pulls the peak of his baseball cap down before pushing the door open.

'Thanks, old man.'

A woman had found a boy soaking and shivering in her Anderson shelter. He wouldn't talk and she thought he'd lost his hearing to the bombs. She took him into the house and put him on a stool by the stove to warm up. She had tried to take his jersey off, to put a towel round his shoulders, but his fists were jammed tightly into his pockets. When she came downstairs with fresh clothes he had gone. He hadn't taken anything.

A young girl outside her front door had caught a glimpse of a boy running up the road as her mother knelt to do up the buttons of her coat – it was a cold day. She didn't see which way he turned at the end.

A seller on Golborne Road heard an animal coughing from under his stall and thought it must be a mongrel sniffing for rubbish. He looked below and saw a boy crouched over a dropped carton of beans, pawing it up from the road. The boy looked up expressionless. The man shooed him away as he would have done a dog.

In rented rooms above a pub in St John's Wood, a woman froze when she heard hammering on the door. It wasn't a client's knock. She thought if she stayed quiet they would think she was out. But the hammering became wilder and it seemed they would beat the door down. She opened it then, not to the police but to a wild-faced boy whose eyes blazed at her. He pushed past and stood in the room full of her things, looking around. He began to scratch his arm and blink purposefully, as if doing so might open up a different view. She opened her mouth to speak but he pushed back on to the landing and heavily down the stairs. The pub door crashed shut and brought a cold gust of air up the stairs. The woman shivered and went back into her room. Her heart was still knocking with the fright. She looked around and wondered what he had been looking for. Her chest, dressing table, mirrors and silk screen sat there, looking too precious against the dirty white walls. She had taken the room on a few months ago, after the last woman had left with a soldier, a woman with troubles, they said.

The boy was picked up that night on Lisson Grove, trying to climb over the gate to the canal towpath. He fought hard and it took two policemen to get him in hand. He wouldn't answer questions. Didn't speak. He spent the night in the police station and it was presumed that he had been damaged by a bombing. He matched no records of the missing in the area. There were institutions for these kinds of children.

Other children on the train didn't take much notice of the boy. Like evacuees, these children were not accompanied, and so played or fought amongst themselves. The journey was long and most slept for a few hours. He didn't join in or sleep but those sitting nearby noticed him drawing on his papers. He drew the same thing repeatedly, a long boat with doors at the back and

portholes along the side. This time names weren't called
out at the station. All the children were taken up to the
street and climbed up on to benches in the back of a bus.
And then were driven out of the city.

The institution was strict with him. If he wanted something he had to learn to ask for it. And so he began to
speak, although never much to anyone else. To the other
boys in his dormitory it sounded as if he was practising
to himself, little mutterings under the blanket after lights
out. Something about him kept them from teasing. Some
said that the brass lock key he kept hooked in his belt was
a torture instrument, that the boy was the son of a pirate.
He acquired a sort of mystery, and the teachers asked no
questions of him either. They had worse cases to deal with.
The boy attended all his lessons, although much of the
time his pale face would be turned to the light from the
window, looking out. Still, he learned to read slowly and
to write a kind of alphabet, the characters made of pains-
taking circles and lines. Strangely uncertain script for a
boy who could draw so well. On the day he left he signed
the name they had given him in these wobbling circles
and lines, and next to it a perfect diagram of a narrowboat
drawn from above. They had found him an apprenticeship
with a cargo company in the Edinburgh docks.

TWENTY-SIX

It is mid-morning of the second Sunday in September and Odeline is on board the return coach from Luton to London Paddington. She arrived at the coach depot with only a few minutes to spare before departure and so has not managed to secure a double seat for herself, or even a window seat. She is squeezed in next to an overweight young woman who prattles stupidly to a child on her lap. The child has fat legs which stick out beyond the partition between the two seats, and it has stared at Odeline without embarrassment since she sat down. The stare is blank and incurious and controlling, as if the child is challenging Odeline to complain to its mother about this invasion of her space. Odeline finds she can't, under this stare, say anything, and so sits on the far side of her seat with her legs in the aisle. Her prop box is wedged in the footwell against the seat in front, her bowler hat in her lap.

The word 'DISAPPOINTMENT' returns to her mind and its letters seem to land there heavily as if dropped from a great height. The letters are hard, sharp-edged, made of welded metal. Particularly the D. In the D there is too much reality.

Her father hasn't invited her to stay with the circus. He

hasn't seen her repertoire. When she asked to show it to him a final time, he had mimed an expression of regret that turned the corners of his mouth down into a mournful upside-down U.

'Next time, *chérie*, next time. I am so sorry we did not find an opportunity on this meeting. You will have to come and see us again.'

He had winked and stepped up on to the steps of his caravan, positioning himself in the doorframe. He lifted a hand to wave as the caravan was towed out of the field, but had gone inside and closed the door by the time it reached the entrance gate. Odeline stood in the field as the other caravans and lorries drove out, leaving muddy scars on the grass and a row of light-blue Portaloos. There were old tissues and cigarette butts stamped into the ground where the steps of each caravan had been. Bits of colour glinted in the dew: empty crisp packets, tin cans, a yellow leather slipper from someone's costume. The shape of the big top was marked by a circle of flattened grass in the middle of the field, silver in the milky morning light. It looked like a pool of water.

She hasn't performed for him, or been invited to join the circus. Equally distressing to Odeline is the fact that her father extracted money from her. She fingers the zip on her moneybelt as she thinks of it.

When the evening circus performance had ended, she left the big top and walked around to the stage entrance, where the other performers were congregated, already half out of their outfits, drinking and talking. Her father wasn't there. She asked a Lycra-clad acrobat who was leaning against a tent rope where she might find Monsieur Odelin.

The acrobat was about the height of her breast pocket and barely looked up at her in reply. His small muscled shoulders lifted and dropped. *'Je ne sais pas,'* he said, and closed his eyelids. Odeline went to her father's caravan. The door was closed and the curtains drawn over the windows. She climbed up a step and knocked on the door. There was no answer, although she could hear talking inside. She knocked again.

'*Oui?*' said a sharp voice.

Odeline stepped down on to the grass.

'*Oui?*' her father's voice said again.

'Hello,' she said. 'It's me, Odeline. I wasn't sure where you were.'

'Ah. I am just conducting an interview here, my dear. I will be ten minutes more.' At this Odeline heard a single peal of high-pitched laughter. She pulled her prop box over to the side of the caravan and waited. And then pulled it further away – she had a sense that she didn't want to be nearby to whatever was going on in there. She sat down, not caring how she looked, and took out her pocket watch. She counted seventeen minutes before the door opened and a woman appeared on the top step. She was wearing a floaty mauve dress with yin-yang signs and sandals. She had brown hair that was longer at the front than the back and a large, loose mouth. She was laughing as she looked back into the caravan: 'I'll make sure it's front page.' She had a camera over her shoulder and a pad and pen in her hand. Odeline felt an instant repulsion. She heard her father's voice say, *'Au revoir, Mmeselle'*, with a long emphasis on the 'elle'. The woman carried on giggling as she trotted down the steps and away over the grass. The lines of her underwear were visible through the flimsy material of the dress.

Her father stuck his head lazily around the door. He was still in his performance trousers, barefoot, with just a white vest on his top half. He watched the woman walk away and flexed his brown toes over the top step of the caravan.

He looked over and saw her sitting on her prop box.

'Hello,' said Odeline.

He came down the steps slowly, his eyes smiling and his hands held behind his back. A little wizard. 'Would you like to sponsor us, Odeline?' he'd said. 'Would you like to be a sponsor of the Arts? Think of it, my dear. We will put your name on the programme. With special thanks. Your name and my name together. You will have the satisfaction of knowing you are keeping the traditions of the Cirque Maroc alive.' He crouched down next to her and raised his eyebrows in mimed wonder. 'Throughout history great artists have only been able to practise with the support of great patrons,' he whispered. 'You will be one of them.'

Odeline stayed sitting absolutely still, with her arms crossed over her moneybelt. On realising she was expected to say something in reply, she cleared her throat, resolved. 'No,' she said. 'I don't have any money for anyone else.'

'So, you are keeping it all for yourself.' Her father had tipped his head to the side. 'My dear girl. I know you have grand dreams in your head. When I was your age I did too. I think I even dreamed of Paris as well!' he winked. 'But your money invested here will be better spent than burning it away on your own fantasies. I am

older than you with more years' experience in this world:
I know its realities. A community like this is the only
way these traditions, these arts, can survive. The only way
they can live on into another generation.' He nodded to
Odeline. 'You understand this?'

'Well, yes,' she said. 'But I don't have any spare money
with me.'

'Did I not see a note or two in there?' He leant forward
and tapped at the strap of the moneybelt, next to Odeline's
hand. 'Some little purple notes?'

Her father put a hand to his chest. 'Every time a circus
disbands another performance art is lost for ever. The
Cirque Maroc is a jewel, and one of the last surviving
showcases for these arts. We are receiving applications
from young talent all over the world.' He paused and
clasped his hands around hers. Odeline looked down and
saw her fingers within the basket of his, the long caramel-
coloured fingers and pink nails an older version of her
own. 'We just want to give them a chance,' he said.

She had found herself untucking her shirt and unzipping
the top of her moneybelt. She felt shamed into giving some
money, as though she should have known that this was
what was expected of her, that this was what she was here
to do. She picked out the rest of the notes in there and he
took them from her hand. 'We are so grateful for anything,'
he said, giving her hand a squeeze. She formulated a question about showing him some of her repertoire but the
words didn't come out.

Later, at the party, there was a bonfire. Two of the
troupe sat on the ground next to it with their legs crossed
around low African drums, which they hit with their

fingertips. Others did mini performances in time to the drumbeat and laughed as they tried to teach each other parts of their own act. There were posts set out in an octagonal formation around the bonfire with strings of coloured lightbulbs running between them like telephone cables. Many of the bulbs didn't work.

Odeline sat a little way outside the octagon on another bench and looked in. It did look like a magical scene. The circus troupe were lit by the firelight, their stage faces washed off but still half costumed. When the two tiny acrobats juggled empty bottles between each other they cheered and when two clowns tried and failed to do the same they roared even louder. The clowns began a waltz around the bonfire. Odeline saw her father's head thrown back in laughter, his mouth stretched open and teeth bared to the sky. She wondered if her repertoire could ever entertain him this much. She hoped he wouldn't ask her to do it then, in front of this audience.

He didn't move from his seat, though, or ask her to do anything. No one from the troupe did either, and now, in the coach on the way back to London, she feels the hard landing of another realisation: they hadn't been interested. She had prepared herself for some initial jealousy; perhaps they would resent the daughter of Odelin the Clown, a rival for his affections and another artist. But she had sat on the bench while they danced, laughed, performed and cheered each other, and she can't remember any of them looking over.

As Odeline stared at the fire, some of the circus workers carried and wheeled things back and forth in the shadows behind her. At one point, the bleach-haired costumier stepped forward into the firelight. She lit her cigarette by Odeline's bench.

'They love him,' she said. 'They totally adore him.'

Odeline followed the woman's gaze to where her father was sitting upright on his bench, with his legs crossed at the ankles and hands held regally in his lap. A small acrobat had his head resting on his knee, others around his feet looked up at him as he enjoyed the spectacle of two clowns chasing each other around the fire. A lithe young woman Odeline recognised as the trapeze artist was watching from behind him, absent-mindedly twisting the spirals of his hair. She rocked her head from left to right to the beat of the drums. Other members of the troupe were entwined around each other on the bench and beside it. Odeline half closed her eyes and they looked like the various heads and limbs of one being, lit up yellow in the firelight.

The woman dropped her cigarette and pressed it into the grass with the toe of a white trainer. 'Work to do,' she said, and walked away. Odeline shifted the bench a little further back into the darkness.

She slept in the big top – her father had presented this to her as a great honour. The circular ringside and rows of benches had already been removed and stacked on the grass outside. She unstacked a bench and dragged it back in, placing it far back from the ring so that the stench of animals would be less immediate. Then she parked her prop box next to the bench and ate Vera's picnic. The panini was soggy from sweating in the ziplock bag but it filled her up and she was grateful. After that she laid herself out on the bench with the soles of her shoes facing the doorway. Her elbows fell off the side and so she linked her fingers over her stomach. She could hear the drumming and laughter continuing at the bonfire. Blurred shadows from outside jumped in the firelight on the walls of the tent. She turned her head away from these and forced herself to sleep.

She was woken by a panicky, fluttering noise. Her eyes sprang open – it was quiet outside and the big top was dimly lit with dawn light. She twisted her head around. There was no one there. She looked up at the dirty slices of yellow and red canvas spreading out from the centre. Their frayed threads hung down into the stillness. Odeline noticed then that the wooden poles around the ring were a veneer; she could see metal platforms at the top and screws along the sides.

She heard the fluttering noise again and saw a small shape swoop across the roof of the tent, from one tent pole to the other. It landed on one of the metal platforms, folded its wings and turned, before swooping back to the other. Its trajectory was the same as a trapeze, dipping in the middle and swinging up to the landing stage. It went back and forth in a rhythm, with a pause between each flight. It was lighter, more effortless and more perfect than any trapeze artist Odeline had ever seen. As it flew, the bird's body curved up at the beak and the tail, shaping itself to the arc it was flying. She watched it back and forth, back and forth, and the big top colours began to grow brighter with the morning sun. When she heard hammering outside the bird stopped flying and Odeline got up quickly. She pulled her prop box towards the doorway and out, where men in shorts and vests were pulling up the stakes around the tent and releasing the ropes.

The sky was a lid of solid blue: there was not one cloud. One side of the big top fell inwards and the entrance flapped down on to the grass. Odeline watched as the whole construction sank slowly sideways, the heavy canvas folding in on itself. It made a ripping sound like thunder. She looked to the back of the tent, where the performers' entrance had been, hoping to see the bird fly out.

Odeline pulls her prop box along the towpath back from Paddington Station. It bumps over the cobbles and the noise grates. It is a stupid thing. A stupid, heavy thing. The plastic handle makes her fingers numb. She stops walking, and looks at it. Black reinforced plastic holding years of collected items. But she has failed to impress the one person who mattered. He has not seen an artist, a protégée in her. He talked of sponsoring young talent and did not think to include her. Her body burns with all the moves, all the mimes she did not show him. She takes tight hold of the handle and swings it round with all her strength. It skids and bounces and then drops off the edge of the towpath into the water. The momentum carries it bobbing into the middle of the canal. For a second she thinks it will float and this annoys her, but then the handle tilts up and the bottom of the box begins to sink. As its sides go under, bubbles travel up to the surface. She imagines water flooding in, washing over the chalkboard, darkening the silk handkerchiefs, saturating the white gloves, the clip-on bowtie, the rainbow feather duster; rusting the harmonica she has hardly played and the roller skates she has never learned to skate on. She imagines the paper roses disintegrating, and the fold of false banknotes. Water soaking the £19.99 Harlequin doll with the bowler hat which is squeezed inside the lid. She feels nothing. The top corner of the box disappears and a green film of water closes over it. A few last bubbles hit the surface and then the canal is still. The prop box is gone. She does not dive in to rescue it, as Ridley dived in for John Kettle. She stands cold-eyed on the towpath and watches it sink.

She walks empty-handed towards her boat. As she comes round the corner to the Little Venice pool the sunlight seems to bounce piercingly off the triangle of water, making liquid stars in Odeline's eyes. The edge of the pool is luminous green with the reflection of the willow tree, so sharp she can see individual leaves. This end of the pool is empty of boats and there is no one on the towpath, a film set after the wrap. As she walks on she sees something new, something out of place: blue and white tape on the towpath beyond John Kettle's boat. What has he done?

She walks slower, wary of what she will see. But John Kettle's boat looks fine, almost celebratory, with pots of silly plants around the deck and gleaming sides. In her absence, the name *Peggy May* has been repainted in white letters, with a flourish added to the tails of both Ys.

The tape is not here: it is around the barge cafe in a triangle where the tables and chairs are usually set out. Odeline goes to it. The tape says 'POLICE LINE DO NOT CROSS' and as she gets closer she sees the cafe doors pushed in with fingers of splintered wood interlinking where they have been smashed across the middle. A lock hangs from the doorframe. She stands at the edge of the tape and she must be swaying slightly because she hears it scratch at her suit trousers. Through the doors a stool is on its side by the counter and the coffee machine is tipped on its face in a pool of something that has seeped on to the floor. Odeline can see broken plates and glass shored up against the counter. And Vera's light-blue shellsuit top in a wet bundle by the doorway.

TWENTY-SEVEN

Things had gone pear-shaped in America. They'd been chucked out and couldn't go back. Buying the boat for Inga, that was Fizz's way of making the best of what had happened. Because he loved her. He really loved her.

And he was so sorry.

Inga's face, the glaze of her eyes as she came out of the police station, it was the worst thing he'd ever seen. She was still wearing the pale linen trouser suit from the day before, now badly creased, and her sandals. She was gripping her sunglasses tightly to her chest. Those tiny shoulders shook silently in the car as he drove her home. He squeezed her hand and it sat cold and limp under his. Barely there. He felt his own heaviness, his pink hammy hand with its big gold rings desperately trying to hold her down as if she might float away from him. She was out of reach and it made him frantic. What had he put her through? She wouldn't say what they had done to her. She wouldn't say what she had told them, or what they had threatened.

They weren't allowed to take anything back with them. They only just had time to organise somewhere for the dogs to go.

Back in Britain they had nothing. Lawyers had hoovered

up all the money and the remainder wasn't enough to buy a place, nothing nice anyway.

Getting a boat had been a brainwave. Inga had grown up with the boats in Stockholm and he knew she was happy on the water. He bought it and kept it a surprise. Persuaded her out of the house down to the boatyard in Harrow where he had arranged to pick it up.

'What's going on, Fizz?'

They walked towards the old packet boat, with its nose swaying gently away from the bank and then back again.

Fizz held out his arms in presentation. 'This is our new home, Ing. We're going nomadic for a while.' She tipped her head and looked at him. 'I'm not joking, my love. She's ours.' Inga looked up and down the length of the boat and took a step nearer, letting her hand rest on the roof. She read the lettering on the side and mouthed the words: the name, the year. When she turned back to him he thought he saw some light flicker behind those pale-blue eyes. For the first time in weeks she looked right at him instead of through.

'We're a pair of hippies at heart,' he said. 'We can pad around barefoot on deck all day, lie out in the sun and get wrinkly.' She almost smiled. 'I promise not to screw things up –' and he pulled her in. He felt her hesitate and then her arms moved slowly around his back. So light he could only just feel the pressure of them. Her shoulders were shaking again. He looked at their reflection in the water and saw the pale column of her body with his huge frame wrapped around it.

Fizz Clements was a big man; big rather than fat, because the extra pounds seemed part of his substance, as vital to his being as the slicked quiff of black hair, now greying, and the bright Hawaiian shirts he wore all seasons. He was a loud man, fond of retelling the old stories. His best one was him and Inga getting married on the beach in San Diego in 1977, both barefoot. 'She looked like an angel,' he'd say, 'I looked like fat Elvis. It was so fucking hot I was melting. Drenched in sweat. She was cool as a cocktail. What was she thinking!'

Inga had been one of the four Swedish girls in Marta's Microphone, the group Fizz had managed in the early 1970s. They'd been a hit in Britain, known as much for their look as for the songs. Four wispy blonde dancing things in floaty clothes, swaying synchronised, loose-limbed puppets. It was a sort of post-hippy look. Fizz had taken them to America, where he released a record. Toured them for a bit. They hadn't worked well there – a bit too Scandinavian, a bit too cold, bit strange. Two of the girls got homesick and eventually the band broke up. The others went home. But Inga stayed out there, and Fizz organised a few small gigs for her, but nothing much. After a quiet gig in Phoenix, he asked if she didn't want to go home too. She looked up from behind her pale curtains of hair and said she felt like she was home, being near to him. 'I don't need anything else.' Hanything, she pronounced it. Her lovely, quiet accent. The first time he held her in his arms he felt like his heart was swelling up so fast in his chest it would explode.

They bought a place in LA and Fizz found a few bands to look after. Inga stopped doing gigs. She seemed happy at home and he did most of his business from there too. In LA business was social and usually done over lunch, which suited Fizz. He could blame his big belly on working too hard. They built a poolhouse with an outdoor bar and a music system, planted palms in the garden. They entertained, Fizz sweating and shouting over the barbecue, Inga swaying around barefoot with the drinks. She had a way of walking on her tiptoes as if there was nothing keeping her weight down. They'd moved their record collection down to the poolhouse and when the guests had gone they'd sit on the sun loungers and listen to old tunes. 'Never been happier,' he'd say last thing at night as he held her to his big beating heart; 'What a morning,' first thing every morning as he pushed himself up in the bed and looked over at her. He would put his hand out and eventually she would link her cool fingers into his. How bloody tiny was her wrist, and skin like honey. What a girl. One day Fizz came home with two retriever puppies and Inga dropped to her knees as they ran to her. Her face beamed up at him. Thump thump thump went his heart.

Standing by the boat he took her shoulders in his hands, felt the birdbone shoulders in his great fat idiot's hands. He would make this a new home for them, he promised her. He would organise for the dogs to be sent over.

'Can you do that?' she asked.

'Sure you can,' he said, not sure. That was his problem, he thought: the promising. It was impossible not to promise the world to this lovely creature.

'I'm so lucky,' he would say, 'to still have you.'

'That's right,' she would say, and smile.

The boat had been owned by an old Government bod who said his boating days were over. Fizz saw an ad for it in the local paper. The old boy'd kept the inside pretty basic with just a bunk bed and a tin hurricane lamp with a glass bowl hanging from a hook in the ceiling. There wasn't even a tap.

They decorated and remembered how fun it was to do a place up. They decked it out like the inside of their poolhouse had been. Groovy wall lights and orange carpet, a black tiled bathroom: showbiz lights. Fizz found a light cord shaped like a mic and got it for Inga. 'Once a popstar,' he said. They put in a fold-down double bed and a wardrobe. They got themselves his 'n' hers pyjamas like they'd had in America. They had their initials carved on the cabin doors. They hired a plumber, put a kitchenette in, bought a drinks fridge and a barbecue. They replaced the worn-out fittings, the decking, the door handles and the glass in the portholes. Fizz got them a fancy music system. The cash flow was drying up but they had to have music. They bought maps and boating books. He said the bonus of being back in England was the pubs. They would do a pub cruise by canal.

Inga knew boats so she did the steering. She looked noble as a queen the way she stood with her hand resting on the tiller, making tiny adjustments back and forth. She loved it. Fizz called her skipper. She was bloody good. She knew how to do the locks and could do the niggly stuff like turning and passing when you only had a foot between boats. He took care of food, drinks and orientation, announcing each new place on the map as they reached it as if over a ship's radio. From Harrow they went down the Grand Union Canal to Bull's Bridge, where they took the southern arm towards Brentford. Ahoy there, Brentford! And then back up from Brentford through Hounslow, back to Bull's Bridge and along the Paddington arm towards Ealing, travelling in the morning then stopping for a big lunch and hanging out for the rest of the afternoon.

The weather was good and the pubs did not disappoint. It felt good to drink proper beer. And to have a laugh. A good laugh. He and Inga spent happy afternoons with fat cold pints on pub terraces. She would turn her face to the sun and he'd make friends, inviting people back to their boat for more drinks in the evening. He'd heave out the barbecue, put the music on. Sometimes he'd get them dancing on the towpath.

Inga didn't seem to mind, she only asked that people not come indoors. That was their private space, she said. Their bed where they slept. It was sacred. But one night they had a gang back from the pub and the heavy warm drops of rain began to hit. 'Come on then,' shouted Fizz and swung back the cabin doors. They all piled in. He kept on serving drinks and people sat on the bed and on the counters of the kitchenette. Someone changed the music and they started dancing again. Fizz noticed a spill on the carpet and looked around for Inga. She wasn't inside. He went out on deck. It was bloody monsoon rain now. Went straight through his shirt.

'Ing!'

He stuck his head back inside the door – she definitely wasn't in there.

'Ing!'

He looked along the towpath and saw her long pale figure on the edge of a deckchair under the trees. She was bent over, arms around her knees. He wheezed over and pushed at his chest as he felt it complain. She was wet through, her linen shirt transparent and clinging to the narrow back and ridge of spine underneath.

'Come inside, darling. You're soaked.'

She didn't answer. He lifted back the dripping curtain of her hair and her face was set behind it. He had a horrible flashback to the LA police station.

'Come on then, my darling.' He pulled at her arm and she snatched it back.

'Nobody inside. That's what I asked, Fizz. That is our space. You can't hold a party in our bedroom. You can't bring strangers in there.'

'I'm sorry, darling. I'll get rid of them. Just come inside now. Don't stay out in this weather. You'll catch something. How long you been sitting here?'

'I don't want to go in there, I don't want to go in.' She hit her shins with the flat of her palm as she spoke, her voice brittle. 'People trampling. All over our things.'

The way she looked scared him.

'I'll get rid of them, love. I'll get rid of them right now.'

He ran back to the boat and felt the same twinge echo in his chest, like a single pluck of a guitar's string. He pushed back the doors and yelled 'Everybody out' again and again, herding them out, stupid drunk and complaining, taking glasses from their hands and jostling them up the steps until they were all gone. He turned off the music and chucked the ashtrays overboard. The barbecue was sizzling in the rain and stacked with shiny charred sausages, chops, burgers. He tipped those into the water too. People stumbled up the towpath and Fizz kept looking back to where Inga was crouched on the deckchair, a pale folded figure in the shadow of the trees. He went back inside and wiped at the kitchen counter with a towel. He put all the cans and glasses into the sink. Their eiderdown was covered in mud and so he stripped it off and shoved it under the bed. Then he grabbed his leather jacket from the wardrobe and rushed back out. He put the jacket over her shoulders and pulled her off the deckchair and on to her feet. She still hung her head. He walked her back to the boat holding the jacket around her.

'I'm sorry. I'm so sorry, my love, my lovely love. I'm so sorry.'

She said nothing.

'Ing?'

She took a breath. 'Nobody in our boat again. Please.'

'Nobody in our boat again,' he said. 'Just you and me.'

That night he lay awake with his fat idiot's arm around her and looked at the cabin roof whilst the rain drummed on. The hurricane lamp creaked on its hook as the wind shifted the boat in the water. Inga's hair was still wet and it soaked through the chest of his pyjamas. Never been happier, he thought of saying, but didn't.

They had enough for one more tank of diesel and that was about it. He couldn't get any more on credit. And he'd lied to Inga about it every time she asked. Fucking fat bloody fucking idiot. He'd been giving out drinks tonight, chucking all their food on the barbecue and showing off the boat like some bloody rock star. Was that what he'd wanted those people to think? Didn't even know

half their names. And they'd trashed the inside of the boat
– his and Inga's gorgeous, groovy, precious boat. All the
money he spent on it. Fucking *idiot*. Pulling out the
barbecue ten thirty at night.

He didn't sleep. Lay there listening to the boat, their
boat, hearing those curious sounds she made. Sighs as she
shifted on the water.

He would have to sort it. It was his mess.

The next morning he got up early and left Inga sleeping.
What a morning, he thought, and couldn't say it. He
walked a mile down the canal to a pub in Hounslow where
the landlord had said something cryptic over a pint a
couple of weeks ago, the kind of thing Fizz recognised
and had ruled out ever getting involved in again. When
the bloke saw him he pulled two pints and took him to a
table in the corner. He explained it all and really it didn't
seem too difficult. He was looking for someone to transport a number of crates up to Ladbroke Grove once a
fortnight or so. Stuff that wouldn't fit in a car and couldn't
risk being unloaded off a van. 'All our business goes by
water. Comes in on the Thames and then out –' he traced
a wiggling line on the table with his finger – 'on the
waterways. You can reach a lot of places by water.'

Fizz was to call some unpronounceable foreign bloke
when he got to the Kensal Road junction and some of his
pals would come and unload the crates and that would be
that. No need to know any more. The landlord opened
the till and stuffed an envelope with cash as prepayment,
and wrote a phone number on it. On Fizz's way back to
the boat the envelope felt shaming hot in his trouser pocket.

He told Inga half the truth about there being no money,

and then said they could earn a bit bringing booze up from the Hounslow pub to Ladbroke Grove. 'It's a cheaper way for the pubs to move it around,' he said, sick at himself, 'no tax on water transport. We'll be using the boat like she used to be used.'

'Is it legal, Fizz?' She looked straight at him and he threw an arm over her shoulder and pulled her in, getting himself out of her eyeline.

''Course it is, my love.'

On the first run he'd been jumpy but it went okay. When they got up to Kensal he made the call from a phone box on Harrow Road. Got through to a swarthy accent who told him to park the boat by some warehouse buildings on the other side of the canal. As Inga brought them into the bank three blokes appeared from the direction of Golborne Road. Two of them were teenagers, fair, shaven-headed and over-muscled. The third one was smaller and skinnier, dark with raked-back hair and stubble. He wore a black leather jacket, jeans and cowboy boots. Sore-looking, pink-rimmed eyes. Fruity cologne. He stepped forward to shake Fizz's hand as Fizz stepped down on to the towpath with the mooring rope. 'Ciao,' he said – it was the accent from the phone. 'The crates are inside?'

'Yeah,' said Fizz, trying to seem cool in front of Inga. The little dark bloke whistled to the two blond machines and motioned them on to the boat.

'My brothers,' he said. Fizz nodded. Right. The bloke went over to the warehouse doors and looked both ways before cracking open the padlock and swinging one door back. Inside was dark, but Fizz could see a tarpaulin laid out on the ground up to the door. He didn't want to look any further in. He turned round to the boat and gave Inga a big smile and a thumbs up. As each man went in carrying a crate, the boss man barked instructions in a language that sounded throaty and harsh. It was over quite quickly. There was another handshake, and a fat envelope. A nod. 'See you soon, friend.'

The boss man said the same at the end of each of their transactions, and not a lot else. More concerned with getting the job done quickly. So Fizz and Inga kept on going up and down between Hounslow and Kensal and after the fourth or fifth journey Fizz relaxed. It was fine. A couple more, then they'd have enough money to stop. It was a relief to have the cash.

They got the boat cleaned, replaced the carpet and stocked up. Fizz wanted to take Inga shopping in Chelsea but she refused. So he went off on his own and bought her a long necklace of amber beads from a costume jeweller's, like one she'd had in LA. She told him off, but he knew it was a keeper. It was round her neck that night and they lifted their table on to the towpath and lit the hurricane lamp. The amber followed the curve of her collarbone and lit up in the lamp's light. Stunning. They ate and he searched for her hand under the table. 'Look at us now,' he said, 'plastic plates on a metal table. Sorry, Ing.'

'We don't need much,' she said. 'Just the odd thing. I'm happy.'

He should have stopped there.

Three days later, another shuttle down to Hounslow

and back, dropped the crates with the man and his thugs. As they pulled away from the bank – a siren. The two crew cuts bolted down the towpath, and Fizz and Inga watched as the boss man snapped the padlock shut and ran after them. Police appeared on the bank, waved the boat towards them.

'What is this?' said Inga, her voice shaking.

Her hand was on the tiller and she steered them in towards the uniforms on the towpath. He went to the back of the boat, tried to take her other hand.

'I'm sorry darling. *Fuck*.'

The police went over every inch of the boat, even took up the decking, went through the engine compartment. They pulled the bedclothes off and knifed a line down the mattress to check inside. They went through the wardrobe, every item. They didn't speak while they were doing this, only to tell Fizz to sit still and shut up. Inga was silent. When they'd finished the search the police took her up to the towpath, questioned her separately. Through the boat's wall Fizz heard her monosyllables. 'No. No. I don't know.' He answered the same, but got blustery and desperate. They wouldn't let him outside to be with her.

Eventually the police left – they'd found nothing. Fizz followed them out and as he stepped off the deck to the towpath, Inga stepped on.

'I don't know what was in those crates, Ing. I honestly haven't a clue.'

She moved out of his reach, went down into the cabin. He clattered down the steps after her.

'I didn't know, Ing. They didn't say what was in them.'

'You told me that they contained alcohol for a pub.' Halcohol. She said this so quietly.

She wasn't looking at him, but around the bits of their life, and he followed her gaze as it took in the wrecked cabin, the mattress slashed with its innards all over the floor, clumps of grey foam clinging to the orange carpet. Some carpet in the corner had been pulled up and a floor-board removed, curved joists of the boat's skeleton were visible underneath. The drawers of their kitchenette had been pulled out and stacked on the floor, the oven door was off; same went for the grille for the extractor fan. The hurricane lamp was on its side on the counter, smashed. Fizz could see the the lid of his barbecue sticking out of the engine room doorway. Their wardrobe was empty, all the clothes on the floor. Fizz's loud shirts, Inga's quiet beiges, her whites.

She walked to the engine room and lifted a plank from above the doorway. She put her arm inside and brought out a handful of notes. 'The police are obviously not so good at finding things.'

'Where's that come from?'

'Some money I put away. I knew we were running out. You always spend everything.' She counted two hundred quid on to the bed. 'This is for you. I am taking the rest. I am going to go and stay in a hotel. Don't follow me.'

He stepped forward to beg –

'There is nothing for you to say, Fizz.' There was an edge in her voice that made him stop. That blankness in her eyes: she had already gone and the more he sweated

and grasped at her the further away she would go. So he
made himself stop and stepped back, managed to ask:

'Will you be back?'

'I don't know. '

'I'll be here.'

'I know.'

She fingered the amber necklace.

'Do you think you should take this back to the shop?'

'No, no. You've got to keep it. It's yours. From me.'

'I do love it.'

She moved forward and put a hand on his chest.

'I do love you.'

He dropped on to the bed as the doors swung shut
behind her.

That night – the first in nine years that they had been apart
– he lay on his back and he heaved. He mauled his eyes
with big hammy knuckles as the tears filled them again and
again and again. His chest was cracking open: the pain came
up through it and along the back of his throat. He choked
on the pain. Twice he thought he heard footsteps outside
and staggered out, but no one. Each time he checked the
ropes were tied properly to the mooring hooks. He mustn't
drift away. He promised he would be here. He had to stay
put.

At dawn he gave up on sleep and began to tidy, folding
their clothes, hanging them in the wardrobe. What would
Inga have to wear in her hotel? She hadn't taken anything
with her. This gave a flush of hope, but then he began
to worry. She hadn't anything waterproof. What if it

started tipping it down? There was nothing to her, his lovely girl.

He pushed his face to a porthole. The sky was clear. No sign of rain. But the worry wouldn't leave him; it was getting harder inside somehow, a barbell lying across his chest.

Heavy.

Pressing down hard on his breath.

He finished doing the clothes, put the drawers back into the kitchenette. But it was an effort. He went into the engine room and screwed the lid back on to the engine compartment. He gripped the handle of the barbecue and as he pulled it up – a new pain: a sharp line down his left side, as if someone had cracked a whip along his arm. And again and again. The pain became a shrill ache that spread to his heart.

He clutched at his chest and tried to push the ache away with the butt of his hand. He looked down expecting to see his heart beating as he fought with this thing. Just saw the rising heave of his chest, heard his panting breath.

This was bad.

He took the doorframe in his other hand and pushed up the steps, through the doors and on to deck. The buildings were spinning around below the blue sky – he saw the double doors of the warehouse and the rectangle of the huge tower block before they spun out of view.

Or was it him, spinning?

He saw the flat green of the water and the concrete slabs of the towpath leading off in both directions slab after slab after slab and at the end near the bridge he saw her figure the long column in white with pale hair the tiniest wrists walking towards him and saw the lovely long legs lift and bend into a run as he spun around again to face the sky dark blue pale yellow burning behind those buildings his legs fold and he goes down bum first and then big fat shoulder hits the floor and head lolls and he is looking along the plank lines at the blue ridge of the boat.

What a morning, he thinks to himself.

What a girl.

TWENTY-EIGHT

For two days Odeline has hardly been able to eat, only nibbling on some stale pieces of crackerbread from a packet on her bedside table. She hasn't left her boat. She has spent most of the time lying in bed looking at the cracked varnish of the buckled planks on the walls. *Chalet style. One of the handsomest houseboats on the water.*

Odeline is in despair. She has mimed this emotion many times before, with woeful eyes and a mouth twisted down into a tragic mask. Real despair feels different – she is not in fact aware of how her face appears. When she looks in the mirror it has no expression at all. It feels as though this real despair is expressing itself internally, somewhere between her heart and her stomach. She imagines a huge metal barrel with rusted edges. If you were to chuck a stone in, it would rattle around the sides and clatter at the bottom. She is an empty echoing barrel.

Her father doesn't want her.

She has no future with the Cirque Maroc.

Ridley doesn't want her. Ridley's not even here.

Her life's work is worthless.

Her prop box is gone.

She has £102.52 to add to her expenses, with still nothing to enter in the cash column of her accounts book.

Her only friend has been taken away.

Of all these, the most terrifying, the most real, perhaps because it is the most recent, is Vera's disappearance. The blue and white tape and the splintered door of the barge cafe, the smashed plates and the heap of sodden clothes, this is the film that plays over and over in her head. The shock of seeing it has not passed, and it seems to contain an even worse reality than her father's rejection, or the unsatisfactory finances evidenced in her accounts book. The world is a cruel, cruel place. She has never liked it, but that was because she'd thought it boring, and then disappointing. Not violent, not cruel, not brutal like this.

When Odeline thinks of Vera, the empty barrel in her stomach begins to spin, violently, the stone hits the sides faster and faster, rising to a terrible drumroll.

She imagines Vera's wrists ducktaped too tightly, her hands puce.

She imagines her crammed into the boot of a car.

She imagines Vera's body in a ditch, a gunshot through her temple.

Perhaps it was Vera's evil brother-in-law who came to get her. Did he have his thugs with him as he threw her around? Did they snigger as he called her names again? Odeline imagines Vera's body rolled into a shallow grave on the side of the motorway. She imagines her flowery skirt billowing as her body is thrown off a bridge into the River Thames. Is he lying in wait for Odeline too, waiting for her to come out from her boat? Will she meet the same gruesome fate?

Odeline has eaten her last crackerbread. At some point she will have to go out for more food. Or she could not.

She could stay lying like this on the bed until her body gives up. There is something magnetic about lying here all day. It is the opposite of what she has told herself to do all her life, with her daily schedule and her go go go. She imagines her skeleton in the suit trousers, collarless shirt and waistcoat being found one hundred years from now. Big shoes hanging off the bones of her feet. The relic of a neglected clown. Quite a poignant image, she thinks.

She imagines she can hear her bones creak as she lifts herself up off the bed. She feels dizzy from being horizontal for so long. She sways slightly, hair rustles the ceiling. The cabin looks different from an upright perspective. So narrow, so small. The faded orange-and-brown-patterned chair appears distant, as if there is a cloud between it and her. The bookshelf looks as miniature as a doll's. She blinks and then checks the cash in her moneybelt. She doesn't bother checking herself in the bathroom mirror, but goes straight to the cabin doors, sliding back the latch and opening them, wincing as the sunlight streams through.

She shields her eyes with a hand and steps up on to the deck. What is this? No brown, rippling canal water. Her boat is sitting on green, as bright as grass. For a second she thinks she has been plucked from her mooring and dumped on dry land, but then sees the stooped blue bridge and the grey-headed drunk leaning on her mangled trolley by the bench. Duckweed – that's what Ridley called it – duckweed surrounding her boat, laid like a carpet along the canal. Her boat is stuck like the other objects poking out of it. A wicker dog basket, a clear

plastic tube of blue styrofoam shapes, hundreds of upright
bottles and cans, half submerged. There are no birds,
nothing moves.

Further up the towpath, by the barge cafe, John Kettle
is taking the lid off a small pot of drawing pins. He jams
his thumb at the clasp and the lid flies off, drawing pins
spray over the towpath and the cafe table where he is
using a pepper mill to weigh down a pile of papers.
'Damn it,' he says desperately, and gets down on to his
knees to start picking them up. He doesn't know why
he bought the coloured ones: they seem childish now
for such a serious thing. When he has them all back in
the pot he lifts a sheet of paper from under the pepper
mill and turns to the barge cafe door, which is hanging
from its top hinge and splintered from halfway down.
He pins the paper to the door and then steps back to
look. Perhaps one should go on the end of the boat too,
in case people can't read the writing from behind the
blue and white tape.

When he sees a tall dark figure in the corner of his
vision he ducks under the tape quickly, with the papers
under his arm. Turning round he sees it is Odeline
walking out from under the bridge. 'You're back!' he
says.

Washed out, jaundiced, great purple bags around her
eyes. 'What are you doing?' she asks.

'I've made some posters to put up,' he says, showing
her one from the top of his pile which reads in black
capitals:

INCIDENT ON SATURDAY
7TH SEPTEMBER PM
BREAK IN AND POSSIBLE <u>ABDUCTION</u>
WITNESSES OR ANYONE WITH
INFORMATION PLEASE CONTACT
J KETTLE VIA THE THE PEGGY MAY
HERITAGE BOAT OR LEAVE A NOTE ON
THE PEGGY MAY HERITAGE BOAT, LITTLE
VENICE MARINA, PADDINGTON

Underneath he has drawn an arrow pointing to the right.

'I did some with arrows pointing the other way too,' he says, 'and I've put them down the towpath to Paddington. Do you know what happened?' he asks. 'Do you know who took her? Thought you were away or I'd have come up to ask. Been asking everyone.'

'No. Where is she?'

John Kettle shrugged. 'Found the barge all smashed up like this Sunday morning. It looked like a bomb had hit, all the chairs and tables knocked over, the doors kicked in. All my plants knocked off the roof.' He waves his hand at a pile of cracked plastic pots on the bank, soil spilling out of them. 'I didn't know what to do. I rang the police from the bridge but they wouldn't tell me anything. I went to this meeting on Sunday and when I came back – all this tape and everything. So they must have come, to check the scene of the crime. I don't know what they found, still haven't seen a copper here. Rang the station again and they put me on hold, for ever. Then said they couldn't give out information. Bloke I spoke to didn't even know where Little Venice *was*.' He looks down at his boots for a second. 'So

I thought I could make some posters. In case anyone saw anything.' His throat tightens. 'She was such a nice woman.'

He checks up the towpath to the right and left and lowers his voice. 'I know for a fact she was sleeping on board the barge, and she didn't want anyone to know it. I wasn't going to dob her in, none of my business. Was never that kind of warden. But I think she might have been under the radar, as it were. In which case the police won't give a damn. They're not going to bother themselves searching around for some unknown who wasn't even on the books. She didn't have family or anyone over here. As far as the world is concerned, she never existed.'

'Nobody knows of you or me either, John Kettle,' says Odeline, in a strangled voice, hitting her stomach with the butt of her fist. 'Nobody knows that *we* exist.'

He stares at her for a moment, and her face begins to crumple. So he risks it.

'Vera told me. Last week – you found your dad. That's where you were off to on Saturday. Wasn't that worth the effort of looking?'

Odeline looks at him. 'I'm not sure,' she says, quiet again.

'Listen, lass.' Her eyes flash in irritation. He tries again: 'Listen, Odeline. Would you sit down?'

He pulls two chairs over from the other side of the police tape, places them opposite one another and sits on one.

'Please?'

Odeline drags hers a little further away before sitting on it. John Kettle rubs his face in his hands, leans forward and takes his cap off. He fingers the anchor insignia at the back.

'When I was a young man in the navy I lost a friend because I wouldn't go and look for him. I've been thinking about it just these last few days, actually, since going to my meetings.'

'What meetings?' asks Odeline, itching to walk off. 'What does this have to do with Vera?'

'Please hear me out. Please . . . The meetings, they're at the church. One through the estates, off the towpath there. Looks like Alcatraz. We talk about different things, give each other support.' He looked up from his cap. 'It's good actually. It's been good. Keeps me out the pub.' He tries a laugh but it comes out thin.

'Anyway, I've been thinking about this time back in Portsmouth, when we were working the submarines, and been thinking that, really, that was when things began to go bad. Sort of lost my way a bit after that.' His voice thickens. 'I told them the story at the meeting on Sunday. They were ever so nice about it.' He sniffs and Odeline grimaces – she does not want John Kettle to start crying on her. Disgusting.

But he takes a breath and levels himself. 'He was my best pal, this chap, we were always at each other's side. We were a double act. I was the straight guy, he was the – he was the clown. Submarining. You don't see daylight for eight, nine weeks at a time. You need to be kept amused. Well, I believe our whole section loved Frank for doing that. The officers let him get away with stuff because they knew he was good for morale. Most of his pranks were harmless: little skits, gentle leg-pulling of the blokes in charge, acting out scenes from the movies with a la-di-da voice for the women's parts. Yellow hair, pointy nose, cheekbones like yours – he could do Garbo, Mansfield, Veronica Lake, all the Hollywood girls. He was funny. Very funny. I was a joker too, but not a performer like Frankie. Bantered all day, but when it came to entertaining the others it was always his show. We weren't allowed music on board so he'd spend most his shift singing, making up rhymes about people. If they took it badly, songs got worse. When we had a few days' leave every couple of months he'd lead the drinkers ashore and end up singing his songs on the bar. He had a good one for me.' And John Kettle begins to sing quietly, rolling his head from side to side:

> *Submariner Kettle*
> *Has a stomach of metal –*

'How is this relevant?'

'Sorry. I'll explain,' says John Kettle. He puts his cap on his knee and lays both hands face up on his lap, opening and closing his stubby, lined fingers, staring down at his soil-rimmed nails. 'I've just been thinking over these things, you see. He was a good friend to me. I didn't have any family around and he'd take me up to his folks for Christmas. Old folks, he had. Their only son, born late in life. Bloody worshipped him. I let them down too. I never got in touch with them afterwards.' He runs a hand over his face. 'Oh damn it damn it. You hear nowadays that people are born that way. But that's not how we used to think of it. Anyway I didn't twig until one night on shore when he, well, had a go at me. Made a pass. In a bar with everyone around. So I hit him about. Dragged him up a wall and knocked that fine nose halfway across his cheek. Had to. You can imagine the names I called him. I was bloody raging. Couldn't have them thinking we were a pair of *faggots*.'

Odeline sprang up.

'I don't have to stay here and listen to your bigoted language, John Kettle.'

'Please,' he said, standing up to face her and rattling his words out. 'Frank. He disappeared – that night. He walked backwards out of the bar, and I can still see him, with a cut eye and his nose bashed in by me, lip already swelling, that tidy blond head, such a mess. Chorus of chanting from the boys. He looked from face to face, all the boys that had been his audience and laughed at his jokes. Some of them still laughing at him now, making gestures, jamming bottles in their mouths. Others mad angry, wanting to pull him apart. He was scared. I knew he was scared. But I shouted after him to go down the docks where he belonged. Where the queers went. I wanted the boys to know I wasn't like him.'

'What has this to do with –'

'He didn't come back.' John Kettle sinks back into the chair and starts fiddling with his hat again. 'He didn't turn up the whole three days we were on shore. One or two of the boys told me to telephone his folks, see if he'd gone up home. Officers asked me if I knew where he'd got to. I let them know he wasn't anything to do with me. Not any more. Told them Frank's doings were none of my business.'

He takes a breath.

'Morning we left, that's when they found him. Face down under the pier by the docks. He'd done his wrists first.'

The shock of this makes Odeline blink. The man floats face down in her imagination, tilting in the black water under the pier. Wet blond hair, body beginning to bloat. John Kettle has put this image there and she feels tethered now by his telling her this awful story. She wants to wriggle out of it, to rewind and be free of it.

He twists his cap and his voice strains into a whine.

'He was my pal.'

'I am not the same as you, John Kettle.'

'I know, I know. But it's the single worst thing of my life, I wish more than anything that I'd at least gone looking. And we're the only ones who might be able to find her, right. Police aren't interested. Vera deserves our help, Odeline. She helped me. She came to get me from the hospital. And it seemed like she was a good pal to you too.'

John Kettle looks up at Odeline. She is standing upright with her hands linked. She looks around to the barge cafe. There is a long pause.

'All right. Where do we start?'

'There was some bloke sniffing around on Saturday morning when you were away. Foreign gent, asking her questions. She seemed rattled.'

'What did he look like?' says Odeline.

'Just foreign, and dodgy-looking. Slick hair, dusky. Tight trousers. Cowboy boots.'

'Leather jacket?'

'Yes.'

'That's her boss. Zjelko,' says Odeline. 'He's a gangster. That's the man who took her.'

TWENTY-NINE

Odeline and John Kettle are marching along the Harrow Road. Odeline walks briskly ahead and in a straight line. Others on the pavement step out of her way or look up surprised as they are knocked. Her shoulders are pushed down and her neck is angled forward. Her gaze is fixed in the direction of travel. John Kettle is in her wake, keeping up, sweating under his cap. He was trying to roll a cigarette as they walked but has given up and is stuffing the bag of tobacco back into his pocket. They are going to the biggest establishment in Mr Zjelko's portfolio, the place that Vera once told her was his headquarters: the Portobello Queen on Elkstone Road.

Odeline is dressed for action. She has rolled the sleeves of her shirt to above her elbows and pushed kitchen roll into the toes of her brogues, in case she needs to run. She has also shortened her braces so the trousers won't flap and trip her up. She is wearing her moneybelt under the shirt and has zipped into it the screwdriver from her mother's toolkit (for 'security'), as well as her notebook and pen (for any details that may be useful if the rescue operation turns out to be more prolonged than this one mission). Zjelko may be keeping Vera locked up in any one of his establishments across West London; it could take more than one afternoon to extract the details of her whereabouts.

The outside of the bar is purple, with a gold crown set above the glass doors. When they get to the entrance, Odeline raps sharply on the glass. John Kettle puts his grizzled, bearded face to it. 'They're open,' he says, and swings the door back. Inside there is a football game on a pull-down projector screen and a pair of men at a table in the corner. The bar stools are covered in spotted white fur like ermine, and there is a giant crown chandelier hanging from the ceiling. The barman is leaning forward on the bar looking up at the screen. 'Where is she?' shouts Odeline, advancing towards him. He jerks upright.

'Excuse us, mate,' says John Kettle, appearing at Odeline's shoulder and trying a friendlier approach, 'We're looking for a lady called Vera. We think Mr Zjelko knows where she is.'

'Well, I don't know where Mr Zjelko is,' says the barman, in a thick, Vera-ish accent. Check the office upstairs.' He points to a door at the other end of the bar.

Odeline and John Kettle climb the wooden stairs to the next floor, their feet in a synchronised march, creaking the steps. There is a men's toilet symbol on a swing door ahead of them and a small empty bar to the right. On the left is another door, slightly ajar, showing a large man with a crew cut sitting at a desk. He is squinting as he deals out playing cards. Smoke curls up from a cigarette hanging at the corner of his mouth.

'That's not the bloke,' whispers John Kettle.

'I know,' says Odeline and thrusts the door back, revealing another equally large, polo-shirted man on the other side of the desk. This one has a short square haircut too, with blond tips. They both look up, incurious.

'Where is he keeping her?' demands Odeline, whipping her head around the back of the door and seeing only a filing cabinet and a mini fridge.

'You have business with Mr Zjelko?' says the man behind the desk in a thick accent. He chucks his head at Odeline and looks across the desk, whistles. The other man laughs.

'That's right,' says John Kettle, trying to fill the rest of the doorway, with his thumbs hooked into the pockets of his jeans. 'Your friend downstairs sent us up. We're looking for Vera.'

'We are leading an investigation into the abduction of a woman on Saturday night from the barge cafe,' corrects Odeline.

'Zjelko's barge?' asks the smoking man.

'Yes,' says Odeline.

'Shit, man,' he says to the blond, who makes a worried face. 'The police know?'

'They have cordoned off the crime scene,' says Odeline.

'Ring him,' says the smoker, lobbing a mobile phone across to the blond, who whips his hands away, letting the phone clatter off the table.

'I don't wanna tell him!'

The smoker exhales and looks back to the doorway. 'Maybe better you speak to him yourself. You can wait in the bar. He will be back, maybe thirty minutes.'

'We don't have time to waste. Where is he?'

'I said you wait here.'

'Where is he?'

The smoker bites on his cigarette. 'You better call Zjelko,' he says across the desk. 'Tell him we have trouble.'

'Let her go find him,' says the blond.

The smoker turns the block of his head back to Odeline. 'Okay, he's at the supermarket.'

'Thanks, pal,' says John Kettle, and Odeline shoots him a look.

'We will go there directly,' she says.

The supermarket is the biggest Odeline has ever seen. It is the size of an airport, she imagines. In Arundel convenience stores there were two aisles and a freezer section. They enter this place through electric doors where people are rattling their trolleys out to the car park, piled high with plastic bags. Beyond the checkouts there is a sign which says 'AISLE 48 CLEANING PRODUCTS'. Forty-eight! Odeline positions John Kettle in front of the electric doors to prevent Zjelko's escape and walks into the huge hangar of bright lights and endless rows of blaring packaging. She summons to her mind an image of the man she saw outside Vera's boat on the morning she got the letter. The shiny hair. The velvety foreign voice – 'Ciao, Vera.'

Repellent man.

She gets to a gap halfway down aisle 48 and heads left towards the centre of the supermarket, whipping her head right and left to look down each aisle. In aisle 7 she sees him: the black hair lacquered back to a nest of curls at the nape of the neck, the shadowed jaw, the leather jacket with the Ferrari motif, the leg-hugging jeans. Cowboy boots. He is reading the back of a juice carton. She approaches and, just a step behind him, smells coconut. She takes a breath and speaks in a cold, clinical whisper to the oiled curls sitting on the leather collar.

'The game is up.'

He does not flinch as she expects him to, but turns around slowly and looks at her brogues, up the length of her trousers, over the wing-collar shirt billowing out from the red braces, up the length of her neck to her chin, over her frozen face and into her eyes. Up close, she sees he has close-set eyes, and thick short hairs around his jaw. The top of his mouth is a line – no lip – and the bottom is a thick, pale pink pad, as if he is wearing some kind of gloss. The lips of his eyelids are thick pink as well, and his crooked nose has a dropped septum, so Odeline can see this same pink on the insides of his nose – it is as if the orifices of his face have been freshly cut. He is still holding the juice carton and has a metal basket looped over the elbow of his leather jacket. At the top of it is a bag of organic granola.

'Who the fuck are you?' The line of his top lip curls to show a gold eye tooth. His eyes are wandering back down her figure.

Odeline delivers her next line faster than she would like, looking at the point of black hair at the top of his forehead, which is at her eye level.

'Don't test my patience, Zjelko. Tell me where she is.'

'Eh?' He shows the gold tooth again. 'You looking for a job or something? I only have cleaning for ones like you.'

Odeline tries her ultimate line, the one she has planned to save for extreme circumstances. She can't believe she is using it this soon.

'I know what kind of business you run, Mr Zjelko.'

'Oh!' He rolls his head back in understanding, showing a bald scar under the stubbled chin. 'Nice voice. So you funny girl?' He takes a step forward and unscrews the cap at the top of the carton, making a click. The coconut smell is stronger now. Odeline moves back and puts a hand to the shape of the screwdriver beneath her shirt. She whips her head to the left and the right. There's only one shopper nearby, a fat girl with a fatter toddler sitting at the top of the trolley, and they're about to turn the corner. Soon this half of the aisle will be empty.

'And what business do you have, funny girl, annoying me now with your stupid voices when I am trying to shop?' He puts the juice carton on to his bottom lip and takes a swig, using a little finger to wipe the orange liquid from the corners of his mouth. She sees wiry black hairs on the backs of his fingers and very pink nails.

'I am a friend of Vera's. I am leading the investigation into her disappearance,' says Odeline, hearing her voice tremble. 'It's time to come clean.' She tries tensing her jaw.

He takes another swig. 'Whatta fuck about some Vera?'

'We have come to take her back. I have a team of people guarding the exits.'

Swig. And then, for an instant, Zjelko freezes – a flash of recognition in his pink-rimmed eyes.

'Vera, from my barge? Vera Novak?'

Odeline is briefly taken aback, this is the first time she has heard her friend's surname. But she doesn't let it throw her – she perseveres.

'Don't test my patience, Zjelko,' she says again. (It was a good line.) 'Tell me where she is.'

Zjelko takes another step forward and puts the juice carton down on the shelf behind her. He lifts his face to hers – it is centimetres away. She can feel the corner of his metal basket pressing into her hip. The coconut smell is overbearing – it has a chemical sweetness at this distance.

'First things.' He lifts a pink-nailed forefinger in the gap between their faces. 'I don't take orders.' He lifts a second finger, holding it together with the first like a gun. 'Second things. I don't take orders from funny-talking girls dressed like crazy people. Third things.' He flicks his thumb out. 'I don't like to be annoyed. I –' he points the gun fingers at the shoulder of his leather jacket – 'give the orders. Now you can fucking tell me what is going on with my barge.'

Odeline sees his eyes drop to her throat and she gulps.

'I just want to know where she is,' she rushes, pressing her head back against the top shelf. There isn't room enough between them to untuck her shirt and access the screwdriver even if she wanted to.

'When she go missing?'

'Saturday night.'

'Shit!' He steps backwards and drops his basket to the floor in the middle of the aisle. 'Shit! We haven't been open since Saturday?'

Odeline shakes her head.

'Why no one tell me? Fucking pigs. I can't believe they do this.' He kicks the basket and takes a mobile phone from the inside of his jacket, flipping it open.

'Who?'

He is flicking his thumb over the buttons. He lifts the phone to his ear, holding it slightly away with his little finger pointing out.

'*Who?*' says Odeline. He knows. He's speaking like he knows.

He kicks the metal basket again and it goes skidding into the shelves opposite.

Odeline steps forward in front of his face. 'Who? Who did this? You said *they*.'

'Is me,' Zjelko says into the telephone. 'You both go down to barge now. Straight away. They fucking *took* her. I can't believe, those fucking *murija*. Ring me and tell me what you see. Check the till. Check appliances. Secure *everything*. One of you stay there and one of you meet me in the office.' He snaps the phone shut, puts it back in his pocket, and retrieves the shopping basket.

'Get out of my fucking way.'

'Who was it? Who took her?'

'Move. Stupid fucking woman.'

He sidesteps Odeline and she spins around to follow him down the aisle.

'You said *they*. Who is *they*? Is she in danger? Is it the brother-in-law?'

He walks faster down towards the checkouts, taking long strides in his tight jeans. Odeline marches behind. They are passing through the refrigerated section. He is muttering to himself, spitting out words. Odeline can't catch any of it. She pulls the bag of granola out of his basket, dashes a couple of steps ahead and drops it on to a shelf of cheeses.

'Who took her?'

He lurches past her and snatches it back, puts it into his basket.

'Whatta fuck are you doing, woman? Fucking leave me alone. And fucking shut your mouth.'

Odeline dives for the basket again, pulls the granola out and takes a tub of Greek yoghurt too, pushes them on to a top shelf next to some packets of ham.

'Where is she? Tell me who took her.'

He pulls the granola and yoghurt off the shelf without much effort and drops them back into the basket. 'You're a crazy.' He taps his head with a bent forefinger, top lip curling in disgust. 'Stop fucking touching my shopping.' He stalks off down the aisle. Odeline puts her hand into the middle shelf of the refrigerated section as she pursues him, taking with her packets of prawns, trays of salmon fillets, vacuum-packed pairs of smoked mackerel. She sweeps all these into her arms and runs forward to dump them in Zjelko's basket.

'TELL ME WHERE SHE IS!' She screams this, stretching her mouth open to be as loud as she can.

He twists round and his forehead is corrugated, his hand rigid as he makes a frantic slashing motion at his neck.

'Shut up your fucking face!' he spits in a whisper, saliva running over the pad of bottom lip.

They are standing by a rack of batteries at the end of the aisle. He looks around; all the faces in the checkout queues have turned to them. 'What is your fucking problem?' He's still whispering.

'TELL ME WHERE SHE IS. I WILL KEEP ON SHOUTING UNTIL –'

'Okay, you can fucking shut up because I don't know where she is anyway.'

'But you said you knew –'

'I know who took her. It was the pigs. They were asking questions last week. They came round to my bar. I told

Vera she has to be careful. That morning even – Saturday
– I go, to tell her.'

'Pigs?'

'*The* pigs. *Murija.* The police.'

'Where is she? In prison?'

'I don't fucking know. No. They take them to detention
centre.'

'Where is that?'

'I *don't* fucking know. West somewhere. Big place. I
never been there. You can leave me alone now. Fucking
crazy woman.'

Odeline steps closer, pushing the metal basket out of
the way. She looks down on the ridges of oiled hair combed
back from the widow's peak, the twitching brows, the raw
eyelids. 'Did you send the police to get her?'

'Do I want my business to be wrecked? Do I want my
cafe closed since Saturday and taking no money? The
fucking pigs in this country want to ruin my life.'

'You are a repellent man,' says Odeline, stepping back
and reversing the gaze he gave her a moment ago – a full
inspection, but working down: the shiny jacket, the thick
legs in their close-cut, womanly jeans, his boots, which
are heeled, at least an inch high.

'Fuck yourself,' he says, and walks to a vacant checkout,
clattering his basket on to the end of the conveyor. He
twists his head away from Odeline and looks unblinkingly
towards the next checkout. The packets of fish are still in
the top of the basket.

Odeline finds John Kettle by the exit, rolling a cigarette.

'Any luck?' he says, popping it into his mouth as he
follows her out of the electric doors.

'It wasn't him who took her,' she says. 'But I know where she is.'

As they leave the car park Odeline hears a rattling and looks round to see John Kettle pushing a shopping trolley on to the pavement behind her.

'What are you doing?'

'It's not for me,' he says, beard clamped around the cigarette. 'It's for a friend.'

Early that evening Odeline goes over to the barge cafe with a plastic holdall that she has bought from Harrow Road. She ducks under the police tape and takes a few steps towards the threshold. She pushes a half-closed door back on its hinges and it smacks against the cabin wall, sending two pigeons flapping up inside the boat. Zjelko's men haven't made it as secure as he'd hoped. The pigeons settle back down to pecking around the broken crockery in the middle of the floor. Odeline hates this pecking: these dirty birds feeding off Vera's misfortune. She stamps at them, clapping her hands. They half fly over the threshold and then flap down again on the towpath, turning in affronted circles.

'Vultures!' shouts Odeline after them.

The till has been taken, so presumably Zjelko's thugs have been here. She goes behind the counter to look for Vera's things. Her apron and a pink tracksuit top are hanging on the back of the toilet door. There are some hairclips in a dish on top of the fridge. She looks in the drawers and around the counters for anything else. Down the side of the microwave, where the trays are kept, there

is a stash of newspaper pages. She pulls them out. They
are individual articles that have been neatly cut out, all
relating to the situation in Vera's country, the horrors
there. There are profiles of the individual leaders, reports
on particular areas and some accounts of UN negotiating
efforts. Odeline looks through them. Some are as small as
a paragraph. Others are pages long, with pictures of burned
buildings and mobs with flags. Many are yellow and
stained from their hiding place.

She unfolds a magazine page: a vivid colour photograph
with a gruesome figure at its centre. The figure is lying
face down across the steps of a building. It wears a uniform,
a green jacket and cap with a badge on the front. The head
is tilted back, an eye half open, teeth showing. A stain has
spread across the back of the jacket. One arm is crumpled
under the body, the other is flung along a stone step. The
legs flop down the steps, one foot folded over the other
as if scratching the back of a heel. Around this figure the
steps are chipped, bullet-bitten. On the bottom step are
the stringy remains of a burnt tyre. Bits of charred cloth
hang from the blackened flagpoles. All the windows of
the building are smashed. A flag has been wrapped around
a statue at the top of the steps. Desk drawers and papers
are washed up against the base of the statue, as if the stone
figure is the centrepiece of a bonfire.

Odeline refolds the picture and stacks it into a pile with
the other articles on the counter. She checks there are no
more papers hidden behind the microwave. There is a
murmuring sound and she looks around before realising
that the radio is on at a very low volume. She brings her
ear down to it; it sounds like a news programme.

She checks underneath the counters but can't see any other personal belongings. She looks at the double doors at the back of the cabin. Odeline had noticed Vera glancing at these sometimes, when she was making hot chocolates. Odeline walks over now and pulls them open. Inside is a long low storage area, about waist height and the length of two cafe tables. A tarpaulin has been laid over the floorboards and there is a mattress taking up most of the floor space, with an open sleeping bag spread across the middle and blankets folded neatly at the foot. A torch tied to a piece of string is pinned to the rafters over the head of the makeshift bed. Crammed in the corner, a cafe chair with some toiletries arranged on it; Odeline can see toothpaste and a toothbrush in a foam cup, some deodorant and a box of washing powder. Underneath the chair seat is a pile of neatly folded clothes, one of Vera's floral skirts at the top. On the other side of the bed, jammed at an angle against the low rafters, is a shallow clothes rack with some socks and underwear hanging off it, and a towel slung over the top. Odeline looks to the corner at the head of the bed and sees a neat row of books, as if on a bookshelf, upright between two glass coffee jars. Leaning against the jar nearest a thin pillow is a photograph.

Odeline crawls in to look at it. It is a black-and-white image of a wedding couple, the man in a dark suit with a flower pinned to his lapel, the woman in a high-collared lace dress and veil. The man has the same crumpled eyes as Vera, and, under his moustache, the same thick mouth. Her father. The couple are standing on a step outside a building with high wooden doors, above which runs some foreign motto. The school perhaps. She takes the photograph and puts it inside the cover of the first book, a red and gold *Reader's Digest* edition of *Jane Eyre*. There are four more books in all, each a *Reader's Digest* edition. She takes the five books, the towel, the toiletries and the rest of Vera's clothes, and unpins the torch from the ceiling. They all go into the plastic holdall. She puts the newspaper articles in there too with the hairclips and the pink top, and after a few moments' deliberation unplugs the radio, wraps it in the towel and pushes it down to the bottom of the bag.

As she lifts the holdall out on to the towpath, she hears the chug of a boat coming under the bridge. She looks up and recognises it – it is the orange narrowboat with white lotus flowers that belongs to Ridley's friend Angela. She is steering and waves at Odeline.

'We missed you on Saturday!' she shouts. 'Come again! We'd love to see more of your work. Fantastic!'

Odeline nods her head vaguely, but the thought of performing is far from her mind right now. She looks down at the holdall with her friend's world inside.

'Will you come?' calls Angela, the boat getting closer.

And then Ridley's head appears over the roof of the cabin, decorated, friendly, unapologetic.

'Hi,' he calls, before noticing the scene around Odeline, the police tape and the fallen tables and chairs.

'What happened?'

THIRTY

Luminous blue bleeds into the sky with dawn the following morning, and the outline of the huge tower block west of the canal becomes definite against it. The green of the willow trees on Little Venice island takes colour, as does the red of the telephone box, the bridge's light-blue railings. The shadows under the bridge are still pooled black. In those shadows, underneath the arch of riveted metal, wire mesh and pigeon feathers, stands Crosbie – steering teacher, community canal worker, boat builder, evacuee boy.

He stands at the edge of the path with his side pressed to the wet wall of brick, the dampness coming through his sweatshirt. His binoculars are again held up against the peak of his baseball cap, looking towards the boat that is moored along the water from the bridge. He has been watching the cabin doors since the girl went inside yesterday evening, after speaking to the tattooed man and the canal warden for a long time on the towpath. He saw all this through his binoculars from the far side of the Little Venice island, but when night fell he moved closer. The porthole lights went out soon after dark and there has been no movement on the boat since then.

He is waiting.

Two days ago, he found numbers for a canal museum
at Braunston in the telephone book at the Camden
Community Boat Centre. He wrote down the wording of
his enquiry and practised saying it out loud. On his shift
he used the Centre's telephone, following the line of
numbers with his finger, pressing the buttons carefully.
His breath went shallow and fast as he heard the line ring.
When it clicked to connect he thought he would slam the
handset down. He read his enquiry out loud, heard his
breathy accent, tried to slow it down as it came out. The
museum woman chatted back to him and he pushed the
handset close in to his ear as he heard that old Walter
Chaplin's boatyard was no more, but Walt's widow still
lived, alone and ancient now, in the cottage by the boatshed. The lady from the museum heard silence and then
the line went dead.

As Crosbie looks at Walt Chaplin's boat now, he reads
her appearance the way others read an expression on a
face, or the tone of a spoken sentence. She is tired, she
has seen enough, she has carried enough. Her time is nearly
done and she pleads to be taken home.

THIRTY-ONE

A few hours later, Odeline is sitting between Ridley and John Kettle in the front seat of a camper van that Ridley has borrowed from 'a good friend'. It is extremely old and has no wing mirrors. The rear-view mirror is redundant as the rear window is boarded up with planks. John Kettle is driving as he is the only one of them with a driving licence. Ridley has the map on his lap. He says he knows where this detention centre is. 'Years of living in the shadows,' he said. 'I've friends who've been in and out of these places.' Ridley has a lot of friends, evidently. His head is sticking out of the window, calling out when it is safe to turn or change lanes. John Kettle does not like to indicate, it seems, blames the clutch every time he stalls and does not brake before turning – the result is that Odeline has been frequently flung against one or other of them. She has nothing to hold on to to keep herself upright so has slumped firmly back into her seat and wedged her knees against the dashboard. John Kettle says 'Excuse me' in an irritating faux-polite way every time he reaches under her feet for the gearstick.

John Kettle swings them on to the motorway and she is slammed once again into Ridley's warm, firm shoulder, which smells of washed cotton. He is wearing a short-sleeved cheesecloth shirt and Odeline, as ever, can't stop looking at the blues and browns of his arm.

She pulls herself upright and Ridley slides the map down the side of his seat.

'We stay on now for six junctions,' he says.

He has still offered no explanation of his recent whereabouts. She has been building up the courage to ask him all journey – now seems as good a time as any to take the plunge.

'Where have you been?' she asks.

'We've been moored up at Kensal Green.'

'The whole time?'

'Er, yeah. These past two weeks.'

'How long are you going to stay there?'

'I'm not sure. We were thinking of going west next week.'

'You and Angela?

'We three. Me, Marlon, *Saltheart*.'

'Is Angela your girlfriend?'

'Ha!' He laughs. 'She was once, a long time ago. Twelve years.'

'How old are you?' says Odeline, looking at the tough lines around his eyes, the tarnished gold of the rings through his eyebrow.

'I don't keep track,' he smiles. 'What'd be your reckoning?'

'Twenty-eight?' she guesses, thinking how old that sounds.

'Bollocks,' says John Kettle.

'Slightly north of that,' grins Ridley, 'but thanks.'

They bump along the slow lane of the M40. The holdall

containing Vera's things is on the floor in the back, wedged between a sofabed and a fridge with its door missing.

Odeline's moneybelt bulges against the waist of her suit trousers. An hour ago she went to the Post Office and released £5,000 from her funds in cash. The money is arranged around her middle in packets of £1,000. She keeps her hands folded over it. She has not told the others of her plan: to use this money to buy Vera's release.

Back at her boat this morning she mentally prepared herself for the rescue mission. She sat on her bed. Reality thumped through with every heartbeat. She thought of Vera and her life. She thought of double doors and the mattress with the sleeping bag and the tiny collection of books. She thought of the photograph. She thought of the clothes rack with the socks and the underwear, the towel. She thought of the toiletries on the chair. She had never apprehended another person's reality so directly. She felt embarrassed at having done so. Until now it has been her rule to keep a safe distance from other people's lives, other people's mundanity and messiness. She had always been repulsed by those sorts of tangles.

Odeline had arranged to meet Ridley and John Kettle at 11 a.m. outside the Lock Inn. She dressed lightly, in shirt, waistcoat, braces and trousers, imagining that her tailcoat might be cumbersome on the journey. When she came up from her cabin with the holdall there was an enormous bird perched silently on her roof. It was a grey heron like the ones she'd seen from the barge cafe during

one of her hot chocolates with Vera. She had never seen a
heron this side of the canal before, so close to human life.

Odeline looked at the heron and it looked back, blinking
along its long yellow beak, closing and opening eyes that
were perfect black dots in perfect yellow circles. It was
standing on one leg, with three yellow talons splayed for
support. This close, it struck Odeline as remarkable that
one twig leg could carry the whole oval bulk of the body.
Its head was folded into its shoulders and Odeline noticed
how the black-edged wings curved back to a point, like
the shape of a tailcoat. Its chest plumage was shaggy and
striped with black, but as she watched, it flattened, the
black stripes stretched, and the heron began to lift its head
and unfurl its neck. Odeline watched as the neck continued
to extend – impossibly long! The bird kept its eye on her
all this time, beak down. It blinked again, at full height,
its shape now a series of long, soft curves.

Odeline didn't hear what John Kettle called out from
behind her but watched in dismay as the bird flinched,
shook its huge wings out and then dipped its whole body
into lift-off. It took two wing beats towards her and then
turned away up the canal, its long legs hanging down and
then straightening behind the body. She watched it go,
ignoring John Kettle, who called her name and then called
it a second time. As the bird reached a steady height over
the water its wings slowed and Odeline imagined the up
and down movements were breaths in and breaths out.
She thought of the badger-haired accordion player on
Angela's boat widening his arms to stretch the accordion
and then bringing them together.

The bird dipped under the far bridge and John Kettle

called out again. She walked past him and on to the pub without answering.

Odeline has no idea whether they are travelling north, south, east or west. Even when Ridley showed her the place on the map she couldn't orient herself. I must get better at geography, she thinks. It will be essential once I am a fully qualified steerer.

They turn off the motorway and swing wildly on to a roundabout in front of an estate car which holds its horn at them as it follows.

'You almost killed us, you stupid man,' snaps Odeline, picking herself up from John Kettle's blue-shirted arm, which stinks of sweat and tobacco, and has bits of soil living in its creases.

'I'd like to see you lot try and drive this bloody death-trap,' shouts John Kettle. He grimaces as he reaches under Odeline's legs and pulls the gearstick down. The engine screams and he jiggles the stick, shunts it back up again. 'Absolute effing tin can.'

'Off here,' says Ridley. And then, 'You did pull out without looking, John.'

'Where's your bloody driving licence then?' He turns the steering wheel with both hands as if he is pulling in a rope. They swing off the roundabout and the estate car's horn trails away. 'Get some driving lessons and then come and tell me what's what.'

'Left in about a mile. I did start learning once and then I thought, there just don't need to be any more cars on the roads.'

John Kettle sniffs.

'Do you disapprove, John?' says Ridley, leaning forward.

'Bloody gypsy,' grins John Kettle through his beard. To Odeline's surprise they both start laughing.

On Ridley's instructions John Kettle takes a left and they drive along a tall wire fence before coming to a barrier in the road. Ahead is a square building painted dirty pink, with small blue barred windows and a brick porch. Other buildings in the same colours stretch out behind it and the wire fence continues around the whole compound. There are small patches of green grass in the car park in front of the central building with rubbish bins positioned on them. It is quite like the motorway service station they visited on the way out of London.

John Kettle leans out of the window and presses a button next to the barrier.

'I'll speak,' says Odeline and leans over him. There is a fuzzy ringtone and then a voice.

'Reception.'

'We are here for a visit.'

'You got a permit?'

'The name is Vera Novak, she is a resident here.'

'Official permits only.'

'We need to park our vehicle.'

'This is a staff car park. Visitor access is by foot.'

'But we're not on foot. We're in a camper van.'

The line cuts out and Odeline reaches forward to press the button again. This time the ringtone fuzzes on and on. She presses it again: the same.

Ridley opens the door and jumps down. 'Why don't you go on and start making the enquiries. I'll help John park somewhere and we'll join you in there.'

'All right.' Odeline shuffles out of the seat.

'Righto.' John Kettle begins shunting the gearstick around. 'Where the bloody hell is reverse?'

Ridley gets the holdall from the back of the van and helps Odeline lift it on to her shoulder. 'Good luck,' he says. 'We'll be quick as we can.'

Odeline walks across the car park crookedly, the holdall straps cutting into her shoulder. She should have worn her tailcoat for extra padding. She keeps one hand resting on her moneybelt. At the entrance to the main building she turns around and sees the camper van shunt violently back into the grass verge behind the barrier: Ridley and John Kettle both give a thumbs-up signal through the windscreen. She walks through a revolving door into the centre.

The reception area is starkly lit with a flecked linoleum floor and rows of blue fabric seats linked by metal bars and screwed into the ground. There are people sitting at intervals along the rows: a withered old couple with two bin bags of clothes on their laps; a man in a turban with a grey plastic suitcase; two young men in jeans sprawled across several chairs; a young woman leaning forward to talk to a child in a pram. At the far end, slightly separate, sit a cluster of people in suits with briefcases, flicking through papers on their lap. They don't look up when Odeline comes in. All the others do.

There is a window opposite the seats, with an officer leaning on a counter below a square clock. Odeline goes straight up and puts the holdall down on the linoleum beside her.

'I'm here to collect Vera Novak.'

'Name again, madam?'

'Vera Novak.'

He taps away at something for a minute.

'Nothing here about a release. Look. Says here her case hasn't even been heard yet.'

Odeline unzips her moneybelt and brings out three of the clear plastic packets of fifty-pound notes. She places them on her side of the counter and, fixing the official with a look she's practised – the look of a seasoned conspirator – she slides them towards the glass.

'I'd like to collect her now, please.'

The officer straightens. 'Madam, you'd better put those away. I'm not sure I understand your meaning and I'm not going to ask. There are other people in this reception area.' He gestures with his eyes to the people on the seats. 'You are making yourself vulnerable, miss.'

Odeline nods – she gets the message – and pulls out another two packets, puts them down on the counter.

'Madam. There are cameras in all four corners of this reception area.' He points to one in the back of his booth. 'I strongly recommend you put those back where they came from.'

'I need to get Vera Novak out of this place.'

'There is a proper process for that, madam. Perhaps you could discuss this with Miss Novak herself. She will have been briefed on the procedure. You might get a visit this afternoon but I can't guarantee it. Name?'

'Odeline.'

'Your full name, please, miss, plus surname.'

'Odeline Milk.' Her throat is suddenly tight. Her nose feels hot and runny. She stuffs the bags of cash back into her moneybelt. 'Are you going to send her back? To her country. It's terrible –'

The officer points along the counter to a stand with leaflets in it. 'Read the information. All legal options are outlined in there.'

'I've brought a bag of her things.'

'They'll have to be checked if you get a visit. When you get called up, take them to the window round the corner.' He points along the counter again.

Odeline takes a leaflet and carries the holdall across to the front row of blue seats. She puts the bag on the floor and places a foot either side, squeezing it tight to guard it from anyone who might think to snatch it. But the people in the reception area don't look especially threatening, even the sprawled young men in ripped jeans have stopped their talk and seem smaller now they are inanimate. The people at the other end in suits keep themselves demonstrably busy scribbling and flipping over their papers. But the rest of the waiting people are inactive; their eyes look ahead and their faces are blank. They look as though they have been there for hours, reduced now to statues under the electric glow of the strip lighting.

The old man in the turban is as still as the others, but his expression can be read – his brow lopsided, his mouth dropped open as if he has just been punched. Odeline knows this look now. That is despair, she thinks, that is the mask of despair. He holds on to the handle of his plastic suitcase, which stands by the side of his chair. He is holding on to it tightly. The skin is strained yellow over his knuckles. She wonders what is in there, and why he is holding on as if it is the only thing in the world keeping him on the ground.

She looks down into the unzipped holdall at her feet. At the top is *Jane Eyre* with an edge of the photograph sticking out. Odeline leans forward and slides it out. Vera's parents in grainy black-and-white. Scrubbed and proud and full of hope. With Vera's eyes, Vera's mouth, framed by the doorway, she thinks, of Vera's school.

It stiffens Odeline's resolve. She will study the detention centre leaflet and work out what to do. She will hire an army of professional people in suits with briefcases to fight their case. She will not let Vera be one of those people swallowed up by the unfairness of the world.

She slides the photograph back in between the pages of the book, and shifts the towel around the books in the holdall so they don't get damaged.

And then she hears a sound, so close it seems to have come from just behind her head, and so familiar she registers it without surprise. It is the sound of her mother's pencil scratching across the columns of an account book, and with it the heavy breathing that accompanied her concentration. Odeline hears it as clearly as if she had just walked into the kitchen in Arundel.

She twists to the right and left to look around her, but there is no one writing with a pencil, no one there on the seats beside or behind her. She knew there wasn't. It wasn't a sound from the reception area of the detention centre, it had come from somewhere else. She knows this more certainly than she has known anything in the last weeks.

And with it she remembers: the top of her mother's head as she bends over the account books at the kitchen table, wiry auburn chunks of hair shaking with the effort of pressing the numbers into the columns. Shoulders moving up and down as she breathes roughly in, roughly out. Eleven-year-old Odeline going to the edge of the table and her mother looking up, the concentration dropping away, her face beaming into a smile. She taps on the table for Odeline to sit down, and Odeline does, hooking her satchel strap over the back of the kitchen chair. She is already tall, her knees press against the underneath of the table. Her mother picks up a big parcel from behind the pile of account books and pushes it across. The parcel has 'INTERNATIONAL MAGIC' written across the top, with a shooting-star motif. Odeline looks up and her mother nods at her to open it, wrapping each hand around the other in anticipation. Tearing open the end, Odeline takes out: a copy of the *International Magic* magazine with a picture of Paul Daniels on the front in a top hat and tailcoat; a magic wand; a deck of cards with the shooting-star motif on the back; a postcard of the nineteenth-century illusionists Maskelyne and Cooke; a pair of glasses with mirrored lenses.

This was the first parcel Odeline's mother ordered, as Odeline's interest was just beginning. Soon she would dress up in her mother's coats and make things disappear up the sleeves – and Eunice Milk would send off for something after every month's pay. She would sit and peer through the catalogues with the same concentration as she peered at her account books.

She remembers this, now; it is right there before her

eyes. And soon there are other scenes. The silent laughter of the woman on the sofa watching Buster Keaton on the television, one hand covering her gaping mouth, the other squeezing Odeline's with excitement. The frowning woman hunched on the sofa stitching 'O.MILK' into the items of Odeline's school uniform with blue thread. The single figure marching, head forward, down the street, thrusting the Arundel Magic business card into people's hands. What a contrast with the circus clown in hemp clothing, worshipped by his troupe, who had asked, eyes twinkling, about the house in Arundel. Quizzed her about the inheritance. Belittled her plans. Tapped at her moneybelt. Turned away before he had finished waving her goodbye.

Odeline feels shame now – a deep, sharp shame – for having been embarrassed by her mother. For having wished for the romance of her father. She could have had no other parent, she sees that now. Her head dips and she feels humility rise up her body, the hotness of having been so deeply wrong. She has not been worthy of such a mother. She has been so far from grateful. She is grateful now. So grateful.

There is a click from above the reception desk and the memory breaks. The hour on the clock has changed: 2.00. Next to the time, the clock's black and white display shows the day, the month and the year. It is a familiar date. Odeline looks down and unzips her moneybelt, taking out three tickets. She unfolds them to check the date and time of the performance. She is missing Marcel Marceau.

THIRTY-TWO

Vera is sitting on her bed, the bottom mattress on an iron bunk in a room she shares with a Kenyan woman, Nadra, who has been here for seven months. She is the Kenyan woman's fourth roommate; all the others have been sent back to their respective countries: Colombia, the Philippines and Lithuania. Nadra has had three different lawyers take her case so far, each one has done nothing and then dropped it. She says that without money it is hard to get the lawyers to stick. She is meeting a new lawyer this afternoon who sounds better than the others. But she's thought that before.

Vera has the room to herself while Nadra meets her new lawyer. This is a relief. She is not used to living so near to another person, with no privacy at all. She finds it very difficult to do things like dress and wash her face in the same room as someone else. And she finds it hard having to talk so much. But her roommate seems happy to have someone to discuss her case with. Vera doesn't have an opinion and finds it hard to think of what to say in reply. The main problem, though, is this: she feels she cannot process what has happened or develop an opinion on her own case until she is safe in a room by herself. This has been her only request since entering the detention centre and it has been refused.

They have given her an outfit of a blue shirt and tracksuit bottoms, which she is wearing now with her trainers.
It is fine. Not too hot. The window in the room is barred
but quite large and can open wide. Looking from the bed
she can see the toilet and sink which annexe the room.
There is graffiti scratched into the annexe wall in various
languages – Vera has counted seventeen different languages
that she can recognise. Most of the graffiti is written in
English, though, and refers to the prison-like aspects of
the detention centre, the treatment of detainees as criminals. Vera is not cheered by this – she would like to write
something beautiful instead of anger and swear words and
complaints. She would like to fill a wall with the Christina
Rossetti poem she once taught her class to recite by heart:

> Come to me in the silence of the night
> Come in the speaking silence of a dream
> Come to me with soft rounded cheeks and eyes as
>   bright
> As sunlight on a stream.
> Come back in tears
> Oh memory, hope, love of finished years.

Vera finds some poetry over-sentimental but has always
loved this. And it is right. All she has now is everything
she can remember.

In some ways this state of affairs is a relief. Even with
nothing, it is a relief to be out in the open. Living in hiding:
there is self-censorship, self-surveillance and fear. You have
to be your own secret police – hardly better than living
under the new regime at home. Now the worst has

happened, she would not change it. This is an odd thing to realise.

When she'd heard the knocking on the barge cafe door she'd thought perhaps it was Mr Zjelko come back to check up on her. He'd been there just before lunch, telling her there'd been a crackdown recently – officials out checking papers. He'd spoken as though he expected her to do something about it; she knew all she could do was pray she'd be lucky. But she didn't expect him to come checking at eight o'clock at night – perhaps he'd discovered she was sleeping on the boat? Had John Kettle told him? She kept still, sitting on her stool at the counter, and turned the radio right down. There was more knocking and some talking – more than one person out there. Had Zjelko brought his thugs? What would he need them for? Her heart started to knock so hard that she could hear it in her head. Each beat muted everything else. She brought a hand to her chest to try and muffle it, keep it in.

'Vera Novak,' said a tired English voice, 'we have reason to believe you are residing in this country on an expired visa. We also believe you are working for a wage without the required documentation.'

'Vera Novak?' the voice repeated.

Vera kept absolutely still.

'Sarge?' said another voice. There was a pause.

'Go in.'

With the first blow to the door Vera tripped off the stool, which clattered underneath her, and pressed herself to the back wall of the barge. As the doors splintered inwards she looked around to check she had left nothing out. There was just her tracksuit top on the back of a chair. Everything else was hidden. There was another blow to the right-hand door and the top half came off its hinges and swung back. A head in a policeman's cap ducked into the doorway to look inside.

'She's here.'

'Bring her in,' said the first voice.

As the man in the doorway kicked open the bottom half of the door and stepped down into the barge, Vera backed along the wall, pulling the stool in front of her.

The policeman lifted his hands up, smiling, as if she was holding a gun. He was tall, narrow-headed, stooped under the barge ceiling.

'Speak any English?'

Vera took the edge of the stool and lifted it towards him like a lion-tamer.

'It's going to need all of us, Sarge,' the man called out. Two more men stepped into the barge and the first man edged towards her.

Remembering this, Vera feels foolish. What did she think, that they could be scared away like pigeons? One of the two new arrivals stood in the doorway while the other sidled along the far wall and reached for the stool legs. 'Come on now,' he said, baring his teeth a little – she remembers the flash of yellow. She pulled away from him and shot back into the corner by the counter. The tall man lunged forward to grab the stool, knocking over the coffee machine and tipping a stack of salad plates on to the floor. They smashed at Vera's feet and she looked down to see the triangles of patterned china washed up around her trainers.

In the end they had shepherded her out like dogs with a sheep. At the threshold the tall man handcuffed her wrist to his. 'No more funny business,' he nodded slowly. 'Quite a little fighter,' he said to the others.

'She looks bloody terrified,' said the one with the teeth.

At least in this place she has access to the news on television. For the first time she can know about everything that is happening at home, not just snippets of radio and other people's discarded newspapers. She has seen terrible images of home. Tanks rolling into villages, along empty streets. Soldiers with flags. Women crying and pleading to the television cameras, lifting their children up to be filmed. They have declared it a civil war. When she told her roommate this, she seemed excited. 'This means you can stay,' she said. She had clasped Vera's hand in her hard, warm palms. 'They will recognise you as a refugee. It is a bad thing to say, but I wish I had your situation. I wish I was running from civil war. For me, it is just my family. And they will send me back to them.'

Vera said, 'But with a good lawyer?'

'Yes. Maybe.'

Nadra looked tired. She squeezed Vera's hand once more and said, 'You must find a good lawyer too. If you have money, pay for one. Then you have a good chance. Better chance than me.'

Vera does not know how to begin to do this. She cannot afford to pay for a good lawyer; she has no money.

And she has no energy. Even the effort of washing has left her exhausted. She can barely manage to shuffle out of her room, along the corridor and down the stairs to the canteen each day for meals. Hiding for so long has taken everything from her. Every day listening out, every day watching out. Her body is heavy as concrete. All she can bear to do is sit on her bunk, and think.

And her thoughts here are turning to home, to life there before the troubles. Was there some hubris in thinking she could carry on learning, could perhaps one day travel? Could continue to follow her curiosity? What was so impossible about this idea of life? Her hopes had not weighed against anyone else's. Her dreams took from no one. She had needed nothing from anybody else, except perhaps to be left in peace.

Peace.

The loss of peace – it swallows up everybody's dreams.

She flinches, interrupted by a loud thud on the door. It swings open and an officer puts his head round, then opens it wide when he sees her sitting on the bed.

'Vera Novak? Visitor.'

THIRTY-THREE

The boat *Chaplin and Company* sits in the water by the bridge at Little Venice. It sits alone. Most of the summer cruisers left a few weeks ago. The duckweed has broken up now, dissolved, lining only the water's edge, hugging its litter – packets, bottles, cans – to the wall of the canal. The day is cloudy but windless, the water is unmoving and shows the bridge perfectly in its green-hued surface. Likewise, the boat's reflection butterflies out beneath it, completely still, discoloured by the water and appearing almost as solid as the boat itself. The canal is quieter now; many of the geese have begun their migrations and the young ducks and moorhens have separated from their parents so are no longer moving around in noisy flocks. There are no birds around the boat, but their faint calls can be heard from beyond the bridge, where they weave between each other below the porthole of the barge cafe, waiting for scraps. There is the distant roar of traffic from the Westway, and the occasional noise of a car or bike on the small roads that run two or three metres above the level of the towpath. A halfworld up, a halfworld apart.

These are the dead hours of mid-afternoon, when the momentum of the day stops, pauses, before tipping on towards the evening. The light is static and it is as if the earth itself has held its turning. These are the longest hours. In the sky above, even the clouds are not moving. Still as a photograph.

But now, from beyond the bridge, there is the faint sound of an engine. It is the phut-phut of a very old motor, rising and falling like the rhythmic turnover of a steam train. Different to the constant drone of modern engines. The sound comes closer and a shape appears below the bridge. It is the low, flat shape of a packet boat. The sound of the motor is amplified as it moves through the blackness under the bridge, and then the boat emerges into daylight. Its bow pushes through the green surface of the canal, folding the water back in lines that travel out and out and wash the hem of duckweed up the concrete banks of the towpath.

The boat moves slowly. As it comes out from under the bridge the line of sunlight moves along it, giving colour. Richly varnished cabin doors at the front have brass handles and hinges. The body of the boat is blue with a red border outline around its sides. There are four shining brass portholes along the length of the boat. In the centre of these is an arc of white writing that reads *Chaplin and Company*, underneath is written *Est. 1936*. The writing gleams so sharply it looks like lacquer. The bowl of the boat is tarred matt black. Old-fashioned rope buffers hang over the side. A man stands at the tiller, baseball cap jammed low over long hair which is as cleanly white as the script on the boat's side. His expression isn't clear, but he is holding himself still. Rigidly still.

Then he pushes the brass handle away and the nose of the boat begins to swing in towards the bank. It is heading for the boat moored there, the one with tired decking, doors bleached by weather, a patchy blue body with chipped paint, yellowed plastic buoys hanging over the side – but whose lettering reads the same. The same arc, the same script, the same date beneath. A faded, discoloured version of the approaching vessel, a watery reflection.

The second boat pulls in behind its twin and the timbre of its motor changes as the stern swings round towards the bank. As the knotted-rope buffers nudge the towpath's edge, the man straightens the rudder and steps down into his cabin. The engine cuts out and the scene is silent again, only disturbed by the boat's wake, which laps briefly at the bank and then subsides. The man steps on to the towpath with rope in his hand and leans down to knot it around a mooring hook. He does all this deftly despite his size, though the exertion shows when he lifts a sleeve to wipe the line of pink forehead beneath his cap, and blows out from beneath a thick white muzzle of moustache. He walks to the front of the boat and knots the bow rope around another mooring hook.

As he straightens he looks at the boat in front and his rounded chest pulls sharply upwards, as if in shock. He takes a step forward. The boats are so close they are almost touching, bow to stern. He brings one hand up and reaches out with it, touching a patch of bubbled blue paint which cracks under his fingers. He runs his hand along the side and around the old, blackened brass of a porthole. The glass is cracked and dusted with dirt. He takes off his baseball cap, his white hair flattened in a circle where it sat, and presses his forehead to the side of the boat. His eyes are closed. He is muttering something.

After a minute the man straightens, looks along the towpath, to the left and right, and then steps aboard the weathered boat. He pulls a small brass windlass from his belt. He touches his fingers to the cabin doors and then pushes the narrow end of the windlass into the lock. With a grunt he wrenches it and splits the white plastic bolt from the wood of the door. The windlass clatters to the deck. He runs his hand up the door and pulls at the top corner. As it opens, he gasps.

He ducks his head and steps down into the engine room.

Immediately, he sees the fold-down shelf that Walt Chaplin used as a bed, and the engine compartment underneath. The engine has been replaced with a three-valve model. The fuel gauge reads empty. All the surrounding wood is new – pine rather than oak. But whoever did it has replicated the engine compartment exactly. A boiler has been fixed on to the internal wall and there is a large black case parked in the corner. But the compass still sits in the ceiling of this room, the bowl of glass murky with dust and flaked paper. He taps at the glass and the needle quivers. He looks around the engine room doorway and sees a bathroom cubicle has been added, with a chemical toilet, sink and showerhead. He steps through to the main cabin and his eyes travel down the length of it. He knows the dimensions, the curves and the corners of it. He has built them himself. He has re-created every inch in oak.

When he was last here the cabin was empty of furniture, just stacked with different crates and sacks of cargo. As he looks around, he feels anger at the objects and built-in units that invade the space. They should not be here. There are pictures stuck to the walls. He walks around the cabin and pulls these down, one by one. They leave pins in the walls and he works these out with his fingernails. He rolls them up and then untacks the strips of film reel stuck to the porthole glass above the bed. He slips these into the middle of the roll and takes it to the engine room, where he posts it out of the porthole on to the towpath. They land on their ends and open outwards as they fall flat. On the top is an image of a clown in white with black ballet shoes, a crushed top hat and a rosebud mouth in a circle of spotlight against a black backdrop. He is listening to something invisible in his palm, his eyes round with wonder.

The man goes to the shelving unit, unloading handfuls of books and videos on to the floor. He tilts the shelves backwards and bumps them up the steps to the deck. Heaves them on to the towpath. He goes back in and stacks the books and videos into piles, carries each pile up to the deck and drops it on the towpath. He picks up the orange and brown chair (with an Arnott's biscuit tin on the seat), lifting it high as he backs up again to the deck. He puts this on the towpath next to the shelves.

Back inside, he can't stop: unplugs the mini fridge from the kitchen and carries this out, then some food packets that have been left out on the kitchen surface. He wheels the large plastic case out of the engine room and fills it with any loose thing he can see: a paper bag of film reels, a postcard of two punks with the message 'WELCOME TO LONDON'. Up to the deck again, he swings the case on to the towpath and goes back down to the cabin. He puts the lid back on a brown cardboard box that is on the bed, and rolls the mattress and quilt around it, then carries this bundle outside to put it next to the other things. There

is a screwdriver on the floor and he starts to unscrew the
bed from the wall. He unscrews, with some difficulty,
the rest of the cupboard units from the kitchen, and the
counter which juts out from the wall. He even detaches
the cooker. He carries these things outside one by one so
as not to knock the cabin doors. It is time-consuming,
back-wrenching work – he hasn't emptied the cupboards,
so each of them is an even heavier task than it needs to
be. He undoes the light fittings between each porthole and
pulls the wiring out from the wall. He unhooks the rhinestone mirror from the bathroom, painstakingly removes
the chemical toilet and carries them outside.

Then he comes back in to unscrew the boiler from the
engine room, takes his sweatshirt off and drags the boiler
along the floor on it. This is the hardest work yet: heaving
it up and over the side of the deck on to the towpath. It
hits the ground with a tinny crack.

There are dark arcs of wetness around the breast of his
shirt and down his entire back, but he puts his sweatshirt
back on, now lined with oil and dirt from the boiler. He
looks around the walls of the main cabin. Against the
bleached, worn planks, the shapes of the cupboards and
light fittings are drawn in rich, shiny varnish.

When he knew this boat the floors were waxed canvas
over oak boards. He bends down and touches the carpet
that is here now, squares of ribbed orange felt that are
faded to yellow in the areas below each porthole. He pulls
at a corner and sees boards underneath; they are pine and
look as though they are in good condition. He pulls harder
and rips up a whole piece of carpet. The glue has dried and
it pulls up easily. Yes, the boards underneath are hardly

damaged. Good colour. He tugs at another corner of carpet, then another, and he moves along the cabin doing this with each square, stacking them as he goes along. When they are all up he takes the squares out and puts them on top of the boiler.

He walks back along the towpath to the boat behind. He goes inside for a few moments and comes out carrying a toolbox, a plastic fuel can and a stack of papers crammed into a plastic bag. The papers are all different sizes and colours, torn at their edges. There are rows of numbers in the corners of some of the sheets and degree angles marked out. The man carries the bag and the toolkit over and puts them on to the deck of the first boat. On the towpath the discarded cupboards are stacked high, watching him. The orange and brown chair waits patiently beside them. As he walks past, he hears a rip beneath his feet. He looks down at the sound. He's torn the corner of the clown poster. He stares at it a moment, and at the other things around.

He makes a decision: drops his toolkit, dumps the fuel can and his bag of papers on to the deck of the old boat. And then, load by load, he takes all of these possessions to the boat behind, the boat he built, carrying them in through the cabin doors, placing them carefully on the varnished wood floor. The kitchen cupboards he arranges in a U shape at the end like she had them, putting the oven in the middle of them and the sink on the right, with the fridge below, still connected to its gas canister. All is as it was. It takes him almost three hours. He screws the boiler to the engine room wall and parks the big black case in the corner. He opens up the bed, unrolls the mattress and quilt on to it, then folds the bed up and props

it against the wall. He sets up the chair with the Arnott's
tin next to it. He pins the picture of the black and white
clown on the wall opposite the bed, pushing the ripped
corner under the edge of the pin. When all these things
are in place, he lays the squares of orange carpet on to the
planked floor of his boat.

When he comes out his face is a mask, unblinking. This
is the moment, the absolute moment of his life. Every
muscle of his body aches. But he has done the right thing.

He walks back along the towpath towards the old boat.
He unscrews a cap on the steering deck and pushes in the
nozzle of his fuel can. Keeps his eyes cast down as it flows
out. Screws the cap back on and leans on his knee to stand.
Walks to the bow and unties the rope from the mooring
hook, then does the same with the rope at the stern,
throwing it on deck before stepping on himself. There is
no wind and the water is still but the boat's nose begins
to turn away from the bank slightly, as if it wants to go.
As if she is ready to go. The buoys nudge gently at the
bank and the boat seems to release, to sink very slightly
into the water, giving a sound like a sigh.

The man knows this sound, he remembers it.

He leans down into the engine room and switches the
motor on. It takes a few seconds to come to life and then
rises to a humming pitch. He blinks his eyes. Thank you.
Thank you. The boat starts to move forward off the
mooring. The man picks up the old windlass from the
deck and tucks it into his belt. He takes hold of the tiller
and touches the handle of the windlass with his other
hand, feeling the familiar grooves. He stands upright and
looks along the roof to the open canal ahead. There are

silent glistening channels running over his red cheeks and into his moustache. The tears run on down and make dark drops on the chest of his sweatshirt. They fade and mix with the oily lines and smudge from the boiler.

The boat is moving into the middle of the water and heads out, away from the barge cafe, the blue-railinged bridge, the willow tree of Little Venice island, the heron standing at the water's edge. Past the balconies of the tower blocks, past the shape of the dirty brick spire in their centre. It travels out past the skateboard park and the allotments, past the eyeless warehouses with their boarded windows, under bridges, past a squat supermarket building. The engine turns over, gently, happily, and it chugs along a blind stretch of canal where a woman walks weightless in crumpled beige clothes, lashless eyes looking out behind pale panels of hair. She lifts a birdlike hand to her mouth when she sees the boat, grips the other around a chain of amber beads hanging from her neck. She stands there, frozen, as it passes her. On and on, the boat travels. It continues out past the last tower blocks, towards the edges of West London, out through once bombed suburbs, past the dockyards, the wharves, and the derelict factories, through unlit patches of countryside and towns where the canalsides have been left to rot, through water edged with litter and industrial waste, where banks of billboards have been built to keep this from view, under bridges and over aqueducts, through tree tunnels of forgotten waterways, through lock and lock and lock.

He does not look back.

The boy will steer the boat home. He will hold a steady course. He will keep on through the night until morning. He will not stop until he has brought her home.

THIRTY-FOUR

Odeline peers through the window of the oven. She has wiped the glass with a cloth but still can't see the sausage rolls in the gloom, only the edge of the foil they are sitting on. There is a button with a bulb symbol on the panel of the oven, but when she presses it, it just clicks repeatedly. She opens the door and sticks out a finger to touch the top of a sausage roll. Stone cold. They should have been cooking now for ten minutes. Why did she not think of testing the oven before tonight?

She turns the temperature dial back to zero and opens the cupboard on the right, where the gas canister sits. It's not connected. She leans on the kitchenette counter to peer behind the unit. At the back of the oven is a cascade of wiring. Nothing is connected to the wall. And there isn't even a socket.

The whole place has come loose. The carpet squares unstuck from the floor. The wardrobe and bookshelves: no longer attached to the walls. The bed which crashes, hingeless, to the floor when she tries to pull it down.

British Waterways. When she came back from the detention centre three and a half weeks ago, she had to admit they'd responded to her complaint impressively. She returned to find they had revarnished the walls, repainted the outside and removed much of the personalised interior she'd protested about. But they didn't finish the job. The plumbing has been only rudimentarily reconnected, so that she has just hot water from both taps in the sink. And this sink is where she has had to wash, floss and brush, since they also demolished the entire bathroom, leaving only the rhinestone mirror hanging on a random wall and the chemical toilet sitting in the open cabin. She has moved it into the engine compartment.

And now the oven. Odeline has already filled in a complaint form at the office in Lisson Grove; now she will have to go back to add this in an appendix. She doesn't have time for these inconveniences – every hour of her day is valuable. In the last three and a half weeks, Odeline has been interviewing a team of lawyers to fight Vera's case. She has settled on a firm called Morpe Partners, who have an 82 per cent success rate. She would have liked to find a higher rate, but this firm, it appears, has the highest available.

If Odeline has to spend every penny of her inheritance, she will. But, at these rates, she has to be certain she has the best possible service. She has interviewed each member of the team and paid for their time as she did so. She wanted assurances that these lawyers would not drop Vera's case, that they would not make false or misleading promises, and that they would use every legal finesse available to make sure Vera is allowed to stay. She has asked each one to give a brief performance of how they would argue Vera's case in court. Those who were unwilling to audition she has asked to have replaced. To lead the case she has chosen a 37-year-old woman who gave a clear and heartfelt account of her parents' own battle for asylum. This woman has a first-class degree and fourteen years' experience in immigration law.

The legal team at Morpe Partners believe that Vera has a good chance – the international recognition of civil war is going to help. Odeline has bought books on immigration law and the asylum process, and goes to their glass-walled offices daily, her notebook full of queries. The legal team have said that they are keen to resolve Vera's situation promptly. But they cannot give a precise date.

Odeline has been to the detention centre only once since her first visit, to update Vera on the proceedings. It is a lengthy journey by coach and she has preferred to use her time constructively at the lawyers' office. But it was good to see her friend. She bought her some hot chocolate powder, some cereal bars, and some *Reader's Digest* magazines that she saw for sale at a stall on Harrow Road. She waited in the visiting room and sat at the same table, the one by the window. Outside, the miserable staff car park with its bins sitting on the islands of grass. And running around the whole compound, the teeth of the tall wire fence.

Vera's squat figure came through a door and lumbered over to the table. She was in the same blue shirt, tracksuit bottoms and trainers as the first visit, and as emotional. As soon as she sat down her eyes began to crease into little pumps, pushing out tears, and her thick lips wobbled. Odeline kept her hands linked on her lap, out of reach. She waited for Vera to stop squeaking into her tissue before continuing with her news.

'They couldn't give me an exact percentage for the case

to succeed, but they estimated between eighty-five and ninety per cent.'

'That is wonderful,' said Vera through the handful of tissue. 'Wonderful.'

'Would you be willing to testify to your mistreatment at the hands of your brother-in-law and the other extremists in your town?'

'Yes,' Vera nodded. 'I can tell them about that.'

'We need to arrange a meeting as soon as possible.'

'How much is this costing?'

'It doesn't matter.'

'Odi, you must not spend your savings on me.'

'Yes I must.'

At this, Vera's lip shook and the tears began to pump out again. Embarrassed, Odeline took her notebook out, but before she could note anything down, Vera had thrown her squishy little hands across the table and was clasping Odeline's, trapping the notebook and pen inside her hot grasp.

'Thank you. Thank you, Odi. You don't know how I am so grateful –'

'All right,' said Odeline and straightened her fingers to escape. 'Can I just write this down?'

'Of course. I am sorry.'

Odeline put the cap of the biro from one end to the other and bent over her notebook.

'I can't believe it,' Vera said, wiping each eyebrow with the tissue. 'I can't believe someone can do this for me. You are a true friend.' Odeline, underlining the words 'Willing to Testify' in her notebook, felt the corners of her mouth pull into a smile. A big, beaming smile, which – she couldn't help it – pulled back to expose her teeth and made her forget what she was writing.

'It makes me happy,' she said, looking up.

But something had caught Vera's eye:

'Odi, new shoes!'

Odeline looks down beyond the tails of her coat at her new plimsolls. Black canvas with an elastic half moon in the centre and a lightweight rubber edging. Another discovery on Harrow Road. £1.50 a pair and an elegant alternative to her brogues. Almost like a tightrope walker's slippers. After wearing them for a morning she had gone back to the stall and bought six more pairs. They were sublimely comfortable, soft and giving, and yet hugged her feet more securely than the brogues ever had. They were so thin soled that she felt she could be walking barefoot, a shoeless joe! And they didn't have the brogue's hard heel – so that now, standing in her boat, she doesn't have to sink her head into her shoulders to avoid scraping it on the ceiling. Life one centimetre lower is a lot easier.

But the sausage rolls! She opens the oven door and lifts them out on the foil. She checks her pocket watch. The minute hand is above quarter to, the hour hand on six. People will be arriving in *under fifteen minutes*. The cartons of white wine are set up in a row along the sideboard but she hasn't even organised the seating yet, or put out glasses, or plates for the sausage rolls, which will have to be eaten cold. Very cold – there are crystals of ice around the bases where they have not yet defrosted. She opens a top cupboard and takes out eight of the tall glasses with sliced limes cascading down the side, and eight lime green formica plates. There is a bag of charcoal in the cupboard behind the remaining plates and she lifts it out, remembering the dismantled barbecue in the end cupboard. Looking into the bin bag with the rusted barbecue parts inside, her heart sinks. She has thirteen minutes to put this together.

There is a tap on the porthole and she looks up to see John Kettle's grinning beard behind the glass. 'Ahoy there!' He wriggles his fingers in a wave. She shoots him a dark look and carries the bag of barbecue parts up, dumping it on the deck. It is windy outside, a brisk autumn evening. The edges of the trees are yellowing and leaves are swirling through the air, landing on the water.

'You cannot look in through people's portholes, John Kettle,' she snaps. 'It is extremely intrusive.'

He straightens. 'I'm here for the party,' he says with the side of his mouth, a rolled cigarette clamped between his lips. He is looking neater than usual, denim shirt tucked into his jeans, which are tightly belted. His top button is done up and a roll of grey-bearded neck spills over it.

'You're early,' says Odeline, and tips the corners of the bag so that the barbecue parts come clattering out.

'What's this you're doing then?' He wanders a step or two along the towpath, towards the front of the boat. His walk is swaying, a sort of sashay. He takes the cigarette out of his mouth with a thumb and forefinger and blows smoke into the air.

'Have you been drinking?' barks Odeline.

'Not today,' he says. 'You have to take each day as it comes. Life is a journey, you know, Odeline.'

'What?'

'But I do have something to celebrate.'

Odeline lifts up the black pan of the barbecue and looks in bewilderment at the jumble of metal parts on the deck.

'Just got back from the Waterways office,' he continues, taking another suck of his cigarette. 'Reinstated!'

'As canal warden?' She picks out the grill and the barbecue tongs, both brown with rust, and rests them down on the deck.

'That is correct. Can't keep a good man down.'

'So you're allowed to harass people legally again.'

'I'm going to do the job properly this time. Really look after things. I've got a plan to do plant boxes down the towpath. Brighten up the whole area.'

Odeline doesn't answer. She is trying to identify which of the metal bars are the legs, and which make the stand for the barbecue pan to sit in.

'Trying to set something up? Need some help from your friendly canal warden?'

'Do you know how these things work?'

'Leave it to me,' he says and jumps on board.

'You can put that out,' says Odeline. 'This is a non-smoking boat.'

John Kettle chucks the fag end into the water and squats down to look at the barbecue parts. 'I'll have this up in no time,' he says. 'Mechanics was my thing. Submariner Kettle, can tinker with metal –'

'I've got to arrange the seating indoors,' she says, stepping back down into the cabin.

'Right you are, lassie. I'll give a shout when we're ready to spark her up.'

Odeline hears him whistling as she unstacks the chairs she has taken from outside the barge cafe. She arranges them into rows of four on either side of the cabin. She has folded the bed up against the wall to make more space. She looks around the interior. Although the low orange and brown chair is still in the corner, it certainly looks far more handsome without all the personalised furnishings it came with. The natural wood floor is stunning: wide boards of varnished pine. The porthole brass and windows gleam now. British Waterways even cleaned the compass glass.

'And we're all set,' calls John Kettle from the deck. 'Bring up your fuel and your fodder!'

Odeline balances the foil tray of sausage rolls on top of the charcoal bag and carries them both up. The barbecue is perched on the deck like a rusty UFO. She slides the foil tray on to the deck and hands the bag to John Kettle, who shakes the coals out into the barbecue pan. 'No meat?' he says.

'There is sausage inside the rolls.'

'Righto. And we need a touch paper, please. Anything will do.'

Odeline goes back inside and looks for some paper to use. She won't waste a page of her notebook, obviously, or the *A–Z*, or her account book, which she is now using to keep a log of lawyers' costs in case they charge for extra hours. (Her mother had warned her about lawyers in the typed pages of instructions that Odeline followed after her death.) She looks in the receipt box that lives

beneath the bed. Clearly she can't use her school certificates, or her birth certificate, or her passport. Or the
letter confirming ownership of *Chaplin and Company*.
Or any of the pages from her mother's daily logic puzzle
books. Or the stack of Arundel Magic business cards
that her mother had printed for her – these are precious
things.

There is one other item in her cardboard box, a brown
envelope containing a letter written in green-ink capitals,
a simple drawing of a house, a signature with a flourish
over the letter O. She takes it outside and hands it to John
Kettle. He pushes it under the coals and takes the lighter
from his shirt pocket to set it alight. The flame eats into
the corner of the brown envelope and then bursts into
dancing orange as it reaches the white paper inside. Odeline
watches as the line of fire crumbles her father's letter to
ash.

A horn booms along the water. Odeline turns to see
two boats coming down the canal in convoy. She recognises
the stacked roof of Ridley's *Saltheart*, the silhouette of
upturned bicycle, wheelbarrow, and string-bound towers
of chopped wood, like an alternative city skyline. The boat
behind is Angela's wide-hipped orange barge. Odeline can
see her at the tiller, hair piled up and buxom like a belle
époque barmaid. 'Quick!' she says, and transfers the
sausage rolls one by one from the foil on to the barbecue
grill.

'You leave this to me,' says John Kettle, picking up the
tongs. 'See to your guests.'

'All right.'

'You're welcome.'

Ridley's boat steers in and he throws a rope across to Odeline as he cuts the engine. 'Feels like the end of summer, doesn't it,' he says, pointing to the sky, the clouds rushing across it. 'Hello, John.'

'Ahoy there, my gypsy friend.' John lifts a hand as he prods a sausage roll into the middle of the grill with the tongs. 'I've good news to share with you once I've finished my shift at the campfire.'

Ridley crooks his eyebrow at Odeline, making the gold rings quiver. He is wearing a sheepskin waistcoat over a vest and a pair of shorts, but the tattoos make him appear cosily sleeved and trousered. 'Pull me in then,' he says, and Odeline pulls the rope through her hands until the *Saltheart*'s steering deck is bumping against her new rope buffers. Ridley ducks his head into his cabin. 'Philip,' he shouts. 'Moor us up the other end.' The tall, suited opera singer steps out from the other end of the cabin and steps a long leg over on to the *Chaplin and Company*, holding the tiller to pull himself across.

Angela's boat is now cruising into the towpath, and Odeline can see that there are more people next to her on the rear deck. The badger-haired man with his accordion slung over a shoulder, the blonde actress with the ear plaits, the fringed poet with the rectangular mouth, and the two identical little girls.

She had forgotten that the children would be coming. It was Ridley's idea to have the music and performance gathering in her newly decorated boat. It is starting to feel like a bombardment, that she is being ambushed from all sides.

Ridley comes out of his cabin holding his bow and

fiddle. 'Mustn't forget this!' Odeline rushes into her cabin
and goes to the sideboard. Should she pour the drinks
now or wait until everyone is on board? She pours four,
squeezing the wine-carton tap until the glasses are almost
full. She goes over to check the bed is sufficiently secure
against the wall. She rearranges the chairs so that they are
slightly further apart. In comes Philip the opera singer
from the rear deck, and Ridley from the front. He puts
his fiddle down on one of the chairs. She can smell burning
pastry from the barbecue outside.

'Would you like a drink?' she says, thrusting a glass of
wine at Philip.

He takes it. 'Very generous, thank you.'

'Would you like a drink?' She hands one to Ridley.

'Thanks,' he says. 'Is John in charge of catering?'

'Yes,' says Odeline, as Angela and her boisterous boatload thump down the steps into her cabin. Her little cabin
with her posters on the wall and her shelves full of books
and her wardrobe full of clothes darned by her mother.
She burns as she sees these people look around, taking it
in. The girls, wearing matching pink dresses, run up to
the bookshelves and run their fingers along the spines.
Hands off! Odeline wants to shout, but Ridley is standing
just by her and she wants to seem relaxed.

'Handsome boat,' says the badger-haired man.

'It's lovely,' says Angela, coming over, her girls gripping on to her myriad skirts. 'Thank you so much for
having us.'

'Would you like a drink?' says Odeline, thrusting out
another glass.

'I think we should drink a toast,' says Ridley, filling

more glasses from the wine cartons and handing one of them to her. He lifts his glass. 'To Odeline, who has been working so hard on our friend Vera's behalf.'

'No, no,' blinks Odeline, feeling them all look at her. She buries her nose in the glass of wine. It smells sharp, like the crate of shoes in the *Costumerie* at the Cirque Maroc.

'Hear, hear!' John Kettle's face appears through the cabin doors in a haze of smoke. 'And the rolls are ready. Shall I bring them in?'

Odeline turns to pick up the formica plates and lay them out on the counter. John comes down the steps slowly, hands under the foil tray of sausage rolls as if he is carrying a crown on a cushion. 'Put them down here,' says Odeline, and he slips the foil on to the edge of the counter. The sausage rolls are flaking, blackened, not quite recognisable, but smell quite good.

'Goodness,' says Angela. 'What delicacy is this? Are they Arabic?'

Odeline starts putting them on to the plates.

'Can I help myself to a drink then?' says John Kettle.

'You can have water.'

'No, thanks, trying to give it up.'

'You can only stay if you don't drink alcohol,' says Odeline, handing him two plates of sausage rolls. 'Give some of these out.' Ridley steps in to help deal out the plates and Odeline turns to fill a glass with cloudy hot water from the sink. 'Here you go,' she says to John Kettle as he comes back to the counter.

'Do I at least get to sample my cooking?' She hands him a plate and he goes over to the low orange and brown chair in the corner and sinks into it, taking a bite of the sausage roll. It leaves black flakes in his beard.

The others have taken seats along the walls of the cabin and are eating. 'Delicious,' says the badger-haired man, lifting half a roll in a salute to Odeline. The two girls are lifting the *Great London Theatres* book from her bookshelf.

'Girls,' Angela says, 'don't touch other people's possessions without asking.'

The girls hurtle over.

'Can we look at the book, please?' says one.

'Will you do the bird act again?' says the other, taking hold of her tailcoat and flapping it up and down. Odeline snatches it back.

'Yes, yes, yes!' shouts the other one, jumping up and down.

Angela laughs and ruffles the girl's head. 'You really loved that bird act, didn't you?' She raises her big eyebrows at Odeline. 'They've been talking about it ever since.'

'It's amazing!' shout the girls in unison, gazing up at Odeline. They are clasping their hands to her.

Their faces are wide and adoring. Beseeching.

They are holding their breath, imploring.

'Perhaps . . . perhaps I could do it again,' says Odeline.

The girls dance around each other, clapping. 'The bird, the bird!'

London's adult audiences may be just as philistine as Arundel's, thinks Odeline. But perhaps its children are more enlightened. Angela shepherds the girls to a seat at the end nearest the bookshelves and Odeline goes to sit opposite. Ridley is standing at the counter with his fiddle and bow.

'Right,' he says. 'Who's up first?'

Green to yellow on the canal as autumn curls the edges of the leaves and lets them fall. Blue to grey as autumn clouds the sky and the water's surface turns to iron, a metal ribbon that runs from west to east and billows out at this triangular junction, this soldered join where three paths meet. If summer beat down on this stretch of canal, compressed and cooked it, then autumn will whistle a breeze through, moving things on. Three boats by the bridge. From the smallest, the handsomest, the most polished and painted, comes the sound of a bow being drawn across strings, the first notes of a slow song, which leak from this boat and travel with the breeze, up, out, along the water.

The woman walking along the towpath towards the bridge, she knows the words. *My funny valentine, sweet, comic valentine.* She stretches her lips and tips her head back to sing, holding the low notes in a deep vibrato. *You make me smile with my heart.* The wheels of her trolley trundle over the slabs of concrete. Her snaffled loafers plant outwards as she pushes. *Your looks are laughable, unphotographable.* Her new trolley is piled high, the racket covers spilling out of the end like flowers from a vase, a half-bottle of brandy in the child's seat at the front. *Yet you're my favourite work of art.* She wears tights and chequered trousers under her floral dress on this cool evening – her burgundy towel is draped around her shoulders. *Is your figure less than Greek?* The temperature will drop tonight as she sleeps. *Is your mouth a little weak?* She will put on all the clothes from her trolley before she lifts out the duvet to lay on top of her. *When you open it to speak, are you smart?* She will pull a red beanie hat with a football crest upon her rustling matt of hair. *Don't change a hair for me.* But still she needs the brandy to carry her through the night. *Not if you care for me.*

This is how it is.

Stay, little valentine, stay.

ACKNOWLEDGEMENTS

I am extremely grateful to Sheila Mossé for her memories of life on board the *Shropshire Lass*, to Rebecca McKenzie on board *Myark*, John on board *Prosper* and to Richard and Geraldine Sear on board *Trafalgar*. Thanks to Joseph Alexander Smith and others for their insights on the asylum process. Any inaccuracies or inconsistencies are my own.

Thanks to my agent and friend Alice Lutyens for taking me on, for all her efforts, encouragement and unstinting frankness. Huge credit and thanks to Alex Bowler whose ideas and vision transformed the book. Thank you to Katie Adams for taking *Chaplin & Company* across the pond, and to Cordelia Calvert and all of the team at Liveright.

For the hours of writing time, thanks to Wednesday Fellowes, Leeanne James and Tracy Daines. For unofficially launching the book in such style, thanks to Natasha Ascott and Lucy Payton. And for your patience, support, spelling suggestions, and for believing this could happen, thank you Nick.